D1292584

DICKENS, VIOLENCE AND THE MODERN STATE

Dickens, Violence and the Modern State

Dreams of the Scaffold

Jeremy Tambling

Reader in Comparative Literature
University of Hong Kong

First published in Great Britain 1995 by
MACMILLAN PRESS LTD
Houndmills, Basingstoke, Hampshire RG21 6XS
and London
Companies and representatives
throughout the world

A catalogue record for this book is available
from the British Library.

ISBN 0-333-63389-X

 First published in the United States of America 1995 by
ST. MARTIN'S PRESS, INC.,
Scholarly and Reference Division,
175 Fifth Avenue,
New York, N.Y. 10010

ISBN 0-312-12684-0

Library of Congress Cataloging-in-Publication Data
Tambling, Jeremy.
Dickens, violence and the modern state : dreams of the scaffold /
Jeremy Tambling.
p.   cm.
Includes bibliographical references and index.
ISBN 0-312-12684-0 (cloth)
1. Dickens, Charles, 1812–1870—Political and social views.
2. Violence in literature.   3. Literature and state—Great Britain–
–History—19th century.   4. Literature and society—England–
–History—19th century.   5. Politics and literature—Great Britain–
–History—19th century.   6. Capital punishment in literature.
7. Social problems in literature.   8. Prisons in literature.
I. Title.
PR4592.V56T36   1995
823'.8—dc20

95–13817
CIP

---

10   9   8   7   6   5   4   3   2   1
04   03   02   01   00   99   98   97   96   95

Printed and bound in Great Britain by
Ipswich Book Co Ltd, Ipswich, Suffolk

For Ackbar Abbas, Antony Tatlow and Jonathan Hall
– not readers of Dickens, but colleagues and readers
of everything else

Contents

Acknowledgements

My debts in general for this book go back very far, and include Sheila Smith and John Lucas, and are mainly to all those who have listened to me on Dickens or who have passed ideas on to me. Elizabeth Crockford Pam Morris, Jeanette King, Stewart Hamblin and Graham Martin all at different times suggested I should write on Dickens. Stephen Wall, who published early versions of the *Great Expectations* and *Dombey and Son* material, in *Essays in Criticism* in 1986 and 1993 was kindly, critical, and supportive. Students in comparative literature at the University of Hong Kong at various times have heard much of this material. Linda Johnson provided useful comments on violent women in the 1860s, a seminar-group on post-modern legal theory chaired by Bill McNeil gave help on the *Great Expectations* material, and Pauline, while keeping her graceful allegiance to George Eliot, has been highly supportive of the enterprise.

A Note on the References

I have quoted Dickens out of various convenient editions. Throughout, I have referred to chapters (and to parts if the novel is so divided) and then to page numbers. Finding the reference by means of any Dickens edition should thus be easy.

Oliver Twist, ed. Kathleen Tillotson (Oxford: Clarendon Press, 1966).

Martin Chuzzlewit, ed. Margaret Cardwell (Oxford: Clarendon Press, 1982).

Christmas Books, ed. Michael Slater (Harmondsworth: Penguin, 1971).

Dombey and Son, ed. Alan Horsman (Oxford: Clarendon Press, 1974).

David Copperfield, ed. Trevor Blount (Harmondsworth: Penguin, 1966).

Bleak House, ed. Norman Page (Harmondsworth: Penguin, 1971).

Hard Times, The New Oxford Illustrated Dickens (Oxford University Press, 1955).

Little Dorrit, The New Oxford Illustrated Dickens (Oxford University Press, 1953).

A Tale of Two Cities, ed. George Woodcock (Harmondsworth: Penguin, 1970).

The Uncommercial Traveller, The New Oxford Illustrated Dickens (Oxford University Press, 1958).

Great Expectations, ed. Margaret Cardwell (Oxford: Clarendon Press, 1993).

Our Mutual Friend, The New Oxford Illustrated Dickens (Oxford University Press, 1952).

The Mystery of Edwin Drood, ed. Margaret Cardwell (Oxford: Clarendon Press, 1972).

Christmas Stories (for 'The Perils of Certain English Prisoners'), The New Oxford Illustrated Dickens (Oxford University Press, 1956).

For biographical details, I have used through the text:

John Forster, *The Life of Charles Dickens*, ed. J.W.T. Ley (London: Cecil Palmer, 1928).

Letters (Oxford: Clarendon Press edition, 1965 onwards).

I have mentioned and referenced a number of critics in my Introduction – Carey, Frank, F.R. and Q.D. Leavis, Marcus, Miller, Hillis Miller, Trilling, Wilson, and have referred to these in the body of the text elsewhere without any further mention. Other writers are noted the first time they are mentioned, and subsequent references appear in the text.

Introduction:
Dickens and Dreams of
the Scaffold

The props of my affections were removed,
And yet the building stood, as if sustained
By its own spirit!

Wordsworth, *The Prelude* (1805) 2.294–6.

Il rêve d'échafauds en fumant son houka.

Baudelaire, 'Au Lecteur', *Les Fleurs du Mal.*

'The "scaffold" ' will suggest numerous ideas, but what have they
to do with Dickens? – apart from the scaffold for capital punishment, which is an important reference point, and the main one for
Baudelaire. I refer to the scaffold for its suggestion of props and
supports, going round a building to keep it up, like the props round
Mrs Clennam's house, or the piles that are gradually letting the old
manufactory where Monks receives Mr and Mrs Bumble sink into
the river ('the rat, the worm and the action of the damp had weak-
ened and rotted the piles on which it stood, and a considerable
portion of the building had already sunk into the water beneath' –
Oliver Twist, 38.249). Such props may be metaphorical, like the
building itself in the quotation from Wordsworth, which is that of
the single subject whose confidence is in himself as such. Dream-
scaffolds suggest for me too the imaginary prisons of Piranesi, full
of scaffolding and bridges over impassable abysses: such a labyrinthine architecture appears several times in Dickens, beginning and
taking inspiration from the impossible dwellings and houses in
the slum areas described in *Oliver Twist*, but giving way to the
terrifying architecture dreamed of by Esther Summerson, by Pip
and by John Jasper. And then, the scaffold is a place of display:
etymologically linked to the word 'catafalque' it suggests a place

1

for bodies, and it is the place where people are turned into inert bodies. Here the scaffolding that sustains a structure lets down the subject, gives way under his or her feet, so that the scaffold incorporates one meaning and its opposite: it supports and it collapses. But then scaffolding is both interior and exterior. Traddles in *David Copperfield* draws skeletons: that is the body as scaffolding. Miss Skiffins in *Great Expectations* is scaffolding itself in her uprightness and self-protection. The scaffold as outside and inside questions the independence of whatever it is that it supports.

As related to the body, supporting it like Tiny Tim's crutch, scaffolding calls attention to the body which it also helps construct; and the body, in the condemned cell or on the scaffold, whether anatomised, dispersed or armoured, is Dickens's fascination. But the body as index to the responsible and individual subject cannot be assumed to be whole, and nor can the subject, which instead depends on the prosthetic, on the artifical, to keep its autonomy. Some quotations from *Martin Chuzzlewit* will illustrate the point. They deal with legs, mainly wooden, which act as the supplements to the body – forms of excess, and ways of demonstrating the incompleteness of the subject and its overlap with forms of scaffolding to keep it together:

> [Mr Pecksniff:] 'It has been a day of enjoyment, Mrs Todgers, but still it has been a day of torture. It has reminded me of my loneliness. What am I in the world? – a ship's boat without a rudder, a barrow without a wheel – a wooden leg without a cripple.'
>
> (9.151, MS reading)

> [Mr Pecksniff:] 'The legs of the human subject, my friends, are a beautiful production. Compare them with wooden legs, and observe the difference between the anatomy of nature and the anatomy of art. Do you know,' said Mr Pecksniff, leaning over the banisters . . . that I should very much like to see Mrs Todgers's notion of a wooden leg, if perfectly agreeable to herself?'
>
> (9.153–4)

> [Mrs Gamp:] 'When Gamp was summonsed to his long home, and I see him a lying in Guy's Hospital with a penny-piece on each eye and his wooden leg under his left arm, I thought I should have fainted away.'
>
> (19.316)

[Mrs Gamp, on not having a daughter:] 'Gamp would certainly have drunk its little shoes right off its feet, as with our precious boy he did, and arterwards send the child a errand to sell his wooden leg for any money it 'ud fetch as matches in the rough, and bring it home in liquor: which was truly done beyond his years, for ev'ry individgle penny that child lost at toss or buy for kidney ones; and come home arterwards quite bold, to break the news, and offering to drown himself if sech would be a satisfaction to his parents.'

(25.404)

[Pip/Pimp, reporting a speech:] '... Shakespeare's an infernal humbug, Pip! What's the good of Shakespeare, Pip? There's a lot of feet in Shakespeare's verse, but there an't any legs worth mentioning in Shakespeare's plays, are there, Pip? Juliet, Desdemona, Lady Macbeth and all the rest on 'em might as well have no legs at all for all the audience know about it, Pip.... What's the legitimate object of the drama, Pip? Human nature. What are legs? Human nature. Then let us have plenty of leg pieces...'

(28.452)

[Mrs Gamp:] 'And as to husbands, there's a wooden leg gone likewise home to its account, which in its constancy of walkin into wine vaults, and never comin out again till fetched by force, was quite as weak as flesh, if not weaker.'

(40.625)

Dickens's investment in the body as mechanical, as having autonomous bits added to it, or having appendages which are more human than it is, has been well charted.[1] Taking the wooden leg as an example, and adding in Silas Wegg from *Our Mutual Friend*, it may suggest some of the following, each of which could be developed or extended from the standpoint of critical theory, (though each implication could be seen as highly contentious):

1. the body as turned into a thing, like a commodity, through the power of capitalism and its reifications;
2. an anti-Cartesianism, whereby the body asserts a life of its own, expressed down to its very appendages;
3. the fear of castration whereby the wooden leg represents the

loss of male potency, and may suggest the sexual fetish – and then it would be a question of how that fetishism links back to the first point and to Marx's sense of the commodity as a fetish. When Silas Wegg reads about misers and hoards of money, his 'wooden leg started forward under the table and slowly elevated itself as he read on' (*Our Mutual Friend*, 3.6. 482), which suggests how commodity fetishism turns a man's scaffolding on. That might be a start, but though Dickens cuts rebellious sons down to size quite drastically (see Simon Tappertit's *two* wooden legs), it is a question for this book whether his writing is marked by castration anxieties;

4. the power of the grotesque, the wooden leg representing a new access of non-human power;

5. the question which is more alive, that which speaks of the anatomy of nature or the anatomy of art. When Mr Gamp's wooden leg lies next to him, which is stiffer? As for anatomy, Mrs Gamp, far from fainting away, donates Mr Gamp's body to science. Mr Boffin calls Silas Wegg 'a literary man – *with* a wooden leg' (*Our Mutual Friend*, 1.5. 49), as though literature is much improved by prosthetics; and

6. as I want to take it here, both the incompleteness of the human and a defiance of the attempt to anatomise, expressed through an undecidability about what is human or not.

The psychoanalyst Lacan discusses the mirror-stage, whereby the subject gains a narcissistic first image of itself as complete and perfect. This 'manufactures for the subject ... the succession of phantasies that extends from a fragmented body-image to a form of its totality that I shall call orthopaedic – and lastly to the assumption of the armour of an alienating identity, which will mark with its rigid structure the subject's entire mental development.'[2] The fear existing in fantasy is of the body as fragment, as dispersed, and Lacan sees Bosch as the painter of fantasies of the body in pieces. The alternative to that is the body as something with hard contours and complete, in the scaffolding provided by 'armour', that 'rigid structure' in which the subject is locked into the schizoid state of 'an alienating identity'. The attempt to become single is productive of a split-off state, and Lacan links aggression to the fear of not being able to stage the single-subject position. Between these two fantasies – of dispersal or of complete unity – there is the necessity for the 'orthopaedic' – that which makes the subject walk upright, stand up straight. The subject goes in for orthopaedic devices: elsewhere Lacan refers to the 'orthopaedics of group relations' (*Ecrits*, p. 70). Social groupings, which are reified through the social spacings of architecture, are one of the principal ways in which the subject learns to walk upright, as normal, a complete subject, as a being with a totality. But the orthopaedic becomes also a grotesque image in itself. Breughel, following from Bosch, has been called the first painter of prosthetics with his depictions of cripples, who add another image of monstrosity to the carnival. There is the grotesquerie involved in trying to outgo the gaps and deficiences which make the single subject impossible, sustained only by scaffolding.

In Dickens, the wooden leg, that example of the orthopaedic, far from ensuring either normality or totality, provides images of schizoid states, of the power of the sexual, of the dominance of deviance. Mrs Gamp, apart from alcohol, relies on two equivalents of the wooden leg – on Mrs Harris, who does not exist in point of fact but who is there in the sense that she represents what 'they' say – what group relations do to keep Mrs Gamp together – and on her umbrella, which cannot be packed on the coach, but 'several times thrust out its battered brass nozzle from improper crevices and chinks, to the great terror of the other passengers. Indeed, in her intense anxiety to find a haven of refuge for this chattel, Mrs Gamp so often moved it in the course of five minutes, that it seemed not one umbrella but fifty' (29.468). Quotation from *Martin Chuzzlewit* could go on happily irresponsible for ever, with writing so grotesquely *risqué* as this, and in the midst of material equally comic, but if deconstruction is definable as an attack on the historically produced (seventeenth to nineteenth century) concept of the 'proper' (including property, propriety, proportion, *amour propre*, things proper, placid and pleasant and legitimacy – all Dickensian themes), it would have to be said that this 'improper' prop for Mrs Gamp (her stage prop) works to deconstruct the sense of the subject having its own proper status, as do Dickens's texts in general, and that it demonstrates the priority of catechresis throughout, the impossibility of finding proper words or of metaphor ever being appropriate.

The wooden leg is deviant, unnatural, illustrating 'the anatomy of art' rather than 'the anatomy of nature' – but it is supposed to be orthopaedic, making people stand and walk correctly. Orthopaedics are provided in group relations and in Lacan's terms come from the Symbolic Order into which the child is inserted – forced to repress difference, made into a single subject – but they are also a matter of state power, where education, the prison, social training and medical practices all work to produce the responsible subject. A picture of 1749 that Foucault reprinted in *Discipline and Punish*, of a sapling bound to a post and called 'Orthopaedics, of the art of preventing and correcting deformities of the body in children', suggests the power of the hegemonic discourse to fit the person to the prosthetic device. The convict's leg-iron in *Great Expectations* symbolises the power of the orthopaedic and of state control. Judge Schreber, who suffered from psychosis, and was kept in an asylum, and whose *Memoirs of My Nervous Illness* (1903) Freud commented on, it seems from the researches of W.G. Neiderland (*The Schreber Case*, New York 1974), suffered from a father who was full of orthopaedic devices for his son to prevent masturbation, to correct posture and to encourage healthiness. No wonder his son provided so much material for Lacan on schizophrenia. The orthopaedic techniques of the nineteenth century are expressed, according to Foucault in *Discipline and Punish*, in the Panopticon as a system of generalised surveillance, which includes punishment, then also through the medical discourses of anatomy and of charting women's bodies and in the construction of sexuality and of sexual types. This may be extended with reference to the powerful colonial practices of Britain in India, in the Caribbean, in China and Hong Kong and in Africa, in the growing power of law, in the development of an information society and in the rapid circulation of information,[3] and in the literary discourse of realism. Through these means, the subject, not dispersed or plural, is brought under firm regulation, and the consequence of it is the armoured identity that makes discussion of violence so relevant in considering Dickens.

My study focuses mainly on Dickens texts post-1848, and there is little in it of the subversively funny but perhaps finally comfortable world of *Martin Chuzzlewit*. Perhaps that is a less regulated world in the end, less so than post-1848 texts. Nonetheless, I do refer to two early texts, largely because they raise so powerfully images of violence – *Oliver Twist* and *Barnaby Rudge* – and I develop some comments on *A Christmas Carol*. When critics discuss the 'later Dickens' they usually refer to a change in writing around the time of *Dombey and Son* (1846–48). As Raymond Williams argues in *The English Novel from Dickens to Lawrence*, those changes may be taken as political, and can be linked to the absence of change resulting from the revolutions of 1848. The 1850s brought in both a period of reaction and a reactionary bourgeoisie who made a narrative of political change seem impossible, and also the *coup d'état* of Louis Bonaparte, Napoleon III, whom Dickens had known and disliked ('Rantipole' he was called in Britain: the name survives in *Great Expectations*). That nothing happened in 1848 of an insurrectionary character, apart from the last Chartist demonstration, shows that the props of the administered state, which were begun to be put in place in the 1830s (though the establishment of the Metropolitan Police in 1829 might also be said to mark the beginning of scaffolding for the modern state), stood firm in a moment of crisis felt everywhere else. The 1850s and 1860s, increasingly interventionist in the power of the state, consolidated a work of modernisation about which Dickens was deeply split.

To see a change in Dickens's work around 1848 suggests that the Dickens I describe becomes more embattled against the forces of modernity which organise social and private life. The parallel is seen in the change in Dickens from the picaresque and improvisatory text to the novel planned overall. *Dombey and Son* was the first novel to use systematic number plans. A state which is strongly administered and justified rationally – which provides its own scaffolding for society – conceals, however, its own violence, its own dreams of the scaffold in the other sense, and that repression is lifted throughout the Dickens texts of the 1850s and 1860s, most especially in *Great Expectations*, the novel with which I start. The violence of the state is expressed in punishment, in imperialist discourse and control of the other, and in a culture of demonstration, in being able to force the subject further and further into self-revelation. But there is a readiness for Dickens's text also to become violent itself in its hatreds and obsessions, this being one significant difference it has from, say, George Eliot's text. There is a violent 'abjection' in Dickens, to use the term of Julia Kristeva (I discuss it principally in relation to *Our Mutual Friend*), a reaction away from otherness, identified with scum and dirt, and identified with the woman and especially the mother, and everything associated with her. Yet despite this revulsion, which is a fear of not being able to establish firm borders for the self, not being able to make the building stand independently, there is also a desire for otherness, however far that may require the subject to deviate from itself. It is what Forster calls, in the context of the boy Dickens's interest in the area around the slum area of Seven Dials, 'a profound attraction of repulsion' (*Life*, p. 11).

If he [the young Dickens] could only induce whoever took him out to take him through Seven-dials he was supremely happy. 'Good Heaven!' he could exclaim, 'what wild visions of prodigies of wickedness, want and beggary, arose in my mind out of that place!'

In the light of Seven Dials (Tom-All-Alone's in *Bleak House*), London becomes, like the area round Todgers's, a 'labyrinth' (*Martin Chuzzlewit*, 9.129). The labyrinth is both what cannot be charted (it is a humanist myth to think that it can be created by a Dedalus: it pre-exists the power of the individual subject who is overthrown by it) and is also what cannot be named, neither by the bourgeois artist nor through the techniques of realism, because everything about it is 'prodigious', unnatural, and any naming would be an act of catachresis. But what is unnameable (the theme is to be discussed further with reference to *Dombey and Son*) is inviting, not least because the unnamed resists the imperialist look of surveillance, the violence of categorisation. The 'attraction of repulsion' governs all Dickens, appearing, for instance, in the fascination with corpses, so many of them unnamed, like the ones fished out of the river or in the Paris Morgue, and with the final violence of death (Sikes and Nancy, the attraction towards capital punishment about which few writers have said so much). But abjection produces a certain fear and set of obsessional attitudes within the text, like Mr Jaggers compulsively washing his hands; an overconcern with cleanliness and separation from filth that is not merely anally fixated but the product of disgust. Uriah Heep with his wet hands in *David Copperfield* is a distasteful figure of 'humble propitiation' that the Dickens text recoils from with fascination, and his effect, as with the abject itself, is to make impossible a separation between the subject and the object. Thus when Uriah Heep sleeps in the next room in David Copperfield's lodgings, he colonises David's dreams, so that David, between sleep and waking, imagines having run him through the body with a red hot poker and then goes in to look at him. 'He was so much worse in reality than in my distempered fancy, that afterwards I was *attracted to him in very repulsion* and could not help wandering in and out every half-hour or so, and taking another look at him' (*David Copperfield*, 25.443–4 my emphasis). Attraction is to what is constructed as monstrous. But the Dickens text colludes in creating monstrosity, as when the 'criminal intellect' is declared 'a horrible wonder apart'. In relation to Jasper, the 'criminal' thus textually constituted, Rosa Bud feels 'the fascination of repulsion' (*Edwin Drood*, 20.175). Such attraction (fascination with the state of repulsion, fascination with the idea that the self feels repulsion) seems to belong in gender terms to the feminine. But there is a fascination in Dickens with violent women, women who feminise the male self. To name some of the violent or angry women in the texts is to suggest their importance: Miss Murdstone, Rosa Dartle, Hortense, Mrs Clennam, Miss Wade, Mme Defarge, Miss Havisham, Mrs Joe, women whose anger is at some point seen as pathological. These women are in no way an index of feminism, but they suggest the primacy of gender issues for Dickens, when violence is so likely to be linked to the impulse to feminise.

In *Great Expectations*, where I begin, there is women's violence to each other, as with Molly and the other woman killed in the barn, or Miss Havisham and Estella, whose rivalry is sensed in Chapter 37 of that novel, and is to be connected with aspects of Miss Wade's and Tattycoram's relationship with each other in *Little Dorrit*. Miss Wade, a 'self-tormentor', deviant sexually and socially, illustrates the text's willingness to produce women as violent and marked by a psychic cruelty which does not distinguish between borders, between hurting the self and hurting others. Violence, then, turns inward. Miss Wade is exceptional in that her self-torments are explosive, revolutionary. Esther Summerson in *Bleak House* continues a put-down of herself throughout her narrative that disavows her own happy ending (marriage, children, status) by returning to the theme of better never to have been born, refusing to acknowledge in her text how this misrepresents her actual situation. Amy, in *Little Dorrit* pursues her own narrative of her father's state even in the time of his riches, so that she drives him back all the time to a reliving of the Marshalsea. The narrative is collusive with her passivity which is at the same time a strategy to bring out her father's dependence on her ('She had no blame to bestow upon him... nothing to reproach him with, no emotions in her faithful heart but great compassion and unbounded tenderness' (2.5.478)). Her tendency to increase the torment she suffers and aggravate her passivity and the need for it is effective in making him whimper and cry and in reducing him to the dependency of a child.

The text backs the self-tormentor, and not just where that is a strategic weapon, and not just with women. It is, in fact, fascinated by people whose aggression is inward-directed. Arthur Clennam's progress to the Marshalsea is death-driven; Pip feels guilt and is also masochistic. His guilt means he feels both criminal and criminally tainted, belonging to and affected by the discourse that creates 'the criminal', but he also seeks out punishment and the desire to be shamed, as in his relationship to Estella. The feminising aspect of this I suggest in writing on *Great Expectations*, but I come back to it with *Our Mutual Friend*, and with Bradley Headstone, committed by his schoolmastering to professional orthopaedics, is a self-tormentor and a masochist – though he is also textually constructed as a 'criminal'.

In none of these instances is the text simple or straight: it is rather riddled by a doubleness which comes from a discursive contradiction. One tendency, exacerbated in masochism, is towards the fragmented body image, towards a dispersal which is potentially everywhere in Dickens, and which appears in spontaneous combustion, and the desire to make the body disappear (through the quicklime in *Great Expectations* and *Edwin Drood*), or by being eaten up cannibalistically, or being torn to pieces as happens to Carker, or through crumbling into powder as happens to the 'buried magnate' of *Edwin Drood* when his coffin is broken into by Durdles's pickaxe:

> The old chap gave Durdles a look with his open eyes, as much as to say, 'Is your name Durdles? Why, my man, I've been waiting for you a Devil of a time!' And then he turned to powder.
> (*Edwin Drood*, 4.29)

Dispersal happens through the use of opium, through the sense of the double, which implies a splitting up of the self, or in schizoid states, or in dreams. The other textual formation is the belief in the orthopaedic, in bourgeois order. It takes many forms: that model of rectitude Miss Skiffins (*Great Expectations*) is all scaffolding. It also has strong gender-implications and can be sadistically violent. In *Our Mutual Friend*, Silas Wegg, 'so wooden a man' (1.5.46) is called 'the wooden leg' (as at 1.5.48). The orthopaedic principle has taken him over completely, and when he secures regular employment with Mr Boffin, he tries to reclaim his leg from the taxidermist Mr Venus, who has bought it from the hospital, saying: 'I shouldn't like ... under such circumstances to be what I may call dispersed, a part of me here and a part of me there, but should wish to collect myself like a genteel person' (*Our Mutual Friend*, 1.7.82). The bourgeois or the upwardly mobile, like Wegg, will never allow for dispersal.

Violence maps onto punishment. Foucault's surveillance model of the Panopticon is often softened into an image of general inspection, rather than being seen as a form of punishing for the purpose of correcting, but it should be stressed that if Dickens is preoccupied with the prison, that implies as a trope for the novels the supremacy of the ideology of punishment. Punishment may be internalised, as in a sadism directed against the self (the self-tormentor image), producing both the armoured ego and its violence in turn. The dominance of punishment has several motivations, though it is hard to think that any can claim justification. Adam Smith, satirised by name in *Hard Times*, proposed that punishment was the rightful 'resentment' of society, where such resentment was a proper moral sentiment.[4] In contrast to this view may be put that of Nietzsche in *The Genealogy of Morals*, for whom the prompting to punish is a feature of *ressentiment*, reflecting its envy and grudge in being reactive, after the event, beginning out of a spirit of disappointment that the event has eluded the grasp of the person who would discipline. Punishment, in fact, has to disguise its envy. The Panopticon represses through its architecture, its arrangements and its concern for impersonality the violence of punishment – that was famously seen in the nineteenth century with the elimination of public hangings. As Weber discusses nineteenth-century rationalisation, imprisonment may be included here as one of its triumphs, where making punishment less open to the public to see it has led to a bureaucracy, to specialised agencies and to a stress on scientific management. Such objectivity conceals the emotional forces already dictating punishment. 'Resentment, outrage, hatred – as well as mercy, justice and forgiveness – continue to feature within these rationalised measures. But they do so in an unexpressed, sublimated fashion, overlaid by a utilitarian concern with institutional discipline and individual management, so that even the most transparently punitive actions are often represented in more "positive" instrumental terms' (Garland, p. 189). Dickens's critiques of the abstractions permitted by Utilitarianism are familiar. So, from *Bleak House* onwards, is his critique of a police force which conceals its animus and class and gender position behind its concern with technique and professional skill. But it is not difficult to see Dickens buying into efficiency and in his pronouncements on capital punishment encouraging a superior technology as well. At such moments he too conceals his own violence.

The blacking factory episode, when the twelve-year-old Dickens was taken from school and made to work while his father stayed in the Marshalsea prison for debt, was Dickens's own punishment, endured proleptically, disrupting the narrative order of crime and punishment, and so, if interpreted masochistically becoming that which would enable all crime, since pain endured masochistically undoes the hierarchies of society which rely on punishment for survival and licenses anything. Yet when I say it was endured proleptically, that assumes a chronology which is contradicted by the fact that Dickens seems to have needed to reinvent and rewrite the account of the blacking factory in adulthood, as an example of Freudian deferred trauma (*Nachträglichkeit*). In the 1840s, Dickens seems to have cancelled out bourgeois marriage and success in favour of returning to that event: 'Even now, famous, caressed and happy, I often forget in my dreams that I have a dear wife and children; even that I am a man; and wander desolately back to that time of my life' (*Life*, 26). Warrens's blacking factory is referred to as early as *Pickwick Papers*, but the need to continue to think about it becomes more intense, perhaps as a means of licensing present or future transgression. It is evident, from Dickens's comments on the episode, preserved in Forster and commented on most by Edmund Wilson and Steven Marcus,[5] that its effect was also repressive, tending him towards the bourgeois and respectable. So its effects were to decode and to recode him at once: to take away all social existence (as he would actually later leave his wife), and even his identity as a man, and to affirm them in a state of difference. The texts are partly aware of their splits in discourse, and cannot take up single-subject attitudes, though I have already suggested that their drive is away from the 'proper', from that which is definable as produced from the single subject. Dickens's reputation from George Eliot and Henry James onwards has suffered in consequence; on this basis he has been found intellectually confined or superficial, prompted only by imagination rather than by thought. In contrast to this I would argue that the conscious intellectual bounds come from someone repeating the limitations of the English national ideology (bourgeois, imperialist, nationalist). But he contests that national discourse out of a sense of difference which relates to the working class and to the underside of bourgeois society. It means that he can only become bourgeois through a violent repudiation of the heterogeneous, the heteroclite, all that for which the punishment of the blacking factory is a symbol, a commitment made for crimes as yet (and perhaps forever) deferred.

Dickens needs to be put alongside not those writers who have more allegiance than he to Victorian social order and attitudes – Thackeray, Trollope, Tennyson, Arnold, Mill, George Eliot – but with those more uncomfortable with it, such as the Brontës, and those outside that ideology altogether. It seems that the lack of an adequately articulated contestatory ideology marks an absence in British nineteenth-century politics. It produces in him his own forms of violence: a willingness to interpret the other, and strong emotional attitudes which will be familiar from his letters and speeches and journalism. There is, too, the more specific willingness to construct people as violent or as 'criminals', where the criminal was created as a discrete character type by the disciplinary technologies of the nineteenth century. Yet these things do not suggest how much he shows up English ideology. As discussions of European realism, which might well afford another context for Dickens, have never adequately taken in his work, his fate – in perhaps a massive recuperation of his work – has been to be identified with an English way of writing, and English critics in particular have replicated the accusations against Dickens that belong to that ideological formation that punished him before admitting him to it, that his writing is superficial and philistine.

It has been therefore a matter of record that most of the interesting writing on Dickens has come from America. British scholarship on Dickens has been formidable and is indispensable,[6] but British academics have no monopoly on scholarship, and this work has not as yet produced corresponding new readings. More speculative criticism outside English ideology is associated with the essay of Edmund Wilson, with Lionel Trilling for his essay on *Little Dorrit*, Steven Marcus (in what I think is the best sustained work on Dickens, *Dickens from Pickwick to Dombey*), J. Hillis Miller, especially for his introduction to *Bleak House*, with Lawrence Frank and D.A. Miller.[7] Nor are these the only ones. English criticism has worked pain-stakingly to build up a social background: Humphry House's *The Dickens World* appeared in 1941, the same year as Edmund Wilson's essay, and the contrast of direction and of attitudes in the two critics towards what counts as proof and what may be constructed as empirical data is illuminating. The most provocative essay in British criticism came with Leavis's essay on *Hard Times* in 1948; but brilliant as this is, it avoids an encounter with Wilson or with any sense of an unconscious in Dickens. The result is that the critic reads the text as a form of Freudian secondary revision

– it is what Dickens might have wished to say he was writing. It is the construction of a 'Dickens'. The same performative skill, erasing the Dickens of violence and hatred as well of 'abjection' takes place in *Dickens the Novelist* (1970).[8] Nonetheless, the writers I have mentioned, while certainly not the only ones, have enabled readings of the text which make it a matter of urgent analysis in the sense that they enable a feeling that the work makes a difference. Agreement with these critics' interpretations is not at all the point.

My own work shows a dependence on as many critics of Dickens as I have been able to read, English and American. In this study, the first chapter on *Great Expectations* is a revision of work I published on Dickens in 1986, and in much more detail now it sets out the ground for much of what follows; it raises issues about the prison, about punishment, violence and masochism and confession, that I pursue throughout the book.[9] Three chapters follow – on *Dombey and Son* where bourgeois progress is seen to be death-driven and needing only to be anatomised, on *Bleak House* and on *Little Dorrit*. The topic in these is the ambiguity of Dickens's response to modernity, to changes that would make further revolution virtually impossible, to the bourgeois revolutions which installed commodity fetishism in the London and Paris of the 1850s as well as a tourist culture (as discussed in *Little Dorrit*). This completes a reading of bourgeois Britain in terms of the fixed vision of a nineteenth-century 'society of the spectacle'. Here Britain is a subject for archaeology and anatomy, but is static, has no possibility of forward movement unless a 'password' can be found. The need for a way through, for some sign that will start things going again, relates to the perceptions in Dickens of the power of the labyrinth, of the sense of 'no thoroughfare', a phrase which reappears continually in the texts,[10] of the sense of paralysis, of vertigo and dizziness, and loss of any proportion. In these moments when the subject seems trapped in the textual *mise en abîme*, perceptions of the self in relation to otherness are overthrown. Several examples appear in the chapters ahead, including David Copperfield, Esther, Pip, Jasper, but I would like to quote an early instance, again from *Martin Chuzzlewit*, from the view from the roof of Todgers's, where 'the revolving chimney pots on one great stack of buildings' seem animistically to interrupt the subject, and to baffle sight of the 'prospect' (that which implies the centred stability of a looking based on architecture, with its confidence in structuring the self and selves).

The man who was mending a pen at an upper window over the way became of paramount importance in the scene, and made a blank in it, ridiculously disproportionate in its extent, when he retired. The gambols of a piece of cloth upon the dyer's pole had far more interest for the moment than all the changing motions of the crowd. Yet even while the looker-on felt angry with himself for all this, and wondered how it was, the tumult swelled into a roar, the host of objects seemed to thicken and expand a hundredfold; and after gazing round him, quite scared, he turned into Todgers's again, much more rapidly than he turned out; and ten to one he told M. Todgers afterwards that if he hadn't done so, he would certainly have come into the street by the shortest cut; that is to say, head-foremost.

(9.132)

The giddiness here, bordering on ecstasy and productive of a death-wish, a disorganisation of the subject who might throw himself into the abyss, suggests a dispersal that is everywhere liable to occur in Dickens, and that is concentrated in the texts of the 1850s and 1860s.

If the orthopaedics of modernity shape Dickens's own attitudes, the last three chapters of the book (Chapters 5–7) form a unity, where the focus is on Dickens's complex reactionary stance towards violence and the state, resistant to dispersal, antagonistic also to the orthodoxies of the modern state and colluding with them which in its own way is repressive, violent, even proto-fascist. In the first (Chapter 5), I compare his two historical texts, *Barnaby Rudge* and *A Tale of Two Cities*. Here the question is Dickens's attitude to two forms of violence: revolution and state violence, both of which centre on the ultimate scaffold – for capital punishment. It detects a proto-fascist violence in Dickens, drawing on, for comparison, Carlyle's *French Revolution*, Victor Hugo's *Last Day of a Condemned Man* and Dostoevsky's *The Idiot*. In the second of these chapters I look at both *Oliver Twist* and *The Mystery of Edwin Drood*, together with Collins's *The Moonstone*. Here the topic is Dickens and colonialism, focusing on the question of the 'other' and how he or she is definable as such, beyond the bounds of the normal which are actually created by a prior act of exclusion. While colonialism is already violent, it also produces a schizoid position which the bourgeoisie adopts because of complicity in the oppressiveness of colonialization, and with the double standards, for home and abroad, that this necessitates. Hence the interest in the double, which this chapter makes much of in relation to opium, and the question is how this schizoid state is replicated in the discursive splits which construct the novelist.

The last chapter centres on an examination of *Our Mutual Friend*, and here I focus on issues of Dickens's own disgust towards those elements of society that are excluded from the normal. Discussion of this novel with its stress on waste and effluence is preceded by a reading of a piece of Dickens's shorter fiction, 'The Perils of Certain English Prisoners' and it discusses both *ressentiment* and Kristeva's 'abjection' – the denial of that which has to do with the body – as characteristics of Dickens's reaction to the other. But the chapter concludes with a reminder of Dickens as himself caught, himself excluded, trapped in the machinery of modernity itself dedicated to the elimination of waste and scum.

1
Prison-Bound: Dickens, Foucault and *Great Expectations*

I wander thro' each charter'd street
Near where the charter'd Thames does flow
And mark in every face I meet
Marks of weakness, marks of woe.

In every cry of every Man,
In every Infant's cry of fear,
In every voice, in every ban,
The mind-forg'd manacles I hear.

How the Chimney-sweeper's cry
Every black'ning Church appalls,
And the hapless Soldier's sigh
Runs in blood down Palace walls.

But most thro' midnight streets I hear
How the youthful Harlot's curse
Blasts the new born Infant's tear
And blights with plagues the Marriage hearse.

Blake, 'London' (1794).

London . . . the seat of inspection.

Bentham (1794)

I

Great Expectations has been called an analysis of 'Newgate London',[1] suggesting that the prison is everywhere implicitly dominant in the

book, and it has been a commonplace of Dickens criticism, since
Edmund Wilson's essay in *The Wound and the Bow* and Lionel
Trilling's introduction to *Little Dorrit*, to see the prison as a metaphor throughout the novels. Not just a metaphor, since the interest
that Dickens had in prisons themselves was real and lasting, and
the one kind of concern led to the other, the literal to the metaphorical. Some earlier Dickens criticism associated with the 1960s, and
Trilling's 'liberal imagination' stressed the second at the expense
of the first, and Dickens became the novelist of the 'mind forg'd
manacles', where Mrs Clennam could stand in the Marshalsea
'looking down into this prison as it were out of her own different
prison' (*Little Dorrit*, 2.31.789). This Romantic criticism became a
way of attacking commentators who emphasised the reformist
Dickens, interested in specific social questions: Humphry House
and Philip Collins, the last in *Dickens and Crime* and *Dickens and
Education* (1962 and 1964). Yet of course that intense concern with
the literal prison is there in Dickens, and it is fascinating to compare the nineteenth-century discourses that inform his examination of it with the twentieth-century work of Michel Foucault, the
historian/philosopher who was also an activist in the Groupe
d'Information sur les Prisons in the early 1970s, which informed his
work on the 'birth of the prison' – the subtitle of *Surveiller et Punir*
– *Discipline and Punish* (1976). This book, though not using Dickens,
takes as its examples for the nascence of the modern prison examples Dickens was well familiar with. A Foucauldian Dickens? In the
light of *Discipline and Punish* it is easier to see how the physical
growth of the modern prison is also the beginning of its entering
into discourse and forming structures of thought, so that the literal
and the metaphorical do indeed combine, and produce the Dickens
whose interest is so clearly in both ways of thinking about the
prison.

Discipline and Punish is perhaps the first of Foucault's books about
modes of power operating in western societies, succeeding his in-
augural address at the Collège de France in 1970, the 'Discourse on
Language', where knowledge is seen as a form of manipulation to
be thought of in the same breath as the word 'power'. Power in the
absolutist state takes its bearings on the body, illustrated in the first
part of the book, but the 'gentle way in punishment' associated
with late eighteenth-century enlightenment thought leads to a change
in the way power is exercised – from 'a right to take life or let live
to a form of power that fosters life, the latter being described as a

power over life, in contrast to the former sovereign power, which has been described as a power over death.'[2] At the end of the eighteenth century, penal codes were drawn up which addressed themselves to the mind of the criminal, defined as a 'delinquent' (p. 251).[3] A personality type is thus created; the change Foucault marks is towards the creation of an entity: a mind to be characterised in certain ways (whereas earlier the body was directly marked), to produce the 'docile body' – 'one that may be subjected, used, transformed and improved' – and thus fitted for new modes of industrial production. A 'technology of subjection' comes into use: Foucault refers to Marx's discussion of the division of labour in this context (p. 221). The arrangement of the bodies of individuals for productive and training purposes is facilitated by the renewed attention given to the mind, to the prisoner as personality.

Foucault's subject is the 'disciplinary technology' engineered in western societies, and the most compelling image in the book is the utopist idea of the Panopticon, an idea left on paper by Bentham, whose sleep of reason producing monsters it was, but nonetheless one of a group of rationally inspired reforms carried out in Europe and North America, which changed prison architecture, and brought about one at least huge change in the nineteenth century: the move towards solitary confinement for prisoners. The Panopticon, with its central tower where the unseen warders may or may not be looking at the several storeys of individually divided-off prisoners, who can see neither their controlling agency, nor the others in the cells, but are arranged in a circle around this surveillance tower, presents the possibility of total and complete control being exercised over the prison's inmates. Philip Collins discusses it in *Dickens and Crime* – a book still useful for its donkey-work, though very undertheorised, and not able to question the role of the prison in western society – and Collins stresses that the Panopticon, while it was itself not to be realised as a project, was to provide the model for all other types of institution: the birth of the prison means the birth of all kinds of normalising procedures, carried out in buildings still familiar today, that all look like the exterior of the nineteenth-century prison. Collins quotes Bentham for his dream of scaffolds, as does Foucault: 'Morals reformed, health preserved, industry invigorated, instruction diffused, public burdens lightened, economy seated, as it were, upon a rock, the Gordian knot of the Poor Laws not cut but untied – all by a simple idea of Architecture!'[4]

In *The Fabrication of Virtue*, Robin Evans finds a coincidence between the emergence of the architect as someone separable from the builder, working with plans and models in the absence of the building itself, and the emergence of prison architecture.[5] The prison itself as something to be specifically designed is a concept dating from the middle to the late eighteenth century, bound up with Bentham and other 'reformers' such as John Howard and with the Penitentiary Act of 1779, an Act whose name implicitly labelled the purpose of prisons as to produce guilt and repentance (hence requiring separate cells, on monastic lines: according to Evans, 'the obsolete term penitentiary referred to a monastic cell, set aside for sinful monks – a place of penitence and remorse' (Evans, p. 119)). Architecture as a way of conceptualising buildings, making them into monuments, making them state concepts, is, for Georges Bataille, a practice closely linked to the prison.

> Architecture is the expression of the very soul of societies, just as human physiognomy is the expression of the individuals' souls. It is, however, particularly to the physiognomies of official per-sonages . . . that this comparison pertains . . . Great monuments are erected like dikes, opposing the logic and majesty of authority against all disturbing elements . . . monuments inspire social pru-dence and often real fear. The taking of the Bastille is symbolic of this state of things: it is hard to explain this crowd movement other than by the animosity of the people against the monuments that are their real masters.[6]

Bataille sees architecture as oppressive to the outsider, Foucault, reading the Panopticon, sees it as oppressive to those on the inside. No wonder Dickens made his arch-hypocrite, Mr Pecksniff, an architect. Architecture with Pecksniff doubles his own production of a facade. Pecksniff might have suggested the Tory politics of Peel (*laissez-faire* before the repeal of the Corn Laws, and Utilitar-ian in character), but perhaps Bentham is the architect signified in the Dickens text. Joe Gargery and Mr Wopsle in *Great Expecta-tions* bring together in their London sightseeing and comments thereon Dickens's very own private prison (the blacking factory), and architecture as an imprisoning ideology, concealing what goes on within:

> '. . . me and Wopsle went off straight to look at the Blacking Ware'us. But we didn't find that it came up to its likeness in the

red bills at the shop doors: which I meantersay,' added Joe in an explanatory manner, 'as it is there drawd too archictooralooral.'[7]

Nonetheless, it is more Foucault on architecture than Bataille that I want to consider. The Panopticon produces a whole architecture which works on those within. Something of its method is at work in *Hard Times* too: its governing idea being thought suitable for schools and factories. In Gradgrind's school, the pupils are so raked that each can be seen at a glance, and each are individuated, though with a number, not a name. Leavis's influential account of this book stresses how Benthamism in Coketown stifles individuality, life and emotions, and the account thus sets Dickens against Utilitarianism. Foucault's argument implies that the Panopticon idea stressed individuality, though not in the idealist manner that the Romantic poets, themselves contemporary with this 'birth of the prison', saw that concept of the individual. The Panopticon's rationale was the sense that each subject of care was to be seen as an individual mind, its differences from others being carefully measured and rationally produced, whereas Romanticism asserts the magnitude of difference as such. Romanticism is inseparable from Utilitarianism, but the latter *manages* the challenge in Romantic discourse. It is a question how far the Romantic novelist is able to see how that Romanticism is inseparable from Panopticism, is indeed even collusive with its oppression.[8]

Alongside the Panopticon's creation of separate sentiences goes a discourse to sustain it – in the formation of the 'sciences of man . . . these sciences which have so delighted our "humanity" for over a century . . . (which) . . . have their technical matrix in the petty, malicious minutiae of the disciplines and their investigations' (p. 226). The social sciences emerge out of what Foucault calls the 'constitution' of this individual with an individual mind, as 'a describable, analysable object' (p. 190), so that the origins of the sciences of man may have their origin in the files of prisons and institutions, 'these ignoble archives, where the modern play of coercion over bodies, gestures and behaviour has its beginnings' (p. 191). This new carceral framework 'constituted one of the armatures of power-knowledge that has made the human sciences historically possible. Knowable man (soul, individuality, consciousness, conduct, whatever it is called) is the object-effect of this analytical investment, of this domination-observation' (p. 305). It is a retreat from this positivist conception that stresses 'man's unconquerable mind' – the conclusion to Wordsworth's sonnet of 1802 apostrophizing Toussaint L'Ouverture, significantly a revolutionary in prison – and that invests the mind with unknowable, unfathomable qualities, as both Dickens and Leavis-like criticism do. The two stresses run together.

Bentham, more than just the inspirer of Mr Gradgrind, is a voice behind a whole new 'disciplinary technology', then, and the Panopticon becomes a metaphor, or, to quote Foucault:

> ... the diagram of a mechanism of power reduced to its ideal form; its functioning, abstracted from any obstacle, resistance or friction, must be represented as a pure architectural and optical system: it is, in fact, a figure of political technology that may and must be detached from any specific use. It is polyvalent in its applications; it serves to reform prisoners, but also to treat patients, to instruct school children, to confine the insane, to supervise workers, to put beggars and idlers to work. It is a type of location of bodies in space, of distribution of individuals in relation to one another, of hierarchical organisation, of disposition of centres and channels of power, which can be implemented in hospital, workshops, schools, prisons.
>
> (p. 205)

As a metaphor, what is implied is that the prison will enter, as both reality and 'type', into public discourse. Trilling's discussion of the prevalence of the prison motif in nineteenth-century literature finds its explanation here. The sense that metaphysically the prison is inescapable – reaching even to a person's whole mode of discourse, creating Nietzsche's 'prison-house of language', so that nothing escapes the limitations of the carceral – is objectively true in the domination of the prison in other nineteenth-century forms of discourse.

What is in question is normalising delinquent mentalities and preserving them as abnormal, since for Foucault, normalising powers succeed best when they are only partially successful, when there can be a marginalisation of certain types of personality, and the creation of a stubborn mentality that resists educative and disciplinary processes. 'The prison, and no doubt punishment in general, is not intended to eliminate offences, but rather to distinguish them, to distribute them, to use them...' (p. 272). Power uses as its prop not the law, but the norm, the standard, and not acts, but identities are named. The law was, however, involved as well: police surveillance grew especially in the 1850s, with as a result the nearly inevitable criminalising of so many sections of the population due to the growth in the number of penal laws.[9] In the Panopticon, that 'mill grinding rogues honest and idle men industrious',[10] identity is created and named. The model prison (i.e. that which practises solitary confinement, either partial and belonging merely to the prisoner's leisure time or total as in the Eastern Penitentiary Philadelphia which inspired Pentonville) is discussed by Foucault in terms of the way isolation becomes a means of bringing prisoners to a state where they will carry on the reform work of the prison in their own person, where the language of the dominating discourse is accepted and internalised.

To come with these insights of Foucault to *Great Expectations* is to investigate two things – how far a nineteenth-century text is aware of this creation of power and of oppression that Foucault has charted and to examine the text's relation to this dominant ideology as Foucault has described it. It is also to read the book as having to do with 'the power of normalisation and the formation of knowledge in modern society', which is how Foucault describes the subject-matter of *Discipline and Punish* (p. 308). The issue of seeing the prison as an essential condition of Victorian society turns on the libertarianism of the prison as inherently oppressive; that much is clear in the novel, with its Hulks, Newgate and transportation, and prisonous houses such as Satis House and even Wemmick's castle. People are held by their emotions, like Magwitch's 'click' in the throat (3.19), but they are also held by a system which machine-like seems ready to trap them: 'suddenly – click – you're caught' (24.198). Miss Havisham is as conscious of her house being locked, like her emotions, as Mr Jaggers is of his house being unlocked; both show awareness of being part of a carceral economy. The prison individuates: you do not shake hands 'except at last' (21.172), i.e. before taking leave of the person who is about to be hanged. Before that, it would be an act breaking down the idea of human singularity.

The prison also has to do with Dickens's registering of the prison being bound up with questions of language and the control of language – which, of course, entails ways of thinking, a whole discourse, and implies as a consequence the modernism of the book's form. Thus in opposition to the modernity that permits the Panopticon, there is a textual modernity of attitude which means that its parabolic narrative is open-ended; that the title hints at the space within it for the reader to construct his/her own sense of how to take it; that, unlike the warder at the heart of the Panopticon, the author is not felt to be directing and encouraging a labelling; that the text resists single meaning. The famous doubleness of the novel's ending is relevant, as is the sense that the reader has only Pip's text to work upon, and that this is certainly not final nor authoritative. In other words, the book shows awareness that to learn a language is connected with the control of knowledge. Dickens's absence of explanation about it only emphasises the extent to which he as author has receded: the novel stands alone, open-ended, marked out by the lack of 'closure' within it supplied by the moralist Dickens.

II

In *American Notes*, Chapter 3 (1842), Dickens reports on visits to the isolation penitentiaries in the United States. He saw the 'Auburn system' derived from New York at work at Boston. The Auburn system was based on the prison at Gloucester, built in the 1780s, which Foucault refers to as not providing total isolation – 'it corresponded only partially to the initial plan: total confinement for the most dangerous criminals; for the others, day work in common and separation at night' (p. 123).[11] Dickens refers also in *American Notes* (Chapter 5) to the prison at Hartford, Connecticut. The 'silent association' system in these places – partial solitary confinement only – he preferred to the Eastern Penitentiary at Philadelphia (*American Notes*, Chapter 7.) The English follow-up to Philadelphia (1830) was to be Pentonville (1842), which is made fun of in *David Copperfield*. But it is not hard to see both systems as related to the Panopticon dream. Dickens found Philadelphia distasteful. He questioned, in a letter to Forster, whether the controllers 'were sufficiently acquainted with the human mind to know what it is they are doing' (letter of 13 March 1842, *Letters*, Vol. 3, p. 124), while *American Notes*, Chapter 7, finds 'this slow and daily tampering with the mysteries of the brain to be immeasurably worse than any torture of the body'. The person must be returned from this state 'morally unhealthy and diseased'. It is halfway to Foucault's gathering of criticisms of the prison that were made in France between 1820 and 1845: indeed, Dickens's comments are sited within those criticisms, commented on in *Discipline and Punish* (pp. 265–8).

George Eliot, commenting on Forster's *Life of Dickens* in a letter of

15 December 1871, recommends it 'because of the interest there is in his boyish experience [an understatement!] and also in his rapid development during his first travels in America ... The information about the childhood and the letters from America make it worth reading.'[12] Both these letters and the revelations of Dickens's childhood came into public knowledge only after the death of the author. It is interesting, however, that they do not lead George Eliot to a revaluation of Dickens: the language of 'development' implies, instead, a 'Dickens' who is a steadily progressing subject, fully known already, and not marked by discontinuities. Nonetheless, even if Eliot is not driven to rewrite her sense of Dickens after reading Forster, the attention to America, somewhere Eliot never visited, might be regarded as interesting. *Martin Chuzzlewit*, the novel which succeeded the American journey, contrasts Todgers's part of London as a labyrinth[13] with the plans for Eden as they appear on paper – 'a flourishing city ... an architectural city! There were banks, churches, cathedrals, market-places, factories, hotels, stores, mansions, wharves; an exchange, a theatre; public buildings of all kinds, down to the office of the Eden Stinger, a daily journal; all faithfully depicted in the view' (21.353–4, and see Phiz's illustration, 'The Thriving City of Eden as it appeared on paper').[14] Eden is panoptical: an architect's dream of the organised city. Philadelphia, the place where Dickens came nearest to seeing the Panopticon *echt*, was panoptical outside the Penitentiary as well: as Dickens wrote, 'it is a handsome city, but distractingly regular. After walking about it for an hour or two, I felt that I would have given the world for a crooked street' (*American Notes*, Chapter 7). This triumph of rational architecture in *Martin Chuzzlewit* I want to say more about before returning to *Great Expectations*.

The 'Eden Stinger' (magnificent title!) is one of a number of papers that Martin Chuzzlewit encounters, along with such titles as the New York Sewer, the New York Family Spy, the New York Peeper, the New York Private Listener and the New York Keyhole Reporter, all of which, apart from the first, suggest surveillance. The Sewer is no different:

Here's the Sewer's exposure of the Wall Street Gang, and the Sewer's exclusive account of a flagrant act of dishonesty committed by the Secretary of State when he was eight years old, now communicated, at great expense, by his own nurse.

(16.255–6)

And there is the account of Professor Mullit:

> He found it necessary, at the last election for President, to repu-
> diate and denounce his father, who voted on the wrong inter-
> est. He has since written some powerful pamphlets, under the
> signature of 'Suturb,' or Brutus reversed. He is one of the most
> remarkable men in our country, sir.
>
> (16.272)

The disappearance of the private self is the point. Nadgett, the secretive London detective of *Martin Chuzzlewit* who knows everything
about everybody, suggests the direction that America has gone in
entirely. The self is constituted as secret in *Martin Chuzzlewit*, Mrs
Gamp saying that 'we never knows wot's hidden in each other's
breasts and if we had glass winders there, we'd need to keep the
shetters up, some on us, I do assure you' (29.464). America is the
society of transparency where everything may fairly be dragged into
the light.

In the movement between Britain and America, *Martin Chuzzlewit*
allows for the Panoptical uncovering of secrets in London through
the detective, but criticises the comparable activity in New York.
'The regeneration of man' (21.348) that the United States stands for,
as Martin Chuzzlewit is told, is 'man' as Foucault sees 'him' being
formulated and given definition at the end of the eighteenth century, as part of the discourse of Romanticism and as part of the
sciences of man that by giving such a full description to which
'he' must conform impose a known identity, which is also a
carceral condition. (The Eastern Penitentiary aimed at the regeneration of man by such means.) An uncertainty about Rousseau's
'natural man', who is individual and solitary and outside society,
a doubt whether such a romantic creature can exist and what
sort of manners 'he' would have, and whether there is any need
for any regeneration is expressed in Martin Chuzzlewit's last
speeches to Elijah Pogram (34.535–6). The accusation is that
Americans have lost 'the natural politeness of a savage, and that
instinctive good-breeding which admonishes one man not to
offend and disgust another'. That dream of innocence is, however,
immediately followed by Martin's other and final charge against
the Americans, and this belongs much more to the Panopticon in
style, suggesting the need to regulate, if not produce, the natural
man:

The mass of your countrymen begin by stubbornly neglecting little social observances, which have nothing to do with gentility, custom, usage, government, or country, but are acts of common, decent, natural, human politeness. You abet them in this, by resenting all attacks upon their social offences as if they were a beautiful national feature. From disregarding small obligations they come in regular course to disregard great ones and so refuse to pay their debts. What they may do or what they may refuse to do next, I don't know, but any man may see if he will, that it will be something following in natural succession, and a part of one great growth, which is rotten at the root.

(34.536)

This passage is so confused that it is hardly necessary to deconstruct it. The Romantic and the Utilitarian are in opposition to each other, so that the word 'natural' is used twice here with opposing senses: it is not clear whether natural man is Romantic and Rousseauistic, or criminal. The social observances which are neglected (refraining from spitting, for example, on the evidence of the novel) are declared to lead 'in regular course' to the non-payment of debts. The *non sequitur* here disguises the point that the preferred image for natural man is bourgeois man – man who pays his debts. Martin, or Dickens, has become Benthamite: Rousseau's natural man would be a Benthamite. Marx's satire against Bentham, who 'with the dryest naiveté . . . assumes that the modern petty bourgeois, especially the English petty bourgeois, is the normal man', is relevant here.[15]

This bourgeois complacency is also the subject of Nietzsche in considering the origins of morality in *The Genealogy of Morals*. In this text, he has a whole essay dedicated to the relationship between making people feel guilty and making them pay their debts: guilt is the only way to make people properly bourgeois and aware that debts must be met. Martin refuses to speculate on what could be worse than not paying debts, but it would seem that a society that is formed on the basis of ensuring that debts are cleared up is half-way towards being panoptical, becoming the society that arrests John Dickens, to say nothing of Micawber, Skimpole and Mr Dorrit. Perhaps the next line in the text, 'the mind of Mr Pogram was too philosophical to see this' intimates the possibility of disagreeing with Martin, and at the beginning of a reading of *Great Expectations* I do not want to foreclose on the question whether Dickens is

part of a discourse that is prepared to will the means towards making people pay what they owe.

What does seem clear is a paralysis before the extent to which
prison reform will go in its effort to reform 'criminals' (including
those who do not pay their debts). The critique of the Philadelphia
Silent System is not one of the prison as a system, questioning its
rationale as a social fact, as the product of a type of thinking. The
point may be made from *Great Expectations*, at a moment where Pip,
in an almost gratuitous moment, is invited by Wemmick to visit
Newgate:

> At that time, jails were much neglected, and the period of exag-
> gerated reaction consequent on all public wrong-doing – and
> which is always its heaviest and longest punishment – was still
> far off. So, felons were not lodged and fed better than the soldiers
> (to say nothing of paupers) and seldom set fire to their prisons
> with the excusable object of improving the flavour of their soup.
> (32.259–60)

Philip Collins links this observation to the riots that took place at
Chatham convict prison early in 1861,[16] and makes it clear that
Chatham represented a heavily reactionary kind of discipline consequent upon the increased stress that prison life received in the
1850s, especially between 1853 and 1858 when, according to Ignatieff,
'convict prisons were swept by strikes, sit-downs, group assaults
on warders, and escape attempts, all designed to bring pressure on
the convict prison directors to eliminate sentence anomalies and
restore transportation instead of imprisonment.' A prison service
which was since 1835 (two years before *Oliver Twist*) becoming
subject to inspection, however ineffectual, was becoming more interventionist and certainly different from the Newgate Pip is describing. Can much be said in favour of this passage? Many readers
of Dickens will assume it to be part of the dominant mode to
be noted in Dickens's speeches and letters: the voice of the liberal
consensus, wanting prisons to be simply neither too hard nor too
easy. But the quotation also gives the register of Pip, who is
historically at the moment when he is furthest away from his
knowledge about the criminal basis of society, most alienated from
his own associations with criminality – hence, of course, the irony
that the chapter closes with Estella's facial resemblance to Molly.
As narrator, is he any better? He seems to have learned nothing: at

least he still wishes to place prisoners below soldiers and paupers, not seeing that both these groups endure the same oppression that makes people prisoners. Pip's language is still, even now, part of that of a 'brought-up London gentleman' (39.319): it belongs to a Victorian dominant discourse. (And 'brought-up' also suggests 'bought-up' and goes along with the equations of property and personality that go on throughout; compare Havisham with Have-is-sham, even Have-is-am, the last the latest development of the Cartesian cogito. The dominators, no less than the dominated, receive their individuality from their position in the carceral network.) If the voice is still so repressed, then it suggests that the text will fail in self-analysis, and that what Pip will say of himself in this carceral society must be read symptomatically.

Those who identify Pip's attitude in the quotation with Dickens's assume there is nothing in the text to qualify what is said here, or else that a plurality in the text allows Dickens to engage in a journalistic point in the middle of Pip's narration. But the utterance could be taken also as trying to capture how Pip thought then, and to be an attempted disavowal, in this most confessional and disavowing of books, of a way of thinking once held. Pip's mode is autobiographical and confessional almost in the Catholic sense of that last word. The reader of *Great Expectations* is able to reject the opinions expressed at the start of Chapter 32 in the light of the reading of the rest of the book. Behind the narrator, does the author asks for a similar dismissal? Is it that behind Pip's confession lies Dickens's own, or Dickens's as the representative of a precisely positioned class, of the liberal petit-bourgeoisie? The novel distances itself from Pip's confessions perhaps in order to listen to Dickens's. But then that one – Dickens's – may itself be refused, be shown to be as relative as the one that it shadows. Confession would be liable to the strictures that Freud makes about it:

When a patient brings forward a sound and incontestable train of argument during psychoanalytic treatment, the physician is liable to feel a moment's embarrassment, and the patient may take advantage of it by asking, 'This is all perfectly correct and true, isn't it? What do you want to change in it, now that I've told it you?' But it soon becomes evident that the patient is using thoughts of this kind, which the analysis cannot attack, for the purpose of concealing others which are anxious to escape from criticism and from consciousness.[17]

Behind the confession is what cannot be confessed because it is outside consciousness or too much inside it: it belongs in the discourse of the society at a level which cannot be directly questioned. An approach to *Great Expectations* cannot rest with finding out what Pip says or what he means. But what is clear is the text's prevailing confessional note. TO BE READ IN MY CELL (13.104) is apt metalinguistically. It comments on the text's sense of the way it should be read, and what Pip thinks it is about. This is not the fictional Augustinian mode of confession, though a 'cell' would well suit the Catholic confession: it is rather that the mode of autobiography fits with Protestant thought. Lionel Trilling comments on the late eighteenth-century 'impulse to write autobiography', saying that 'the new kind of personality which emerges ... is what we call an individual: at a certain point in history men become individuals.'[18] Confession in autobiography is constitutive of the subject for him- or herself – but as Foucault would add, it would be 'subject' 'in both senses of the word',[19] since it is the means whereby the dominant discourse is internalised. Foucault continues: 'The obligation to confess is now relayed through so many different points, is so deeply ingrained in us, that we no longer perceive it as the effect of a power which constrains us; on the contrary, it seems to us that truth, lodged in our most secret nature, "demands" only to surface.' Interest in the prison, in the cell which has that private space which must be filled by the individual who must fit it, and interest in autobiographical confession: these two things converge.

For *Great Expectations* is certainly about the creation of identities, imposed from higher to lower, from oppressor to oppressed. From the first page there is the 'first most vivid and broad impression of the identity of things', where a considerable amount of naming goes on – 'I called myself Pip and came to be called Pip'; where the seven-year-old child names 'this bleak place overgrown with nettles' as 'the churchyard' and similarly characterises the marshes, the river, the sea, and himself as 'that small bundle of shivers growing afraid of it all and beginning to cry' who 'was Pip'. The phrasing of the last part suggests that the act of naming the self and the outside world which also constitutes it is a rationalisation, an incomplete and unsatisfactory way of labelling what resists formulation. The external world is set over against the child, alienating it, making it shiver and cry (as also Magwitch shivers and weeps, 3.19). The self is misnamed from the beginning, minimised;

and gross acts of naming take place thenceforth, from Mrs Hubble's belief that the young are never grateful, not to say 'naterally wicious' (4.26) to Jaggers saying that boys are 'a bad set of fellows' (11.83). Wopsle and company identify an accused with the criminal (Chapter 18), Pip sees himself as George Barnwell, and receives a number of descriptions and names – Pip, Handel, 'the prowling boy' (21.174), 'you young dog' (1.5), 'my boy' (3.19), 'you boy' (8.63), 'you visionary boy' (44.362). Anonymity, though not the absence of naming, hangs over Mrs Joe (defined through the husband), Orlick, whose name Dolge is 'a clear impossibility' (15.111), Magwitch – Provis at all times to Jaggers, Trabb's boy, Drummle – the Spider, the Aged P and Mr Waldengarver. The power of naming confers identity: Q.D. Leavis's analysis sees the power as one that implants guilt.[20] That guilt-fixing belongs to Foucault's Panopticon society, and indeed the sense of being looked at is pervasive. Pip expects a constable to be waiting for him on his return from taking the food to the convict, has the sensation of being watched by relatives at Satis House, has his house watched on the night of Magwitch's return, has Compeyson sit behind him in the theatre (where he himself is watching), and is watched by the coastguard and the river police in the attempt to take off Magwitch (none of the friendship here with the police implied in the 1853 article 'Down with the Tide': the Dickensian hero is shown here as in flight from the agents of law). Where such spying is an integral part of the book, the sense of being someone constituted as having a secret to hide is not far away. Pip feels himself a criminal early and late, and Orlick tells him he is: 'It was you as did for your shrew sister' (52.423) – this coming from the man who has tracked Pip constantly, and shadowed Biddy. Reflecting the first chapter's growth of self-awareness – where the child is crying over his parents' grave, as though not just feeling himself inadequate, but as already guilty, already needing to make some form of reparation – Magwitch says that he 'first became aware of himself down in Essex a thieving turnips for his living' (42.344). Jaggers identifies Drummle as criminal – 'the true sort' (26.217) – and encourages him in his boorishness and readiness to brain Startop. His method of cross-examination is to criminalise everyone, himself resisting classification, no language being appropriate for one as 'deep' as he. 'You know what I am, don't you?' is the last comment he makes after the dinner party where he has hinted that Molly (whom he owns) is a criminal type. The question is to be answered negatively, for he is like the unseen watcher in the central tower of the Panopticon, naming others, but not named himself. (His centrality is implied in the address of his office while that he leaves his doors unlocked when he leaves his house makes him like the Panopticon warder who may or may not be on duty: no one can be sure.) He is in the position, as criminal lawyer, of power, conferring identities, controlling destinies. Not for nothing are those criminals in Newgate compared to plants in the greenhouse, and regarded with the scientific detachment that for Foucault is part of the 'discourse of truth' of nineteenth-century positivism.

Identities become a matter of social control and naming: Estella might have turned out one way as one of the 'fish' to come to Jaggers's net, yet she is constituted differently (though almost as nihilistically) by the identity she receives from Miss Havisham's hands. Pip remains the passive victim whose reaction is to blame himself for every action he is in: his willingness to see himself as his sister's murderer (Chapter 16) is of a piece with seeing himself characteristically unjust to Joe. Q.D. Leavis's account of the novel works against those which see the book as 'a snob's progress'; her emphases are useful in suggesting that it is *Pip* who sees himself thus, and that now he is 'telling us dispassionately how he came to be the man who can now write thus about his former self' (p. 291). But the 'us', by eliding the 1860s readers of the text with these who come a century later, implies that there is a central, ahistorical way of taking the text: a liberal-humanist ideology underwrites this assumption which also implies that there is some decent norm Pip could approximate to which would untie all his problems. It thus assimilates all historical differences, at the least, to the notion of the free subject, who is at all times accessible to decent human feelings – and capable of reaching a central normality. If what Q.D. Leavis said were the case, Pip would have reached some degree of 'normality' by the end of what has happened to him before he starts narrating. He is not a central human presence, but a writer whose text needs inspection for its weakness of self-analysis, for he never dissociates himself from the accusations he piles on himself at the time of the events happening and afterwards. In Wemmick's and Jaggers's character-formulations of people as either 'beaters or cringers' he remains a cringer, unable to recognise Herbert's genial view – 'a good fellow, with impetuosity and hesitation, boldness and diffidence, action and dreaming, curiously mixed in him' (30.248). That positive evaluation is beyond him: his self-perception makes him oppressor, while, more accurately, he is victim. Foucault stresses how the healthy individual is defined in relation to that which has been labelled as delinquent, degenerate or perverse; and his studies of madness, of the birth of the clinic and of the prison all meet in this: 'When one wants to individualise the healthy normal and law-abiding adult, it is always by asking him how much of the child he has in him, what secret madness lies within him, what fundamental crime he has dreamed of committing' (*Discipline and Punish*, p. 193). On this basis, Pip might be said to be the creation of three intersecting discourses: he remains something of the child – his name, a diminutive, establishes that; he is never in a position, he feels, of equality with anyone else; his dreams of the file, of Miss Havisham hanging from the beam, of playing Hamlet without knowing more than five words of the play, his nightmarish sense of phantasmagoric shapes perceived in the rushlight in the Hummums, and his sense of being a brick in a house-wall, or part of a machine, 'wanting to have the engine stopped, and my part in it hammered off' (57.458) – all proclaim his 'secret madness'. His sense of criminality is fed by virtually each act and its consequences that he undertakes.

A victim of the language system, only on one or two occasions does he reverse the role and become implicitly the accuser; one is where he prays over the head of the dead Magwitch: 'Lord be merciful to him a sinner' (56.457) where commentators such as Moynahan have found something false. It is inappropriate, but it seems to belong to the Pip whose sense of himself is not free enough to allow himself to deconstruct the language system he is in. The odd thing is not that he fails to see himself as the sinner, as in the parable (Luke 18), but that he should want to name Magwitch as such. But that act of naming is a reflection of the way the dominated have no choice but to take over the language of their domination – to continue to beat, as they have been beaten, to continue to name disparagingly, as they have been named. That act in itself continues to name Pip – implicitly, as the Pharisee, of course. The question the novel asks is what else he might do: he seems caught. The self can only retreat from that dominant discourse through schizoid behaviour, as happens with Wemmick and his dual life-styles, yet does not the Castle's existence betray the prison's presence still in Wemmick's thinking? He, too, has not got away.

A second time when the language of Pip's oppression becomes one to oppress another is at the end of the book where he meets the younger Pip and suggests to Biddy that she should 'give Pip to him, one of these days, or lend him, at all events' (58.490). To this Biddy responds 'gently' 'no', but her answer might well have been a horrified one in the light of what surrogate parents do to their children in the book: Pip is offering to play Magwitch to Biddy's child. He has learned nothing: he is a recidivist, unaware of how much he has been made himself a subject of other people's power and knowledge. Magwitch similarly 'owns' Pip (39.319) as he says with pride: as a member of the class marginalised and set apart by the Panopticon society, he has had to take on those dominant oppressive values, and talks the same language of property. It is a mark of his social formation, which, after his experience in England in relation to the gentleman Compeyson, is continued in Australia when, as he puts it, 'the blood-horses of them colonists ... fling up the dust over me as I was walking' (39.318) which conditions him to speak as he does, and make him a post-colonial figure, forced into reaction – 'blast you every one, from the judge in his wig to the colonist a-stirring up the dust, I'll show a better gentleman than the whole kit of you put together' (40.330).

It is the cruellest irony for Pip that he must disparage himself and praise Joe so constantly in his narration. Pip has no means of assessing the forge and the village life independent of his own given language. Nothing more is given of the forge in the novel apart from Pip's perception of it, and the absence of such a thing makes the torture for Pip, the prisoner in the Panopticon societal prison, the more refined. For it remains as a deceptive escape for him, although one that he cannot endorse (so that his intention to go back and marry Biddy is self-oppressive), and any step that he takes, either of accepting or rejecting it, remains a compromise. The split is caught in the scenes leading to his going to London in the first instance, and a compromise is dictated to him by the dividing nature of the society as prison. For Foucault argues that there is no 'knowledge that does not presuppose and constitute at the same time power relations' (*Discipline and Punish*, p. 27). That is, the birth of the prison ensures that there is no common language – no means of making a value-judgement which is outside the terms of a particular set of power-relations. The methods of deployment of power are various, as are the social groupings; indeed *Great Expectations* displays something of that variousness. What Pip finds to be true of himself is the result of the way he has been set up; at the same time, he does not possess terms to think about a different way of life – the forge – that are not themselves instrumental for control over that way of thinking. Difference is not allowed for. The illusion he is given is of seeing things whole, but to the very end he cannot see the forge way of life as something different from his, and one that his own language formation cannot accommodate from the moment he got to Satis House. The modernity of the novel lies in this area: Dickens commits himself to no view about Joe or Biddy, or Pip, but writes rather a *Bildungsroman* where the expectation that the hero will learn through experience is belied, and not only by the title.

In this most sociologically interactionist of novels, it is recognised that the self can use no other language than that given to it. What liberty there is is suggested by Orlick, who cringes after Joe beats him, beats Mrs Joe and secures her cringing. Orlick, through a certain upward mobility derived from his association with Compeyson (though that could be a cringing relationship) changes from the cringer (paid off by Jaggers from service at Satis House) to being the accuser of Pip in the sluice-house. He perceives he has been marginalised, in some ways defined as delinquent, a 'hulker' (15.113), and he comments on this, 'you [Pip] was favoured and he [Orlick] was bullied and beat' (53.423). Out of that crazed imperception, he lashes out at Pip: the reverse action to Magwitch's who almost equally arbitrarily identifies Pip with himself. Orlick, compared to Cain (15.112), and Magwitch, called Abel, the original hunted-down figure, go in opposite directions: what unites them (as it links them with Pip) is their sense that they are the watched, the ones under surveillance. Orlick's reactions to Pip look like Nietzsche's *ressentiment*,[21] that quality that Foucault has made much use of in discussing the origins of the impulse towards power. Dickens's 'cringer' is like Nietzsche's 'reactive personality': for Nietzsche, it is characteristically this type that, fired by resentment, tries to move into the legislative position. Orlick's rancour is born out of the inability that those watched in the Panopticon society have (since they have been put in individual cells, they cannot see each other) to read their situation as akin to that of other marginalised figures.

Pip refers to Orlick's use of the word 'jiggered'. 'When I was younger, I had a general belief that if he had jiggered me personally, he would have done it with a sharp and twisted hook' (17.130). Jiggering and 'jaggering' may suggest forms of aggression, but to 'jigger' is defined by the OED as 'to make a succession of rapid jerks, said of a fish struggling to free itself from the hook' and it cites an angling example from 1867: 'when a fish jiggers or keeps up a constant jag, jag, jag, at the line . . .' To be jiggered is also to be tired out (OED, 1862) or to ruin, and a 'gigger' is a prison. It looks as though Pip takes a passive for an active: Orlick too is caught. His being jiggered associates him with Jaggers: the OED giving the meaning of pedlar or carter for a 'jagger', which reduces Mr Jaggers, while 'to jag' is also to jig like a caught fish: in this game of jigger-jagger, the text exposes Jaggers as also empty, even caught. Hence, in Chapter 20, the irony of the Jew Pip sees. (The language is doubtless racist, and normalising, but it is also worth noting that Orlick is compared to the Wandering Jew as well as to Cain.) He is 'performing a *jig* of anxiety under a lamp-post [suggestive of the gallows] and accompanying himself, in a sort of frenzy, with the words, "Oh Jaggerth, Jaggerth, Jaggerth! all otherth ith Cag-Maggerth, give me Jaggerth"' (20.165). 'Cagmag' means offal, and can be used negatively of a person. But in a minute this suitor, who is working for 'Habraham Latharuth, on thuthpithion of plate', learns that Jaggers is 'over the way', i.e. against his client, and he is reduced to crying out 'if you'd have the condethenthun to be bought off from the t'other thide . . .' (20.166–7) and dancing in frenzy. Orlick dances at Biddy; dancing also suggests the fate of the person strung up. Jiggers, jaggers and cagmaggers all come together here in a virtual interchangeability of names and stations – where only bribe-money distinguishes offal from value, where the Jew and Orlick both represent marginalised types, where Jaggers's status is only so exalted because he has been bought up, certainly having nothing to do with abstract notions of justice or worth. 'Over the way' sets a 'great gulf' between the rich lawyer and Abraham Lazarus (the word play on the rich man and Lazarus in the parable of Luke 16 is obvious), and the gulf is equivalent to those on either side of the Panopticon, but it is an opposition which the names and word-play show as being nothing but the effects of power in society.

Thus the production, and reproduction, of oppression is what the book charts. Orlick attempts to move over to the other side in the Panopticon, and from the attempted assumption of that position, turns against Pip. Magwitch's acquisition of money is his attempt to move to the other side, to create a Pip, whom he surveys. In fact, he remains for ever the criminal. Nor can Orlick change, and though he is in the county jail at the end, the replication of the book's past events seems safe with him when he is released: he really has no alternative, and as such he remains an apt commentary on the course an oppressed class must follow. Pip, in terms of status, moves over to the other side, in Panopticon terms, but his social formation is already firm, and basically he cannot change either: the events in the second part of his 'expectations' are an aberration from what he is in the first and third parts. Ironically, since he is cast there as guilty, what he is at those points is preferable to what he becomes in the second part.

As the recidivist, he wishes to be given Biddy's child, which would start again the whole cycle of oppression; and self-oppressive to the end, he writes out his autobiography – one that remains remarkably terse as to its intentions and its status as writing and which, while beautifully written, rolls out as though automatically the product of a consciousness that remains fixed. There is, in *Great Expectations*, implicit commentary about the mode of autobiography. Autobiography defines the subject confessionally; it puts upon it the onus of 'explanation', makes it prison-bound: a state that proves naturally acceptable to so much Romantic writing, where the tragic intensity of those who have to inhabit alienating spaces or constrictions can be defined as the source and inspiration of their reality. 'We think of the prison' – Eliot's reading of F.H. Bradley in *The Waste Land* suggests that the essence of humanity is that it is confined, this is its common condition. In contrast, Foucault's analysis stresses the prison as the mode that gives the person the sense of uniqueness, the sense of difference from the others. In that sense, autobiography becomes a mode that helps reproduce the discourse that the Panopticon society promotes – though with a twist. In Pip's case, subjugated as he is by these discourses, the mode becomes a vehicle for self-reflection, and for very moving writing, but how much else? There is not the self thinking and moving from there into an area of thought where it can question the terms of its language, but instead the self continuing to reify its own status, to see it as an isolated thing. It continues a divisive trend. Not only is Pip's autobiography one that is markedly end-stopped in the sense that there is no feeling for a future, no way in which there can be a further development of the self, so that experience seems to avail nothing, but that cut-offness exists too in Pip's relations with others, with those surrounding him, save perhaps with Pumblechook, and there it is hardly difficult to see. It is appropriate that Miss Havisham should say to him 'You made your own snares. *I* never made them' (44.358). It is manifestly untrue as a statement, and especially as far as the second sentence goes, which Miss Havisham corrects later with her own confession (Chapter 49). But Pip seems to receive this analysis and can't see that to individualise the issue in this way won't do. *Great Expectations* comes close to suggesting that in an understanding of a society, the concept of the individual is unhelpful, that what is important are the total manipulations of power and language by whatever group has the power of definition and control. Autobiography provides an inadequate paradigm.

The final irony of *Great Expectations* is that it displays the bankruptcy of Pip's efforts to understand what has happened to him. Just as he reads names and identities from tombstones, and no writer (it is an emphasis I want to pick up in later chapters) is more aware of tombstones and writing as epitaphic than Dickens, his utterance comes from beyond the grave, arresting the traveller ('Pause you'), like a voice from the tomb, like Magwitch's, indeed:

> This was a memorable day to me, for it made great changes in me. But it is the same with any life. Imagine one selected day struck out of it, and think how different its course would have been. Pause you who read this, and think for a moment of the long chain of iron or gold, of thorns or flowers, that would never have bound you, but for the formation of the first link on one memorable day.
>
> (9.73)

The 'memorable day' of the novel's first page and the first visit to Satis House come together; these two 'selected' days also repeat each other (chains of iron with Magwitch, of gold with Miss Havisham), as though contradicting the idea that days may be seen as specially selected or memorable. Narratively, the passage wishes to find a day when a first link was formed, but this is impossible, for the memorable day mentioned at the beginning of the passage may well not be the 'one memorable day' of its ending, which may be, instead, that of the meeting with the convict. A designation of a day as memorable tries to fix it, but the technique of the novel is to keep going back, as in the narratives of what happened twenty-five years previously, and thus to imply that narrative 'links' are always already in place; there is no start, even though Magwitch 'started up from among the graves' (1.4) and no possibility of a 'pause' except under the assumption of being struck dumb, as though by a voice from a tomb.[22] Confessional narrative tries to give a complete coherence, however displaced the completeness may be, but the price for that is a speaker as though struck dumb himself, like his sister, unable to speak of himself as he is at the time of writing, remaining someone who seems not to have gone beyond the emotional state documented in the writing.

Miss Havisham too thinks of herself as dead and replacing the bride-cake which is rotten and spider-eaten: 'This is where I will be laid when I am dead. They shall come and look upon me here' (11.85) and she appoints the places for her relatives: 'Matthew will come and see me at last . . . when I am laid on that table. That will be his place – there, . . . at my head. And yours will be there! And your husband's there! And Georgiana's there! Now you all know where to take your stations when you come to feast upon me' (11.88). The language is both that of anatomy – the corpse is to be exposed to all – and of cannibalism. Anatomy relates to Dickens's lifelong interest in the morgue, but it is also part of the Panoptical gaze, where the deep secrets of the body are opened up, and where an absolute truth about the self is assumed. Anatomising may be linked to images of eating the other: Miss Havisham on the table replicates Pip as a 'four-footed Squeaker' (4.27), taking the place of the pork on the Christmas table, with his throat cut by Dunstable the butcher (the second time Pip's throat has been threatened in the text) and further repeats the role of Magwitch as being 'sauce for a dinner' (5.34). In considering herself as the corpse, Miss Havisham antici-pates the corpses hunted for in *Our Mutual Friend*, the next novel of Dickens, and the economy associated with corpses in that text, but it is also true that she is marked out by a hatred of her body, which might suggest Julia Kristeva on abjection, (and which I will come back to, especially in discussing *Our Mutual Friend*). Having been shamed on her wedding-day, she thinks of herself as worthless: her self-loathing, and loathing of her body, so no one sees her eat, and allowing herself to burn to death and to be associated with rotten-ness are all forms of self-hatred which have much in common with abjection.

Looking, eating and being eaten all come together. The young man with Magwitch sees Pip and wants to eat him; the hare hung up by the heels seems to wink at Pip as though both are to be eaten/hung up (2.16); the cattle, also designed for slaughter, seem to accuse him in the morning mist (3.17). Newgate and Smithfield are associated (19.163-4), and the legal system is cagmag, rotten meat. Miss Havisham 'devours' Estella 'the beautiful creature she had reared' (38.300). Miss Havisham's body is to be eaten after death – but her death has virtually already occurred – as a metonymy for her money which is the thing really wanted.[23] Her body was never desired by Compeyson: only her money. The refusal of the body here, which is repeated when the 'Spider' Drummle takes Estella in marriage and misuses her, means that the body is seen always as dead, like Jaggers's death-masks, so that in this Panoptical society, there is death associated with confession, with surveillance, with knowledge of the other, and with property and personal relations, which involve treatment of the other as a dead thing, and an equivalence between that knowledge of the other which is akin to anatomising and that control over the other which is anthropophagy.

III

For Q.D. Leavis, *Great Expectations* is about relationships between guilt and shame induced in the child. Pip feels guilt with his involvement with the convict, shame in relation to Miss Havisham and Estella. At Satis House, he is 'humiliated, hurt, spurned, offended, angry, sorry – I cannot hit on the right name for the smart' (8.63). After he is apprenticed, he feels 'ashamed of home' and dreads the idea that in some unlucky hour, 'I, being at my grimiest and commonest, should lift up my eyes and see Estella looking in at one of the wooden windows of the forge. I was haunted by the fear that she would, sooner or later, find me out, with a black face and hands, doing the coarsest part of my work, and would exult over me and despise me' (14.106, 107–8). This is an erotic fear, connecting social shame ('beggar my neighbour') to the fear of being seen working at the forge, probably inadequately clothed: shame is the fear of being found wanting in masculinity, and this connects with all the male violence that runs through the text as a desperate attempt to compensate the self for its inadequacy.

The fear Pip expresses, which may also be a desire, a wish to be humiliated by this imaginary Estella, replicates an experience of the young Dickens in the blacking factory, when his father came in when he was working at the window, working so hard (with Bob Fagin) that people would stop and watch. When John Dickens and the relative who gave the young Dickens employment quarrelled, and Dickens left, Dickens writes that 'it [the quarrel] may have had some backward reference, in part, for anything I know, to my employment at the window.'[24] If it did, the father's petit-bourgeois sympathies were on top: the boy might work, but work must not be defined in working-class terms. The secrecy of the middle class must be maintained.

Shame has been discussed in terms of fear of being looked at – which would link it to the whole operation of the Panopticon – and has been connected, too, to fear of being regarded with contempt (Dickens being watched at work in his 'prison' as a child by a father who could come and go as he pleased, Pip being watched by Estella), and as a result, being abandoned.[25] If a distinction may be maintained between guilt and shame, shame sets up a self that watches the self all the time with disapprobation, so that it makes the narcissism of looking in the mirror impossible (as in Lacan's mirror-phase), and from a masculinist standpoint, it is felt to feminise. Guilt, which Freud calls 'the most important problem in the development of civilization', he defines as 'fear of the superego'.[26] And what is the superego? It comes into play as an instinct is renounced in the face of a superior, external authority, and it replaces that authority.

> Originally, renunciation of instinct was the result of fear of an external authority: one renounced one's satisfactions in order not to lose its love. If one has carried out this renunciation, one is, as it were, quits with the authority and no sense of guilt should remain. But with fear of the superego the case is different. Here instinctual renunciation is not enough, for the wish persists and cannot be concealed from the superego. Thus, in spite of the renunciation that has been made, a sense of guilt comes about ... Instinctual renunciation no longer has a completely liberating effect; virtuous continence is no longer rewarded with the assurance of love. A threatened external unhappiness – loss of love and punishment on the part of the external authority – has been exchanged for a permanent internal unhappiness, for the tension of the sense of guilt.
>
> (p. 320)

Guilt makes the ego side with patriarchy, so that for the male it enforces masculinity. In that sense the statement about prison conditions in Chapter 32, already quoted, comes from guilt: from the need to side with a societal superego. Writing in the 1840s about himself and his childhood experience in the blacking factory, Dickens said: 'I know how all these things have worked together to make me what I am.' It is a confidence belonging to the *Copperfield* period, akin to that expressed so often in *The Prelude* (1850), Wordsworth's autobiography. Yet the declaration does not preclude the shame that made the incident one completely closed off from even his family who did not know about it till after his death. In that bourgeois confidence, much is repressed. *Great Expectations* is different in having no such confidence, in showing the production of guilt and shame in the child.

For Freud, 'civilization' has to repress the aggressive and the sexual instincts. Or as Mrs Joe, who has aspirations towards the petit-bourgeois class, puts it, 'People are put in the Hulks because they murder, and because they rob and forge, and do all kinds of bad; and they always begin by asking questions' (2.15). The word 'forge', which has application to Compeyson, brings Pip near to the Hulks: forgery and the forge link at the level of language. Mrs Joe is the agent of civilisation, but more: she stands for the text's violent women, and this issue links to that of masochism. Her repression of Pip is as violent as the violence she seems to fear (her repressiveness suggested in the pins and needles with which she armours her apron, an unconscious form of self-defence, futile since she is struck from behind). She has a Panoptical drive herself in being a 'spy and listener' (15.113) and a sense of civilisation as protecting and regulating by processes of law, as when she tries to shame Joe into violence – 'What was the name [Orlick] gave me before the base man who swore to defend me?' (15.114). And she watches the fight between Joe and Orlick: she provokes both men. In the same way, Estella watched Pip and Herbert fight, and Miss Havisham watched Pip and Estella play cards, and Pip be beggared.

When Mrs Joe argues with Orlick, the text becomes reflective about women's violence:

> 'What did you say?' cried my sister, beginning to scream. 'What did you say? What did that fellow Orlick say to me, Pip? What did he call me, with my husband standing by? O! O! O!' Each of these exclamations was a shriek; and I must remark of my sister, what is equally true of all the violent women I have ever seen, that passion was no excuse for her, because it is undeniable that instead of lapsing into passion, she consciously and deliberately

took extraordinary pains to force herself into it, and became blindly furious by regular stages . . .'

(15.114)

Joe has then to fight Orlick and knock him out, and Orlick responds by the attack on Mrs Joe by hitting her with that instrument of orthopaedics and control, a convict's leg-iron. Mrs Joe is the un-loved wife married by Joe for the sake of Pip; perhaps looking after Pip means she has no children of her own – she may be, even in her violence, a victim, who treats her assailant with 'humble propitia-tion' 'such as I have seen pervade the bearing of a child toward a hard master' (16.123), demonstrating that she has never been more than a child. The attack on her foregrounds something concealed in her attempt to be 'everybody's master' (15.113). Whatever the narrational violence that assimilates her with 'all the violent women I have ever seen' and makes her violence simply worked up from her will, the text points to a syndrome of injured women turned violent or propitiatory, and may even suggest a desire in the nar-rator for them: Estella, Molly, Mrs Joe, Miss Havisham (another woman sabotaged by a brother) described in language assimilating her to Mrs Joe as appearing to have 'dropped, body and soul, within and without, under the weight of a crushing blow' (8.62 – the text thus aligning Compeyson and Orlick in violence). What of Estella's violence? Pip receives nothing but physical or mental cruelty from her, and her glacial sternness, repression of sensuality and statue-like features align her with the northern Venus fantasised by Sacher-Masoch in *Venus in Furs* (1870). Her violence, which is crushed by Bentley Drummle's beatings (perhaps that is what she seeks out through marrying him), is what Pip wants for the shame it induces. Mrs Joe treats Pip and Joe with contempt, which makes her anger sadistic, but more importantly her hysterical behaviour is maso-chistic and a public (as opposed to belonging to the private and secret space enforced by Panopticism) sexualisation of her body: 'Here my sister, after a fit of clappings and screamings, beat her hands upon her bosom and upon her knees, and pulled her cap off and pulled her hair down . . .' Miss Havisham tortures her body equally, in two chapters, 38 and 49, with Estella and with Pip. Estella virtually denies her body's existence (29.237–8), what she calls her 'tenderness', but she marries a man calculated to torture the body and so to sexualise it.

Freud at first considered masochism a craving for punishment from the superego. But masochism is also a problem in that it suspends the pleasure principle – the avoidance of unpleasure and the obtaining of pleasure. The pleasure principle sounds strongly rationalist and Utilitarian, and Freud's *Beyond the Pleasure Principle* (1919) has importance in proposing a death-drive which counters this pleasure principle. Death is the defeat of rationality, and indeed of any model of thought which thinks in terms of subjectivity, depth and inwardness. Masochism could be linked to that death-drive, as a form of undoing the drive that produces the subject marked out by rationality and depth – the very model produced by Utilitarianism (constructing people as subject to the rationality of the pleasure principle, marking them out by depth through the machinery of the Panopticon). Freud's rationality made him think of the death drive as an older regressive instinct, but the undoing of the organisation that the pleasure principle implies is a defiance of the economy of rationality.[27] In this appears the use of masochism as a way of undoing the single subject formed through the constituting powers of the Panopticon.

In contrast to Freud's primary attaching of masochism to sadism, as an activity of the ego desiring the punishment of the superego, Gilles Deleuze describes masochism as separable from it, as an undoing of punishment, since that and the fear it produces secures societal order and patriarchal hierarchy. Deleuze suggests that male masochism comes from violence enacted by the woman, not by the punishing father, which would link it to the feminine.[28] It emanates not from the superego, but from the mother of the oral phase, who is associated at that stage both with boundless giving and with pain perceived from the standpoint of the narcissistically demanding child. It is the memory of this that is articulated in masochism, where the Oedipalised child 'punishes' the father in him (the superego) who has negated the power of the woman.

In *Great Expectations*, the sister and Miss Havisham embody aspects of the devouring mother, and Estella is the figure fantasised as omnipresent and giving character to everything about whom Pip thinks masochistically. Pip has a fantasy of the vengeful return of his sister when the convict returns, and Orlick's attack on him, blaming him for what happened to her, may also be seen as contributing to his masochistic fantasy of the return and dominance of the woman causing pain. Orlick's attack on Mrs Joe might be seen as akin to anal rape, and analogously, his sadism to Pip – 'I'll have a good look at you and a good goad at you' (53.422) – reads like male rape. Heroes in literature, though they may suffer, are not imagined as victims of sexual abuse, certainly not willing it, but that Pip walks into this situation suggests how much he has been opened up to sexual suffering at the hands of the woman, how much he has been feminised, just as feminity marks his utterance to Estella: – 'the rhapsody welled up within me, like blood from an inward wound' (44.363). His confessional narrative is akin to an 'admission' of being raped – from the moment when he is seized by the convict, (himself a feminised figure of tears and shivers and with the memory of the violent woman Molly behind him, the woman he thinks destroyed his child), and is threatened with the cannibalistic young man. He is taken over completely – 'done very brown' (15.108 – cooked, or rolled in excrement) in London by having his fortune made for him. The masochistic feminine *par excellence* in the text is Miss Havisham who describes giving 'your whole heart and soul to the smiter – as I did' (29.240), an act of violence which the text's statement about violent women would make into a series of acts of will-power. But then, if Pip has been feminised, the statement about violent women turns against himself, and is yet another example of a wish for punishment.

While the attraction to the cold woman and the interest in the violent woman as masochistic is a new and transgressive note in the text, this does not exhaust the text's attention to violence. The boy Herbert's violence, no doubt induced by Estella's objections to him (29.236), is codified according to 'regular rules' (9.91), and thus made bourgeois. Violence is implicit in the state's 'gentle way of punishment', in its activities which oppose the self's aggressive instincts and operate as the superego, claiming to know the murderous and transgressive thoughts of the self and inviting that self to further degrees of aggression against itself through the mechanisms of guilt. In Dickens, the state is no less violent than the subject of the state. Jaggers 'tames' Molly in an act of obviously psychosexual violence, just as Orlick secures Mrs Joe's silent acquiescence to him through horrific violence. Both produce docile bodies. These different subjects – different as regards their position in relation to Panoptical power – both find productive a form of violence towards women, one of which may perhaps be codified as a normalising of the marginal gypsy, the other being aggression towards the woman who can rely on nothing save the normalising procedures of Panoptical society.

The shamed subject, the subject of the Panoptical gaze, has to

find a way out through violence, where this implies the loss of a
sense of shame, and in this sense the violence, which forces people
out of their subject-positions, is overcoded by a masochism. When
Magwitch says to the sergeant, 'Now the Hulks has got its gentleman again, through me' (5.37), referring to Compeyson, it is after
they have been fighting at the bottom of a ditch, both like 'two wild
beasts' as the sergeant says. Violence of this sort rejects shame, and
Magwitch's statement is a resistance to the usual form of naming
associated with prison-power, which, as in their joint trial (42.349),
automatically diminished Magwitch and elevated Compeyson. Pip's
fight with Herbert, Joe's fight with Orlick (and putting his fists up
to Jaggers), Pip's struggle with Miss Havisham (Chapter 49) as she
runs at him in a destructive blaze which may well be vengeful
passion or sexual repression broken out,[29] and the final struggle
underwater of Magwitch and Compeyson (Chapter 54) are all repetitions of this. So is the fight of Molly and the strangled other
woman (Chapter 48), though that violence is capped by a margina-
lising which I have pointed out, a project of the text's Benthamism
and its normalising strain: Molly is constructed as having gypsy
blood in her. Jaggers's trick with Bentley Drummle, which is to
incite him to violence at the table in an exposure of self (26.216) is
suggestive of the novel's technique: to arouse the aggression that
may continually be seen to work against the 'cringers', enforcing
shame upon them. Fighting, by taking place in mud or water or fire
and amongst cinders or brambles, has thus been constructed in a
powerfully elemental manner, and it usually has the character of
representing the oppressed striking back. As such, it is a form of
violence which works in contrast to the state and societal violence
operant in Panoptical power. When Dickens writes in *Oliver Twist*
that Fagin, after being condemned to death, was taken into prison
and 'here he was searched, that he might not have about him the
means of anticipating the law' (52.360), the point is made that there
is a contest of who has the right to be violent operant here: self-
violence is not allowable, state violence is.[30]

   In so far as the novel identifies with violence, it is separate from
the bourgeois Dickens. Whatever liberalism affects the book – as in
the 'poor dreams' that nearly save Mr Jaggers in spite of himself, or
in the way that Pip seems to enjoy a reasonable bourgeois existence
in the Eastern Branch of Herbert's firm – is not central nor does
interest in character sanction belief in the individual as ultimately
irrepressible. Rather, the idea of the Panopticon as the chief model

for the formation of any individuality in nineteenth-century Britain makes for something much more complex and gives rise to the sense that the formation of individuality is itself delusory as a hope. It is itself the problem it seeks to solve – through its way of dividing a society and separating it. To that diagnosis, which demands a consideration of power structures in society such as Foucault gives, and which draws attention to language as a way of making the person prison-bound, the autobiographical mode of *Great Expectations* bears witness, keeping the narrator in the prison. Just as Wemmick's father and his pleasant and playful ways, and the possibility that Jaggers himself might one day want a pleasant home, ensure that the prison's durability is not in question: these individual escapes, by staying within the limits of the individual idea, address, effectively, no problem at all. Failing breaking the power structure, a structure which the text is also collusive with, the only way out is violence.

2

'An Impersonation of the Wintry Eighteen-hundred and Forty-Six': *Dombey and Son*

I

When Ruskin wrote after Dickens's death that 'Dickens was a pure modernist – a leader of the steam-whistle party *par excellence*',[1] he both gave an early use of the word 'modernist' in English and identified him with railways and railway power, which are central to *Dombey and Son*. The reference in that novel to the railway's 'mighty course of civilisation and improvement'(*Dombey and Son*, 6.65) fits with Asa Briggs's singling out the word 'improvement' as a key word for the historical period, and it allows Leavis to argue that the railway as a symbol in the novel is the 'triumphant manifestation of beneficent energy'.[2] Steven Marcus takes the railway a little differently as 'the great symbol of social transformation', so that he reads the novel as about change.[3] Without referring to Ruskin he argues that 'it is universally acknowledged that the idea of growth or development is one of the chief conceptions of the present epoch. Nothing is more characteristic of the *modern* habit of mind, perhaps, than its tendency to think in terms of this idea' (p. 319, my emphasis).

If Dickens is to be thought of as a modernist, it fits with the immediacy of the situations described in *Dombey and Son* (1846–48), particularly thinking of the years of railway speculation, which reached high-fever point in 1846–47. It also belongs with the changes frequently commented on in Dickens's writing itself at or around the time of *Dombey*. These are implicit even in the non-picaresque, non-character-centred title, *Dealings with the Firm of Dombey and Son, Wholesale, Retail and For Exportation*. Finally, the modernity of the text fits with the 1848 revolutions in Europe.

Dickens's letters on the revolutions in Paris and in Italy record his total enthusiasm, and add interest to the point that much of *Dombey and Son* was written abroad (in Lausanne and Paris), and that the novel followed upon a sojourn in Italy, where Dickens commented on Venice, with contemptuous reference to those who see the times as 'degenerate' because 'a railroad is building across the water at Venice; instead of going down on their knees, the drivellers, and thanking heaven that they live in a time when iron makes roads, instead of prison bars, and engines for driving screws into the skulls of innocent men' (quoted, Marcus, p. 306). Here indeed Dickens's true hero was the Ironmaster. The reference to torture in Venice anticipates Mrs Skewton who indeed becomes a 'driveller' after her stroke, and her nostalgia for 'those darling bygone times' from which 'how dreadfully we have degenerated' (27.375), and makes Dickens an apologist for the modern.

On 26 June 1846, the repeal of the Corn Laws was given its third reading in Parliament; on 27 June in Lausanne, uprooted from his home and from London, Dickens 'began Dombey'. The triumph of Free Trade in Britain itself signals a modern development. But it is not agreed, in criticism of *Dombey and Son*, that the text identifies with modern free-trade industrial developments. What is implied by the existence of the firm Dombey and Son? F.R. Leavis sees Dombey as a prototype of Gradgrind the Utilitarian, 'the new money-power', representative of the 'England whose prevailing ethos is that of *Hard Times*' (Leavis, p. 7). This would align Dombey with Peel and the Free Traders of 1846, making Dombey something of a modernist himself and his firm a contrast to the East India Company, whose powers as a protectionist organisation were disappearing in the face of the pressures for free trade. He is also a contrast to Sir Barnet Skettles, who as an MP hopes to 'touch up the Radicals' (14.196) who were, of course, pro-Free Trade. If Dombey is a modernist, the contrast with his 'old-fashioned' son is indeed piquant.

But this view of Dombey is contested, for instance, by Humphry House, and by Robert Clark who suggests that it is Carker who represents the expansionist capitalist – who would free trade with Edith, of course – whose spirit of capitalism is 'a threat erupting within the established house of mercantilism'.[4] This criticism makes much of Dombey's apparently negative attitude to the railways – in which some criticisms of the novel, usually concentrating on the destruction of Staggs's Gardens, have joined. Nina Auerbach, for example, sees the railroad as the sphere of the mechanical and masculine rather than the organic and feminine. It too is part of a closed and regulated system, without flowing and diffusing beyond one. 'Like Dombey ... the railroad embodies phallic force ... [it] has no private language; its voice is deafeningly public. ... its shrieking linear progress makes us turn with relief to the secret, private sphere of feminine dissolution.' [5]

If the text endorses Florence's passivity, it would then be anti-modernist. But I think Auerbach's reading simply wishes a set of concepts onto the railway. By pinning its development to the power of patriarchy, she diminishes its explosive potential, which though it may indeed be shaped by patriarchy does not simply function in its favour. The sense of the railroad's dynamism as it changes everything might be more profitably compared to Marx's awed praise for the modernising force of the bourgeoisie as described in *The Communist Manifesto* of 1847:

> Constant revolutionizing of production, uninterrupted disturbance of all social conditions, everlasting uncertainty and agitation distinguish the bourgeois epoch from all earlier ones. All fixed, fast-frozen relations, with their train of ancient and venerable prejudices and opinions, are swept away, all new-formed ones become antiquated before they can ossify. All that is solid melts into air ... [6]

The uncertainty and agitation would link, of course, with the new proliferation of joint-stock companies and their speculations, which fits directly with Dombey's world.

If Dickens presents the values of old-fashioned mercantilism, with a fascination for the railways which is mixed with nostalgia, the novel suggests that Dombey's destiny is ultimately to be replaced; that the collapse of his firm is historical and a matter of inevitable change, not simply produced from a different kind of money-power. But if the novel can be read as presenting Dombey as a modern free-trader, as I think it can, the challenge it presents is more radical, since there can be no evasion of the power represented by modernity, and this in itself has profound implications for the extent to which the novel can allow itself to be aware of its issues – for example, those of imperialism and of the sexual politics engendered by modern capitalism which extend to the Victorian family home. Thus Suvendrini Perera discusses the novel in relation to imperialist expansionism in the 1840s. The repealing of the Corn Laws in 1846 had the effect of opening up foreign markets to British traffic in a new way: the implications of repeal were not merely domestic (e.g. affecting Ireland and British agricultural interests), though that is the way they are customarily represented. They licensed a huge if informal imperialist expansion.

In considering this argument, it is relevant that Walter Gay and Florence go to China immediately after they are married, and this fits in the context of the British–Chinese Opium War of 1840, waged after the Chinese government ordered the confiscation of opium which was being smuggled into China from India by British merchants. The Liberals and Radicals supported the war in the spirit of arguing that England was fighting for the opening of trade to all nations. The Radical Joseph Hume argued in the House of Commons in July 1840 that 'from the moment British subjects at Canton were placed in prison to the danger of their lives the Chinese became the aggressors', and he defended the war since the approximity of China to the 'Burmese empire' meant that the 'peace of India greatly depended on our vindicating British supremacy before China'.[7] It is interesting to recall that according to Captain Cuttle, Walter Gay was rescued from the 'Son and Heir' by a 'Chinese trader', where he was regarded with favour 'and so, the supercargo dying at Canton, he got made (having acted as clerk afore), and now he's supercargo aboard another ship, same owners' (56.747). Florence's honeymoon on a ship to China would have been spent amongst quantities of opium. Britain's exploitation of China, which I will return to in considering *Little Dorrit*, fits with the free-trade note of *Household Words* and that journal's attitude to China, calling the Chinese 'a people who came to a dead stop' in comparison to Britain, with its Great Exhibition, an 'Exhibition of the moving world' (*Household Words*, 5 July 1851). The discourse of the non-modernity of the Chinese is also a basis for imperialism. And certainly, the personae in the drama of the Opium War seem present in *Dombey and Son* – the East India Company is just round the corner from Dombey's offices (4.36) and an East India Director 'of immense wealth' but with no more substance than a tailor's dummy, is invited to Dombey's 'housewarming' (36.489). But the text embodies several other buried histories of colonial intervention. The Dombey firm trades in hides (1.2) which suggests a connection with Buenos Aires. Mr Pipchin's death from a failed speculation in the Peruvian mines is a reminder of the importance of Peru as a mineral-producing region. Lima opened as a port to the British in 1822, received loans from British joint-stock companies in the 1820s, suspended interest payments on loans in 1825, and sent companies which had invested in Peru into liquidation. (This was part of a commercial crisis running throughout the winter of 1825–26, resulting from speculation mania, and serving as a background to *Little Dorrit*, which is set around 1825.) Similarly Walter Gay is sent out to Barbados, the site of considerable controversy since the emancipation of the slaves there in 1833, the fall of sugar production during the 1830s and 1840s, and the British government passing the Sugar Equalisation Act in 1846 removing protection on sugar from the West Indies. Major Bagstock's silent, anonymous 'dark servant' comes from either the East or West Indies, in both of which places Bagstock has been. And such phrases of Susan Nipper that she is 'a black slave and a mulotter' and 'I may wish, you see, to take a voyage to Chaney, Mrs Richards, but I mayn't know how to leave the London docks' (5.53, 3.29) are fine reminders of how much the language of trade and empire is in the discourse of the text.

Perera's essay suggests that the conflict between Dombey and Florence is a 'displacement' of mercantilism's impact, and that 'the operations of mercantile capital are measured mainly in their social and human cost to the metropolis' as opposed to their impact on the countries colonised by such firms as Dombey and Son.[8] This argument implies that, however real the father/daughter conflict, its resolution in terms of the change to Mr Dombey that occurs at the end deflects attention from the true enormity that exists in the firm's existence and that the narrative legitimates by its silence the imperialism it treats of at its margins. This reading seems right, though I find it inconsistent that it should also see Dombey as representative of 'old-style mercantilism' (p. 611), and I want to add to its argument that the novel's narrative of the family is effectively a legitimating one covering up issues of empire and preventing their consideration, by pointing out that it fails to deliver just such a narrative of domestic change.

Problems with the narrative of *Dombey and Son* begin with the way no Dickens novel has more starts and stops and acts less like a railroad in terms of possessing a single direction. A progressive narrative based on patrilinear succession is undone by the text which destroys Paul Dombey after the fifth monthly part, having setting out from his birth to do just that. The 'Son and Heir' goes down in more than one sense, in its literal one by effectively removing another central character, Walter, from the novel's direction. Dickens originally intended Walter Gay, the surrogate son (as 'brother' to Paul and Florence), to have a Hogarthian fate as a kind of Idle Apprentice, which would, of course, have made the narrative's resolution impossible. But the inconsistency of the change whereby Walter comes back means that both narrative possibilities for him are equally arbitrary: character development follows no consistent line to which either novelist or reader can feel committed. Similarly, the process whereby the businessman can be humanised depends on a violent change of genre – from realism to melodrama. Leavis argues for the 'unreality' of the events surrounding Edith Dombey, Carker, Alice Marwood, Mrs Brown and the 'bought bride' theme in contrast to the tracing of the birth and death of Paul Dombey, and though it may be argued that the handling of the repression of women and their sexuality in Edith and Florence requires a different genre, that of melodrama, in which to do it, changing from the earlier dominant realism, it is noticeable that the switch also coincides with another change. That is the bringing into further prominence of an older form of caricatural writing (Toots, Cuttle, Mrs MacStinger), which represents a move to a sub-eighteenth-century style, regressing from modernity. In these contradictory forms of writing may be seen narrative moves that threaten the single linear presentation of Dombey as a character and make his presentation plural. Any change he may undergo loses consistency in relation to a first and dominant sense of him when the text itself changes all around him in modes of conceptualising character and action. It is simply not the same character who changes.

II

To illuminate this contradictoriness which disallows change and to illustrate both its essentiality to Dickens and its impossibility, I want to refer to an earlier text of the 1840s, *A Christmas Carol* (1843), whose main character anticipates Dombey in his self-exclusion and attitude to business and to money. The change involves the secular conversion of Scrooge, who becomes the benevolent businessman, as good as his word, the new Mr Fezziwig to his clerk Bob Cratchit and the patriarch in relation to Tiny Tim, whose crutch stands as an important metonymy for social deprivation, a hint of the text's concern with the 'condition of England' question. Tiny Tim's allegorical status is confirmed by the appearance of the boy and girl, Ignorance and Want, who come out from under the skirts of the Spirit of Christmas Present. The words of the Spirit are crucially concerned with the need for change, change from those who live in the industrial city, whose doom is otherwise threatened:

> 'Beware them both, and all of their degree, but most of all beware this boy, for on his brow I see that written which is Doom, unless the writing be erased. Deny it!' cried the Spirit, stretching out its hand towards the city. 'Slander those who tell it ye! Admit it for your factious purposes, and make it worse. And bide the end!'
>
> (p. 108)

I will return to this passage, but will fasten first on the problem in the change that Scrooge undergoes. For the Benthamite and Malthusian Scrooge, the personification of Economic Man, to become like Fezziwig, his first boss, or like the Cheeryble brothers in *Nicholas Nickleby* would be an impossibility: he would immediately go out of business. These bosses are no more than children: the narrative of the conversion of Scrooge is also impossible both in prescriptive terms and in the likelihood of it happening. As an impossible change it can only be produced by two narrative tricks, one of which is to present the change in the form of a dream and ghost story and merely to record, not show, the change afterwards; the other is by the text working, as Marcus puts it, 'by a kind of regression; its mode resembles *Pickwick Papers* and *Oliver Twist* more than it does the work of the period during which it was written' (p. 272). The text lapses into an escapist mode which refuses modernity, represses it even. Going back in time, which literally happens with the episode of the Spirit of Christmas Past, allows for simpler solutions and evades the challenge of the modern.

But *A Christmas Carol* is more complex than Marcus's account suggests since the narrative design permits two resolutions of Scrooge's situation. He can be converted: that is the celebratory and non-sustainable Christmas-pudding closure, or as the Ghost of Christmas Future shows him, he can go on and die in a state of anonymity. This possibility is presented to him when the last of the Spirits conducts him into a part of the city corresponding in type to the vision produced earlier of Ignorance and Want. The shop where old rags are bought, like Mr Krook's in *Bleak House*, is run by 'old

Joe', who seems to be a pawnbroker, and here the charwoman, the laundress (Mrs Dilber) and the undertaker's man all meet, having rifled Scrooge's body and things, even replacing the shirt in which he was laid out by a cheaper one made of calico. The Spirit goes on to show Scrooge the bare bed where the corpse lies, as yet unrecognised by Scrooge as his; finally the Spirit moves to the churchyard, which in description fits Nemo's in *Bleak House*. But unlike Nemo – no name – the Spirit points Scrooge to the inscription on the grave, which is his own name, so that in terror Scrooge asks that he may 'sponge away the writing on this stone' (p. 126). The words recall those of the Spirit of Christmas Present, already quoted, about the writing on the brow of the boy. To erase the writing would be to eliminate the name, and naming in Dickens has a power of imposing character, eliminating subjectivity and mis-naming (Scrooge is indifferently called 'Scrooge' or 'Marley').

The narrative of the last of the Spirits fits then with a writing which the protagonists are unaware of: the boy as Ignorance cannot see what is written on his brow: Scrooge comes to the recognition that he is identical to the despised figure of finance capital only when he confronts his own tomb. It is the novelist who sees these things, just as it is the novelist who shows the middle class the wretched poor parts of the city. The Spirits are suggestive of the power of the realist text to show something the bourgeois world does not want to see. That world is also given a fantasy ending in the Fifth Stave of *A Christmas Carol*, but in the other narrative provided by the last of the spirits, importantly paratactic so that connections are made by Scrooge himself while the Spirit remains silent and certainly not answering Scrooge's question whether these are 'the shadows of the things that Will be, or . . . shadows of things that May be, only' (p. 124), there is the demise of all Scrooge stands for. He is destroyed as the embodiment of the business ethos of the bourgeoisie. He is the spirit of 'the city' where this is no longer the generalised city but really the City, i.e. London, 'in the heart of it, on 'Change, among the merchants' (p. 111). In the vision of the working-class who see him off there is a striking sense of Marx in *The Communist Manifesto* referring to the bourgeoisie producing, in the proletariat, its own grave-diggers. The vision may be repressed by the writing of the Fifth Stave, where Scrooge wakes up to find himself alive and well on Christmas Day, but the ambiguities that hover over the last two chapter titles offer two possible conclusions, 'The Last of the Spirits' and 'The End of It' which leaves the question open: what narrative is Dickens writing really? What 'end' is the city to 'bide'? Or better, what possibility of change is there when a narrative already seems written? The issue of 'change' returns, and it is noteworthy that Scrooge's own financial success depends on his existence in the world of ''Change' where that word is only a contraction of 'Exchange'. It is the place for the swapping of money as empty signifiers – Paul Dombey asks 'What is money after all?' – so that 'exchange' guarantees no alteration of narrative.

As in *A Christmas Carol* there seems to be a double movement in *Dombey and Son* – refuting the possibility of change as much as it overtly deals with it. Modernity may be identified as much with death as with progress: that is what the conscious text must resist as a belief. Thus the names 'Dombey and Son' and 'Son and Heir' point to a patriarchal narrative of regular succession and linearity. Paul Dombey, the infant, is named both for his father and his grandfather, and the change in Mr Dombey's personal narrative is this: he 'had risen, as his father had before him, in the course of life and death, from Son to Dombey' (1.2). A prescriptive narrative exists in names which have been pre-written and to which individual identities have to fit. In cancelled passages from Dickens's manuscript, Dombey, in the elation of being a father, savours the name 'with his eyes half-closed as if he were reading the name in a device of flowers' – which would certainly be a proleptic moment, a suggestion of the death of the boy and hence threatening the death of the narrative itself. He further ponders, needlessly, as it turns out, on the 'inconvenience in the necessity of writing "junior" . . .' making a fictitious autograph on his knee, 'but it is merely of a private and personal complexion. It doesn't enter into the correspondence of the House. Its signature remains the same' (1.1, 2). Identities and signatures do not fit, do not 'correspond'. The prior power of writing, which is there before individual characters are aware of it, and imposes itself on those who are the subjects of it, suggests the power of history – or 'Time and his brother Care' – to control, to 'set some marks' on the face and the brow (1.1). It is not just Paul who has to be a Dombey and 'a man' (11.145). Paul himself describes his father as 'Dombey and Son' (12.153) and the implications of this are profound: that the child is father to the man, that Mr Dombey cannot pass off the responsibility of anything onto his son, but must be the child he wants to have himself (as Scrooge has to go back on his childhood). He must contain in himself his own child-likeness and must establish his future for himself. And if 'and Son' also allows for the idea that 'son of . . .' means having the same character as another, wanting to possess that character, Carker, certainly a modern if not an aesthete with his villa in Norwood hung with pictures, in imitating Mr Dombey might be thought of as the son, in an Oedipal narrative where he cannot secure Edith for himself.[9]

The name 'Dombey and Son' is coercive in its import on Dombey, Paul and Carker, to say nothing of Florence, and the naming power, which originates with the patriarchal firm not only misnames, as is seen with the various names Dr Parker Peps gives to Mrs Dombey, but leaves out the whole category of the feminine, as when Polly Toodle becomes Richards. She is not only masculinised but also, curiously, given a name which unconsciously fits with 'Dickens'. (The number of people called 'Dick' in the novels comes to mind here.) It is as though the novelist makes an identification of himself with the mother's body, that which sustains, and which allows the existence of the patriarchal narrative by preserving the 'son'. 'Dombey and Son' implies a narrative whose essence is the preservation of patriarchy as well as its constitution – there is no patriarchy until there is a son. Mr Dombey rejoices that the 'house will once again . . . be not only in name but in fact Dombey and Son' (1.1) but the connection of signifier and signified cannot be made so easily, since the 'house' is ambiguous, both the firm and the home, both the office in the city and the 'house' in the 'region between Portland-place and Bryanstone-square' (3.24), which is the firm's 'home-department' (part of the title of Chapter 3). Patriarchal narrative exists by its repression, firstly of the mother's body – she dies barely noticed – and secondly of the daughter (according to Mrs Chick, Florence will never, never, never, be a Dombey' – (5.50)) who also acts as mother to Paul. Thirdly there is the suppression of the nurse, the mother figure. Miss Tox, would-be mother, is only elevated to the godmothership of Paul 'in virtue of her insignificance' (5.49).

Many readings of the novel have fastened on the exclusion of the daughter, usually basing themselves on Miss Tox's words immediately after Paul's death, 'that Dombey and Son should be a Daughter after all' (16.225). But it is also interesting to focus on the prior exclusion of the mother, like Mrs Gradgrind in *Hard Times*, remembering that it is the mother's existence, rather than simply the daughter's, which shows how patrilinear succession – and by extension, linear narrative itself – is based on repression or exclusion of an otherness embodied in the mother. Mother and daughter represent a heterogeneity which does not, by its excess, fit a pre-set narrative: 'what was a girl to Dombey and Son? In the capital of the House's name and dignity, such a child was merely a piece of base coin that couldn't be invested' (1.3) – something that does not fit Mr Dombey's entirely homogeneous text, like the Dickens text itself, whose whole principle is excess. An inability to name, which pairs with misnaming, goes with an attitude to class (Dombey cannot refer to Mr Toodle by name) and operates against women. Dombey writes Paul's epitaph as 'beloved and only child' (18.237) in a parapraxis which leaves out Florence, just as Mr Gills has no recollection of the woman who walked into his shop within the last few days, though he can remember the man (4.41).

But if the text is thus sensitive to repression carried out through naming, it may be asked if it also fails to name things. Dickens's texts *do* name, as in 'This boy is Ignorance, this girl is Want' and naming and misnaming, if they are both here, would point to a doubleness of desire. Misnaming is repressive, but the desire to name is, on the contrary, part of a culture marked out by demonstration and showing. This may be connected to Michel Foucault in *Discipline and Punish*, which I have discussed in Chapter 1, reading the nineteenth century in terms of its Panopticism, its desire for a total vision where nothing will be opaque, where all can pass under the supervising eye of the state. It may also be linked to the wish, already apparent in *A Christmas Carol*, that narrative must make connections, however repressed these may be by those in the city whose response to such narrativising is, in the words of the Spirit of Christmas Present, to 'deny it'. In which case, the culture of demonstration, of removing repression and repressed links, would fit with aspects of modernity.

I would like to illustrate this by commenting on two famous passages, set pieces from the book, almost operatic, from Chapters 20 and 47. In the first, Mr Dombey travels from Euston station in London to Birmingham on a line actually opened in 1838 and perceives the railway as the 'type of the triumphant Monster, Death'. That act of naming, which is in one sense misnaming, represents his own alienated vision as the man in mourning, whose own melancholy in any case denies connections with the outside world. (In the same way, Carker's glimpses of the railway in Chapter 55 are strongly suggestive of his alienation, and both men's sense of the railway may be activated by a death-wish.) The railway embodies speed and democracy, as the appearance of Toodle as the stoker on the train suggests, and classlessness, for in 'piercing through the heart of every obstacle' in revolutionary fashion, it 'dragg[ed] living creatures of all classes, ages and degrees behind it' (20.275). Speed motivates this novel: for example, killing Paul Dombey as early as the fifth number, necessitating a memorandum to himself for no. 6: 'Great point of the no. to throw the interest of Paul *at once on Florence*' (*Dombey*, 840). And speed belongs to a revolutionary politics and one of modernity, where that implies change or the ability to bring things – including space and different spaces – more under control.[10]

As the train nears the industrial Midlands, in the present-tense narration 'everything around is blackened', the blackening belonging to the imagery of death. The language recalls the portrayal of Ignorance and Want:

> There are jagged walls and falling houses close at hand, and through the battered roofs and broken windows, wretched rooms are seen, where want and fever hide themselves in many wretched shapes, while smoke, and crowded gables, and distorted chimneys, and deformity of brick and mortar penning up deformity of mind and body choke the murky distance.
>
> (20.277)

The paragraph concludes with a sense that the railway may be the new spirit that shows things, replacing the Spirits of *A Christmas Carol* who show things to Scrooge, and may be suggestive of the novelistic writing itself:

> As Mr Dombey looks out of his carriage window, it is never in his thoughts that the monster who has brought him there has let the light of day in on these things, not made or caused them. It was the journey's fitting end, and might have been the end of everything; it was so ruinous and dreary.
>
> (20.277)

It is not the end of everything since journeys end in lovers' meeting (Chapter 21, Dombey and Edith), but in the indirect free discourse of the last sentence the impossibility of change – the finality of the 'end' – is also entertained as a possibility. And such an ending would be part of another, frightening, narrative which this novel cannot entertain, but must repress, in the name of concentrating on change.

In the description of the train's journey, there is a slippage: the 'monster' the first four times it is referred to in the section is identified with death and not with the train, but by the end, in the phrase 'the monster who has brought him there', it is the railway itself, as earlier, 'the carcasses of houses, and beginnings of new thoroughfares, had started off upon the line at steam's own speed, and shot away into the country in a monster train' (15.218). The monster stands outside nature: that is the definition of what the monstrous means. As the train becomes the monster, it works to undo the whole idea of nature as something which can have a separate existence. Indeed it rather organises and shapes nature. The 'railway world' as it is called in Chapter 15 is not only one of timetables and speed, generating in its turn the need for accurate watches and electric telegraphs, it marginalises 'old roads and paths' (20.276) and reverses perceptions of time and place. Such is the effect of the plunging into tunnels, the train being at one time above the earth and the next moment beneath it. Historically, the railroads in the 1830s and 1840s shaped landscapes: cuttings, embankments, bridges, tunnels implied profound changes which modernised the country. Everything becomes visible, within a culture of 'monstration'. The railway gives shape to a society which is becoming Panoptical, regulated, even by accurate clock-time, and 'monstration' and the 'monster' fit together. And hence the train journey is presented not just from the single vision of Mr Dombey seated in his carriage on the train; it is everywhere at once, just as the present tense used in this section implies a changed attitude to time, where things have to be seen simultaneously, and linearity of description or narration is a limitation. The writing of this passage illustrates the reversals in operation:

> Away, with a shriek, and a roar, and a rattle, plunging down into the earth again, and working on in such a storm of energy and perseverance, that amidst the darkness and whirlwind the motion seems reversed, and to tend furiously backward, until a ray of light shows its surface flying past like a fierce stream. Away once more into the day, and through the day, with a shrill yell of exultation, roaring, rattling, tearing on, spurning everything with its dark breath, sometimes pausing for a minute where a crowd of faces are, that in a minute more are not: sometimes lapping water greedily, and before the spout at which it drinks has ceased

to drip upon the ground, shrieking, roaring, rattling through the purple distance!

(20.276)

The speed in the tunnel which apparently puts things in reverse and sends them backward suggests not only a sudden awareness of time as an issue of modernity but also that no one perspective is enough to be aware of what is happening: the vision from the tunnel has no explanatory power; another more multiple one must be sought. Hence the perspectives here are plural, belonging both to the person inside the train and to the person outside, who watches it go through 'the purple distance'. The literariness and pictorial quality of that last phrase suggests that the train cancels out by its 'tearing' out a particular way of seeing things, an older representation. The power of the train, like the power of technology in Heidegger (a source for Foucault) in his essay 'The Question Concerning Technology', is to enframe nature, to dispose and arrange it all around itself in new landscapes, just as the time registered by Dr Blimber's clock punctuates utterance and so gives character to utterance: 'How, is, my, li, tle, friend, how, is, my, lit, tle, friend!' (11.145). Noticeably, in this paragraph the train is not named at all, and is only characterised by the pronoun 'its'. It names, as it were, by dominating while remaining unnameable, escaping the impulse to name that would imply a control over it. And since it escapes naming, the passage shows the impossibility of full and single representation, the impossibility of seeing things whole.[11]

Dombey denies what the railway has shown ('it is never in his thoughts'), which suggests his repression and makes him incompletely modern. But in the second passage I want to use, from Chapter 47, another imagined society voice says of the sights of the degraded city when they are shown to her, 'I don't believe it' (47.619), and here what may be seen, what it is possible to see, and what is not is examined more discursively. The isolation of Dombey and Edith in their mutual pride, which prohibits a wider gaze and which opens the chapter, leads into five paragraphs beginning with the question 'what Nature is', and asking 'how men work to change her'. Here are the first two paragraphs:

It might be worth while, sometimes, to inquire what Nature is, and how men work to change her, and whether, in the enforced distortions so produced, it is not natural to be unnatural. Coop any son or daughter of our mighty mother within narrow range, and bind the prisoner to one idea, and foster it by servile worship of it on the part of the few timid or designing people standing around, and what is Nature to the willing captive who has never risen up upon the wings of a free mind – drooping and useless soon – to see her in her comprehensive truth!

Alas! Are there so few things in the world about us, most unnatural, and yet most natural in being so! Hear the magistrate or judge admonish the unnatural outcasts of society; unnatural in brutal habits, unnatural in want of decency, unnatural in losing and confounding all distinctions between good and evil; unnatural in ignorance, in vice, in recklessness, in contumacy, in mind, in looks, in everything. But follow the good clergyman or doctor, who, with his life imperilled at every breath he draws, goes down into their dens, lying within the echoes of our carriage wheels and daily tread upon the pavement stones. Look round upon the world of odious sights – millions of immortal creatures have no other world on earth – at the lightest mention of which humanity revolts, and dainty delicacy living in the next street, stops her ears and lisps 'I don't believe it!' Breathe in the polluted air, foul with every impurity that is poisonous to health and life; and have every sense, conferred upon our race for its delight and happiness, offended, sickened and disgusted, and made a channel by which misery and death alone can enter. Vainly attempt to think of any simple plant, or flower, or wholesome weed, that, set in this foetid bed, could have its natural growth, or put its little leaves forth to the sun as GOD designed it. And then, calling up some ghastly child, with stunted form and wicked face, hold forth on its unnatural sinfulness and lament its being, so early, far away from Heaven – but think a little of its having been conceived, and born, and bred, in Hell!

(47.619)

An argument which starts with the Romantic implication that there is a prior original Nature soon turns that into a near-impossibility, concluding that it may be 'natural to be unnatural'. The section seems quite ambiguous. The last phrase quoted refuses, cancels out, the power of an originary nature in the same way that the railway as the 'monster', the outside-nature, challenges the very existence of an independent nature as it crosses the countryside. It perhaps reveals that it exists only as an ideology. In case this reference to a refusal of the idea of nature seems too strong, Wordsworth's sonnet of 1844, 'On the Projected Kendal and Windermere Railway', should be recalled, remembering its citation in *Dombey and Son*:

> Is then no nook of English ground secure
> From rash assault? Schemes of retirement sown
> In youth, and 'mid the busy world kept pure
> As when their earliest flowers of hope were blown,
> Must perish; – how can they this blight endure?
> And must he too the ruthless change bemoan
> Who scorns a false utilitarian lure
> 'Mid his paternal fields at random thrown?
> Baffle the threat, bright scene, from Orrest-head
> Given to the pausing traveller's rapturous glance;
> Plead for thy peace, thou beautiful romance
> Of nature, and, if human hearts be dead,
> Speak, passing winds; ye torrents with your strong
> And constant voice, protest against the wrong.[12]

The sonnet would, by implication, firstly convict Dickens of Utilitarianism – itself a new word of 1827; secondly, it would see 'change' as destructive, and thirdly present a vision of family continuity which protects the power of patriarchy ('paternal fields') that the novel does its best to question. The novel's way with it is short indeed:

> But Staggs's Gardens had been cut up root and branch. Oh woe the day! when 'not a rood of English ground' – laid out in Staggs's Gardens – is secure!
>
> (15.219)

The spirit of this sets the modern Utilitarian against the Romantic. The irony it plays with is that 'Staggs's Gardens' is a paradigm not of nature but of urban squalor. However Wordsworthian the appeal to 'Nature', the text does not, practically, and especially in this comment in Chapter 15, allow for a consideration of 'nature' outside the way it has already been enframed by human change.

In Chapter 47, in the next and second paragraph of the section, the 'natural' is declared to be only possible to the person who can 'rise up on the wings of a free mind'. In a situation where 'the magistrate or judge admonish[es] the unnatural outcasts of society',

– the agents of surveillance in society are at their customary work of disciplining and punishing – it is not simply the outcasts who are to be pronounced unnatural. Unnaturalness belongs to all those whose vision is partial. But in any case, the phrase 'the unnatural outcasts' may be either a pleonasm or an oxymoron. It may suggest that some outcasts are naturally so, and some are unnaturally so (e.g. through being falsely judged and sentenced), but in any case that all judgements are equivocal, as in the case of Edith and Alice Marwood. The effect is to confuse the distinction between what is natural and what unnatural. And this too may be related to modernity. A specific example of this confusion exists in the new creation of London suburbs, such as those where Harriet and John Carker have their house – 'the neighbourhood in which it stands has as little of the country to recommend it, as it has of the town. It is neither of the town nor country' (33.455). And if 'unnaturalness' is so universal, it makes it impossible to think in terms of the 'natural', for this is unobtainable; it provides an instance of the impossibility of a return to an origin, which supposes, too, that there is no ability to give a narrative which has a progression from one state to another.

In not wanting to go back to origins, the narrative becomes modern: this is the spirit which refuses to give a source for the name 'Staggs's Gardens', rather playing with the impulse that wishes to find it out, mocking it out of the novelistic confidence that has created the name with total arbitrariness:

> Some were of opinion that Staggs's Gardens derived its name from a deceased capitalist, one Mr Staggs, who had built it for his delectation. Others, who had a natural taste for the country, held that it dated from those rural times when the antlered herd, under the familiar denomination of Staggses, had resorted to its shady precincts.
>
> (6.66)[13]

In keeping with this playfulness with the rationality involved in tracing histories back to their source in nature, the text shows a potential to go beyond the necessity of connecting everything. Yet the text also wishes to show. In its next paragraph it envisages imagining what the filthy air would look like if it could be seen (the opening of *Bleak House* is anticipated here), and compares that imagined sight with the 'moral pestilence' which it is suggested also hangs in the atmosphere. And such a train of offences includes 'nameless sins against the natural affections and repulsions of mankind'.

The ambiguity involved in 'nameless sins' is important. Sins which are nameless cannot be sins if what they are is not known, but the paragraph realises that it cannot show moral pestilence that is rising and accumulating; if it did what would come to light would be what is 'nameless': nameless because not named in polite society (where people can say 'I don't believe it'), and nameless because it must not be brought to demonstration, even if it could be. The text is asking for the nameless to be named by showing it, but in a context which makes it clear that the nameless would continue to be that – unnamed – because it would not be proper or natural to carry out the naming. And yet what is proper and what is natural are not synonyms. The proper is the sphere of the person who says 'I don't believe it'. To invoke the natural reveals a belief that there are some things which ought not to be named, which admits therefore that there are things which a text must repress.

Repression as a concept fits the subjects of *Dombey and Son*, almost visualised in the image of the 'cold hard armour of pride in which [Mr Dombey] lived encased' (40.538). For Steven Marcus, the novel's interest in change, which would entail a break from the repression of the armoured ego, comes from a concept of 'nature and of civilization as being in a condition of dynamic flux which is determined primarily from within' (Marcus, p. 319). In contrast to Marcus's sense of repressed subjects comes Foucault's idea of modernity not permitting repression, but forcing subjects into the open, writing upon them descriptions of their being and subjectivity which they must live up to. Repression or monstration: which concept better describes the narrative drive behind *Dombey and Son*?

Foucault's analysis of nineteenth-century sexuality in *The History of Sexuality* begins by taking issue with Steven Marcus in *The Other Victorians* (1966) and his Freudian view that the nineteenth century may be explained in terms of its repression of sexuality. For Foucault it is not repression but the active bringing to light of forms of sexuality that constitutes the drive within the century. And for Foucault, this culture of demonstration, bringing things into discourse, is part of a will towards domination and reduction of the subject. Modernism thus proves double-edged, showing things up that ought to come to the light, but then repressing them in the name of the 'natural repulsions of mankind'. In that way, Dickens's modernism is ambivalent.

To explain this as it works in *Dombey and Son*, it is worth going back to the 'monster death' section of Chapter 20. It was written at the moment when Dickens was leaving Paris for London. Dickens's time in Paris was marked by an interest in visiting the morgue, doing this as everything else 'with a dreadful insatiability' as Forster comments – an insatiable appetite which in its drive might be allegorically compared to that of the train absorbing everything, 'drinking' even as it speeds through the countryside. The body of one old man with grey hair seen at the end of December 1846, Dickens himself allegorised as though extracting meaning from the corpse and then reading back from that: 'he lay there, all alone, like an impersonation of the wintry eighteen-hundred and forty-six' (*Life*, pp. 445, 449, 450–1).[14]

The figure is made like the Spirit of Christmas Present in *A Christmas Carol* seen at the end of his life: Scrooge notices his hair is grey just before commenting on the figures of Ignorance and Want, as though the death of Christmas and the death of the year fit with the imminent doom in the city. In the light of that melancholy, the sense of death all around – including the bourgeoisie as dead – and the desire to probe death and read meaning into it as it is laid out in the morgue, it seems no coincidence that Paul Dombey's death followed on. Part 5 of *Dombey*, (Chapters 14–16) which finishes with Paul's death, was completed on 15 January 1847. Part 4, which begins with the six-year-old Paul going to Dr Blimber's establishment (Chapter 11), was written after Dickens had moved with his family to Paris (20 November 1846) and started by 6 December. This, not *The Battle of Life*, the 'official' 'Christmas Book' for that year, was effectively Dickens's Christmas offering for 1846, when Paul, like another version of Tiny Tim (but who *did* die) 'sat as if he had taken life unfurnished, and the upholsterer were never coming' (11.149). The child's death and the deaths in the morgue go together, and bring out the subtext of *A Christmas Carol*, the death of Scrooge.

Perhaps these activities of visiting the morgue and writing may be connected more theoretically. Reference to the morgue recalls one of Foucault's most memorable studies: *The Birth of the Clinic* (1964). It treats of the interest in the corpse and of anatomising the corpse which medical science developed in the early part of the century, headed by the revolutionary doctor Bichat. Foucault's argument concentrates on the absolute knowledge of the subject that death is thought to provide, as this is conceptualised by Bichat and his fellow doctors. The ultimate, full truth of the person – the fullest demonstration of what he or she is – is provided by their individual death. In death nature is seen in its truth – which is another way of saying that nature is defined as that which is unnatural, as death itself.

Dickens amongst the bodies in the morgue points to an interest in anatomy, in the sense that the fullest truth about the person's nature seems to be revealed by their death. Anatomy might have been a subject of horror: as with the murderer recorded in the *Newgate Calendar* – 'I have killed the best wife in the world, and am certain of being hanged, but for God's sake don't let me be anatomised.'[15] It connects Dickens with radical new scientific developments outlined by Foucault as far as France is concerned: as far as Britain goes, it is relevant to recall that Bentham, Panoptical in thinking to the last, insisted – thereby breaking the law but helping to change it – that his own body should be opened up and anatomised after his death. In 'opening up a few bodies', as Bichat advised, the whole structure and truth of the body and hence of the subject would become plain. The railway, which lets light into dark areas, which makes, in potential, no part of the country ('no nook of English ground') separate from its influence, is double in effect: both changing perception and fixing it. If it is the monster death in type, that echoes and records Mr Dombey's repressed sense on his journey of what modernity means – opening things up powerfully, shamelessly. But it also fits another sense of the text: that to open things up is to find them dead, to discover in doing so that they have lost something vital.

Dickens recollects going like a *flâneur* – 'an idler' – into the Paris morgue in 'Some Recollections of Mortality' (1863), and watching the people looking at a dead body. 'There was a much more general, purposeless, vacant staring at it – like looking at waxwork, without a catalogue, and not knowing what to make of it. But all these expressions concurred in possessing the one underlying expression of *looking at something that could not return a look* (*The Uncommercial Traveller*, 192). The Morgue has already, in the essay, been referred to as a 'Museum' (191), a suggestive commodity/death image I will return to in considering *Little Dorrit*. But the sense of a look at something that cannot look back is strongly suggestive of the Panopticon, and implies a dominance which is also the power to interpret where there can be no return, no opposition. If the other idlers cannot make anything of what they see, that is not the characteristic of the realist novelist whose look is by definition not superficial, but one that goes beneath. It is committed to taking the house-tops off (47.620), which recalls the point that etymologically a detective is someone who takes the tiles off the roof. Or the novelist turns anatomical.

It is a question how much there is of the anatomist in Dickens, though *A Christmas Carol*, especially in the scenes with the Spirit of Christmas Future, gives the opportunity to read people's lives in the light of their deaths, and the writing of Doom on the boy Ignorance's brow either marks him off for death, and thus characterises him as a figure of death-in-life, or suggests that he means death to those he comes in contact with. (Both things are true of Jo in *Bleak House*.) Something of the finality of the anatomist is also in *Dombey and Son*. In her dreams, after she has heard of Walter's drowning (which links him the more firmly with her brother through the imagery of the waves and what they were always saying), Florence sees her father dead and Walter 'awfully serene and still', while Edith, like the Spirit of Christmas Future, takes her to a dark grave. 'And Edith pointing down, she looked and saw – what! – another Edith lying at the bottom' (35.487–8). It is strikingly anticipative of Esther Summerson discovering her mother cold and dead; it suggests death as the fullest revelation of character, pulling down the mother's body, as patriarchal narratives do by implication, as though the original dead mother (Fanny Dombey) were turned into a degraded Edith, and Edith as a split subject (like Lady Dedlock) were turned into a single one through her death. In that sense it is immaterial that Edith does not die, though, like her cousin Alice, 'another Edith', who dies in Chapter 58, her death was intended.[16] In this dream, her death already has been shown, and the novel's commitment for her is death-centred. So also with Carker on the railway platform, just before he turns to see Dombey and falls under the train, there comes the comment, 'Death was on him. He was marked off from the living world, and going down to his grave' (55.743). 'Marked off' recalls the earlier references to writing, the sense of the body being written upon by a text which both knows its subject, and constructs it in a way it must follow and be subject to. The fullest revelation of what he is and has always been comes at the time of his death.

Thus to return to Chapter 47 and to the ending of the set piece on 'what Nature is', it may be noticed how it hovers between alternative desires for repression and demonstration, between an older form of writing which appeals to 'nature' as a sanction which will announce some things as thoroughly 'unnatural', and a modernity which might even name the sins which are unnamed. The passage closes with a reminder of what *A Christmas Carol* provided: asking for a 'good spirit who [will] take the house-tops off, with a more potent and benignant hand than the lame demons in the tale and show a Christian people what dark shapes issue from amidst their homes, to swell the retinue of the Destroying Angel as he moves forth among them' (47.620).

The text requires this good spirit, as though recognising that the novel is not identical with it and with what it would show, as though asking for another novel. But the result of such a demonstration of what is inside the Victorian home would be that:

> ... men, delayed no longer by stumbling-blocks of their own making, which are but specks of dust upon the path between them and eternity, would then apply themselves, like creatures of one common origin, owning one duty to the Father of one family, and tending to one common end, to make the world a better place.
>
> No less bright and blest would that day be for rousing some who have never looked out upon the world of human life around them, to a knowledge of their own relation to it, and for making them acquainted with a perversion of nature in their own contracted sympathies and estimates; and yet as natural in its development when once begun, as the lowest degradation known.
>
> (47.620)

The language, which is anticipative of George Eliot (*Middlemarch*, chapter 81 – the moment when Dorothea rouses herself to look out of her window after her night on her bedroom floor), is that of demonstration, asking people to look around them and to relate to that (and 'relate' suggests supplying for oneself a narrative: filling in the gaps in narrative that prevent connection). But its powerful rhetoric suggests a will to close off issues in a form of repression. The use of repetitions particularly may well signal an uncertainty which hence requires repression. It appeals to nature in a romantic way; it addresses the idea of a common origin and common telos founded upon a natural unity of people considered as 'one family' where the model for the family seems to be patriarchal and economic, like the Dombey family; it preaches meliorism, as the railways promise nineteenth-century 'improvement'. It represses any sense of difference, especially class difference: it asserts that people would arouse themselves to a common goal. The result of a Panopticism that will 'show [something to] a Christian people' is that people will repress their differences and work to one 'common end'.

Returning to the language of the Spirit of Christmas Present, the 'common end' here would represent the desire to avoid the end which is 'Doom' – an ending figured also in the railway as Death. The fear seems to be that there can be no change for the bourgeois world, that its course is deathwards. This may reflect 1840s fears of revolution coming about from people whose character of 'Ignorance' (so defined by the middle classes), or whose social marginalization, like Alice, means that they have no investment in bourgeois values. If *Dombey and Son* hovers between a modernity which wishes to show everything and another desire to repress, it seems that repression wins here because of the fear of the end. This suggests that the drive to show a conversion, a change in Mr Dombey, is also a wish to turn the bourgeoisie away from an imagined doom. That possibility of change is something that the text cannot fully endorse. The contradiction in *Dombey and Son* would be that if it became truly modernist, it would show everything, not leave things unnamed. But such a movement would also be attended by the fear that there would not be much that was left alive, that the Dombey world could not be reformed or changed, but would succumb to the triumphant monster death.

3

'A Paralysed Dumb Witness': Allegory in *Bleak House*

There were things to gaze at from the top of Todgers's, well worth your seeing too. For first and foremost, if the day were bright, you observed upon the housetops, stretching far away, a long dark path: the shadow of the Monument: and turning around, the tall original was close beside you, with every hair erect upon his golden head, as if the doings of the city frightened him.

Martin Chuzzlewit, 9.131

I

In this chapter, I look at a resistance in Dickens to the surveillance and control of modernity, a resistance through allegory. Allegory in Dickens seems an obvious subject: his reliance on the 'humours' mode of writing associated with Jonson and Bunyan makes it already tendentially allegorical. But that mode of writing is associated with unitary meanings, with stability and closure and the assigning of fixed subject-positions. Allegory as an other (*allos*) way of speaking, a secret language in which public meanings are inverted, rather suggests the doubleness of a text, which is public speech, or private, secretive if it is deliberately read for allegoresis. And if speech is in any case already 'other', as Lacan for example suggests, not immediate or transparent, that decision is preempted; everything becomes allegory.

Two possibilities of allegory exist in Dickens's *Bleak House*. A realist writer confronts modernity, and part of the text (Esther's narrative) in its realism resists the otherness of allegory with its fracturings of the self and speech into non-identity and non-readability. But allegory is a device used consciously within the text's sustained public narrative – the *other* 'portion of these pages'. It undermines

71

that narrative, and Esther's portion too, in its apparent immediacy and transparency, by an awareness of madness and delirium and by implying that all the text is already in a position of 'otherness'. In *Bleak House* (1852–53) there seems a subversion of realism, an investment in undoing its fetishistic and stabilising promise of the continuance of 'all that is solid', to quote again the famous Marx formulation that I will come back to.

There was allegory too in *David Copperfield*, written before *Bleak House*. Betsey Trotwood comments on Mr Dick's fixation on the execution of Charles the First as being his 'allegorical way' of expressing his own problems with his madness and his past, the recollection of which is painful to him. Perhaps the nineteenth-century project of writing the historical novel finds its justification here. Autobiography can only be written through allegory, where a psychic 'great disturbance and agitation' (14.261) linked to Mr Dick's illness has to be thought through by reference to the political and the public. That sphere and its disorder is productive of private neuroses: it is the argument of the effect that repression has that is given by Freud in *Civilization and its Discontents*. For Mr Dick, allegory links the two forms of 'agitation', political and revolutionary and mental; but also by repressing the pain of recollection through its displacements it becomes a means of covering over aporias within psychic life, and enabling the existence of a narrative of the self.

Another form of allegory, and a prompting to think about it in relation to the nineteenth century, comes from the 'Tableaux Parisiens' in Baudelaire's *Les Fleurs du Mal* (1857), written as Haussmann radicalised the modernisations of Paris which had begun in the 1830s and 1840s, and which Dickens noted in his account of the Dedlocks in Paris in *Bleak House* (Chapter 12). The dream-city, 'fourmillante cité, cité pleine de rêves' of 'Les Septs Vieillards' is unreal because of change. In 'Le Cygne', 'La forme d'une ville / Change plus vite, hélas! que le cœur d'un mortel':

> Paris change! mais rien dans ma mélancolie
> N'a bougé! palais neufs, échafaudages, blocs,
> Vieux faubourgs, tout pour moi devient allégorie,
> Et mes chers souvenirs sont plus lourds que des rocs.

(Paris changes! But nothing in my melancholy has altered! New palaces, scaffolding, blocks, old neighbourhoods – all for me becomes allegory, and my dear memories are more heavy than stone.)[1]

If everything changes in Paris, that 'capital of the nineteenth-century' which is 'other' to 'London' – the first word of *Bleak House*, and the 'other' capital of the century – then there is no stable identity to be spoken of, and everything has the same ontological status: being only allegory, scaffolds only, dreams. This articulation of *melancholy* and *allegory* seems basic to *Bleak House*, as with Baudelaire it receives its most important study in Benjamin's discussions of allegory in the *Ursprung des deutsches Trauerspiels* and the *Passagenarbeit* of the 1920s and 1930s. The *Passagenarbeit* reads Baudelaire, the poetry and such essays as 'The Painter of Modern Life' (1859–60), to identify melancholy with the ability to read everything of modernity as transitory, allegorical, shifting.[2]

In Dickens's autobiographical fragment, probably written during the period of *Dombey and Son*, Dickens makes his own comment on changes in London, with reference to the blacking factory:

> Until old Hungerford-market was pulled down, until old Hungerford-stairs were destroyed, *and the very nature of the ground changed*, I never had the courage to go back to the place where my servitude began. I never saw it, I could not endure to go near it. ... In my walks at night I have walked there often, since then, and by degrees I have come to write this.
>
> (*Life*, p. 35, my emphasis)

In the modernised London Dickens speaks of, the old prison of the blacking factory exists as allegory. I connect this writing with *Dombey and Son* because of the description of the uprooting of Staggs's Gardens:

> The first *shock* of a great earthquake had, just at that period, rent the whole neighbourhood to its centre. Traces of its course were visible on every side. Houses were knocked down, streets *broken through* and *stopped*; deep pits and trenches dug in the ground; enormous heaps of earth and clay thrown up; buildings that were undermined and shaking, propped by great beams of wood ... Everywhere were bridges *that led nowhere, thoroughfares that were wholly impassable*, Babel towers of chimneys, wanting half their height; temporary wooden houses and enclosures in the most

unlikely situations, carcases of ragged tenements, and fragments of unfinished walls and arches, and piles of *scaffolding*, and wildernesses of bricks, and giant forms of cranes and tripods standing above nothing. There were a hundred thousand shapes and substances of incompleteness, wildly mingled out of their places . . . *unintelligible as any dream.*

In short, the yet unfinished and unopened Railroad was in progress; and, from the very core of all this dire disorder, trailed smoothly upon its mighty course of civilisation and improvement.

                              (*Dombey and Son*, 6.65, my emphases)

The changes to Staggs's Gardens are welcomed because they might allow for the possibility of forgetting: they change things, but through a violent power which represses the way things have been. Yet also, within this writing, a double movement will be noticed. The first paragraph arrests movement; the second allows for it. The first paragraph is dream-like, and evokes Mr Dick's great 'change and agitation'. In the equivocal state in which things are, everything could be under construction or returning to Benjamin-like ruin. The second paragraph allows for progress and modernity. In the two stages which are implied by the two-paragraph structure, a crisis is faced and resolved; arrest becomes motion; repression is freed and the self moves forward. In discussing *Dombey* I have already suggested the text hesitates between repression and showing. Both seem to me evoked and combined in this section, and I will return to discuss it further, later in the chapter, in relation to an episode in *Bleak House*.

Change is not however quite solidified: the railway is not yet in progress in Chapter 6 of *Dombey*; the landscape is as unintelligible as a dream. Modernity is also unreal, or can be seen as de-realised. Benjamin's *Passagenarbeit* quotes from Dickens as well as Baudelaire, seeing him as the *flâneur* in the streets of both Paris and London. The streets, the crowd, the city Dickens describes as his indispensable 'magic lantern' (*Baudelaire*, p. 49; cp. Dickens's *Letters*, 30 August 1846, 3. 612). The city is the place of bright illusion, but also unknowable, the screen on which to project images which belong entirely to private subjectivity: as the Memorandum book (1855–65) considered a story 'representing London – or Paris, or any other great place – in the new light of being actually unknown to all the people in the story, and only taking the colour of their fears and fancies and opinions. So getting a new aspect, and being unlike itself. An *odd* unlikeness of itself' (quoted, Hillis Miller, p. 293). Here interpretation is all: there is no knowable city beyond the allegories or images which are impressed on it. This 'new' idea of Dickens goes further than the 'magic lantern' image in a direction opposite to that of realism. But then the magic lantern already subverts realism by inscribing everything as illusion. The image of the city and its commodities as optical illusion produced through a magic lantern is what Benjamin calls the 'phantasmagoria'. He follows Marx on commodity fetishism in *Capital*:

> a definite social relation between men ... assumes ... the fantastic form (*die phantasmagorische form*) of a relation between things.

Here commodities themselves must be seen as phantasmagoric:

> In order ... to find an analogy, we must have recourse to the mist-enveloped regions of the religious. In that world the productions of the human brain appear as independent beings endowed with life, and entering into relation both with one another and the human race.[3]

For Dickens and Baudelaire nineteenth-century bourgeois reality is destabilised, seen as the phantasma. The city becomes allegorical. Only the factory remains real, though all the ground has been torn up and another architecture has taken its place.

The supreme emblem of modernity is the commodity, displayed in a new fashion in London in the 1851 Great Exhibition, the presentation of the triumph of bourgeois values and of Britain's escape from the European revolutions of 1848–49. It displeased Dickens: 'I have always had an instinctive feeling against the Exhibition, of a faint inexplicable sort' (*Letters*, 27 July 1851, 6.448). The commodity displayed in the Crystal Palace, that real and transparent triumph of architecture, was the fetishised object torn from any connection to the worker and excluded from a narrative of its production, which thus cancels out not only economic realities, but time and the object's relation to the past and present. According to Benjamin, the Baroque allegorist used the emblem in seventeenth-century drama to de-realise the apparent form and structure of social existence, reducing its forms to the empty characteristics of the death's head. But in the nineteenth century 'the devaluation of the world of objects in allegory is outdone within the world of objects itself by the commodity'. The commodity in its unreality (like 'the world of fashion' represented by Lady Dedlock, fetishised in her turn by the pictures of her possessed by Guppy), already does the work of allegory in the nineteenth century. Hence the task of allegory is to work on dead, commodified, fetishised reality:

> Allegories represent what the commodity makes out of the experiences which men of this century have. The allegorical mode of intuition is always built on a devalued phenomenal world. The specific devaluation of the world of things, which occurs in the commodity, is the basis of the allegorical intention of Baudelaire.[4]

Capitalist society is shown as reified in *Bleak House*: the eighteen lawyers who 'bob up like eighteen hammers in a pianoforte, make eighteen bows and drop into their eighteen places of obscurity' (1.54) are accordingly like allegorical emblems, fitting the commodified existence of relationships between people turned into relationships of money (as in 'Jarndyce versus Jarndyce'). Nonetheless the emptying out of life and significance into things, and ruined things at that, which is characteristic of the allegory of *Bleak House* works to undo fetishised reality. Like Baudelaire, Dickens devalues the object and the objectified world back to the ruin, back to detritus, like the unusable objects Mr Krook in *Bleak House* compulsively collects. London is seen under the sign of the ruin.

The modern is melancholic, since melancholy is the tendency described in Benjamin's book on the *Trauerspiel* to disconnect, to see a breakdown between signifier and signified. The melancholic gaze reverses belief in progress into its opposite; this vision does not integrate signifier and signified as the Romantic symbol supposedly does.

> Whereas in the symbol destruction is idealized and the transfigured face of nature is fleetingly revealed in the light of redemption, in allegory the observer is confronted with the *facies hippocratica* [death's head] of history as a petrified, primordial landscape. Everything about history that, from the very beginning, has been untimely, sorrowful, unsuccessful, is expressed in a face – or rather in a death's head.

(*Origin*, p. 166)

When history is seen as the pre-historic we are back to Dickens's 'the waters had but newly retired from the face of the earth and it would not be wonderful to meet a Megalosaurus, forty feet long or so, waddling like an elephantine lizard up Holborn Hill' (1.49). The mud, the dust – 'the universal article into which [Mr Tulkinghorn's] papers and himself, and all his clients, and all things on earth, animate and inanimate are resolving' (22.359), the Megalosaurus, the houses crashing down in Tom-all-Alone's, the Jarndyce case are all examples of an entropic movement in *Bleak House*, fitting the reversals implied within Baudelairian allegory. References to fog and rain, and to the ice and snow amidst which Lady Dedlock lives metaphorically and dies literally, suggest by their abolition of recognisable places, as complete as any modernisation process of Haussmann, a history which is that of a petrified, primordial land-scape. Allegorically it seems that the nineteenth century, in which the novel's characters move, has not yet begun to be history; it remains frozen nature. Spontaneous combustion – a supremely allegorical subject – hollows out both history and man as a concept and collapses their importance into nothing. The death-chamber of Nemo suggests the traces melancholy leaves behind (the room is full of the smell of opium), and suggests the return to the death's head, the central emblem of the *Trauerspiel*: the fire-grate is called a 'rusty skeleton' and 'no curtain veils the darkness of the night, but the discoloured shutters are drawn together; and through the two gaunt holes pierced in them, famine might be staring in – the Banshee of the man upon the bed' (10.187–8).

'Poverty' allegorised as the death's head, staring with 'gaunt eyes' presides over Nemo, the 'law-writer', in death, as though allegory had power over writing itself, undoing it. With its associations of madness, of 'disturbance and agitation' and with its relationship to narrative and narrative aporias, allegory even appears in *Bleak House* as a virtual person, the frieze in the ceiling in Mr Tulkinghorn's chambers being named Allegory, and given a proper name status, like Poverty, Rumour and the Fashionable Intelligence. The para-lysed status and the madness of allegory need emphasising: the possibility that allegory is incapacitated either from uttering any-thing, or from being intelligible.

These signs of incapacity appear most startlingly in Chapter 48 of *Bleak House*, which answers to the discovery of Nemo's death in Chapter 10. In this section, Mr Tulkinghorn's murder is discovered by anonymous people who come to clean his rooms. The classic figure in the ceiling fresco, 'the Roman', points at the Gothic scene below. The narrative imagines him first gesturing at the almost full bottle of wine, and at 'an empty chair, and at a stain upon the ground', horrified like the 'face' of the Monument in *Martin Chuzzlewit*, almost like a parody of Benjamin's angel of history, who has eyes staring, mouth open and wings spread, as though in shock.[5]

> An excited imagination might suppose that there was something in them [the objects on the floor] so terrific, as to drive the rest of the composition . . . in short the very soul and body of Allegory, and all the brains it has – stark mad.

The illustration by Phiz which accompanies chapter 48 shows no body, but just an empty space: it is an allegory, a picture of a picture, of the Roman in the allegory looking down at something missing: at the lack of a signified. Something missing – which is suggestive of a deficiency in the signifier, its madness – looks at something missing. Signifier and signified have for ever come apart.

Pointing also suggests writing, as when Esther reads from St John's Gospel 'how our Saviour stooped, writing with his finger in the dust, when they brought the sinful woman to him' (3.66). Jesus' action is like a performance of a parable, allegorical itself, suggestive of *Bleak House*'s stress on dust and on deaths like spontaneous combustion which produce further dust; as allegory it induces paralysis in Miss Barbary: as though pointing to her as marked for death, for the dust, it deprives her of motion. This fits with what Paul de Man refers to thinking of the effect of the writing on gravestones that seems to call out to travellers, as with 'STRANGER PAUSE' (*Edwin Drood*, 4.28). The epitaph is an example of *prosopopoeia* (it speaks as though a mask or face has been conferred on the writing) and de Man speaks of 'the latent threat that inhabits prosopopoeia, namely that by making the dead speak, the symmetrical structure of the trope implies, by the same token that the living are struck dumb, frozen in their own death.'[6] But in Dickens, not just the reader, the addressee, but Allegory itself is arrested. As in *David Copperfield*, allegory is connected with madness, with a way of knowing which cannot be given an allowable and sanctioned epistemological status, as though, like Jo, it knows nothing.

Such a breakdown is apparent, too, in Benjamin, the parataxis of his statement repeating the collapse of relationship between allegory and meaning: 'Allegories are, in the realm of thoughts, what ruins are in the realm of things' (*Origin*, p. 178). Allegory comes both from the failure of rational thought that thinks in terms of its own self-possession, and it memorialises that failure by being the record of ruin. But the sense of madness clearly goes further than this mere lack of ability to achieve rationality. Madness involves not only the loss of the single-subject position and loss of control, where the borders of the self are not delineated, and the self is taken over, but also an hallucinatory sense of doubleness and of everything of reality being seen in 'other' terms.

Allegory is not only as though mad, but called 'a paralysed dumb witness'. The phrase operates literally for the figure on the ceiling and evokes the nature of writing as allegory, evoking a sense of deprivation and loss of faculties. Here, Paul de Man might be the apt commentator, discussing in 'Autobiography as De-facement' the possibility of autobiographical writing in Wordsworth, suggesting how fractured such writing would be and referring to the prevalence in his text of figures of deprivation, maimed men, drowned corpses, blind beggars, children about to die, that appear throughout *The Prelude* [which] are figures of Wordworth's own poetic self. 'They reveal the autobiographical dimensions that all these texts have in common. But the question remains how this near-obsessive concern with mutilation, often in the form of a loss of one of the senses, as blindness, deafness, or, as in the key word of the Boy of Winander, *muteness*, is to be understood, and consequently, how trustworthy the ensuing claim of compensation and restoration can be' (*The Rhetoric of Romanticism*, p. 73).

The image of 'defacement' works with the pun on 'figures', meaning people, and the tropes which run through writing and structure it. Both are disfigured. De Man sees allegory as a key to narrative, where allegory suggests 'the failure to read', just as the similar 'tropological narratives' – narratives relying upon 'figures' – show 'the failure to denominate'.[7] To take an allegory as pointing *to* something, as it does in the ceiling frieze, is already to have imposed a reading. De Man's sense of allegory evoking unreadability draws from Benjamin's in inspiration, though with this strong difference: that in de Man the disfiguring of the figure which Wordsworth mimes in his poetry through his deprived solitary figures is a part of language and its temporality, and not part of a history of modernity, as it is in Benjamin. In de Man, unreadability is discovered so that narratives turn out to tell the story of how it is impossible to read them. Both these aspects – Benjamin's and de Man's – seem to work in Dickens, but it may still be necessary to choose between them.

The possibility of reading seems to be frustrated in *Bleak House*, a text which records the *illisible* nature of everything in Chancery. And, going with de Man for a time before returning to Benjamin and recalling his comments on Wordsworth, which I have just quoted, *Bleak House* seems equally concerned with mutilation. Paralysed dumb witnesses include Miss Barbary, inflexible in life after her stroke, when she gives no 'sign' that she knows Esther, and in death: 'her face was immovable. To the very last, and even afterwards, her frown remained unsoftened' (3.67). She appears as an allegorical death-mask. There is Sir Leicester Dedlock's stroke, the Smallweeds' incapacity, Phil Squod's crippledness, Esther's blindness during her smallpox and her disfigurement which makes her autobiography indeed involve a 'de-facement', Guster's fits, Miss Flite's madness, Caddy Jellyby's deaf and dumb child. To these may be added Krook's illiteracy, Tom Jarndyce's depression and suicide, Jo's ignorance and death and Hortense's passion which makes her walk barefoot on the wet grass. All witnesses to the nineteenth-century world of *Bleak House* are incapacitated, ruined. An important theme was suggested when Oliver Twist became an undertaker's mute: a silent and silenced witness to a whole series of corruptions. Though it seems most marked in *Bleak House*, where the deaf and dumb child comes at the end (Chapter 67) to defeat the text's narrative closure, bodily deprivation is everywhere in Dickens: Mrs Clennnam in *Little Dorrit* repeats her earlier paralysis when she falls to the ground and becomes like a statue as her house collapses in front of her eyes. Mrs Skewton in *Dombey and Son* becomes a grotesque puppet after her stroke. John Carey (p. 87) compares the 'paralysed dumb witness' to Mrs Joe, struck down by Orlick, unable to give witness to the identity of her attacker save through drawing the hammer on the slate. Reading back from *Great Expectations* to *Bleak House* with this in mind means that Allegory actually points to the dead Mr Tulkinghorn as allegorising himself: allegory as autobiography: he is a paralysed dumb witness to his own murder. Mr Tulkinghorn dead is the expression in allegory of what he was before in life, the withdrawn depository of noble secrets. His death plays out what he was before.

If Allegory in the ceiling points out the emptiness of what it signifies it is liable to the charge that in itself it is incapable of signification. That could be placed in the context of writing as marked by default, unable to come to full expression, haunted by the sense of its own loss and paralysis. Thus the following paragraph of Chapter 48, which also concludes it, gives a statement continuing this sense of impotence, that the Roman 'pointed *helplessly* at the murderous hand uplifted against his life [a hand pointing to a hand] and pointed *helplessly* at him, from night to morning, lying face downward on the floor, shot through the heart' (48.721, my emphasis).

Deconstructive readings of the novel, reading from Hillis Miller's sense of the text as 'a document about the interpretation of documents', have taken it as dealing with the impossibility of closing on any interpretation – unable to conclude, as Esther finishes with her declarations of what she does not know and her speculative 'even supposing' which completes the text but not a sentence. Knowledge is deliberately presented as fractured, 'mad', lacking an epistemological guarantee which would make it usable in realism. Hence the ambiguity of Allegory pointing, as do many fingers in *Bleak House*, whether in the text, or in illustrations (Krook pointing out his letters, Jo at the churchyard, Bucket, Mr Guppy at the scene of spontaneous combustion, for instance). Pointing fits with the production of the single subject in the nineteenth century, to surveillance, to control and to the power of the police – to everything Panoptical.

Such a production of the subject fits with literary realism. Pointing with the index finger indicates and is accusatory and discriminating, singling out: it individualises, it invites confession. The Roman pointing may have come from God creating Adam in the Sistine Chapel ceiling, which would make Allegory patriarchal indeed. It may also evoke *Othello*, a play which seems to be behind *Bleak House*, for Bucket refers to it when he tells Mrs Snagsby, 'Go and see Othello acted. That's the tragedy for you' (59.863). The Moor, standing in the place of all jealous people, fears being demonstrated to be a monstrous object – 'the fixed figure for the hand of scorn / To point his slow unmoving finger at'.[8] At the same time, with the incident in Chapter 16 when Jo points out to the disguised Lady Dedlock the burial place of Nemo, Dickens's directions to himself in the 'number plans' make the episode generative of other moments:

Jo – *shadowing forth* of Lady Dedlock in the churchyard. Pointing hand of allegory – consecrated ground.

I emphasise 'shadowing forth' for it is suggestive of allegorical thinking itself. The chapter is the first which says Allegory points (he does not point in Chapter 10). In Chapter 16, Allegory seems to point out of the window, and had Mr Tulkinghorn followed the indication, he would have seen Lady Dedlock in disguise. Lady Dedlock wonders if Nemo looked like Jo in his poverty – the identification between Nemo and Jo was established in Chapter 11 – and the episode closes with Jo pointing beyond the bars of the churchyard to the grave in which Nemo lies. A suggestive set of identifications is set up – between Allegory and Jo, between Jo and Nemo and between Lady Dedlock and Nemo, since she is eventually to be found dead in this place (Chapter 59).

One figure and one episode shadows forth another, while 'shadowing' means following someone as a detective, so that the allegorical intention by which identities are mapped onto others also involves the pursuit of a narrative closure which fixes a final identification and utters a final truth. In Chapter 48, 'Closing In', the closure is Tulkinghorn's murder, as though the final truth of a person is that which they are revealed to be in the moment of death. In discussing *Dombey and Son*, I commented how the nineteenth-century medical gaze inspired by Bichat singles out the organism as achieving its most exact state in death. For Foucault, in this new nineteenth-century discourse:

> That which hides and envelops, the curtain of night over truth, is, paradoxically, life, and death, on the contrary, opens up to the light of day the black coffer of the body: obscure life, limpid death.[9]

The modernist aim, as in Baudelaire, to reduce the hard alienating reality of the nineteenth century to allegory opposes the equally modern wish to fix identities in death by the dismissal of their shadowy otherness.

Deaths in *Bleak House* are frequent, and allow for the pointing finger of the other. But the deaths of Gridley, Jo and Richard are of one kind, and those of Nemo, Krook, Tulkinghorn and Lady Dedlock of another. The first three are obviously interpretable, but the last four are discovered dead in an atmosphere of mystery which invites detection, the tracing of what has brought them to this point. Detection stands as the exposure and elimination of their difference. Krook's body literally escapes tracing or the anatomising that the Bichat-inspired doctors of *The Birth of the Clinic* would have loved to practise. Hence, perhaps, the irritation on the subject of spontaneous combustion on the part of G.H. Lewes, who wrote on Bichat in 1853 in *Comte's Philosophy of the Sciences*. These deaths – Nemo, Krook, Tulkinghorn, Lady Dedlock – belong to those who kept secrets, and their deaths point to a possibly central truth about them, missed before but now to be produced from their deaths, however difficult. A further death which is only alluded to provides a clue: Mr Tulkinghorn in his impenetrability 'perhaps spar[es] a thought or two for himself, and his family history, and his money, and his will – all a mystery to every one – and that one bachelor friend of his, a man of the same mould and a lawyer too, who lived the same kind of life until he was seventy-five years old, and then, suddenly conceiving (as it is supposed) an impression that it was too monotonous, gave his gold watch to his hair-dresser one summer evening, and walked leisurely home to the Temple, and hanged himself'. (22.359).

This bachelor friend waits to have his whole life read and speculated on, including his relationship to Tulkinghorn, in the light of the manner of his death. But like Nemo, the friend is never seen alive: if Krook's body is not found in death, Nemo's was not in life:

> And all that night, the coffin stands ready by the old portmanteau; and the lonely figure on the bed, whose path in life has lain through five-and-forty years, lies there, with no more track behind him, that any one can trace, than a deserted infant.
>
> (11.196)

The coffin, the portmanteau which is like a coffin and the body which conceals its secrets are all in alignment. No Derridean 'trace', no writing (recalling Jesus writing within the dust) points the way to him. He has no more name than the Roman except this allegorical one of Nemo, and he is only revealed at all in a death which both baffles and invites speculation. In Tulkinghorn's death, all that could reveal the truth is allegory.

This unknowability exists most famously in the scene of spontaneous combustion (Chapter 32 – 'The App*ointe*d Time' – my emphasis). More than scientific belief is being strained: epistemology itself is under question in writing this event. Spontaneous combustion is allegorical, and allegory here has a further justification, related to the politics of the novel and to its desire to escape realism's demands. Indeed, whereas allegory has been presented as something defective, marked by privation, it is also, and especially here, a means of undoing a form of writing that has confidence in its representational and demonstrative ability.

Allegory appears in the last paragraph of Chapter 32, which makes the conclusion of the account of spontaneous combustion different from the realism involved in the discovery just before of 'all that represents' Mr Krook. The writing turns to an older episteme of the body with its tendentially allegorical 'humours', and makes the body here the body of the state, in Shakespearean mode:

> The Lord Chancellor of that Court, true to his title in his last act, has died the death of all Lord Chancellors in all Courts, and of all authorities in all places under all names soever, where false pretences are made, and where injustice is done. Call the death by any name whatsoever Your Highness will, attribute it to whom you will, or say it might have been prevented how you will, it is the same death eternally – inborn, inbred, engendered in the corrupted humours of the vicious body itself, and that only – Spontaneous Combustion, and none other of all the deaths that can be died.
>
> (32.511–12)

G.H. Lewes, as though he were the 'Law-writer' himself, publicly contested, on the grounds of realism, the possibility of this death in the *Leader* of 11 December 1852, after the publication of the monthly part:

> As a novelist, [Dickens] is not to be called to the bar of science; he has doubtless picked up the idea among the curiosities of his reading from some credulous adherent to the old hypothesis and has accepted it as not improbable.[10]

The *Leader*, Lewes's own journal, had given the word 'realism' its first use in relation to art in its issue of 27 April 1850. Objections to the possibility of spontaneous combustion in the style of Lewes are inserted by Dickens dialogically into Chapter 33 when describing the inquest on Krook, but this was insufficient for Lewes, who urged him in a further issue of the *Leader* to 'get things right'. He was asked to add a qualifying statement to the Preface to *Bleak House* when the complete novel appeared. But the Preface begins by defending the text's authentic treatment of Chancery and continues with reference to 'my good friend MR LEWES' in an anxiety to preserve the text as realist before concluding with the disavowal of realism in the statement 'I have purposely dwelt upon the romantic side of familiar things.'[11]

This is an implicit discarding of the ordinary, of what George Eliot would call 'the most *solid* Dutch sort of realism' (my emphasis) in a decade when she had begun her reviewing by asking for 'earnest study' of the laws of nature and 'patient obedience' thereto.[12] There is a self-distancing from realism with its concomitants of linear narrative and plot. The contradiction in Dickens between realism and non-realism is a split between two discourses, where realism was becoming hegemonic. It fits that Dickens was accused by reviewers in 1853, after the conclusion of *Bleak House*, of 'fail[ing] in the construction of a plot' (*The Illustrated London News*) or 'discarding plot, while ... persist[ing] in adopting a form for his thoughts to which plot is essential' so that 'the series of incidents which form the outward life of the actors and talkers has no close and necessary connexion' (*The Spectator*).[13]

The 1850s discourse of realism links to post-1848 developments, when revolution had been defeated. The revolutionary possibility appears at the end of Chapter 1, when the empty court of Chancery is locked up:

> If all the injustice it has committed, and all the misery it has caused, could only be locked up with it and the whole burnt away in a great funeral pyre – why, so much the better for other parties than the parties in Jarndyce and Jarndyce!
>
> (1.55)

This burning away, which is fulfilled in spontaneous combustion, would also finish linear narrative, which obeys a sequentiality based on linear time, by 'blast[ing] open the continuum of history' as Walter Benjamin puts it in the 'Theses on the Philosophy of History'. Benjamin notes that 'the great revolution introduced a new calendar' and that in the July revolution, 'on the first evening of fighting it turned out that the clocks in towers were being fired on simultaneously and independently from several places in Paris' (*Illuminations*, pp. 263–4). The clocks are the symbols of state power and control – control through the new 'realism' of clock-time, and this firing attacks realism itself; revolutions alter clock-time, while realism affirms it, but in *Bleak House*, the nineteenth century is 'the moving age' (12.211), and this compels the acceptance of linearity in narrative time. Revolution is impossible, as it would be post-1848, surviving only in the energy of Hortense, who to Esther appeared like 'some woman from the streets of Paris in the reign of terror' (23.373). It can only come back in allegorical form, in spontaneous combustion, where the old rottenness immolates itself.[14]

Spontaneous combustion answers to Mr Dick's 'allegorical way of putting it' when he connected his mental upheaval to the English Revolution. In discussing *Dombey and Son*, I referred to Marx who spoke of the bourgeois epoch in ways that anticipate Mr Dick's 'great disturbance and agitation', words which are as appropriate to revolution as to mental breakdowns and the loss of memory, and which run counter to Eliot's solid Dutch realism:

> The bourgeoisie cannot exist without constantly *revolutionizing* the instruments of production, and thereby the relations of production and with them the whole relations of society. Conservation of the old modes of production in unaltered form, was ... the first condition of existence for all earlier industrial classes. Constant *revolutionizing* of production, uninterrupted *disturbance* of all social conditions, everlasting uncertainty and *agitation* distinguish the bourgeois epoch from all earlier ones. All fixed, fast-frozen relations, with their train of ancient and venerable prejudices and opinions, are swept away, all new-formed ones become anticipated before they can ossify. All that is *solid* melts into air, all that is holy is profaned ...[15]

Much here is recalled, if unknowingly, in *Bleak House*: Lady Dedlock's 'freezing mood' (2.57), and the Ironmaster's 'restless flights' (28.450) which, productive of 'everlasting uncertainty' are manic in themselves. The adjective allows for that, and the noun connects the Ironmaster most seemingly incongruously, to the mad Miss Flite. Something of the craziness of Mrs Jellyby may also be there. But the sense of hope in modernity that breathes through the *Manifesto of the Communist Party*, long before Marx evokes the yet further hope of working-class revolution, is heavily qualified by *Bleak House*. Lady Dedlock's freezing mood comes from her dissociation of herself from her class: she emblemises the failure of connection that revolution would have established. If Mr Krook's death suggests that all that is solid melts into air, which would be the hope of the allegorist (as allegory makes that happen), and if the pursuit of Lady Dedlock suggests that all that is holy is profaned, these are not in Dickens the unequivocal signs of hope, that they were for Marx; their significance is double. They are things to make 'the very body and soul of Allegory . . . stark mad'. If Allegory is mad, then following the logic of post-1848 events, it may be in *Bleak House* the record of alienation. As Benjamin said Baudelaire was, it is 'nourished by melancholy' (*Baudelaire*, p. 170). Melancholy is systemic in the text: in Lady Dedlock being bored to death, in Esther being told she had better not have been born and Caddy Jellyby wishing she were dead; in Mr Bucket's mourning ring (22.364); in the narrative of the failed relationship of Miss Barbary and Boython, and in Ada and Richard's depressed condition. These things fit with the overt madness, despair and suicide in the text.

With the movement to allegorical writing with spontaneous combustion, the text renders something unrepresentable, and unrepresented since only traces of Mr Krook are to be found. It is the impossible event whose impossible existence and non-possible representation defeats the pretention to linear narrative, disallowing movement from step to step, save through the commitment to the continuum allowed through realism. But the idea of linear narrative in any case is undermined, rendered false, by Esther's conclusion which reveals that she has been happily married for seven years to Allan Woodcourt. His interest in her she suppresses in much of the earlier part of her narrative. To write a narrative at all, Esther must become duplicitous, casting herself as the deprived person she is not: autobiographical statement rests upon a deception or repression.

The aporias within linear narrative which are thus opened up, and stressed within the allegory of spontaneous combustion, are confirmed by the tendency in *Bleak House* to see everything regressing to the fragment and the ruin. Here Benjamin, not de Man, is a more useful point of reference. It is not just a question of allegory disabling epistemology, even when the form of knowing that what the text at times makes impossible is the reductive kind of knowledge that Foucault anatomises. Rather, I have singled out in Benjamin the movement that so reads in order to make everything allegorical. That fluidity comes from a Medusan gaze which paradoxically petrifies the object, reducing it, turning it back in time. In the fragment thus discovered appears what the 'Theses on the

Philosophy of History' calls 'that image of the past which unexpectedly appears to man singled out by history at a moment of danger' (*Illuminations*, p. 257). Here allegory enables the production not of some complete whole or a statement which would entail the realisation of some subjective intention, but of some other, heterogeneous image. When Benjamin declares that 'the work is the deathmask of its conception',[16] subjective intention is relativised by being frozen into an otherness which is also allegorical, as the death-mask is the prime example of allegory for the Baroque. The death's head over the ruined and dead Nemo, the opium-addicted law-writer with no identity, his identity a disguise, suggests the end of subjectivity – a subjectivity that in this case may be suggestive of the death of the author: Dickens as Nemo.

II

Many years ago, when I was looking over Piranesi's Antiquities of Rome, *Coleridge . . . described to me a set of plates from that artist, called his* Dreams, *and which record the scenery of his own visions during the delirium of a fever. Some of these . . . represented vast Gothic halls; on the floor of which stood mighty engines and machinery, wheels, cables, catapults, etc., expressive of enormous power put forth, or resistance overcome. Creeping along the sides of the walls, you perceived a staircase; and upon this, groping his way upwards, was Piranesi himself. Follow the stairs a little farther, and you perceive them reaching an abrupt termination, without any balustrade, and allowing no step onwards to him who should reach the extremity, except into the depths below. Whatever is to become of poor Piranesi, at least you suppose that his labours must now in some way terminate. But raise your eyes, and behold a second flight of stairs still higher, on which again Piranesi is perceived, by this time standing on the very brink of the abyss. Once again elevate your eye, and a still more aerial flight is descried; and there, again, is the delirious Piranesi, busy on his aspiring labours: and so on, until the unfinished stairs and the hopeless Piranesi both are lost in the upper gloom of the hall. With the same power of endless growth and self-reproduction did my architecture proceed in dreams.*

De Quincey, 'The Pains of Opium',
Confessions of an English Opium-Eater

The labyrinth is drunken space.
Denis Hollier, *Against Architecture: The Writings of George Bataille*, p. 59

For Dickens the allegorist and hallucinated dreamer for whom the analogue may be that of the opium-state in which Nemo dies, a further gloss may be provided by Lewes's essay 'Dickens in Relation to Criticism' (1872). For Lewes, Dickens works in his novels by hallucinatory means. In him 'sensations never passed into ideas' and he 'never connect[ed] his observations into a general expression, never seem[ed] interested in general relations of things',[17] a comment which fits with the criticisms of lack of plot in *Bleak House*. Lewes called Dickens 'a seer of visions' and said that in no other perfectly sane mind had he observed 'vividness of imagination approaching so closely to hallucination' (p. 59). After speaking parenthetically about hallucinations in the mad, he continues that in Dickens:

> *revived* images have the vividness of sensations . . . *created* images have the coercive force of realities, excluding all control, all contradiction. What seems preposterous, impossible to us, seemed to him simple fact of observation.
>
> (p. 61)

Lewes is going back over – at least unconsciously – the ground of spontaneous combustion, and continuing to attempt to describe Dickens's allegory within the language of realism, by referring to 'observation'. Lewes argues that Dickens's power over his reader was hallucinatory, that the 'unreal and impossible' figures of his hallucinatory imagination by the process of hallucination affected the uncritical reader with the force of reality. The realism is fake, *not* grounded in observation, despite the fact that Lewes can record Dickens saying to him that 'every word said by his characters was distinctly *heard* by him'. Lewes the realist comments:

> I was at first not a little puzzled to account for the fact that he could hear language so utterly unlike the language of real feeling, and not be aware of its preposterousness, but the surprise vanished when I thought of the phenomena of hallucination.
>
> (p. 66)

Dreams – 'a subject which always interested him and on which he had stored many striking anecdotes' (p. 72) – and hallucinatory reality intersect in Dickens. As reversals of linear time operate in the text (another solidity melted into air), his dreams seem proleptic in character.

Lewes relates Dickens dreaming one night after one of his public readings of being in a room 'where everyone was dressed in scarlet. (The probable origin of this was the mass of scarlet opera-cloaks worn by the ladies among the audience having left a sort of *after-glow* on his retina.) He stumbled against a lady standing with her back towards him. As he apologised she turned her head and said, quite unprovoked, "My name is Napier." The face was one perfectly unknown to him, nor did he know anyone named Napier. Two days after he had another reading in the same town, and before it began, a lady friend came into the waiting-room accompanied by an unknown lady in a scarlet opera-cloak, "who", said his friend, "is very desirous of being introduced." "Not Miss Napier?" he jokingly inquired. "Yes; Miss Napier." Although the face of his dream-lady was not the face of this Miss Napier, the coincidence of the scarlet cloak and the name was striking' (Lewes, pp. 72–3).

Dickens hallucinates, just as, for Marx, present relations between people are phantasmagoric, made real only by a communal illusion, and the solidity of bourgeois reality is insubstantial. Lewes grants the likelihood of hallucination in Dickens, but not the likelihood of Dickens's 'characters' being in any sense real. It is as though, despite the disavowal, he was more willing to grant the possibility of Dickens not being completely sane than that his own estimate of the real might be wrong.

But Dickens might have been closer than Lewes wished to allow to madness, in calling dreams 'the insanity of each day's sanity' (*Uncommercial Traveller*, 132). And sanity seems to be a metonym for George Eliot's word 'real' and her realism. Describing her narrative procedure she writes:

It would be the death of my story to substitute a dream for the real scene. Dreams usually play an important part in fiction, but rarely, I think, in actual life.[18]

Lewes objects to *Bleak House*'s madness. Realism is the attempt to evade or avoid ideas of alienation by attempting to speak from a centre and a position of sanity. In the same way, J.S. Mill's reference to 'that creature Dickens' (Collins, p. 95), objecting to the 'vulgar' portrayal of the bourgeois feminist Mrs Jellyby, is a voice of hegemonic realism and a refusal of alienation as something reaching everyone, including the bourgeoisie, and making them melancholy-mad. Yet, importantly, Esther Summerson condemns Mrs Jellyby, which may imply that her judgement is also alienated, since Esther is the depressive whose attempt is to become as realist as possible. Her account of her delirium is typical: it is narrated in such a way that whatever its unconscious, it will come back to a sober and scientific, if not Positivist, sense of what is happening:

> ...I am almost afraid to hint at that time in my disorder – it seemed one long night, but I believe there were both nights and days in it – when I laboured up colossal staircases ever striving to reach the top, and ever turned... by some obstruction, and labouring again. I knew perfectly at intervals, and I think vaguely at most times, that I was in my bed; and I talked with Charley and felt her touch, and knew her very well; yet I would find myself complaining 'O more of these never-ending stairs, Charley, – more and more – piled up to the sky, I think!' and labouring on again.
>
> Dare I hint at that worse time when, strung together somewhere in great black space, there was a flaming necklace or ring, or starry circle of some kind, of which I was one of the beads! And when my only prayer was to be taken off from the rest, and when it was such inexplicable agony and misery to be a part of the dreadful thing?
>
> Perhaps the less I say of these sick experiences, the less tedious and the more intelligible I shall be. I do not recall them to make others unhappy, or because I am the least unhappy in remembering them. It may be that if we knew more of such strange afflictions, we might be the better able to alleviate their intensity.
>
> (35.544)

The first of these allegorical dream-visions where Esther has two consciousnesses is parodied by Mrs Sparsit's 'allegorical fancy' in *Hard Times*, when she imagines and wishes a future for Louisa, descending to her ruin (allegory for Mrs Sparsit being a performative move, a strategy in thinking). The inspiration for both staircases is Piranesi in Coleridge's version as rendered by De Quincey: the delirium draws, like Esther's father's opium-taking, from *Confessions of an English Opium-Eater,* a text written for its account of opium-induced dreams. Esther embodies the experiences of male romantics. Opium-eating and hallucinatory states, and the phantasmagoric sense and opium-induced death, all come together: Esther repeats her father's alienated state of which this might be said to be an analeptic account. Nemo – 'no name' goes with the disfigured face, another alienation, which she has to identify with and become accustomed to, repressing the knowledge that she had been different in looks (Chapter 36). Physical appearance, too, melts into air: her autobiography, like Nemo's, is one of defacement.

De Quincey absorbs Piranesi in this *mise en abîme* of ascent and of the abyss which is without beginning or end. Piranesi's *Carceri d'invenionze* are prisons full of scaffolding, but also labyrinths, and these are distinguishable in *Bleak House.* A prison – even, symbolically, Chancery – is consolatory since it may be escaped from; but the labyrinth cannot be escaped from, for it is the condition of language as excess (the signifier in excess of the signified), a condition which cannot be mapped, a loss of self; it is like Wordsworth's 'unfathered vapour' which overtakes the traveller during the crossing of the Alps:

> Imagination! lifting up itself
> Before the eye and progress of my song
> Like an unfathered vapour – here that power
> In all the might of its endowments, came
> Athwart me; I was lost as in a cloud,
> Halted without a struggle to break through . . .[19]

This space which has no origins or beginning or end, like the London fog, an entity which cannot be signified or put in its place, comes down not as a principle of organisation but as disrupting the self. The realist text deals with the prison: Esther in her state of delirium which belongs to another kind of text, intuits something else: ecstasy, dizziness.[20]

In De Quincey's opium-dreams, 'space swelled, and was amplified to an extent of unutterable and self-repeating infinity.' Dickens's texts allow for such expansions and explosions and repetitions of space and time – Uriah Heep 'seemed to swell and grow before my eyes; the room seemed full of the echoes of his voice and the strange feeling (to which perhaps, no one is quite a stranger) that all this had happened before, at some indefinite time, and that I knew what he was going to say next, took possession of me' (*David Copperfield*, 25.441). The explosion of everything is what the film-maker Eisenstein notes in discussing Piranesi.[21] The connection is the more interesting since Eisenstein also discusses montage in Dickens, and montage the post-modernist architect Manfredo Tafuri calls 'the explosion of the shot' – 'when the tension within the shot reaches its peak and and can mount no further, then the shot explodes, splitting into two separate pieces of montage' (Tafuri, p. 56). There is a basic montage pattern to Esther's dissociated state of mind. Explosion is a basic word used for describing Piranesi – the explosion of architecture, of perspective, of a single vision. These things are also characteristic of Dickens, and I think they may be seen in the passage describing the break-up of Staggs's Gardens in Chapter 15 of *Dombey and Son*, itself a passage reminiscent of a Piranesi-like imaginary prison, and full of images of thoroughfares that go nowhere, that cannot be traversed or passed. In *Bleak House*, images of explosion work through spontaneous combustion, through allegory, through dream, through plurality of narrative and through the pursuit of the dizzying and the ecstatic.

Esther's other dream-vision is the fear that '*I* was one of the beads.' With a hard solidity as a 'bead' she is firmly fixed within the symbolic order: taking her place with the other beads as no more than a metonym for them. This perception of being in a fixed subject-position goes with the dreamer being able to observe the 'I' from a position of otherness. The illness perpetuates a sense of doubleness she already has, as in the moment before she becomes ill:

> I had for a moment an undefinable impression of myself as being something different from what I then was.
>
> (31.484–5)

This state of difference is allegorised by the physical disappearance of the self in spontaneous combustion in the very next chapter (Chapter 32). The impression Esther has of being different recalls her dream-state of Chapter 4 where Ada's identity disappears first, and 'lastly, it was no one, and I was no one' (4.94). Esther's realist text, a narrative of firm discoveries about the people around her and discovery of the secrets surrounding her birth rejects the allegorical potentialities of dreams. Hence the last sentence describing her delirious visions commits her to a scientific explanation of dreams, repressing their unconscious. Esther's 'I do not recall them to make others unhappy or because I am the least unhappy in remembering them' echoes Dickens on the blacking factory – 'I do not write resentfully or angrily, for I know how all these things have worked together to make me what I am' (*Life*, 35). The blacking factory was Dickens's labyrinth, from which he never got out. Perhaps both statements conceal a resentment within them; Esther, one star in her entrapment in the labyrinth, suggests another star: Estella, and a male fantasy of escape:

> For, when I yielded to the temptation presented by the casks, and began to walk on them, I saw *her* walking on them at the end of the yard of casks. She had her back towards me, and held her pretty brown hair spread out in her two hands, and never looked round, and passed out of my view directly. So, in the brewery itself ... when I first went into it, and rather oppressed by its gloom, stood near the door looking about me, I saw her pass among the extinguished fires, and ascend some light iron stairs and go out by an iron gallery high overhead, as if she were going out into the sky.
>
>   (*Great Expectations*, 8.65, MS reading)

In contrast to the girl who does not need to balance as she walks on casks (so her gesture suggests), Esther refuses dizziness and pre-serves balance by disallowing the otherness she is aware of: first by burying her doll when leaving Miss Barbary's (3.70). Burial sug-gests both death and repression: repression of melancholy persists throughout her stay at Bleak House; she gives melancholy no voice (unlike Mr Jarndyce), but continues to bury the doll, as it were, through her narrative. Yet in her 'fancy' she goes back to her days at her godmother's house (6.131) and recalls 'the days of the dear old doll, long buried in the garden' (9.178). She has already said that she 'almost always' dreamed of the days in her godmother's house (9.172) and both sets of statements about the dreams are placed in the text in conjunction to characters existent from her past. Firstly, Jarndyce has just spoken of Boythorn's near marriage, which it is later revealed would have been to Miss Barbary. Sec-ondly, the chapter which follows the statement gives the death of Nemo (Chapter 10). Memory asserts itself unconsciously and cre-ates an impossible narrative where the anonymous narrative of Chapter 10 perpetuates Esther's dream-memories of Chapter 9 by unfathering her. This sense of an 'other' to Esther's narrative appears elsewhere in the text: at the end of Chapter 6 she goes to bed, but not, it seems, to dream; and Chapter 7 opens 'While Esther sleeps, and while Esther wakes, it is still wet weather down at the place in Lincolnshire' (7.131) as though this montage establishes a link between two states of her own consciousness and the events which are outside her control and her narrative. Yet the word 'link' is ambiguous, for links are nowhere made in the text, and there is no point at which the laying of the two narratives side by side makes sense to anyone within either. There is no password to go from one narrative to the other. The agency most likely to join the two together would be the police.

Esther's first sight of Lady Dedlock brings an association of 'the lonely days at my godmother's . . . when I had stood on tiptoe to dress myself at my little glass, after dressing my doll.' The return to Lacan's Imaginary state, associated with the mother, is continued in the sense that Lady Dedlock's face is 'like a broken glass to me, in which I saw scraps of old remembrances' (18.304). The fragmentariness accords with several things in *Bleak House*: with autobiography as an impossible attempt to gather up fragments, but where the body must be left in pieces and a self can only be composed through loss, like the burial of the doll, and with the sense of pervasive ruin in the book. It fits too with the character of interpretation which is to take 'slight particulars' which only become something 'when they are pieced together' (50.742). The face of the mother fits also with the doll as the other, and everything here suggests both the plural identity that Esther cannot permit herself, and the sense of otherness which is at the heart of allegory, that 'other' form of speaking. And fragmentariness means that the material from Esther's 'portion of these pages' and the material from the unknown other narrator do not fit together into a whole, but that everything remains incomplete between them.[22] Esther says she finds it curious to write 'all this about myself! As if this narrative were the narrative of *my* life!' (3.73–74). But which is 'this narrative'? And is it one or two? One attends the other with all the slippages and displacements of the dream-work.

Esther's attitude to a dream-state which would like to dismiss it contrasts implicitly with the other impersonal narrative which uses allegory. Esther's attitude encourages realism, but sanity for Dickens cannot be continuous: it *must* have its other. Both Esther and Lady Dedlock rebut the servant Hortense who would be an other to both of them. Having been dismissed by Lady Dedlock, she wishes to become Esther's servant, and as the surrogate servant to both of them she kills Tulkinghorn, acting out both of their unconscious and unrecognised desires to repress all knowledge of the mother's past.[23] The 'shadowing' commented on before means that the self is not simply delineated as single, but is inseparable from others, as Esther's 'unknown friend to whom I write' (67.932) helps to construct her autobiographical existence. Otherness marks allegory, the dream image and the state of madness alike. Dreams and allegory work together as part of a hallucinated imagination whose quality is to read reality in a way Lewes cannot accept: that is, it allows for the unreality of what it sees, and accepts that what it works with may not be readable by the standards Lewes applies.

Esther's dissociation and alienation may be compared with Dorothea's in *Middlemarch*, weeping on her honeymoon in Rome. The passage owes something to *Bleak House*, though I am not concerned to prove influence. Rome embodies a 'stupendous fragmentariness' which 'heightened the *dreamlike* strangeness of [Dorothea's] bridal life' and everything in the city, including Eliot's version of Allegory – 'the dimmer yet eager Titanic life gazing and struggling on walls and ceilings' jars Dorothea 'as with an electric shock':

> Forms both pale and glowing took possession of her young sense, and fixed themselves in her memory even when she was not thinking of them, preparing strange associations which remained with her through her after-years. Our moods are apt to bring with them images which succeed one another like the magic-lantern pictures of a doze; and in certain states of dull forlornness Dorothea all her life continued to see the vastness of St Peter's, the huge bronze canopy, the excited intention in the attitudes and garments of the prophets and evangelists in the mosaics above, and the red drapery which was being hung for Christmas spreading itself everywhere like a disease of the retina.[24]

Dorothea encounters modernity in the Eternal City, and for the rest of her life (she is, then, dead now) it creates a montage-effect in her, splitting her consciousness. Benjamin discusses modernity in terms of the experience of shock which has become the norm of experience. In Baudelaire, he sees a close connection between 'the figure of shock and contact with the metropolitan masses' (*Baudelaire*, p. 119). 'Shock' characterises the 'earthquake' in Staggs's Gardens, and the contact with the crowd is like Dickens's 'footpassengers, jostling one another's umbrellas, in a general infection of ill temper' (1.49). Dickens stumbling across people in his dream suggests George Eliot's resistance in *Middlemarch* to what Benjamin sees in modernity – 'a new and urgent need for stimuli' which, in terms of twentieth-century film is met as 'perception in the form of shocks' (*Baudelaire*, p. 132). Yet resistance to modernity is not possible. Dorothea tries to take possession of herself and the passage quoted tries both to universalise through the classic mode of realism ('our moods') and to give scientific-positivist explanations ('a disease of the retina' – like Lewes commenting on Dickens's dream of scarlet). In these ways the self maintains its Cartesian autonomy, and controls the images it receives. But the passage belongs to modernity nonetheless. Dorothea's weeping is the melancholy and deprived sense of loss of autonomy, her subjectivity – awakened and constructed on the basis of her sexuality – left in ruins, the turning of everything to fragments of which the ruins of Rome are only one visible reminder, the invasion of the self by images. All for her, too, becomes allegory.

Realism, considered in contradistinction to Dickens, names the form of writing whose allegorical status is suppressed, that is its non-readability, or non-identity with what it purports to describe. Non-identity is more teasing in that objects themselves lose identity – becoming part of a phantasmagoria, a magic-lantern show. The combustion whereby both self and object disappear in terms of their discrete separate identities operates with Esther and Dorothea alike. These women – significantly marginal figures in gender-terms, marginal like mad Mr Dick(ens) the allegorist – hold on tenaciously to realism, but their lives are allegories of modernity. And allegory registers its own failure adequately to describe what it points to.

4

Finding the Password:
Little Dorrit

In *Great Expectations*, Pip says he never saw his father or mother, 'and never saw any likeness of either of them (for their days were long before the days of photographs).' This early literary reference to photography is to portraits of people who are loved, not landscapes or artistic compositions, and it relates photography to death. In the absence of the photograph, Pip deduces their appearance in a fantastic way from the writing on their tombstones. Writing and the photograph seem to be set against each other. But the statement does not free Dickens's novel from the photographic: in fact it draws attention to it. Pip, who reproduces his father as being another Philip Pirrip, writes from after the moment of photography.

Photography, after Daguerre's prototypes of 1839, within ten years became associated with custody and supervision of prisoners and was used for their identification. The paralysed dumb witness Mrs Joe identifies Orlick with the letter T: the hieroglyph becomes a password, though no policing action follows. *Great Expectations* is concerned with description, identity, naming and memorialising. Character description is baffled. Mr Pumblechook's question 'What like is Miss Havisham?' (9.68) produces Pip's Gothic fantasies about her, all lies. Compeyson, the author of the violence of the novel's primal scene, remains undescribed throughout the text, and when found dead is 'so horribly disfigured that he was only recognizable by the contents of his pockets' (55.445). Writing and photography, both graphic activities, are not finally different in this text: Miss Havisham in her last meeting with Pip says to him with reference to the tablets on which she has written instructions, 'My name is on the flyleaf. If you can ever write under my name, "I forgive her," though ever so long after my broken heart is dust – pray do it' (49.395). Miss Havisham's name on the tablets functions like a photograph: this substitute mother to Pip imagines Pip keeping the tablets like a souvenir or a relic, and writing underneath the memorial of the person. Reference to the photograph in *Great Expectations* provokes the question how photography changes the nineteenth-century novel. It associates the realist text with surveillance and the police, turning it more towards detective fiction as a metalanguage for discussing a power of apparent precise identification and for the isolation of Edgar Allan Poe's 'man of the crowd'. Individuality is enforced: George Eliot's image is photographic when in *Middlemarch* she refers to Dorothea's discovery of the otherness of Mr Casaubon – 'that he had an equivalent centre of self, whence the lights and shadows must always fall with a certain difference'. In naturalism, texts turn towards description, and to passivity before the facts. Passivity may also be related to melancholy and to loss of affect. *Great Expectations*'s melancholia is shadowed in Pip's 'first most vivid and broad impression of the identity of things' (1.3) which links identity to death ('this bleak place overgrown with nettles was the churchyard'), while personal identity is also overthrown as something substantial and discrete in the lines 'this small bundle of shivers growing afraid of it all, and beginning to cry, was Pip.' The child's Blakean 'weeping in the evening dew' with no memory of his parents compares with the mournful text produced from the standpoint of the ending, where, as if aware of the fixing power of photography, he writes a history which he cannot alter.

Little Dorrit (1855–57) is also not free of the photographic. Its background was the Crimean War (1854–56), which was imperialist in that it aimed at the limitation of Russia's foreign policy and the safeguarding of the northwest passage into India, which Russia's expansion at the price of the Ottoman Empire threatened, and in that it intended to show the superiority of British institutions and British power over both American democracy and European authoritarian regimes. The Crimea was modern warfare in that it was the first war to be photographed. Its existence in representational form in Britain existed side by side with its status as an event in the Crimea.[1]

The opening of *Little Dorrit*, despite its use of colour, I believe imposes a photographic method of observance onto its description of a landscape in 1825:

Thirty years ago, Marseilles lay burning in the sun, one day.

A blazing sun upon a fierce August day was no greater rarity in southern France then than at any other time before or since.

Everything in Marseilles, and about Marseilles, had stared at the fervid sky, and been stared at in return, until a staring habit had become universal there. Strangers were stared out of countenance by staring white houses, staring white walls, staring white streets, staring tracts of arid road, staring hills from which verdure was burnt away. The only things not to be seen fixedly staring and glaring were the vines drooping under their load of grapes. These did occasionally wink a little, as the hot air barely moved their faint leaves.

There was no wind to make a ripple on the foul water within the harbour, or on the beautiful sea without. The line of demarcation between the two colours, black and blue, showed the point beyond which the pure sea would not pass; but it lay as quiet as the abominable pool, with which it never mixed. Boats without awnings were too hot to touch; ships blistered at their moorings; the stones of the quay had not cooled, night or day, for months. Hindoos, Russians, Chinese, Spaniards, Portuguese, Englishmen, Frenchmen, Genoese, Neapolitans, Venetians, Greeks, Turks, descendants from all the builders of Babel, come to trade at Marseilles, sought the shade alike – taking refuge in any hiding place from a sea too intensely blue to be looked at, and a sky of purple, set with one great flaming jewel of fire.

The universal stare made the eyes ache.

(1.1)

This passage has been interpreted as about surveillance: the power of the sun as the Panoptical eye (though it does not shine in the prison).[2] But it is a curious surveillance that leaves the prison out. If there is surveillance, it is analogous to that of the photograph, and the universalism of the stare suggests the world wholly encoded by the power of photography, fixing and changing the faces of strangers (note the metathesis in 'st*r*angers were st*r*ared out of countenance'). Total visibility (no blinking) seems to be projected here with no relief for the eye. It is worth comparing this description of Marseilles with a guide of the early 1850s:

Contemplated from the block of arid rocks that shelter its port, its tile roofs form an immense reddish tapestry on which the sun of the Midi pours in torrents its brilliance and warmth. Nowhere an oasis of verdure where the eyes can rest; even the surrounding countryside is bare; the pale olive trees and delicate-foliaged

almond trees which surround the numerous villas on the out-
skirts of Marseille are not enough to enliven the spectacle. Inside
the walls of the city there is no grandiose monument to captivate
one's admiration; but the sea is there, with its majesty. It curls
about in all directions, as if to embrace the city.[3]

The red tiles have become white in Dickens, as part of the impress
of death on the scene. The sea, which might give relief, cannot be
looked at, nor does it in Dickens do anything so human as to embrace
the city. But the tourist description does not notice the black of the
'abominable pool' whose filth is analogous to that of 'the deadly
sewer' which ebbs and flows through London (1.3.28). Black, blue,
purple – these are sharply individuated, with no shadow, no dark
side which would imply only partial visibility. The photograph kills:
total visibility, like the realist project, gives life under the sign of
death, and the city with its *lacuna* in the centre – the black pool –
gives back its death as the produce of the same technology and
commerce that produces the photograph.

The stasis suggested by the photograph and death may be added
in to the feeling of political and personal melancholia that marks
Dickens's texts post 1848. A Romantic discourse speaks in Dickens's letters of the time of *Little Dorrit* of feeling emptiness and loss.
There is a felt need to break a monotony which in this text is established through Marseilles/the Marshalsea, and which is otherwise
unbreakable. Let me return to this sense of immovability through
the photograph. For Roland Barthes, in *Camera Lucida*, the photograph gives not the effect of the real, but the Real itself – 'in
Photography I can never deny that *the thing has been there*'. The
photograph goes beyond symbolisation and evokes the thing
itself – *'flat death'*. Barthes's earlier arguments in 'The Structural
Analysis of Narratives' (1966) on realism being an effect – giving
the effect of the real – are taken away in photography, which also
has a relationship with death. The film theorist Christian Metz
summarises this relationship, saying that the photograph typically
memorialises people no longer alive; secondly that the photograph
is always of someone who has died in the sense that they are no
longer the same person; lastly that it abducts the object out of the
world into another world and another kind of time.[4] The kind of
sad joke that the photograph plays is replicated in *Little Dorrit* by
Flora Finching, the 'statue bride', immobile in her past, unable
(through the stifling power of patriarchy) to live in the present:

trying to regain access to her is analogous to trying to establish the person via their photograph. The photograph moves towards what Barthes calls 'indifference' (p. 94) – flat, platitudinous, out-on-the-surface, Blanchot's *folie du jour*. The photograph, in *Camera Lucida*, emphasises absence, death. It also places the subject, by its effect of total openness, almost beyond the realm of the signifier, beyond symbolisation, beyond art, where this would evoke desire and the unconscious. Colin MacCabe, discussing George Eliot, sees the realist desire for a total explanation as neurotic: arguing that her novels show the drive towards a coherent explanation which will repress the existence of any parapraxis, any disruption to the continuity of being.[5] Here is the total openness of signs, the total visibility which is the already known, *the déjà vu*, the *déjà lu* as dead. The photograph is the fetish that wards off death by recalling death.

'Staring' in *Little Dorrit* belongs to death, and to the tourist mode. Marseilles, where Herbert Pocket travels on business (*Great Expectations*, 39.310) was a port of entry into Europe: and is a port of entry into the novel. France's colonisation of Algeria gave Marseilles a new status in the nineteenth century: this is alluded to on the first page of *Little Dorrit*, in the first of two non-accidental references to the tower of Babel. Mr Meagles thinks of Marseilles in terms of revolution and the Marseillaise, but that is all past. The only radical figure in Marseilles is Miss Wade: an English version of the anger displayed by Mme Hortense in *Bleak House*, and a sexual revolutionary. Her anger against the prison (and Marseilles fits with the Marshalsea) gives this the trace of being a revolutionary novel:

> 'If I had been shut up in any place to pine and suffer, I should always hate that place and wish to burn it down, or raze it to the ground.'
>
> (1.2.23)

Dickens, for whom the conduct of the Crimean war focused particular hatred for unreformed institutions, for aristocratic rule and abnegation of responsibility – the 'Nobody's Fault' theme of the text – expresses a wish for revolution in his statement in a letter of 1855, imagining a possible future:

> And I believe the discontent to be so much the worse for smouldering instead of blazing openly, that it is extremely like the general mind of France before the breaking out of the first

Revolution, and is in danger of being turned by any one of a
thousand accidents . . . into such a Devil of a conflagration as
has never been beheld since.

(*Letters*, to A.H. Layard 10 April 1855, Vol. 7, p. 587)

Yet this follows on a comment on 'the alienation of the people from
their own public affairs' which hints at the impossibility of revolution. Such alienation could not become explosive, because the
silent majorities are alienated from awareness of their real conditions. Where, in the perception of what Marseilles is, commerce
can replace politics, the atmosphere is already post-modern, belonging to Guy Debord's 'society of the spectacle' – which fits the photograph – and fittingly Chapter 2 introduces tourism through the
Meagles family and Tattycoram. Meagles, with whom I would like
to begin for his fetishistic sense of reality, tells Clennam why they
are tourists: it is to counter a morbidity in their daughter, a frailty
associated with 'this time of her life':

'. . . This is how you found us staring at the Nile, and the Pyramids, and the Sphinxes, and the Desert, and all the rest of it;
and this is how Tattycoram will be a greater traveller in course
of time than Captain Cook.'

(1.2.20)

But it is not just the travellers who stare. The Sphinx (though it is
not the same sphinx as Oedipus's, I think the connection can be
made) poses a question as much as the travellers who look at her.
The Sphinx is the last thing to be looked at if the project is to stay
'amused'. Mr Meagles's empty 'staring' poses no question, and
allows none to be put back to him, but in contrast to him, and to
the 'staring' of the first page, I offer an indirect commentary on
that, from a text thirty years later than *Little Dorrit*, Nietzsche's *Beyond
Good and Evil*, which suggests that a mutual looking which is also
a questioning is the character of modernity:

The will to truth, which is still going to tempt us to many a
hazardous enterprise; that celebrated veracity of which all philosophers have hitherto spoken with reverence: what questions
this will to truth has already set before us! What strange, wicked,
questionable questions! It is already a long story – yet does it not
seem as if it has only just begun? Is it any wonder we should at

last grow distrustful, lose our patience, turn impatiently away? That this sphinx should teach us too to ask questions? *Who* really is it that here questions us? *What* really is it in us that wants 'the truth'? – We did indeed pause for a long time before the question of the origin of this will – until finally we came to a complete halt before an even more fundamental question. We asked after the *value* of this will. Granted we want truth: *why not* untruth? And uncertainty? Even ignorance? – The problem of the value of truth stepped before us – or was it we who stepped before this problem? Which of us is Oedipus here? Which of us sphinx? It is, it seems, a rendezvous of questions and question-marks. – And, would you believe it, it has finally come to seem to us that this problem has never before been posed – that we have been the first to see it, to fix our eye on it, to *hazard* it? For there is a hazard in it and perhaps there exists no greater hazard.[6]

Little Dorrit has in it the modernity of the 'will to truth', alongside the no less modern mystificatory power of ideology and commodity fetishism. Can such mystification be countered through the 'will to truth', which drives scientific, positivist thinking – prompting even Arthur Clennam's 'I want to know' (1.10.113)? The will to truth sets out to know and uncover, treating life as it appears on the surface as deception. In Nietzsche, it seems that the Sphinx's questionings become focused in modernity, evoking an Oedipus whose will to truth begs the question, Who wants to know? Coming from the Sphinx (but Oedipus is also interrogating her), that raises issues of sexual difference. Why is it 'the truth' – something without shadows, transparent, photographic – that is wanted? For when the Sphinx gets her answer, which resolves ambiguity and plurality (the riddle) into singleness (including the singleness of the denial of sexual difference) she kills herself; when Oedipus gets *his* answer, he blinds himself. Oedipus and the Sphinx represent different epistemologies. Despite the Sphinx's oppressiveness, which fits the imperatives of the will to truth, her way of asking and Oedipus's will to truth are different, since she depends on deception focused in the ambiguity of the riddle, which can only be resolved by Oedipus finding a password which will fit (this is not the same as the truth), and he depends on flattening out (a form of violence) the riddle's difference and discontinuity in his answer. Both forms of epistemology are present in *Little Dorrit*, and the text moves between them.

Mr Meagles and Nietzsche could hardly be greater contrasts. Yet their alternative forms of seeing respond to each other. Mr Meagles takes his daughter Pet abroad for her health, reasons which are linked to her feelings for Henry Gowan, from whom he wants to separate her (1.17.209). Tourism is the evasion of an issue which is sexual in character. In the repressed existence where the daughter is fetishised as a 'pet' and the shadow-daughter, Tattycoram, not given a proper name, it is not surprising that the latter turns to a lesbian relationship with Miss Wade in an attempt to free herself from patriarchy – while Pet marries into the appallingly class-ridden world that her father really admires. He looks – and the tourist gaze is the will to truth – but he could not survive the challenge of being looked at, which is what the opening page of *Little Dorrit* shows taking place.

The tourists live by evasion after they have received the pass-word to go:

> They made little account of stare and glare, in the new pleasure of recovering their freedom . . .
>
> (1.2.21)

And just as staring suggests the impulse to capture and fix reality, as in the photograph, Mr Meagles has his souvenirs:

> There were antiquities from Central Italy, made by the best modern houses in that department of industry; bits of mummy from Egypt (and perhaps Birmingham); model gondolas from Venice; model villages from Switzerland; models of tesselated pavement from Herculaneum and Pompei, like petrified mince veal; ashes out of tombs, and lava out of Vesuvius; Spanish fans, Spezzian straw hats, Moorish slippers, Tuscan hair-pins, Carrara sculpture, Trastaverini scarves, Genoese velvets and filagree, Neapolitan coral, Roman cameos, Geneva jewellery, Arab lanterns, rosaries blest all round by the Pope himself, and an infinite variety of lumber. There were views, like and unlike, of a multitude of places; and there was one little picture-room devoted to a few of the regular sticky old saints, with sinews like whipcord, hair like Neptune's, wrinkles like tattooing, and such coats of varnish that every holy personage served for a fly-trap. . . . He was no judge, he said, except of what pleased himself; he had picked them up, dirt-cheap, and people *had* considered them rather fine. One man . . . had declared that 'Sage, reading' . . . to

be a fine Guercino. As for Sebastian del Piombo there, you would judge for yourself; if that were not his later manner, the question was, Who was it? Titian that might or might not be – perhaps he had only touched it. Daniel Doyce said perhaps he hadn't touched it, but Mr Meagles rather declined to overhear the remark.

(1.16.193)

A new emphasis appears in *Little Dorrit*, though it is hinted at in earlier novels – the power of the commodity. Behind the fetishised objects are other ornaments in Mr Meagles's own room: 'a pair of brass scales for weighing gold and a scoop for shovelling out money'. Reproduction culture and capitalism go together, and both are associated with the fetishising of people; for the description of symbols of commerce is followed by a picture, equally souvenir-like, of the two daughters – one now living, one now dead – aged about three. Can the two states be distinguished? As Clennam looks closely, the picture is supplemented by another two. Pet stands framed in the doorway, reduced to the commodity by being turned into a picture. (The positioning is repeated in the first appearance of Mrs Merdle from behind a curtain (1.20.238), where the theatricality suggests that she self-fashions her own commodification.) The second is that of the reflection of Tattycoram outside the door (not in the picture) which Clennam sees in the mirror adjacent to the picture. Her anger is a contrast to the fetishised emotions of the daughter. It threatens to take over from that picture, to act as the challenge to it. Her frown 'changed [her] beauty into ugliness' (1.16.194) but Clennam's valuation which says that works from a standard of beauty set up by that which is displayed on the wall. Tattycoram's look is a stare that probes and questions that valuation.

As an intrusion into the *mise-en-scène*, Tattycoram, as the supplement to Pet (she was brought into the family to substitute for the dead sister), threatens to replace the fetishised female, little child – 'Minnie' – pet and woman in one, and to show the priority of the existence of her transgressive energy and anger. Her intrusiveness is into *Little Dorrit* itself, where she must be recontained at the end into a bourgeois acceptance of her servant status, and a rejection of her sexuality as a 'madness' (2.23.811). At the time of Tattycoram's repentance, Little Dorrit, as much fetishised as the portrait of Pet, is shown to her by Mr Meagles, as though she also was in a picture – 'You see that young lady . . . that little, quiet, fragile creature . . .' (1.23.812).

Signs of the commodity and of conspicuous wealth are everywhere in the book, from Mr Dorrit's wealth, down to the choice Mr Merdle makes between borrowing a mother-of-pearl penknife and a tortoise-shell, one in order to cut his throat (2.24.701). Perhaps he rejects the first on account of its aesthetic appearance: perhaps it has too feminine associations for him. And Mr Meagles did not have to go to Egypt to see the pyramids: treasures from them were displayed in 1821 in the Egyptian Hall, Piccadilly, hyped by Belzoni's *Narrative of the Operations and Recent Discoveries Within the Pyramids* (1820).[7] Belzoni (1778–1823) was the self-made archaeologist: a showman (a weightlifter) turned excavationist. The same year, 1821, Champollion deciphered Egyptian hieroglyphics, and thus inaugurated not only Egyptology and the opening up of Egypt to the west (Pip and Herbert work at Cairo), but the idea of reading the unreadable, which Lacan compares to the achievement of Freud in reading the language of the unconscious.[8]

I shall return to Egypt's relics, and to deciphering by means of a password, but want to add to the sense of a museum culture that hangs over *Little Dorrit*. The portrayal of London in Chapter 3 is suggestive of an old, dead country, requiring people to be tourists within its museum character. This is reinforced by the thirty years' gap that is emphasised in the text, between the time of narrating and its events. Museum-culture is mentioned through the reference to the South Sea Islands sculptures acquired by the British Museum in the 1850s. Acquisition of curios has the character of the dominating will to truth, which is a will to possession, but these fetishes have the power to interrogate the staleness of commercial London on a Sunday evening:

> Everything was bolted and barred that could by possibility furnish relief to an overworked people. No pictures, no unfamiliar animals, no rare plants or flowers, no natural or artifical wonders of the ancient world – all *taboo* with that enlightened strictness that the ugly South Sea gods in the British Museum might have supposed themselves at home again.
>
> (1.3.28)

This passage, though it bears witness to its own Eurocentrism, shows a cultural cross-over. The rationalism of Europe, its scientific progress, sanctions anthroplogy as a quasi-imperialist discourse that can 'read' the significance of these 'ugly South Sea gods' (calling them ugly: an aesthetic judgement like that which calls Tattycoram ugly when she is angry). Their power of taboo (a word brought back to Europe by Captain Cook) is instant immediate punishment of the person who touches. Yet what society could hold more taboos than this rationalist Victorian Britain? Dickens 'others' his own society: makes it an object of anthropological investigation; makes its *taboos* – italicising that word as if to make a feature of its technical sense – part of its strangeness, in a defamiliarisation of London.

Reference to the taboo could be taken further, and linked with elements in what Nietzsche calls his 'attack' on nineteenth-century Christianity, *The Genealogy of Morals* (1887), which discusses *ressentiment*, the institutionalising of guilt and bad conscience and the 'ascetic ideal'. All these are associated with Christianity: the ascetic ideal being what it promotes in terms of character. It uses 'poverty, humility, chastity' as its slogans (*Genealogy of Morals*, 3.8.243), and the 'ascetic priest' 'confronts existence' as a labyrinth where order must be (re)imposed – 'treat[ing] life as a maze in which we must retrace our steps to the point at which we entered or as an error which only a resolute act can correct.' Nietzsche continues, looking at the strangeness of nineteenth-century society:

> An observer viewing our terrestrial existence from another planet might easily be persuaded that this earth is simply an ascetic star, the habitation of disgruntled, proud, repulsive creatures, unable to rid themselves of self-loathing, hatred of the earth and of all living things, who inflict as much pain as possible on themselves, solely out of pleasure in giving pain – perhaps the only kind of pleasure they know . . . An ascetic life is indeed a contradiction in terms. Here we find rancour without parallel, the rancour of an insatiable power-drive which would dominate, not a single aspect of life, but life itself, its deepest and strongest foundations.[9]

The description fits Mrs Clennam, but it characterises most of the people of *Little Dorrit*, picking out their capacity to make themselves miserable (Fanny, Miss Wade, Arthur Clennam, for example) out of a bitterness against life which makes them feel that they have missed something and need to control it. Nietzsche identifies the ascetic ideal with an interpretive aim (3.23.284) – the will to truth whose rigour comes from the ascetic ideal (3.24.288–9). In *The Gay Science*, section 344, he calls it also the will to death, as though philosophy, by opposing mind to body, and knowledge and truth to knowledge gained sensuously, and in confronting the play of pleasure by the pursuit of reality, sides with death.

So much of this may be used to read *Little Dorrit*, the deathliness of which comes from two sources. One, the commodification of reality. Secondly, the will to truth. This will to truth is identified with the ideology of Christianity by the sabbatarian practices of the London described in the text. *Little Dorrit*'s strategy of resistance to this will to death is – as with *Bleak House* – to dematerialise reality. Commodification does that too: reifying everything (turning Mrs Merdle into 'the Bosom', denaturing people into abstractions – Society, Bar, Bishop and Physician). Commodification serves as a substitute for Mr Meagles's experiences as a tourist – indeed it constructs those experiences, as the classicising Mr Eustace's guide-book does for Mrs General's. It takes away existence, however, in mystified form: the commodity is the fetish, and the fetish is there to prevent insight into its constructed and fictitious nature. It denatures while all the time suggesting that this is where life is. Marx wrote about the 'fetishism which attaches itself to the products of labour as soon as they are produced as commodities':

> A commodity appears at first sight an extremely obvious, trivial thing. But its analysis brings out that it is a very strange thing, abounding in metaphysical subtleties and theological niceties . . . As soon as [the table – Marx's example of the commodity] emerges as a commodity, it changes into a thing which transcends sensuousness. It not only stands with its feet on the ground, but in relation to all other commodities, it stands on its head, and evolves out of its wooden brain grotesque ideas, far more wonderful than if it were to begin dancing of its own free will.[10]

Every product of labour becomes 'a social hieroglyphic' ready to be 'deciphered' in a process of demystification. Dickens in contrast to the fake life of commodification, here and earlier in *Bleak House*, has the 'destructive character' as Benjamin discusses this:

> The destructive character sees nothing permanent. . . . What exists he reduces to rubble, not for the sake of the rubble, but for that of the way leading through it.[11]

The destructive character appears in a writing that in Chapter 3 cuts out the speech of the waiter, making it unintelligible, and suggests as Clennam walks out into the street that London is a place for anthropology, ready to become a museum:

> Passing, now the mouldy hall of some obsolete Worshipful Company, now the illuminated windows of a Congregationless Church that seemed to be waiting for some adventurous Belzoni to dig it out and discover its history; passing silent warehouses and wharves, and here and there a narrow alley leading to the river, where a wretched little bill, FOUND DROWNED was weeping on the wet wall; he came at last to the house he sought.
>
> (1.3.31)

The house (Mrs Clennam's) is found as though through a process of archaeology. This London of emptied-out fragments where Clennam walks home is uncanny, *unheimlich*, a place of absences and shadowy hauntings which cannot quite be read. The bill on the wall in the rain with its dreary rhyme which enforces repetition is an allegorical *Trauerspiel*-like emblem, pointing to the de-realised dead body, ungendered, unnameable, like the 'nobody' that runs through several chapter titles, as a survival from a working title for *Little Dorrit*, *Nobody's Fault*. 'Nobody' is even genderless: it is Clennam, but in the chapter called 'Nobody's Disappearance' it is also Tattycoram and Pet. This London, which is a place for no body but a dead body – a nemo, no one – is unreadable, indifferent in its signification, its details only existing in their factuality:

> He went up to the door, which had a projecting canopy in carved work, of festooned jack-towels and children's heads with water on the brain, designed after a once-popular monumental pattern
> . . .
>
> (1.3.31)

So much for Baroque ornamental swags and putti, emblems of craziness to fit with the craziness and records of madness inside the Clennam house. The motivation in the writing is to ruin things, to leach them of life, just as the 'stare and glare' of a commodified vision constructs things as dead and people as part of a museum-culture. This is carried to its furthest extent in literal terms, in the scene of the mortuary of the convent of the Great Saint Bernard in the Alps (2.1). Dickens visited this in 1846, and wrote about it to Forster, commenting on his feeling of liminality, as though he had 'died in the night and passed into the unknown world':

Nothing of life or living interest in the pictures, but the grey dull walls of the convent. No vegetation of any sort or kind. Nothing growing, nothing stirring. Everything iron-bound and frozen up. Beside the convent, in a little outhouse with a grated iron door which you may unbolt for yourself, are the bodies of people found in the snow who have never been claimed and are withering away – not laid down or stretched out, but standing up, in corners and against walls; some erect and horribly human, with distinct expressions on their faces; some sunk down on their knees; some dropping over on one side; some tumbled down altogether, and presenting a heap of skulls and fibrous dust. There is no other decay in that atmosphere . . .

(*Letters*, 6 September 1846, 4.618–19)

The stasis here is like Marseilles under the sun's stare, and 'iron-bound' is significant. Dickens calls this 'the most distinct and individual place I have seen.' Individuality is identified with death: what constitutes people as single subjects is death. In the novel, the living travellers, the tourists on their way to Italy, are shadowed by the dead ones in the convent mortuary, whose traces they have seen in the crosses in the snow on their way.

While all this noise and hurry were rife among the living travellers, there, too, silently assembled in a grated house, half-a-dozen paces removed, with the same cloud enfolding them, and the same snow-flakes drifting in upon them, were the dead travellers found upon the mountain. The mother, storm-belated many winters ago, still standing in the corner with her baby at her breast; the man who had frozen with his arm raised to his mouth in fear or hunger, still pressing it with his dry lips after years and years. An awful company, mysteriously come together! A wild destiny for that mother to have foreseen, 'Surrounded by so many and such companions upon whom I never looked, and never shall look, I and my child will dwell together inseparable, on the Great Saint Bernard, outlasting generations who will come to see us, and will never know our name, or one word of our story but the end.'

The living travellers thought little or nothing of the dead just then.

(2.1.433)

The last sentence recalls both the earlier 'they made little account of stare and glare . . .' and the way the Meagles view experience.

The dead shadow the living as the Meagles shadow their live daughter by her dead sister, projecting on her her morbidity. Pet Meagles's fear of Miss Wade is uncanny, a fear of the other, expressed as a fear of being shadowed: she retreats from Tattycoram when she gathers she has seen Miss Wade – 'I feel as if *someone else was touching me!*' (1.16.194, my emphasis). Pet is 'a spoilt child' (1.16.198) – but spoilt by patriarchy and its own relation to death. This side-by-side quality of living and dead does not necessarily suggest a binary opposition within the text of life/death, or truth and reality/social falseness, the real and natural, especially in art/the fake. These sets of oppositions are invalidated by a sense that both sides of the opposition have been constructed. Amy Dorrit and Pet Meagles: Pet and Tattycoram: all are constructed in their social reality, as is the dead sister. There is simply no natural reality the text wishes to present. The living are near to the dead in the sense that the text cannot support any sense of a firm separation between them.

Amy too is not a 'natural' form of goodness: the text makes her the prison child. Her lack of physical presence, of sexuality, or Tattycoram-like energy and ability to talk back are not necessarily to be seen as the fetish-like attributes of the ideal, natural woman. She is made aware of her subjectivity being constructed in the sense she gains that her life cannot be put together into a narrative, as in this episode in Rome:

> Little Dorrit would often ride out in a hired carriage that was left them, and alight alone and wander among the ruins of old Rome. The ruins of the vast old Amphitheatre, of the old Temples, of the old commemorative Arches, of the old trodden highways, of the old tombs, besides being what they were to her, were ruins of the old Marshalsea – ruins of her own old life – ruins of the faces and forms that of old peopled it – ruins of its loves, hopes, cares and joys. Two ruined spheres of action and suffering were before the solitary girl often sitting on some broken fragment; and in the lonely places, under the blue sky, she saw them both together.
>
> Up then would come Mrs General; taking all the colour out of everything, as Nature and Art had taken it out of herself; writing Prunes and Prism, in Mr Eustace's text, wherever she could lay a hand; looking everywhere for Mr Eustace and company,

and seeing nothing else; scratching up the driest little bones of antiquity, and bolting them whole without any human visitings – like a Ghoule in gloves.

(2.15.612)

Being a tourist in Rome, as ruined and antique as Egypt, is alienating: tourism for her does not have the stabilising features it has for Mr Meagles. And what she sees is not under the power of mystification: she looks with the eyes of the destructive character. She is a split subject, despite Mrs General's best ministrations to varnish everything and give it a surface. Splitting may be glossed from Wordsworth:

> A tranquillising spirit presses now
> On my corporeal frame, so wide appears
> The vacancy between me and those days
> Which yet have such self-presence in my mind,
> That, sometimes, when I think of it, I seem
> Two consciousnesses, conscious of myself
> And of some other Being.
>
> (*The Prelude*, 1805, 2. 27–33)

The poet focuses on vacancy, because there is no single subject on the other side of the gap: only a split consciousness, engaged in an act of specular contemplation, conscious of itself and conscious of some other being. Go back as far as he will, Wordsworth cannot find a single subject. The vacancy is always there. In *Little Dorrit*, Amy sees the ruins of old Rome but these in turn become also 'the ruins of the old Marshalsea'. The prison and ancient Rome come together, as they do in Piranesi's *Carceri*. The Marshalsea, which opened on its latest site in 1780 (a date of apparently almost primal significance for Dickens), closed in 1849, and the Preface to the novel records a sense of its ghostliness, but though there is a ghostly awareness of that at the back of this passage, it is not the main point. Rather, the Marshalsea is constituted by a *vide*: it is riven by ruin. Since Amy was born there, it might suggest that the Marshalsea is the mother. According to Julia Kristeva, considering the process of abjection, in which the subject tries to effect a separation from the mother in order to constitute itself as a separate, bounded ego, even the mother in the pre-Oedipal stage cannot be contemplated as a unified object. She too is split, which is what enables and

effectuates a separation from her, quite independent of the workings of patriarchy. Amy contemplates the mother as gone, as that
which cannot be held onto in any unified sense. But the sense of the
mother as a not coherent whole is inseparable from the melancholia
of abjection, and from the consequent failure to constitute herself as
a separate being.[12]

Certainly the record of the past that comes before her is one of
negation: if even the old Marshalsea is seen as a ruin, there can be
no approach to the past as to something complete and sustaining.
The other 'ruined sphere of action and suffering' the text speaks of
is her present life, in the state of riches, the life she tries to narrativise
in the two chapters called 'A Letter from Little Dorrit' (2.4, 2.11).
What sustains her is broken (the fragment); what she sees is vacancy
– the 'lonely places'. The reference to 'the blue sky', recalling
Marseilles, puts this description of the desolate into the context of
modernity: in this world everything is on display, under the sky.
Hence Amy is not alone: Mrs General comes up as a simulacrum
of the mother, a parodic figure whose own ego annihilates Little
Dorrit's.

To show Amy thus split is the text's gender-awareness: Amy
is like Esther Summerson (and like the later Dorothea in *Middlemarch*, also in Rome),[13] alienated in a way that is distinct from,
say, Clennam's. His focus on wanting to know gives him a belief
in the possibility of being a unified single-subject, and of creating
a narrative. In Amy, lack of coherence is annihilating and renders
movement back to the past in terms of memory impossible, as
much as it makes her not a centre, though her name is placed at
the centre of this text.

II

Like *Bleak House* and *Great Expectations*, this novel looks back from
the time of its setting to a past encrypted in its present – and therefore also encrypted in the time of writing the text. Its project is the
discovery of that past in its bearing on the future. But significantly
it avoids a final unveiling, it evades an adventurous Belzoni, for it
leaves things unsaid to Arthur Clennam that he wants to know.
These things are known by Amy and by Rigaud, who, Welsh suggests,[14] acts as his violent double, tracking down and 'closing in'
on Mrs Clennam while Clennam is powerless in prison. Clennam

begins with a weight of guilt which is only shaken off by a sur-
cease of the inquiry. This Oedipus ends up not knowing: there is
a break with the will to truth.

Clennam begins by saying that he has no will (1.2.20), connecting
will with 'purpose' and 'hope'. His upbringing, combining Puritan
tastes with capitalist motivations, shows the triumph in him of the
ascetic ideal, where this entails a death-drive: as Nietzsche puts it
at the end of the *The Genealogy of Morals*, 'man would sooner have
the void for his purpose than be void of purpose.' Like Pip, Clennam
is masochistic, in the sense that he has no resistance to the machine-
like power in which he was caught ('always grinding in a mill I
always hated'), but unlike Pip, there is no punishing woman from
whom punishment can be received which would turn masochism
into a resistance and a critique of that ideology of repression and
enforcement of guilt. The statement 'I have no will' is an expression
of a desire as much as a statement of fact: there is a wish for self-
punishment, and he is not alone in the death-drive which attracts
him to the Marshalsea: it is repeated in Amy's melancholia, Mrs
Clennam's paralysis, in Merdle's suicide, even in the comic writing
of John Chivery's epitaphs. The arrested quality of everything within
Little Dorrit points to a drive towards the end which is not distinguishable from the will to truth. But here it may be worth pausing
over Clennam's accidie and his feeling that reparation needs to be
made for or by his father. The guilt and the lack of will may well
be a displacement for something else that fits the textual unconscious. What has the Clennam House been doing in China for twenty
years? What has the commodity Arthur has been dealing in been?
Flora Finching mentions tea chests (1.13.152) but a historical Clennam
would have been one of those selling opium to buy tea. The hero
is more guilty than he allows consciously, and the text's resolution of the secrets of the Clennam house does not quite explain
that guilt: more remains encrypted in the text in a resistance to
interpretation.[15]

Another narrative is necessary. Both tea and opium required trade
with China, which was conducted by the East India Company till
1833, when pressure for Free Trade ended its monopoly. The trade
surplus Britain had with India, as a result of flooding India with
British textiles, which also meant the destruction of India's indig-
enous handicraft, could not be matched in China, for China's willingness to sell tea had to be reciprocated by Britain selling silver:
the Chinese market was not to be touched by British goods.

Indian-produced opium, however, bought up by the East India Company could serve instead of silver. The opium produced, according to the French missionary Jean-Henri Baldus, 'a mind brutalised, a body enfeebled, the premature death of the smoker followed by the sale of all his and his wife's and children's worldly possessions and their descent into a life of misery and crime – these are the normal consequences of this fatal passion.' But Baldus added that the Europeans cared little about this, 'and particularly the English, in whom love of humanity never prevails over love of gain'. (This corresponds to Mr Pancks's declaration of the 'whole duty of man in a commercial country' (1.13.160).) Baldus, however, lets his own discursive formation slip when he argues that the Chinese take to the drug too easily, as a sign of their inner condition, for 'in all things they are decidedly inferior to the European, whom indeed the Lord seems to have regarded as his second chosen people'.[16]

The East India Company gave its attention to China when it could no longer send cotton goods to Britain from India. Opium fetched a substantial revenue to the British Raj. The loss of silver China suffered impoverished that country. The British government made an estimated £3.5 million per annum through tax revenues on tea during the years of the nineteenth century up to the Opium War of 1840–42 (and made a comparable amount from the sugar industry, which flourished in proportion to the increase in tea drinking). Opium was brought into China in the boats of such companies as Jardine and Matheson: a firm dating back to 1782. Jardine and Matheson wanted to break the East India Company monopoly in order to make China take British textiles: Samuel Jardine was to become an MP ('Mr McDruggy' in *Sybil*), urging further free trade upon the nation. Those British merchants whose toehold in China was in Macao, the Portuguese colony, and in Canton itself, precipitated the war with China when in 1836 opium was supressed by the Qing dynasty. Palmerston's defence in Parliament in 1849 of the rights of free trade – selling narcotics – is memorable:

'I wonder what the House would have said to me if I had come down to it with a large naval estimate for a number of revenue cruisers to be employed in the preventive service from the river at Canton to the Yellow Sea for the purpose of preserving the morals of the Chinese people who were disposed to buy what other people were disposed to sell them.'[17]

It is reflected in the rhetoric of Lord Decimus Tite Barnacle in *Little Dorrit*, who may well be Palmerston himself, 'in the odour of Circumlocution' (no password is therefore likely to come from him) 'with the very smell of Despatch Boxes upon him' (like an archaeologist), defending British Free Trade (allied with the fraud of Merdle) from any inspection:

> [he] had risen to official heights on the wings of one indignant idea, and that was, My Lords, that I am yet to be told that it behoves a Minister of this free country to set bounds to the philanthropy, to cramp the charity, to fetter the public spirit, to contract the enterprise, to damp the independent self-reliance of its people.
>
> (1.34.405)

The War gained Britain Hong Kong and further ports for trade: a later war of 1856–60, written in the very period of *Little Dorrit*, enforced the legality of opium to be sold in China.

But the text is silent on opium, except that Arthur Clennam comes back to London with an ascetic sense of the need to make reparation, just as he thinks of Mrs Clennam mentally saying about Mr Dorrit, 'he has decayed in his prison; I in mine. I have paid the penalty' (1.8.89). It is as though he would like to say the equivalent himself. Such guilt may belong to the suppressed knowledge somewhere that China had, by 1839, two million opium addicts. The 'social problem' novel treated opium in working-class Britain, in *Mary Barton* and *Alton Locke*, but silence or circumlocution about Clennam's trade suggests contradictions in Victorian ideology: a bad conscience at work. Opium in nineteenth-century literature supports a schizoid view of reality and evasion from it via the power of dreams. A drug whose exploitative use enforces silence on the middle classes drinking tea is the marker of separation from bourgeois life, as in Nemo, or in Mr Merdle taking laudanum before his suicide (2.25.706), or as in *The Mystery of Edwin Drood*, it evokes unconscious criminality (as also in *The Moonstone*). The displacements are significant, for the addicted become criminal while un-inebriated England, drinking its tea and making it the emblem of the nation, becomes criminally violent towards China, subverting it from within by selling it addiction in a nihilistic trade where the existence of the commodity conceals the point that this trade has the void for its purpose.[18]

Imperialism and the will to truth are akin. There is an imperialist gesture in the Meagleses looking at the Sphinx: no wonder he refers to Captain Cook. If the staring is photographic in character, that fits with the status of photography – with the point that the Sphinx *was* frequently photographed: 'The photographs depicting the "empty" spaces of Palestine and Egypt become themselves an important (visual) tributary of the progress of empire, the photographs depicting the exotic Other become fuel for the *mission civilisatrice*.'[19] Not surprisingly, Edwin Drood is on his way to 'wake up' Egypt, as de Lesseps began to do in 1859. So if *Little Dorrit* breaks with the will to truth, it does not do so consistently. The presentation of Doyce's single-minded doggedness, the statement about Physician, 'Where he was, something real was' (2.25.704), Clennam reviewing his life and asking what he has found that is real, and the answer coming back, 'Little Dorrit', as she enters his room (1.13.165) – these are examples of a textual drive towards the will to truth that would be death-dealing in demanding single straight answers. But they are part of a different discourse, one which is less aware of modernity, or of the issues of post-modernity which are raised by the text – that there can be virtually no approach to the real where the real has been so thoroughly mystified, as in the existence of the commodity, and its representation in photographs. Mystification means rather that the terms of the real are already enshrouded in ideology.

Yet the text also holds back from the will to truth, and responds to Nietzsche's question, 'Granted we want truth: *why not rather untruth? And uncertainty? Even ignorance?*' by showing value in not knowing, even in being deceived. Yet to be content with deception involves accepting mystification through the fascination of the commodity for consumption. 'Consumption' had been a term with specialised use in eighteenth-century political economy, but its importance as a concept appears mainly in the nineteenth. As applied to the disease of the lungs and as applied to the shopper as a consumer, consumption means 'to take away with,' 'to use up entirely': consumer goods are there for their complete abolition, their removal through use. Opium and tea are consumer goods, like the cigarettes Rigaud smokes in prison (1.1.7) which are a marker of modernity.[20] But consumption exists beyond the level of the commodities consciously described and satirised in *Little Dorrit*, and the word 'consumption' implies that capitalism works to empty out and to take away completely.

Silence about the China trade suggests mystification at work in the text, just as Dickens could criticise the conduct of the Crimean war, yet not see that it was imperialist in character. Hence the arguments sound weak with which Clennam disengages himself from the business by declaring the 'House' out of date (1.5.46). The tea and opium trade was not dying in the nineteenth century. Nonetheless, there are reasons behind Clennam's contention. The 'House' image recalls *Dombey and Son*, and in making it 'a mere anomaly and incongruity', there is the replacement of its ethos by Mr Merdle's, the financier, the 'world-famed capitalist' (1.21.250). According to the OED, the word 'capitalism' was first used in 1854, in *The Newcomes* – though James Mill had used it in 1821.[21] As a date 1854 is relevant: a thoroughly coherent system is in place in the moment of conceptualising *Little Dorrit*. One form of capitalism replaces another. As Benjamin puts it, 'With the upheaval of the market economy, we begin to recognise the monuments of the bourgeoisie as ruins even before they have crumbled.'[22] The Clennam 'House' is as much a ruin as the ruins of old Rome: in capitalist production, everything is swept aside for a new thing (and Merdle too is dead by the end of the novel). The investment the text makes is in the House as empowered by an ideology – Evangelical, Utilitarian – which it presents as deliberately primitive, more fitting to be dug out by archaeologists than to be written about in a contemporary sense. It is the mystificatory ideology of the will to truth, prompted by the Christian ascetic ideal. The text, despite having that collusion with the will to truth commented on already, also shows that, so that no other Dickens text attacks Christianity as an ideology so strongly. The animus is focused in several ways, of which I will take two: through Mr Dorrit in the Marshalsea and through Mrs Clennam.

I will discuss Mr Dorrit and his imprisonment first. He defines what being a Christian means in the astonishing chapter 'Spirit' where his son tries to snub Clennam for not giving him money. He describes this put-down as showing 'a proper spirit' (1.31.375), where 'proper' is a very loaded word (propriety, property, and *amour propre*). But this attitude Dorrit calls 'monstrous', even 'parricidal', and says that his spirit will not endure it. The critique he makes in the speech that follows shows the power of a reading of *King Lear* for Dickens: indeed, it shows the only way a text like *King Lear* could exist in the nineteenth century, linked to the impotent rage of a father anxious to preserve some bourgeois gentility in a prison-bound situation, where all the mystique of patriarchy is disappearing. Dorrit argues as 'the Father', who would see rebellion towards himself (or subversion of his methods of securing testimonials) as anti-Christian:

> 'I point out to you, sir, with indignation, that – hum – the – ha – delicacy and peculiarity of your father's position should strike you dumb, sir, if nothing else should, on laying down such – ha – such unnatural principles. Besides, if you are not filial, sir, if you discard that duty, you are at least – hum – not a Christian? Are you – ha – an Atheist? And is it Christian, let me ask you, to stigmatise and denounce an individual for begging to be excused this time, when the same individual may – ha – respond with the required accommodation next time? Is it the part of a Christian not to – hum – not to try again?' He had worked himself into quite a religious glow and fervour.
>
> (1.31.377–8)

Christianity is declared to be the property of the likes of Uriah Heep, a slave religion that seeks patronage and crawls towards those in a higher position. In doing this, it can only be associated with *ressentiment*. It supports the status quo in that it gets its power by such crawling.[23] It is nihilistic in that it accepts the priority of an invisible cash relationship that it sees as being the only thing that binds members of a society together: in that it is just the same as the supposedly anti-Christian doctrine of Utilitarianism with its 'cash-nexus'. And it is complicit with the class-rule of capitalism. In contrast, Miss Wade hates patronage (2.21.663). But her refusal of it makes her deviant.

The mystificatory power of Christianity appears in Dorrit's self-righteous enactment of a fervent religious position. He does not just describe Christianity in this speech as a system of patronage, he shows its power to control him. The irony is that Dorrit is held in prison for debt, and in Chapter 1, I recalled, via *The Genealogy of Morals* (2.4), Christianity's cultivation of consciousness of guilt as instrumental to ensure the repayment of debts. And Christianity may pray 'forgive us our debts as we forgive our debtors' but this is disingenuous, as forgiveness is meant to ensure a bad conscience since the person forgiven is to feel indebted and guilty for ever more. Here it is interesting that the prayer 'forgive us our debts' is said to be the one 'too poor in spirit' for Mrs Clennam to pray. She is quite a trooper. Her preference is: 'Smite thou my debtors, Lord, wither them, crush them, do Thou as I would do, and Thou shalt have my worship; this was the impious tower of stone she built up to scale Heaven!' (1.5.47). At least she could never be a Uriah Heep. Her interpretation of the Bible might be an instance of what Machiavelli calls 'reading the Bible sensibly' – taking Christianity for its intentional sense, not for its ideological mystification. Mrs Clennam does, after all, interpret Christianity as being fundamentally to do with punishment and its evasion. For Nietzsche, the learning of guilt and the learning of pain are inseparable, and both serve to ensure the repayment of debts: 'it is in the sphere of contracts and legal obligations that the moral universe of guilt, conscience and duty took its inception' (*Genealogy*, 2.6, 197). The body has to pay in order to teach the mind to remember ('do not forget'). The law under which John Dickens, Mr Micawber and Mr Dorrit suffer is one which confined the body (it could not repossess the property of the debtor). If Christianity simultaneously avows and disavows the importance of debts, it is not free from cruelty either mental or physical. Mrs Clennam's putative prayer invokes torture of the body – and that includes her own.

Amy's reaction to Mr Dorrit's release belongs to the discourse that soon would end imprisonment for debt.[24] Clennam is glad that he should pay his debts, while she feels that it is hard 'that he should have lost so many years and suffered so much, and at last pay all the debts as well. It seems to me hard that he should pay in life and money both.' Clennam's response is 'My dear child':

> 'Yes, I know I am wrong,' she said timidly, 'don't think any worse of me; it has grown up with me here.'
>
> The prison, which could spoil so many things, had tainted Little Dorrit's mind no more than this. Engendered as the confusion was, in compassion for the poor prisoner, her father, it was the first speck Clennam had ever seen, it was the last speck Clennam ever saw, of the prison atmosphere upon her.
>
> He thought this, and forbore to say another word. With the thought, her purity and goodness came before him in their brightest light. The little spot made them the more beautiful.
>
> (1.35.422)

Presumably Little Dorrit thinks she is wrong in relation to the dominant Christian ideology, and identifies Clennam with it, just as Clennam looks at her within the terms of that Christian discourse. The text would then give the unstated sense that both it and Clennam in so far as he follows that ideology are wrong: it is asking to be read sensibly, to demystify the sacral suggestions that gather around Amy, which are only purchased at the price of limiting her. Or it might suggest that the reading which marks her off in terms of spots and purity is violently repudiatory of life, in so far as it equates a completed Amy (as it also envisages a satisfactorily acquitted Dorrit) with someone who is absolutely pure. The rhetoric is dismissive of the body, and recalling the earlier suggestion that the Marshalsea is the mother for Amy, it may be that the body, the mother and impurity are deliberately staked against their violent exclusion by the ascetic ideal imposed by Clennam and by other normalising agents of society.

Nonetheless, this reading of an awkward crux in the text is still unsatisfactory, missing its basic complicity with Clennam's viewpoint. The awkwardness of the discussion is only resolved by Amy's voice giving way in the next paragraph to sleep, so that the argument is foreclosed, and she becomes a liminal, haunting figure, on the margins, lacking a firm sense of conscious subjectivity and unnoticed, her earlier comments almost dream-like. That sense of the woman haunting male dominant discourses is the nearest the text approaches to vindicating the woman whose discourse is thus left out.

Amy as a haunting shadow is suggestive, for it is particularly her characteristic in relation to the Clennam house. When Affery learns the secret of the house, she thinks that Arthur's mother is in it, hidden like a Bertha Mason, and she connects this with the sounds of the house being like the uncanny rustle of ghosts, 'making signals', 'marking the walls' (2.30.785). (The sounds the house makes are its gradual falling apart.) The only woman who haunts the house is the Amy who is almost invisible there, and Affery's description is suggestive of Amy's form of indirect discourse. It makes her the ghost who brings down the house.

Mrs Clennam, too, shadows Mr Dorrit. Each are in their prison, he in the Marshalsea where she has effectively confined him, she in her paralysed body and armoured ego and with the prop supplied for her of a wheelchair, while her very house has also to be propped up. Her presentation is as a horrific male fantasy of the woman. Her 'stony head-dress' (1.3.34) in the context of the way she is described makes her Christianity Medusan. But Christianity is inseparable from other religions and other fetishes. She sits 'with the impenetrability of an old Egyptian sculpture' (1.5.47). We are back to the Sphinx and the opening of *Beyond Good and Evil*: while the image, which also indirectly recalls the gods in the British Museum, is decorated a little later when she frowns at Clennam fixedly 'as if the sculptor of old Egypt had indented it in the hard granite face, to frown for ages' (1.5.48).

Something appears in Mrs Clennam of 'what really is it in us that wants the truth'. Mrs Clennam has found out the truth in detecting her husband's affair with Arthur's mother. She has possessed the child, allowing the mother to go mad ('slowly hunted [her] to death' – 2.30.779), finally confining her in a madhouse. In a repetition of this act of suppression, she stops the young Arthur Clennam in his romance with Flora Casby (thereby making Clennam a repetition of his father). Having constructed Arthur as a figure of guilt, she sends him away to China, thereby bringing about the mother's death. Both women are deprived of him in a tabooing action belonging to the ascetic ideal, while the empire serves as a scapegoating place for the atonement of imaginary sins. Finally, she has suppressed a codicil to Gilbert Clennam's will. The will to truth involves a need to make reparation for this last action, which Arthur intuits (1.8.89), and she operates taboos against her own body, as also against love and 'the Arts' (2.30.779). Her will to truth is mystified and mystificatory: her commercialism she calls Christianity.

The codicil she has repressed gives money to the woman's patron's brother's youngest daughter. The patron was Frederick Dorrit, the daughter deprived of money is Amy, who is thus like Oliver Twist in being deprived of a fortune. Generationally, this makes Amy and Arthur's mother the same: just as Pip comes as close as possible to marrying Estella as his virtual sister in *Great Expectations*, Arthur comes close to marrying his mother, though a mother twenty years younger than he is. But such a quasi-incest is overlaid by another feature of repetition. Arthur replicates his father, even down to being 'irresolute' (1.15.181), a quality also shared by Mr Dorrit (1.6.58). Amy replicates the unknown singer in the role she occupies in relation to Frederick Dorrit, yet here again the text is reactionary, for Amy is 'not professional' as Mrs Merdle notices (1.20.239). She is a daughter who has not been put on the stage, unlike her sister Fanny. While the text's naturalism with regard to Amy in size and undernourishment deserves respect, it also breaks with a pattern that is also carefully established. In nonartistry, in being the kind of woman even Mrs Clennam might endorse, as also Mr Gilbert Clennam, the text settles for repression, and endorses patriarchy which indeed it shields.

So Arthur never finds out the truth: Mrs Clennam wants it kept from him and Amy agrees. Arthur Clennam intuits that the House has a secret it should confess, but he exemplifies the partiality of the will to truth, its mystified quality, for his instinct is the Christian one to protect the patriarch: 'if my father had erred, it was my first duty to conceal the fault and to repair it' (2.27.721). Yet the father has been complicit with Mrs Clennam in keeping back the codicil to the will. The text silently endorses the deception, and its similarity in plot here to *Oliver Twist* is suggestive. The novel keeps Amy Dorrit poor, as Oliver's father keeps Oliver poor on probation, which delivers the message that it is money, not poverty that corrupts. The text backs a mystified petit-bourgeois position which claims the importance of morality being possible independent of any class-position.

But the atmosphere of death is on the patriarch too. He is seen always from the standpoint of being beyond death. Death makes him like his picture which, like Hamlet's father, appears 'dark and gloomy, earnestly speechless on the wall, with eyes intently looking at his son as they had looked when life had departed from him, [which] seemed to urge him awfully to the task he [Clennam] had attempted' (1.5.54). He is like Allegory in *Bleak House*, or like the Ghost in *Hamlet*, especially in the psychoanalyst Nicholas Abraham's reading of and addition to the play, where the Ghost's conscience is not easy. He was a Hamlet himself: significantly, his guardian was his uncle, and he repeats the failures of the old patriarchy: now Arthur Clennam is also Hamlet. The father's last words repeat his uncle's, who 'reduced to imbecility, at the point of death', 'labour[ed] under the delusion of some imaginary relenting towards a girl' (2.30.778), as Mrs Clennam puts it, and therefore added the codicil to his will. Now Arthur's father, at the point of death, says to Arthur, 'your mother' (1.5.35), and the Shakespearian echo of the Ghost's charge to Hamlet – 'Taint not thy mind, nor let thy soul contrive / Against thy mother aught' may be deliberate, but not necessarily appropriate. Does the patriarch mean Mrs Clennam or Arthur's mother? Who does this password reach?

The effect is to bring the two women together, Arthur's mother and Mrs Clennam, in a reminder that neither is named. Both had a claim to be called 'Mrs Clennam', in Arthur's mother's case since she went through 'a desecrated ceremony of marriage' (2.30.776) with Clennam. And who is Mrs Clennam? At one point she signs herself to Arthur 'M.C.' (2.28.752). Does M mean mother? or Mrs? Or is it a first name? And C?

Here the text resists deciphering: M.C. remains unread. Nonetheless, the other woman, haunting the house and annihilating it in its literal and ideological character is Arthur's mother. Not present in the house as an immured gothic heroine, but shadowing it like the nameless frozen mother in the Alps, she affects it by the power of the letters D.N.F. written on the watch. These letters evoke speech from the patriarch, but he is finally speechless. Like Mrs Joe's letter T, these letters are a password. But all depends on translation. The image in the text of Marseilles as Babel, and the reference to Mrs Clennam's 'impious tower of stone' which also implies Babel, both suggest the necessity for finding a 'true language', to recall Benjamin on 'the task of the translator'.[25] D.N.F. 'might be almost anything' according to Blandois (1.30.355), who speculates that the letters stood for 'some tender lovely fascinating fair-creature'. And perhaps they do; but Mrs Clennam then gives them a meaning. The 'cypher' is a password to the history of the house: the sentence 'Do Not Forget' being part of the love letter Arthur's mother wrote which M.C. found (2.30.775).

Translation thus would expand in four ways: it would imply the language of the unnamed woman who is Arthur's mother – her words to Clennam senior which Mrs Clennam now is compelled to use. It is Mrs Clennam's way of recalling the past self-justifyingly, punishing herself for general faults in a displacement of another fault she cannnot recognise, and for continually making her husband feel guilty. It has the meaning Flintwinch gives it – 'You know very well that the Do Not Forget, at the time when his father sent that watch to you could only mean, the rest of the story being then all dead and over, Do Not Forget the suppression. Make restitution' (2.30.782). Since the words also recall the Ghost to Hamlet in his mother's closet they also further encrypt the text, giving the sense of an older generation that cheats the younger and that cheats itself, and that passes debts on to be paid. The words pass on to Arthur Clennam the burden of being Hamlet. Such are the benefits of patriarchy.

For Lacan in his programmatic bravura essay of 1953, the 'Rome discourse', which demonstrates his belief in the power of the password:

the unconscious is that chapter of my history that is marked by a blank or occupied by a falsehood: it is the censored chapter. But the truth can be rediscovered; usually it has been written down elsewhere.

The first site for writing Lacan mentions is:

> in monuments: this is my body. That is to say, the hysterical nucleus of the neurosis where the hysterical symptom reveals the structure of a Language and is deciphered like an inscription . . .[26]

Reading the monument gains further meaning from Champollion's translations of hieroglyphics. The body, as with Mrs Clennam, has become the hysterical nucleus of a neurosis. Early, Mrs Clennam baffles interpretation – 'her severe face had no thread of relaxation in it by which any explorer could have been guided to the gloomy labyrinth of her thoughts' (1.5.45). The password would make it intelligible and reanimate the body. The possibility of interpretation would free the woman from being simply the monstrous masculine. She would instead become a subject with a history, an intelligible figure both wronged and wronging, lost within the labyrinth, not in control of her subjectivity.

For the cypher D.N.F. is a prompting to memory, a prompting also contained in its message. The password encrypts the memory of the dead woman. The cryptology that is performed whereby her narrative comes out is also the freeing from paralysis of Mrs Clennam, who almost undergoes a Freudian 'talking cure' in that she insists on giving the narrative herself of an injured older woman, 'cold as the stone but raging as the fire' (2.30.772). D.N.F. deconstructs the distinction between debtor and creditor. Mrs Clennam is described as denying herself food, 'placing the act to her credit, no doubt, in her Eternal Day-Book' (1.5.52), but the credit she gives herself by punishing herself through deprivation, and that she feels she earns by punishing sin 'as a servant and a minister' (2.30.775) is also a debt she pays that she knows is not enough. She ends her defence of herself by addressing the watch, as if speaking to its face, where that becomes the face both of the husband who has sent her the watch, and of the other woman (since her text is there) – 'she [Amy] herself was innocent, and *I might not have forgotten* to relinquish it [the money] to her, at my death' (2.30.780, my emphasis). The violence of self-torture has been her means not to forget that she is a debtor: she has paid in body, following the ideology of nineteenth-century punishment for debt.

Yet the idea of the password is more problematic than simply a means towards a solution. The password to which Lacan referred suggests the importance of recognition by the other: it is the word of release that the person in the confessional wishes to hear (like 'I forgive her', the password Miss Havisham wants to hear in a world where everything has stopped at twenty to nine) – but the conditions of confession mean that he or she never can receive such release, such permission to pass out of the labyrinth. Unconscious confession is a password for oppression: Lady Dedlock's 'Who copied that?' when she recognises Nemo's handwriting is a password for Tulkinghorn, making him begin his researches. And the password goes backwards and forwards like the palindromic 'Sweet marjoram', the deceptive password of health in *King Lear* – or like Pip's name, whether Philip Pirrip or Pip, in *Great Expectations*.[27] 'Recalled to Life', and 'Acquitted' are two ambiguous passwords in *A Tale of Two Cities*. And the word may be missing. Mr Dick lacks the password to get past King Charles's head. The Chinese in the opium-den in *Edwin Drood* says something significant to Jasper, but the word is 'unintelligible'. Then, too, a password can be deceptive in encouraging its addressee simply towards a confirmation of the self: in that sense the password that Pip receives in *Great Expectations* is important in not doing that; it comprises Wemmick's message 'DON'T GO HOME' (44.379). It sends Pip on another *unheimlich* journey altogether, defamiliarising him. (Mr Tulkinghorn in *Bleak House* is also imagined to receive the same message on the night of his murder, but to ignore it to his cost.)

And negatively, the password, as Lacan uses it, suggests that fragments may fit together. Lacan believes in the power of language as affect, having the potential of a password, a *tessera* (Wilden, p. 43). The *tessera* is a token of recognition, a password, and may be compared with the word *sumbulon*.[28] I have referred to the reading of signs as a translation, but in discussing *Bleak House*, I referred to Paul de Man on the incompatibility of bringing together the two broken parts of the one object (plate or vessel) which when united would form the symbol, the complete object which those fragments comprise. The incompatibility of the two narratives of *Bleak House* is followed in *Little Dorrit* by one narrative whose action involves the incommensurability of the past with the present: the impossibility, therefore, of reparation.

And the palindromic structure of the password suggests, in the conditions of post-modernism, a simple reversibility of signs. Reversibility is the fear in Piranesi's *Carceri*: in those labyrinths the ambiguity of space means that depth and height change places. The fear in Baudrillard (and this may be one that the name Pip confronts already, as though *Great Expectations* was itself post-modernist) is that such reversibility will partake of the nature of the Möbius strip – that is, that it leads nowhere. As Baudrillard puts it:

> We are in a logic of simulation which has nothing to do with a logic of facts and an order of reasons. Simulation is characterized by a *precession of the model*, of all models around the merest fact – the models come first, and their orbital ... circulation constitutes the genuine magnetic field of events.

The result is that 'all [signs] are true, in the sense that their truth is exchangeable.'[29] The possibility of the reversibility of the password makes problematic Lacan's distinction between empty and full speech, making the advent of a true speech that he aspires to a phallogocentric dream, a will to truth.

Yet in moving towards closure, *Little Dorrit* assents to the password. The hold of the past is partially broken, fitting the melancholy drive of the text to escape from the stasis it analyses. A password allows for interpretation and frees events to allow movement, getting Mrs Clennam out of her wheelchair and allowing a moment when repression can be undone by speech. The possibility of reversal is also a commitment to a narrative which believes in change. But in this text, as in *Bleak House* and *Great Expectations*, that narrative of change is also, perhaps, delusory, a record of things happening where there is no conviction that there can be any change, or where change could be only under the monological authority of the police. In those circumstances, the only interpretative possibilities are those which break down the separate moments of insight into allegory, and read not for a total interpretation, but for a momentary gleam. Even the photograph, wrenched out of a time-sequence and given an anonymity by its new positioning outside linear history, belongs to that fragmentariness which may be read adventitously, and to effect, however temporarily, by some new Belzoni.

5

Dickens and Dostoevsky: Capital Punishment in *Barnaby Rudge*, *A Tale of Two Cities* and *The Idiot*

You were to have no capital punishment, but were first to sweep off the face of the earth all legislators, jurists, and judges, who were of the contrary opinion.

Edwin Drood, 6.45

Whenever the history of the abolition of the death penalty in Britain is written, Dickens often takes a position of honour for his hostility towards public executions, which were outlawed during his life, in 1868, just as the number of offences for which hanging could take place was reduced from 200 in 1820 to two by 1861: either treason or murder. The abolitionist movement, associated with Bentham and the Utilitarians, newly empowered through the Radical MPs of the Reformed House of Commons after 1832 is a less familiar narrative. Dickens between 1840 and 1849 – the year that Dostoevsky faced a firing squad – moved from abolition to a position, which he argued in letters to *The Times*, of demanding execution within prison walls. John Bright (Mr Honeythunder in *The Mystery of Edwin Drood*) argued that Dickens wanted assassination rather than public execution, and was motivated by 'mere longing to put someone to death'.[1] So Dickens dreamed of scaffolds, according to Bright. Movements for abolition, usually led by William Ewart, came before Parliament first in 1840, then in 1849 and 1850, 1856, 1864 and 1868. Dickens in the 1850s and 1860s moved further and further away from the abolitionist position.

Those who favoured private capital punishment were either abolitionists who considered that this was the only practical step on the way to abolition, or those who set themselves against the carnivalisation of violence represented by public hangings, and their objections fitted with prudery and belief in repression. I have referred to modernity in terms of a culture of demonstration which may be associated with the Panopticon. A shift away from public hanging in so far as it is associated with prudery and repression seems to move outside these terms, and has led commentators to call Dickens increasingly reactionary in the 1850s and 1860s. In fact, in the 1860s there were passed a number of Acts with bearings on Dickens's positions: the 1861 Act which made murder, effectively, the only crime punishable by hanging, the 1862 ending of public whipping, the end of transportation in 1867 and the ending of imprisonment for debt in 1869. These Acts were indeed aspects of modernity in that they brought into the light criminality in more strongly defined terms. The eighteenth century had the death penalty for numerous offences, but the recommendations of a jury and the judge's discretion meant the commutation of many of these sentences. The 1861 Act meant that the judge had no power to commute: the death penalty was now fixed and the criminal now defined as such. Putting punishment behind prison walls, as with whipping and hanging, only reified the prison as a separable entity, for there was now no interchange between society and the prison as in the Marshalsea in *Little Dorrit*. Changed laws about debt meant that no longer the offence – being unable to pay – but the character and honesty of the debtor now came under review. Eighteenth-century law in its practice of commuting sentences made for 'a lottery of justice' according to Samuel Romilly, the Utilitarian reformer in 1810. Wilberforce said in 1812 that it produced 'a sort of gambling into vice'.[2] The reforms of the 1860s, in contrast, did away with the uncertainty principle.

There is a whole epistemic shift, in Foucauldian terms, between Dickens writing about punishment in *Oliver Twist* and *Barnaby Rudge* and in *A Tale of Two Cities*. In the first two, Dickens makes hanging central, bringing out its characteristics of inducement to shock and fascination. *A Tale of Two Cities* (1859) repeats much of the ground of *Barnaby Rudge* (1841), but with certain striking differences which I will describe and then account for, finally, however, comparing the treatment of capital punishment in Dickens with the way it is discussed in Dostoevsky's *The Idiot* (1869). In this novel, capital punishment is imagined vividly, from the standpoint of someone undergoing it, and I want to draw on this account in order to stand away from Dickens and to find a critique of his way of conceptualising it: a critique which itself must be 'read'.[3]

I

Both *Barnaby Rudge* and *A Tale of Two Cities* open in 1775 and continue after five years in 1780 (Chapter 33 for *Barnaby*, Book the Second for *A Tale*). *A Tale of Two Cities* goes on from there to the French Revolution and to the events after the September Massacres (1792). Both texts also double back to the 1750s – 1753 and 1757 – and both contain a virtual equivalent to a primal scene – a murder. In *Barnaby Rudge* it was a double murder, since which time the murderer has been on the run, and his son, Barnaby, has been born an idiot, as though this was the result of his father's villainy. In the case of *A Tale*, it was a rape and a murder. The rape has been committed by the Evrémonde brothers as a virtual act of incest practised towards the feudal daughter: this is again a sin of the father, and as with Barnaby, it brings the son, Charles Darnay, very close to execution. Both texts, then, have an eighteenth-century context, derived partly from Scott's *The Heart of Midlothian*. Both, like that text, put a prison, a crowd and a riot at the centre, and engage with the proper use of law. *A Tale of Two Cities* opens both its first two books with an account of violence practised by criminals such as highwaymen and with state violence – the practice of exposing heads on Temple Bar, for instance – and soon shows itself to be strongly anti-eighteenth century:

> Altogether the Old Bailey, at that date [1780] was a choice illustration of the precept that 'Whatever is is right,' an aphorism that would be as final as it is lazy, did it not include the troublesome consequence, that nothing that ever was, was wrong.
>
> (2.2.91)

The sadism of the crowd that watches trials like plays in Bedlam is touched on, as is the sadism of eighteenth-century punishment for treason. Darnay will:

> 'be drawn on a hurdle to be half hanged, and then he'll be taken down and sliced [castrated] before his own face, and then his

inside will be taken out and burnt while he looks on, and then his head will be chopped off and he'll be cut into quarters.'

(2.2.91)

Gaspard's fate as the murderer of the Marquis is likely to be similar, and Dickens and Foucault at the beginning of *Discipline and Punish* discuss the same material – the execution of Damiens in 1757 – which both might have derived from Voltaire, who would have been one of the 'new philosophers' the Marquis refers to (2.9):

'They even whisper that because he has slain Monseigneur, and because Monseigneur was the father of his tenants – serfs – what you will – he will be executed as a parricide. One old man says at the fountain, that his right hand, armed with the knife, will be burnt off before his face; that into wounds that will be made in his arms, his breast, and his legs, there will be poured boiling oil, melted lead, hot resin, wax, and sulphur; finally that he will be torn limb from limb by four strong horses. That old man says, all this was actually done to a prisoner who made an attempt on the life of the late King, Louis Fifteen.'

(2.15.200)

Parricide is the subtext of *A Tale of Two Cities* and the law of the father displays itself in spectacle which is acted out on the body. In both historical novels, the father condemns, kills, maims, petrifies (cp. castrates) the son: Steven Marcus's reading of *Barnaby Rudge* is excellent for this (Marcus, pp. 169–212) with regard to the earlier text. The result in *A Tale of Two Cities* is that the son *must* annihilate the father correspondingly, as Lawrence Frank argues. The Oedipal conflict emerges as an identifiable issue out of the revolts of the two texts. The theatrical nature of state and patriarchal power was also felt by Dostoevsky, when on 21 December 1849, he and fourteen other revolutionaries were put through a mock execution by the order of Nicholas I, who was willing to commute their sentences but wished to demonstrate the power and forbearance of patriarchy. The aide-de-camp carrying the pardon had to arrive on horseback to the place of execution in Semenovksy Square in Petersburg, to complete the theatricality of power.[4] *The Idiot*, which contains an account from Prince Myshkin of an encounter he had with a person who was to be shot for a political crime, and then after waiting for twenty minutes was given a reprieve, is often connected with this, and the text as a whole circulates round the question of the *condamné's* state of mind.[5]

The eighteenth century, with its absolutism (which Dostoevsky still suffered under in 1849) is identifiable as the period of the father, like Blake's Nobodaddy, imposing guilt, and the Gordon Riots presage the French Revolution, calling forth from Dickens identification with the son: 'I have let all the prisoners out of Newgate, burnt down Lord Mansfield's and played the very devil. I feel quite smoky' (*Life*, 169). The Gordon Riots are discussed by Peter Linebaugh, who brings out some extraordinary details about them.[6] He argues that they were centred against the rich, which increases the force of Hugh – the bastard, the illegitimate son of Lord Chester – and his turning of the rioters' cry 'No Popery' into 'No Property, brother' (38.288). They turned Bentham into a self-styled military hero when he joined the Lincoln's Inn militia to defend property. They put an end to executions going in procession to Tyburn, so that from 1783 onwards, all executions took place outside Newgate since it was now seen as too dangerous for crowd control for the state to use such a drawn-out public spectacle as before in order to assert its hegemony. In firing Mansfield's house in Bloomsbury Square (*Barnaby Rudge*, Chapter 66), they attacked 'the leading exponent of British imperialism' (Linebaugh, p. 358) and Linebaugh suggests that the power of the American War of Independence motivated some of the rioters. Joe Willet loses his arm in fighting 'at the defence of the Savannah, in America, where the war is' (72.555), so that he is mutilated in the defence of the patriarchal imperial power which at the same time cuts him off, and returns him to fight against the rioters as a servant of patriarchy for ever. But Linebaugh's most interesting comment, not made with *Barnaby Rudge* in mind, is that the riots 'stimulated a new theory and practice of securing private possessions' and provoked Joseph Bramah's *A Dissertation on the Construction of Locks* (1781) – a new science of making locks for doors and safes and prisons. Keys had associations of magic and the devil: new keys after 1780 meant that superstition strengthened respect for private property (Linebaugh, pp. 365, 367). *Barnaby Rudge* has a locksmith as its hero, as a Carlylean figure of 'know thy work and do it': the novel was nearly named for him, and his adherence to work is celebrated in Chapter 41. Class status and a bourgeois respect for property are already in place, proleptically, in this nineteenth-century 'tale of the riots of 'eighty' and Varden as 'father' to Simon Tappertit preserves the power of patriarchy himself, and fittingly receives Joe Willet to be his son-in-law. Property is defended, both at home and in the Empire. (For Dickens on locks, see Carey, *The Violent Effigy*, pp. 119–21.)

I shall return to the importance of the lock and key, but already it is clear that a whole ambiguity exists in Dickens's writing on the Gordon riots: they do not stay as historical material; they cannot be as endstopped as the Porteous riots are in *The Heart of Midlothian*, nor does it suffice that the text gives place to anxieties about Chartism in the 1830s. Rather, they show the relationship between patriarchy and property to be dependent on hanging. The historical Edward Dennis, the public hangman, was pardoned for his role in the riots, but of course he is hanged in Dickens's text. Hanging is thus validated within the text's closure, though on the way it is exposed to much ridicule. Dennis defends it as Protestant (37.284–5), which would align it with the protestant ethic and the spirit of capitalism, and the text comments, in indirect free discourse, how he has 'taken up arms and resorted to deeds of violence, with the great main object of preserving the Old Bailey in all its purity, and the gallows in all its pristine usefulness and moral grandeur' (70.536). The gallows is the national phallus, and, unlike the Maypole, it is not to be cut down. In aligning hanging with nationalism, opposing it to what he supposes to be Popish means of execution, and further seeing it to be a form of character-building, as in the scene where he addresses the condemned prisoners in Newgate like a sergeant-major with the troops (perhaps at the Salwanners) (Chapter 65), Dennis suggests inadvertently the non-punishment oriented reasons for keeping hanging: if you lose hanging, the country loses face. Capital punishment is the assertion of the state's dignity and its claim to individuality, hence it may be further dignified by becoming invisible, given more the status of the fetish, by being put behind prison walls.

In the other historical novel, *A Tale of Two Cities*, not only eighteenth-century punishment which dismembers the body is rejected, but the references to the crowd in the French Revolution, and to the machine-like precision with which executions are proceeded with in the Terror, may imply a rejection of spectacle. Dickens himself witnessed a guillotining (see Carey, pp. 11–22). Spectacle, as Foucault suggests, has to do with society as a body, where State power can use theatricality – though it works covertly and secretly as well – and where everything seems to exist on the surface, at the level of the body. It is not clear that Dickens was ever really an abolitionist in any case, and it is worth going back on the terms of the debate he participated in in 1849 on abolition versus private hanging. Writing to the abolitionist Charles Gilpin on 15 November 1849 – just a month before Dostoevsky was to undergo the theatrical power of a mock public execution – he says:

> I believe that the enormous crimes which have been committed within the last year or two and are fresh, unhappily, in the public memory, have indisposed many good people to share in the responsibility of abandoning the last punishment of the Law.
>
> (*Letters*, 5.648)

There is a space here in which Dickens's own convictions allow for hanging. Two days previously, and again on 17 November, Dickens wrote to *The Times* about the 30,000 present at the hanging of the Mannings and about their behaviour, which he regarded as depraved. His ideal is that the criminal should exist after sentencing in 'dread obscurity':

> I would allow no curious visitors to speak with him; I would place every obstacle in the way of his sayings and doings being served up in print on Sunday mornings for the perusal of families. His execution within the walls of the prison should be conducted with every terrible solemnity that careful consideration could devise . . .
>
> The 'mystery' of private execution is objected to, but has not mystery been the character of every improvement in convict treatment and prison discipline effected within the last 20 years? From the police van to Norfolk Island [a reference to transportation], are not all the changes that make the treatment of the prisoner mysterious? His seclusion in his conveyance hither and thither from the public sight, instead of his being walked through the streets, strung with 20 more to a chain . . . His being known by a number instead of by a name, and his being under the rigorous discipline of the associated silent system – to say nothing of the solitary, which I regard as a mistake – is all mysterious. I cannot understand that the mystery of such an execution as I propose would be other than a fitting climax to all these wise regulations . . .
>
> (*Letters*, 5.653–4)

Douglas Jerrold, an abolitionist, and friend of Dickens, who had said that 'the genius of English society would never permit itself private hanging: the brutality of the mob was even preferable to the darkness of secrecy,' replied to Dickens on November 20 that:

> It seems to me that what you argue with reference to the treatment of the convict criminal hardly applies to the proposed privacy of hanging him. The 'mystery' which, in our better discipline, surrounds the living, is eventually for his benefit. If his name merge in a number, it is that he may have a chance of obtaining back the name cleansed somewhat. If it be proved ... that public execution fails to have a salutary influence on society, then the last argument for the punishment of death is, in my opinion, utterly destroyed.
>
> (Quoted, *Letters*, 5.650, footnotes 2 and 6)

With Dickens's desire to perpetuate mystery, and even (Mr Gradgrind take note) the encouragement of use of numbers instead of names, compare a statement about individuality early in *A Tale of Two Cities*. Here investment in secrecy and mystery becomes normative and constitutive of identity, and the experience of prisoners has become a pattern for considering how everyone's experience is carceral:

> A wonderful fact to reflect upon, that every human creature is constituted to be that profound secret and mystery to every other. A solemn consideration, when I enter a great city by night, that every one of those darkly clustered houses encloses its own secret; that every room in every one of them encloses its own secret; that every beating heart in the hundreds of thousands of breasts there, is, in some of its imaginings, a secret to the heart nearest it! Something of the awfulness, even of Death itself, is referable to this. No more can I turn the leaves of this dear book that I loved, and vainly hope in time to read it all. No more can I look into the depths of this unfathomable water, wherein, as momentary lights glanced into it, I have had glimpses of buried treasure and other things submerged. It was appointed that the water should be locked in an eternal frost, when the light was playing on its surface, and I stood in ignorance on the shore. My friend is dead, my neighbour is dead, my love, the darling of my soul, is dead; it is the inexorable consolidation and perpetuation of the secret that was always in that individuality, and which I

shall carry in mine to my life's end. In any of the burial-places of this city through which I pass, is there a sleeper more inscrutable than its busy inhabitants are, in their innermost personality, to me, or than I am to them?

(1.3.44)

This is the metropolis as necropolis, but there seems a wish to bring things near: it is not the alien city which is stressed but 'my friend, my neighbour, my love'. In this extract there is the assumption of an 'I', speaking in a 'brooding first-person utterance' which is 'never heard again in the novel'.[7] This 'I' invests itself with an individuality 'which I shall carry . . . to my life's end', in an assumption of strong personal identity. But that is linked with repression, for the word 'secret' accumulates a further association when in Book the Third, Chapter One – 'In Secret' – the term is elucidated to mean solitary confinement. The prison meaning exists in 'encloses', in 'shut with a spring' (like a door) and 'locked in an eternal frost'. The importance of locks and keys comes in here: they guard individuality.

If death is both 'consolidation and perpetuation of the secret' contained in a person's 'individuality', as though it was only death which really fulfilled what the person always was, then individuality as death-like becomes 'wonderful', 'solemn' and 'awful', and the last sentence of the quotation makes for mutual death: neither the narrating 'I' nor the bodies entombed nor the busy inhabitants can yield up anything of their 'innermost personality.' The other – or the self – exists as a shut book, or as water iced over on the surface when that surface seemed to promise a sense of depths and of an unconscious – of 'buried treasure and other things submerged'.

Thus repression comes back via the word 'submerged', which recalls the words of the Marquis – 'Repression is the only lasting philosophy' (2.9.153). There are several implications here: these are words of advice for a feudal landowner, but they are also suggestive that the melancholy desire of the narrating voice entering the city by night is that individuality should be thus identified as carceral, unobtainable. Behind the statements of fact, the repetitions of 'is dead', lies a wish: that identity should be protected, never surrendered to another.

This accounts for the double movement within the text. It is a repressed text and a text about repression, and I shall come back to why it invests so much in that. But it belongs as a limit case of repression, for the context of the Revolution in Carlyle's *The French Revolution* suggests that political repression cannot be separated from a psychoanalytic cathexis. Since 'the philosophy of Mr CARLYLE's wonderful book' motivates *A Tale of Two Cities*, as the Preface indicates, reference to Carlyle illuminates how revolution breaks with repression, making the protection of enclosed individuality impossible.

In *The French Revolution*, Sans-culottism comes from beneath, 'many-headed, fire-breathing'[8] as a monstrous thing that challenges the ability to articulate what it is: it asks 'What think ye of *me*?' The conservative voice within the narrator of *The French Revolution* is challenged by the violence of change, while being forced to admit the pure contingency of order and habit:

> Rash enthusiast of Change, beware! Hast thou well considered all that Habit does in this life of ours; how all Knowledge and all Practice hang wondrous over infinite abysses of the Unknown, Impracticable; and our whole being is an infinite abyss, *overarched* by Habit, as by a thin Earth-rind, laboriously built together?
>
> But if 'every man,' as it has been written, 'holds confined within him a *mad*-man, what must every Society do; – Society which in its commonest state is called 'the standing miracle of this world'! 'Without such Earth-rind of Habit,' continues our Author, 'call it System of Habits, in a word, *fixed ways* of acting and of believing, – Society would not exist at all ... And now, we add in the same dialect, let but, by ill chance, in such ever-enduring struggle, your 'thin Earth-rind' be once *broken*! The fountains of the great deep boil forth; fire-fountains, enveloping, engulfing. Your 'Earth-rind' is shattered, swallowed up, instead of a green flowery world there is a waste wild-weltering chaos; which has again, with tumult and struggle, to *make* itself into a world ...

(1.3.40)

Carlyle quotes himself out of *Sartor Resartus*: the text is a debate where different voices speak, making for the end of repression (here virtually the same as 'Habit'), and showing that the 'Earth-rind' in the narrating voice is indeed broken. The sense of revolution as chthonic is paralleled in Freud's use of Juno's words in *Aeneid*, 7.312 as an epitaph to *The Interpretation of Dreams*: 'Flectere si nequeo superos, Acheronta movebo' – 'If I cannot bend the higher powers, I shall stir up Hell.'[9] According to Freud, 'This line of Virgil is intended to picture the efforts of the repressed instinctual impulses,'[10] and its appeal to hell and to the Medusa-like Allecto suggests the way the woman works when confronted by a patriarchy that blocks her. But the statement receives further interest as, according to Schorske, it was also the epigraph to Ferdinand Lassalle's *The Italian War and the Task of Prussia* (1859) which was asking for an uprising against the Habsburgs, and Lassalle himself, according to the *Interpretation* (p. 408) 'came to grief over a woman'. The political-revolutionary and the sexual map onto each other, but above that, the quotation from Virgil is being read both as a political demand for revolution and as a statement about the nature of the repressed – and, in addition, as though to link revolution to Oedipal struggle, Freud deliberately relates the subject of his dreams to his reaction to his father's death, 'the most important event, the most poignant loss of a man's life' (*Interpretation*, p. 47).

In Dickens, though not in Carlyle, the subject of the revolution and the Oedipal struggle overdetermine each other. Carlyle depends on the revolution as the monstrosity from below which makes it 'the astonishment and horror of mankind; a kind of Apocalyptic Convention, or black *Dream become real*; concerning which History seldom speaks except in the way on interjection' (3.2.1, pp. 193–4). This nightmare is outside History which is seen in *The French Revolution* to be separate from Revolution. It disrupts history's sense of causality, and its linear continuum. In a chapter entitled 'Cause and Effect', which sees this as an empty 'Formula', the text concludes, 'Let no man ask History to explain by cause and effect how the business proceeded henceforth. This battle of Mountain and Gironde, and what follows, is the battle of Fanaticisms and Miracles; unsuitable for cause and effect' (3.3.1, pp. 244–5). In the Revolution, subjects are decentred from their sense of being in control of their destinies and able to see how cause and effect operate for themselves: they awake:

> amazed at the noise they themselves *make*. So strangely is Free-
> dom, as we say, environed in Necessity; such a singular Som-
> nambulism, of Conscious and Unconscious, of Voluntary and
> Involuntary, is this life of man.
>
> (2.3.1, p. 410)

The decentring of the rational self, then, comes about, as in Freud's Copernican Revolution, from the destabilising effects produced by the unconscious as it invades the conscious with its sense of commanding necessity. *The French Revolution*, like much of Dickens (*Bleak House*, *Edwin Drood*), is written in the present tense, and Carlyle's rejection of the past tense is worth quoting in this context:

> For indeed it is a most lying thing that same Past Tense always: so beautiful, sad, almost Elysian-sacred, 'in the moonlight of memory,' it seems, and *seems* only. For observe, always one most important element is surreptitiously (we not noticing it) withdrawn from the Past Time: the haggard element of Fear! not *there* does Fear dwell, no Uncertainty, nor Anxiety; but it dwells *here*; haunting us, tracking us; running like an accursed ground-discord through all the music-tones of our Existence; – making the Tense a mere Present one!
>
> (3.2.3.204)

Writing 'history' in the present tense involves a refusal of distance, where 'distance' might be mapped onto Walter Benjamin's definition of the 'aura' associated with traditional art as 'the unique phenomenon of a distance, however close it may be'.[11] Traditional history-writing keeps the aura and so shields the person from the event, enables a stabilising of the self, which is repression. The present tense by its sense of anxiety which is not abolished, but runs from the past to the present, suggests the ongoing power of a trauma. In *The French Revolution* there is no sense of negating the power of fear, uncertainty or anxiety: lives are made Gothic by the prevalent sense of haunting that makes existence not one, not harmonious but characterised at all times by 'ground-discord'. Nothing can be allowed to recede into the past tense.

Something of the violence of an ongoing trauma is hinted at in the Preface to *A Tale of Two Cities* when the drama of *The Frozen Deep* articulated with:

> a strong desire to embody it in my own person; and I traced out in my fancy, the state of mind of which it would necessitate the presentation to an observant spectator . . .
>
> . . . Throughout its execution [the idea] has had complete possession of me; I have so far verified what is done and suffered in these pages, as that I have certainly done and suffered it all myself.

Dickens did not 'act' Richard Wardour, then in *The Frozen Deep*: he *embodied* the character in an act of identification which continued into the novel writing, where he was 'possessed' by it, which implies the loss of identity, and as it were went through a revolution himself. As there could be no separation between past and present for Carlyle, there could be no separation between the sufferings of the fictional Richard Wardour/Charles Darnay (another C.D.)/Sydney Carton (dying for the love of Lucy Manette as Wardour dies for the sake of Lucy Crayford) and Dickens. The writing hardly admits of repression, of the idea of distance. The passage I have quoted on individuality, from the novel's third chapter, recoups both, however, writing and repression, making individuality irreversible, like death, investment in which – and this would include an attitude towards capital punishment – is the only lasting philosophy.

II

The legacy of the Indian Mutiny of 1857, which I discuss in the next chapter (and of 'The Perils of Certain English Prisoners', the Christmas story Dickens wrote about it in 1858, and which I will discuss in the last), work to construct Dickens in terms of repression. The *ressentiment* of 'The Perils,' contemporary with *A Tale of Two Cities*, is bitterness that the self has been deprived of its autonomy and needs to be buoyed up with a feeling of interiority and individuality. But a dual drive, not just rancour, works through *A Tale of Two Cities*. The strong identifications with Carlylean revolution impel a struggle towards liberation from the sense of being bound in to the past with its violence and to the *ressentiment* that produces. Equally strong impulses as the reactive ones generated by the armchair-imperialist produce no triumph but only the defeated son and the father who cannot forget his past.

Darnay tries to escape his past, assumes his mother's name and tries for a new identity in London where he will not compete with the patriarchy of Dr Manette: hence the contradictions with which he speaks to the old man when he is asking him if he can marry Lucie: '... sharing your fortunes, sharing your life and home and being faithful to you to the death. Not to divide with Lucie her privilege as your child, companion and friend; but to come in aid of it, and bind her closer to you, if such a thing can be' (2.10.164). The pretence is that patriarchy can survive intact the revolution involved in Lucie marrying Darnay. Not only can it not, inherently, but it cannot because on the wedding-day, Manette discovers the identicality of Darnay with the Evrémondes who committed rape and murder and had him 'buried alive' for eighteen years. As though proleptically, Darnay has been tried in London for treason (= parricide) before he has thus again injured Dr Manette, however unconsciously; but then, when the Revolution comes, he is drawn back to his duties as patriarch to his French estate, and is arrested and tried twice in France. His second French trial condemns him on the strength of the document of Dr Manette, testifying against the Evrémondes. As a 'son' he wrote it against the father: as a father he hears it read out and it condemns the son. In Carlylean terms, 'the Revolution, like Saturn, is devouring its own children' (*French Revolution*, 3.4.8.329). The Revolution is that aspect of monstrous modernity which demonstrates that relations exist under the sign of Saturn, and that they cannot be held otherwise. To keep away from the French Revolution is to try to avoid an encounter with modernity.

The return to France is part of an unconscious compulsion to repeat. It is part of a death drive, on which the narrative comments, referring to prisoners waiting to be guillotined:

> Similarly, though with a subtle difference [from the prisoners engaged in a 'little concert'] a species of fervour or intoxication, known without doubt, to have led some persons to brave the guillotine unnecessarily, and to die by it, was not mere boastfulness, but a wild infection of the wildly shaken public mind. In seasons of pestilence, some of us will have a secret attraction to the disease – a terrible passing inclination to die of it. And all of us have like wonders hidden in our breasts, only needing circumstances to evoke them.
>
> (3.6.310)

'Hidden' recalls the passage on individuality in Book the First, Chapter 3, and suggests the power of repression.

Similarly, there is Dr Manette's compulsion to repeat, an unconscious act when he has suffered the shock to his patriarchal status from the loss of Lucie to Darnay. He goes back to his prison occupation of shoemaking, thus cancelling out his present existence. He repeats the trauma of the past; these anxieties cannot be kept in the past tense. Mr Lorry in Book the Second, Chapter 9, 'An Opinion', tries something like the talking cure on Dr Manette, and Manette assures him of the cessation of this 'blacksmith's work' as Lorry calls it (the whole passage is suggestive for *Great Expectations* and for the schizoid state that Pip feels himself to be in). It can only come back through a repetition of 'a strong and extraordinary revival of the train of thought and remembrance that was the first cause of the malady'. Such a repetition occurs in the third trial when the deposition that Dr Manette has written is read out; the last glimpse of Dr Manette, significantly present tense, is 'this is he; this helpless, inarticulately murmuring, wandering old man pointed out' (3.13).

The overlaying of eighteenth-century revolution by nineteenth-century repetition, which is structured by the failures of the 1848 revolutions, writes into the text its own sense of anger and *ressentiment*. The sharpening of the grindstone, in the context of the preparations for the September Massacres, witnessed from above by Lorry and Manette, evokes a hatred of the spectacle, and evokes a racist vocabulary which is suggestive of the *ressentiment* of 'The Perils of Certain English Prisoners':

> The grindstone had a double handle, and turning at it madly were two men whose faces, as their long hair flapped back when the whirlings of the grindstone brought their faces up, were more horrible and cruel than the visages of the wildest savages in their most barbarous disguise.
>
> (3.2.291)

The spectacle is of the breakdown of individuality, sexual difference and sanity: an outbreak of the monstrous where 'the eye could not detect one *creature* in the group free from the smear of blood' (my emphasis). A 'stain' works through, of Dionysiac wine and blood, which subsumes personal identities: 'men in all sorts of rags, with the stain upon those rags; men devilishly set out with spoils of women's lace and silk and ribbon, with the stain dyeing those trifles through and through'. The response it evokes is similar to that of Dickens on the Indian mutiny:

> And as the frantic wielders of these weapons snatched them from the streams of sparks and tore away into the streets, the same red hue was red in their frenzied eyes; – eyes which any unbrutalised beholder would have given twenty years of life, to petrify with a well-directed gun.
>
> All this was seen in a moment, as the vision of a drowning

man, or of any human creature at any very great pass, could see
a world if it were there.

The stress is on what the eye sees: this is like Carlyle's 'eye of
history' (*French Revolution*, 1.1.2.7) looking down. But Carlyle's eye
is affronted by revolution; it cannot account for it. Further, it looks
into other eyes, which are revolutionary, frenzied, red. Mr Lorry's
face as he looks is 'ashy', as though with the mark of death, and the
vision is described as being that of a person *in extremis*: drowning, or struck dumb, like the 'paralysed dumb witness' of *Bleak
House*. The reference, then, to an 'unbrutalised beholder' may be
deconstructed: no one could view this without being somehow
annihilated, so that any shooting would be an act of brutality (as
an act of violence would be in any case), and the act would also be
one of desperation (giving twenty years of life). The hatred here is
confessed to in the impossibility of the shooter not being brutalised; this confessional nature does not make it the less violent, even
proto-Fascist.

'Petrify' recalls the earlier chapter 'The Gorgon's Head' where
the stoniness of the Marquis's chateau is evoked – 'as if the Gorgon's
head had surveyed it, when it was finished, two centuries ago'
(2.9.149). At the end of that chapter another significance is added:
another stone face has been added to the chateau, since the Marquis
has been assassinated during the night. Setting in stone evokes both
perpetuation of a sight, as well as death, with the further meaning
derived from Freud of castration, that which is associated both with
the woman's threat to the male, in patriarchal ideology, and with
the Oedipal threat, father to son. In the context of its appearance
here it is strongly overdetermined. The desire is to freeze the action,
to end the spectacle, to stop the grindstone going round (with all its
implied sense of 'revolution'), to castrate the revolutionary sons, to
blunt their knives. The polymorphously perverse bisexuality of the
revolutionaries – part of their monstrousness which makes them
look like women – is to be stabilised in death. The city will indeed
become no different from its 'burial-places', which was how it was
viewed, how indeed it was wished to be, in the passage on individuality of Book the First, Chapter 3.

The desire is for statuary, not for living beings. Forster's description of Maria Manning, the Swiss murderer who was executed
with her husband in November 1849, is worth comparing, especially as she is linked to *A Tale of Two Cities*. She was an inspiration

for Hortense in *Bleak House*, who was also derived from a Carlylean reading of the women in the French Revolution – the Menads (the title of Chapter 4 of Book 7 – 'The Insurrection of Women'). Mme Defarge rewrites Hortense as Hortense reinscibes Maria Manning:

> You should have seen this woman ascend the drop, blindfold, and with [a] black lace veil over her face – with a step so firm as if she had been walking to a feast. She was *beautifully dressed*, every part of her noble figure finely and fully expressed by close fitting black satin, spotless white collar round her neck loose enough to admit the rope without its removal, and gloves on her manicured hands. She stood while the rope was adjusted as steadily as the scaffold itself, and when flung off, seemed to die at once. But there was nothing hideous in her as she swung to and fro afterwards. The wretch beside her was as a filthy shapeless scarecrow – she had lost nothing of her graceful aspect! This is heroine-worship, I think!
>
> The doctor who exd [examined] the bodies after death and who said he had never seen so beautiful a figure, compared her feet to those of a marble statue...
>   (Forster to Bulwer Lytton, quoted *Letters*, 5.643, footnote 4)

The articulations of a fetishising look (the face is avoided) and the sexualisation of the woman by Forster (her *noble* figure... *fully expressed* by 'close-fitting' satin), and the sense that she might be a figure to follow into death ('heroine-worship' comes in the same decade as Carlyle's *On Heroes and Hero-Worship*) are also matched by the awareness of her as passive, and the object of a scopic look from the doctor. Her beauty, as opposed to that of her husband, whose scarecrow-like appearance shows that state power has had its way with him, has 'castrated' him, is literally that of a corpse, stone-like, rendered classical in the comparison the doctor makes. It is that beauty that is desirable. It may be compared with the moment in *The Idiot* when the Prince is shown the covered-up body of Nastasya Filippovna, surrounded by disinfectant and by jewellery:

> At the foot of the bed some sort of lace lay in a crumpled heap, and on the white lace, protruding from under the sheet, the tip

of a bare foot could be made out; it seemed as if it were carved out of marble, and it was dreadfully still. The prince looked, and he felt that the longer he looked the more still and death-like the room became. Suddenly a fly, awakened from its sleep, started buzzing, and after flying over the bed, settled at the head of it.

(*The Idiot*, 4.11.652)

Here the dead woman, victim of patriarchy directly and indirectly, replicates the dead Christ of Holbein, the subject of Ippolit's reflections in his 'Explanation' (3.6.446–7). The corpse nature of the cadaver is denied by the American cloth fetishistically arranged over her, but asserted by the fly buzzing. The absolute horror of this is inseparable from the epilepsy dominant in *The Idiot*, since epilepsy includes, in the moments preceding it, an extraordinary heightened awareness. This is the argument of Elizabeth Dalton whose study of *The Idiot* draws on Freud's meditation on Dostoevsky's gambling in 'Dostoevsky and Parricide' to relate the condition of epilepsy to punishment from the superego which is read as analogous to castration anxiety. The sense of castration is magnified in the move in *The Idiot* from describing death by firing-squad to death by guillotine. According to Dalton:

> This transformation reveals more clearly the meaning of the punishment fantasy that unites the scenes of execution and epilepsy. Castration would of course be the punishment for wishing to replace the father, but it would also represent a reconciliation with him, a way of at last placating this terrible father and being loved by and united with him in final passivity. This fantasy . . . means . . . the ego would give up its claims entirely and allow itself to be annihilated by guilt.[12]

A gun that petrified the bodies engaged in dionysiac, orgiastic revolt, would, then, carry out the wishes of a discourse that tried to complete the repressive equation of individual = death = statue. Such a discourse could only emanate from someone who is dying ('the vision of a drowning man'), coming from a repressive eye of history that is cowed by what it sees and must therefore attack it, and desperate, trying to escape, moving away from the alternative history which we may describe as revolutionary. Earlier it was characterised as the voice of *ressentiment*; it is also a dying voice.

The fulfilment of that voice is in Sydney Carton, where the text strives to make nihilism into positive affirmative Christianity.

III

According to Ippolit (*The Idiot* 3.5.423), Prince Myshkin is collecting material about capital punishment, just as Dostoevsky's text engages with executions throughout. This is not only through the discussion of Myshkin's friend whose sentence was commuted (1.5.86–8), but through the early discussion of guillotining (1.2.46–8), and through Myshkin telling Adelaida to paint the face of a man just before he is guillotined (1.5.90–3). The execution of the Countess Du Barry is talked about by Lebedev (2.2.227–8), and above all there is the death of Christ, seen from the standpoint of Holbein's picture of the entombment (3.6.446–7). Nor are these the only instances of discussion of execution. But what appears dominant in Dostoevsky is the moment of intense subjectivity with which the 'criminal' feels his or her last moments, an intensity that goes beyond all limits and that allows for no caesura:

> ... and all the time he knows everything and remembers everything; there is one point which one can't forget and one can't faint, and everything goes round and round, round that point. And to think that this goes on to the last fraction of a second when his head already lies on the block and he waits and he *knows* and suddenly he hears the iron come slithering down over his head! He must certainly hear that! If I were lying there, I'd listen for it on purpose, and I'd hear it. There is only perhaps one tenth part of a second left, but one would certainly hear it. And, imagine, there are still some people who maintain that when the head is cut off it knows for a second that it has been cut off – what a thought! And what if it knows for five seconds?
>
> (1.5.92–3)

The moment of impossible knowledge is comparable to the second before the epileptic fit:

> ... the very second in which there was not time enough for the water from the pitcher of the epileptic Mahomet to spill, while he

had plenty of time in that second to behold all the dwellings of Allah.

(2.5.259)

An objective account of a fit is offered at the moment which Myshkin has his: characterised by a scientificity comparable with accounts of guillotining – or of orgasm:

> It is a well-known fact that epileptic fits, the *epilepsy* itself, come on instantaneously. At that instant the face suddenly becomes horribly distorted, especially the eyes. Spasms and contortions seize the whole body and the features of the face. A terrible, quite incredible scream, which is unlike anything else, breaks from the chest; in that scream everything human seems suddenly to be obliterated, and it is quite impossible ... for an observer to imagine and to admit that it is the man himself who is screaming. One gets the impression that it is someone inside the man who is screaming ... The sight of a man in an epileptic fit fills many ... with absolute and unbearable horror, which has something mystical about it.

(2.5.268)

The horror, which is that of fear of a schizoid state, fear of being separated so that the self does not link up with the self, is analogous to fear of being guillotined. It has been prepared for by the account given of the guillotining of the Countess Du Barry. 'Vainly whimpering' in Carlyle's account (1.1.4.25), in *The Idiot* she screams *'Encore un moment, monsieur le bourreau, encore un moment'* (2.2.228), and is called *'misère'* for it.[13]

The word *misère* goes back to Victor Hugo's *Dernière Jour d'un condamné* (1829) where it is used repeatedly. Victor Hugo's short narrative is a substantial source for *The Idiot*, and it seems evident that it must have influenced Dickens too. Described by Hugo as an abolitionist document, it goes through the first-person fragmentary meditations of someone condemned to death, first of all giving the account of his feelings for the five weeks before his execution, and then turning to his last day alive. Who the man is does not appear: he seems, however, bourgeois, with a young daughter, and in a vision he has of previous condemned men who have passed through his cell and left their names on the walls, he sees them each bearing his severed head in his left hand and carrying it by the mouth, for the hair had been removed; each raises his right hand at him, except the parricide (whose right hand would be cut off prior to execution). The suggestion has been made that the *condamné* is a parricide himself,[14] which would link *A Tale of Two Cities* to this theme.

The Hugo material is suggestive for 'A Visit to Newgate' in *Sketches by Boz*, which concludes with a man spending his last night on earth in Newgate, and for the account of Fagin's last night alive (*Oliver Twist*, Chapter 52). *Sketches By Boz* says 'Conceive the situation of a man, spending his last night on earth in this cell' and then in the next sentence imagines a man in a state of 'feverish restlessness', now 'lost and stupefied'. As the sketch continues, the man's life is narrativised: the journalism is replaced by an imagining of a *condamné*. He is forty-eight; his wife's existence is sketched out; his life appears bourgeois; in his meditations he ends by sleeping and dreaming of how he used to be with his wife, and then:

> The scene suddenly changes. He is on his trial again: there are the judge and jury, and prosecutors, and witnesses, just as they were before. How full the court is – what a sea of heads – with a gallows too and a scaffold – and how all those people stare at *him*! Verdict, 'Guilty.' No matter; he will escape.
>
> (*Sketches*, p. 214)

But the dream of escape is followed by awakening, and 'he is the condemned felon again, guilty and despairing; and in two hours more will be dead.'

In this courtroom, the crowd is inseparable from the one watching the execution. The gallows is in the courtroom, and the emphasis is on the power of the gaze, as in *Oliver Twist*:

> The court was paved, from floor to roof, with human faces. Inquisitive and eager eyes peered from every inch of space. From the rail before the dock, away into the sharpest angle of the smallest corner in the galleries, all looks were fixed upon one man – the Jew. Before him and behind: above, below, on the right and on the left: he seemed to stand surrounded by a firmament, all bright with gleaming eyes.
>
> He stood there in all this glare of living light . . .
>
> (52.358)

The imaginary figure of *Sketches by Boz* gives way to Fagin, and later to Darnay and to Magwitch, all on trial for their life. The mirror over Darnay's head in the dock, to throw the light down upon him (*Tale*, 2.2), here takes the form of eyes which have become mirrors and spotlights, enforcing transparency upon the figure in the centre. At the end of the chapter, Oliver and Mr Brownlow emerge from Newgate to see the crowd already waiting, so that the chapter circles round from its start to close at the same point, save for the new carnival emphasis:

> A great multitude had already assembled; the windows were filled with people, smoking and playing cards to beguile the time; the crowd were pushing, quarrelling, and joking. Everything told of life and animation, but one dark cluster of objects in the very centre of all – the black stage, the cross-beam, the rope, and all the hideous apparatus of death.
>
> (52.365)

The chapter ends here, before the execution, but that has already been rendered, as though proleptically, in the account of Sikes hanging himself before the gaze of the crowd in Chapter 50. The violence of the crowd is referred to in that chapter with the account of how it nearly lynched Fagin, and how he clung to the officers (341). Lynch-law is regarded with fascination in *Oliver Twist* (the chase after Oliver in Chapter 10, and the discussion of the 'passion for hunting something' in that context makes the comparison) and no detective is needed when the crowd itself turns detective, as though punishment is being presented here as the due that is owing to an outraged society. And the novelist spurs the reader on through playing on violence, to make the reader another of the crowd, another pair of eyes. When Sikes is trapped and killed, caught in his own *machine infernale* of the rope he has put round his neck in order to let himself down, the text supports such machinery. As he hangs, 'the old chimney quivered with the shock, but stood it bravely' (347). The phallic scaffold remains in control, or remains controlled by a machinery of justice.

It is different with Ippolit's meditation on Holbein's Christ:

> Looking at that picture, you get the impression of nature as some enormous, implacable, and dumb beast, or, to put it more correctly, much more correctly, though it may seem strange, as some

huge engine of the latest design, which has senselessly seized, cut
to pieces, and swallowed up – impassively and unfeelingly – a
great and priceless Being . . .

(3.6.447)

The 'machine' suggests the guillotine, or the railways, which Lebedev
sees as Apocalyptic – 'the star called Wormwood' (3.4.409). (In
Dombey and Son, perhaps Dostoevsky's source, the railway acts
analogously to the guillotine, with Mr Carker.)

The fascination throughout *The Idiot* is in states of consciousness
that go beyond even the liminal, that are involved with shock. The
desire is for a further attachment to the body, even *in extremis*. The
will to go beyond the 'normal' bounds of feeling makes Dickens in
contrast in *A Tale of Two Cities* very end stopped at least in desire.
The two rivals, Myshkin and Rogozhin, cradling each other in
homoerotic embrace next to the body of Nastasya Filippovna offer
a startling contrast to the pieties with which *A Tale of Two Cities*
ends, with its protection of bourgeois marriage. The desire to have
punishment (epilepsy being like being guillotined) that licenses crime
runs through *The Idiot*, reversing narrative order, and, potentially,
the order of one of Dostoevsky's most famous titles. That desire to
have punishment first, which is masochistic, defeats patriarchal order
altogether. Myshkin imagines the *condamné*'s brain working hard at
such a moment, 'like an engine going at full speed' (1.5.92). Execution
is longed for: the man who in his last few minutes reflects on the
preciousness of time – which involves a transgressive opening up
into unlimited experience – ends up praying 'to be shot as quickly
as possible' (*The Idiot*, 1.5.88). The desire to prolong the experience
of the fragmented body beyond death for perhaps five seconds
fits chiasmically with the moment of heightened sensation before
execution: the pattern is transgressive pleasure followed by punishment which is wished for, followed by a horrified desire to perpetuate the pleasure because the punishment has taken place.

In contrast to the face of the man going to the guillotine that
Myshkin imagines, Carton's stance is ultimately one of resignation
(the 'peacefullest man's face ever beheld' at the guillotine, looking
'sublime and prophetic' – 3.15.403). Reading Dickens in the light of
Nietzsche would suggest that what the text proposes as a solution
– i.e. the nobility of self-sacrifice, following on from the model of
Christianity – is itself the problem. Carton opts for suicide as the
end of a defeated life, and is motivated by a mixture of pity and

love for Lucie. This could be compared with Myshkin's disastrous attempts to intervene for the best in people's lives, as with Nastasya Filippovna, but Nietzsche on pity is suggestive:

> Whenever people *notice* that we suffer, they interpret our suffering superficially. It is the very esence of the emotion of pity that it strips away from the sufferings of others whatever is distinctively personal. Our 'benefactors' are, more than our enemies, people who make our worth and will smaller. When people try to benefit someone in distress, the intellectual frivolity with which those moved by pity assume the role of fate is for the most part outrageous; one simply knows nothing of the whole inner sequence and intricacies that are distress for *me* or for *you*.[15]

Carton belongs to the 'religion of comfortableness' and his death is an evasion of his own accidie, sublimating this into self-sacrifice. Or Nietzsche's comments on Socrates as suicide might be compared, where suicide assumes that the value of life has been gone into and set aside:

> One must reach out and try to grasp this astonishing *finesse, that the value of life cannot be estimated*. Not by a living man, because he is a party to the dispute, indeed its object, and not the judge of it; not by a dead one, for another reason. – For a philosopher to see a problem in the *value* of life thus even constitutes an objection to him, a question-mark as to his wisdom . . .
>
> One would have to be situated *outside* life, and on the other hand to know it as thoroughly as any, as many, as all who have experienced it, to be permitted to touch on the problem of the value of life at all: sufficient reason for understanding that this problem is for us an inaccessible problem.[16]

In terms of the ideology of the text, the Dickens who assumes that the individual is unknowable, absolutely other, has slipped through the narrative of Carton into another position: that Carton can make some assessment of his life's value and of Darnay's and Darnay's family's value and can act accordingly. At the end Carton substantiates a bourgeois ideology centred round the family. The assumption is that an assessment can be made of different values, where even the text itself has refused to be explicit about Carton's motivations for action, inscribing the unconscious of his actions by a conventional nobility at the last. But it can be said that the text turns what it elsewhere recognises as a neurotic drive towards death (referred to in discussing Book the Third, Chapter 6) into the language of sacrifice.

Carton's final speech is put doubly in quotation marks, with two conditions imposed – as what he might have said, and if he had been prophetic. He envisages a future for Paris after the Revolution, and a future for the lives for whom he lays down his life. The Darnays' son will be called Sydney. He will become a just judge and bring his own son, also called Sydney:

> ... with a forehead that I know and golden hair, to this place – then fair to look upon, with not a trace of this day's disfigurement – and I hear him tell the child my story with a tender and a faltering voice.
>
> (3.15.404)

There is to be no heir for Charles Darnay: he is excluded from the prophetic future. The repressed rivalry of Carton and Darnay for Lucie Manette is won by Carton. The grandson is to be tied back to patriarchy through the power of pity which is bound up with telling an idealising historical narrative. The prophecy must envisage Paris of the 1840s: if so, its projection of tranquillity is strikingly inaccurate. Even without the knowledge of the 1848 revolution, and the manipulations of the state that were to follow with Napoleon III, there is something fake about the absence of the guillotine. If Paris is no longer disfigured by the guillotine, this is because the lobby for private executions wins, so that the images of the city conceal the nature of state power and state violence and become so much kitsch. The violence of modern state power has not, however, been eliminated. The text cannot conceal its own kitsch in repressing so much, but it proclaims a symptomatic *ressentiment* – making a virtue out of weakness and inability to alter things – in this language of sacrifice.

But it is possible to read the text differently, responding to the covert way in which Carton gains ascendancy over Darnay. John Kucich suggests how, when reading Dickens in the light of Georges Bataille, and drawing on the drive that Bataille isolates towards an expenditure which is not utilitarian, bound by prudent economy – 'productive expenditure'.[17] This other expenditure emphasises loss, does not avoid the danger of death and its horror, is creation by means of loss, and is therefore called *sacrifice* by Bataille. Kucich reads Carton and Darnay as both motivated by a risk-taking which belongs to this other form of expenditure. Thus in Carton saving Darnay by his own sacrifice there is an element of the *potlach* (Marcel Mauss's term, in *Essay on the Gift* (1925) for the gift offered by tribal leaders which defies a rival by its exorbitant nature). In the same way Prince Myshkin is outside the circle of productive expenditure and his folly belongs to the impulse towards excess, which affects Nastasya Filippovna disastrously. Carton's *potlach* beggars Darnay by his act of giving, but for Kucich, the originating impulse in Carton is his drive towards self-destruction, and this is legitimated in the text by his rivalry with Darnay, which:

> ... is necessarily present in Carton's death to give point to the expenditure, to give it significance. Through his death, Carton finds the same satisfaction that appeared aggressive in the beginning of the novel; the second time he saves Darnay's life, he displaces Darnay in Lucie's eyes as the man willing to sacrifice his life for the sake of others. Without the tension of this rivalry at the same time – as something that Carton both triumphs in and renounces at the same time – Carton's death would indeed seem a savage, suicidal waste.

> (Kucich, p. 119)

Kucich's argument draws attention to masochism governing relationships present everywhere in Dickens as a strategy of control over others. But he overplays the language of resolution of crisis, and it is significant that his argument about Carton concludes by incorporating his excess and non-productive expenditure back into a bourgeois mode by making it serve a utilitarian purpose. This fits his text's dual emphasis on excess and restraint, but it means that the excess may be deconstructed – it is already characterised by a bourgeois interest which can be linked to *ressentiment*. At the moment of writing *A Tale of Two Cities*, Dickens separated from his wife and cultivated Ellen Ternan. But this gesture of repudiation of bourgeois culture was itself heavily protected: Dickens never became known as the writer marked out by libidinal excess, and protected his reputation as the bourgeois writer by a strategy of secrecy, by maintaining several houses, by disappearing to Paris. The text and the life repeat this repudiation of risk. Dickens, unlike Dostoevsky, was no gambler. The secondary impulse towards restraint takes over and becomes primary and governs his attitude towards the violence of capital punishment.

6

From *Jane Eyre* to Governor Eyre, or *Oliver Twist* to *Edwin Drood*

In British culture ... one may discover a consistency of concern in Spenser, Shakespeare, Defoe and Austen that fixes socially desirable, empowered space in metropolitan England or Europe and connects it by design, motive and development to distant or peripheral worlds (Ireland, Venice, Africa, Jamaica), conceived of as desirable but subordinate. And with these meticulously maintained references come attitudes – about rule, control, profit, and enhancement and suitability – that grow with astonishing power from the seventeenth to the end of the nineteenth century. These structures do not arise from some pre-existing (semi-conspiratorial) design that the writers then manipulate, but are bound up with the development of Britain's cultural identity, as that identity imagines itself in a geographically conceived world.[1]

I

The scope of this chapter is the normalising power of empire and its violent side-effects. Post-colonial approaches to nineteenth-century British texts, for example Edward Said's in reading *Mansfield Park*, find imperialism the other scene of their domestic setting and politics. Texts become complicit, in their silence or half-revelations, with imperialist violence, or, in a deconstructivist move based on this, they show the metropolitan centre of imperialism to be riddled with the signs of the heterogeneous power and resistance of the empire itself.[2] There is, however, a predictability in some of the moves of this critical writing, whose effect confirms for the critic both the history he or she is looking for, and the reading of the

155

historical present that is supposed to be the aim of a criticism centred on history. The deconstructive move itself, which finds the colonialist the haunted and demonic figure, ends up by re-centring the text it was supposed to take out of the metropolitan context. As an example, take Suvendrini Perera, discussing *Edwin Drood* in her book *Reaches of Empire* and linking it with De Quincey's opium-eating. What does she mean when she concludes that 'the imperialist was of necessity the true opium-addict', and that knowledge of this 'not only had to remain concealed in imperial policy but also had to be displaced through skilful projection'?[3] What strategy allows her thus virtually to annihilate the addiction of the nineteenth-century Chinese? What morality supervenes to make her think that the addiction of the bohemian De Quincey (or in *Edwin Drood* that of Jasper) makes any kind of comment on the historical disempowering of colonised subjects – put down not through the force of De Quincey's writings which *do*, admittedly, mix opium with empire, but through the operations of a military force and at the point of a gun? The effect is to confirm the metropolitan centre. The writer becomes the imperialist, although the text deconstructs that position by showing the attendant anxieties of empire. In Perera's case, this makes her press for the Thuggee reading of *Edwin Drood*, and even to bring on the goddess Kali – where Dickens does not – as a 'presiding spirit' (p. 119). The homoeroticisings of male relationships in *Drood*, discussed by Eve Kosofksy Sedgwick, produce in Perera's even stronger but derivative reading a Jasper 'feminized' and homosexual (p. 113). Attention to the textual unconscious replaces an attention to what the text does say: thus Perera soon refers to 'Edwin's contempt for . . . the "womanish" musician Jasper' (p. 119). Where has the contempt and the femininity come from, except from speculation made by Edmund Wilson which has now been elided with the Dickens text? Of course what the text says may be a displacement of repressed material, but at least it can be argued with. Perera's *Edwin Drood* is the product of a secondary revision which reads a possible unconscious for the real one. Of course, criticism of *Edwin Drood* runs into the sands when the critic has to bring about the closure Dickens's death prevented, by speculation on what might have happened, and the critic-detective who presses towards a solution will therefore not want to ignore the textual unconscious in producing a reading. But the danger is of assuming a knowledge of what the contents of that unconscious must be, and how the text can be articulated towards a reading of it. A new positivism succeeds a text-based one: a positivism that asserts implicitly that it knows what the political unconscious is, and how therefore we must read *Edwin Drood*.

I begin this way with an animus towards the criticism that makes its own suspicion into a new orthodoxy, because at the same time I recognise its importance, and it influences this chapter. The opium, the Orientalism, the anxieties and the homoeroticism are there, and I want to read both *Oliver Twist* and *The Mystery of Edwin Drood* in the light of them, and mainly for the discourses at the margin of these texts, for their offstage imperial narrative. It is the West Indies in *Oliver Twist*, as it was in *Mansfield Park*, and Ceylon in *The Mystery of Edwin Drood* ('that part of the world is at a safe distance' Drood says (8.59) as though challenging its influence to show itself). But *Edwin Drood* also evokes Egypt after 1859, when the Suez Canal project began, and post-Mutiny India and China, which was opened up to Britain by the Opium Wars (1855–58), an imperialism brought about partly through the agencies of Sir John Bowring, whom Dickens consulted for information about opium amongst the Chinese.[4] Opium is a subject of *Edwin Drood*, and recalls Collins's *The Moonstone*, which I also want to use for comparison. In line with *The Moonstone*'s use of Indians, there is the argument which I have referred to, that Jasper may be a member of the Indian cult of Thuggee, strangling Drood with his scarf. The discourse of 'Thuggee' is an example of Orientalism, of the constitution by the British (Captain William Sleeman, who suppressed the cult by 1848) of a Indian secret society of criminals with its own unique mystique. The reification of such groups of resisting Indians into a sect with its own rules associates with Foucault's sense of the power of the dominant to create the criminal; nonetheless perhaps the need to construct the existence of such groups belongs to a real, though less articulated opposition to British rule which could only frighten the coloniser. Perhaps Jasper represents a literal 'return of the repressed' – the repressed colonised subject. Perhaps he is a product of miscegenation.

What is clear is Dickens's interest in the backlash caused by empire. The Indian intellectual Ashis Nandy, also cited by Perera,[5] discusses the long-term damage that colonialism did to British society (apart from what it did to the colonised society), and lists four destructive effects. Firstly:

It began to bring into prominence those parts of the British political culture which were least tender and humane. It de-emphasised speculation, intellection and *caritas* as feminine, and justified a limited cultural role for women – and femininity – by holding that the softer side of human nature was irrelevant to the public sphere.

Its tragedy was 'the tragedy of the younger sons, and the women' and those who did not fit into British life. Monks in *Oliver Twist* is an elder brother pushed into younger brother status: Mr Rochester in *Jane Eyre* is a younger brother. Secondly, it produced a false sense of cultural homogeneity. Thirdly, it led to underdeveloped emotions, and emotions that could not recognise themselves under the appeal to duty and religion. Lastly, it caused colonisers to impute to themselves magical feelings of omnipotence and permanence.[6]

Nandy illustrates the fate of the person who did not fit the hegemony established through colonialism – particularly after the hardening of attitudes caused by the Indian Mutiny in 1857 – by reference to Oscar Wilde. He ran foul of the Marquess of Queensberry, the father of Wilde's lover, Lord Alfred Douglas. Wilde made his homosexuality not just a matter of sexual preference, but, more scandalously, the index of his refusal of conventionality. This was the Marquess of Queensberry who in 1867 established the rules of competitive boxing, thus making for an endorsement of the British culture's masculine self, 'defining and demanding rule-bound violence and conformity to that ultimate virtue of aggressive British masculinity, sportsmanship' (Nandy, p. 44). Boxing features in *The Mystery of Edwin Drood* with Honeythunder and the Rev. Mr Crisparkle, sexless and a boy for ever because he has controlled his aggression by his sportsmanship, helping establish a dominant masculinity which informs the text, and in so far as it is endorsed by the text, along with such a figure as Mr Tartar, it suggests a narrowed sense of what it is to be male in this society. And Nandy's negative comments on the British as colonisers could have an application to Dickens in bringing out his violent self-righteousness, of which more later, with regard to India. But those who, as Nandy suggests, are simultaneously disempowered as well as empowered by colonialism are the preoccupation of this chapter: younger brothers, those whose contact with the colonies has affected them so that they are like Neville Landless, 'at once hunter and hunted' (8.55), split as to their identity; those whose exposure to colonial rule and to the fantasies of Orientalism imposes on them a schizoid state, unable to articulate the officially sanctioned violence that rules the colonies but that cannot be spoken of back home.

This schizoid state is a subject of *Oliver Twist* (1837–38), and is dramatised in the figure of Monks, a man characterised by frequent lapses out from consciousness. This kind of personal parapraxis, which we will find repeated in other figures whom I discuss in the chapter, dramatises the schizoid state which exists at the macrolevel of society. I will first trace it through with *Oliver Twist*, which opens with the death of the mother (like *Dombey*), and ends with her memorial, so that like *David Copperfield*, it concludes with 'Agnes', in both novels spoken of in a church context. Oliver (whose surname may be Leeford, or Fleming, or Twist or Brownlow), is the second son of Edward Leeford, also called in a textual parapraxis Edwin Leeford (51.350), which encourages the reader to make connections with *The Mystery of Edwin Drood*. Edward Leeford was forced into marriage (as Edwin Drood was to be) to a woman ten years older, given over to 'continental frivolities' – a loveless marriage defined in terms of a 'clanking bond' and ending in loathing (49.332). Leeford's oldest attachment was to his friend Mr Brownlow, who was to have married his sister (she died on her wedding morning, as part of this novel's commitment to the passive and non-sexual, which is defined as purity). Leeford ends his marriage by taking up with a recently widowed naval officer with two daughters, Agnes, and, much younger, Rose (Maylie). He contracts a marriage with Agnes (like Rochester with Jane Eyre: a bigamous one), but has to go to Rome where a relative's death leaves him a fortune, and where he dies. The son from the first and proper marriage, also Edward Leeford, but called Monks, is twelve when his father dies, and already marked out by a 'rebellious disposition, vice, malice and premature bad passions' (51.351).

Secretly, the father made a will, where most of the money was to go to Agnes's child, 'if a boy, only on the stipulation that in his minority he should never have stained his name with any public act of dishonour, meanness, cowardice or wrong'. The father, having performed his own act of dishonour, shows a schizoid tendency with regard to his son: a continuation of the split-off state of mind that is a subject of this chapter. The wife destroyed the will after his death, telling Monks, by now eighteen and living in London where he 'associated with the lowest outcasts' (51.352), what she had done and making him swear vengeance on Agnes's issue. But Monks left for the West Indies to his own estate 'to escape the consequences of vicious courses here' (49.335) not to come back till a few months previous to these revelations. On his return he sees Oliver in the street on the day he is arrested and recognises him (26.171). After being foiled from his destructive intentions towards Oliver, he is last heard of 'in a distant part of the New World' where he 'once more fell into his old courses, and after undergoing a long confinement for some fresh act of fraud and knavery, at length sunk under an attack of his old disorder, and died in prison' (53.365).

The gaps in this narrative need supplementing. The West Indies are mentioned before Monks appears: Mr Brownlow has gone there to find him (Chapter 22). The text makes the West Indies part of its cultural coding, with the housekeeper's son clerk to a merchant there (14.83), or as when Mr Grimwig refers to a man who was hung in Jamaica for murdering his master (14.88), evoking the whole world of resistance to colonialism, and in Charley Bates's comments on the food he has brought, with their totally casual critique of the way that the West Indies were being worked for cash crops:

> 'Sitch a rabbit pie, . . . sitch delicate creeturs, with sitch tender limbs, Bill, that the wery bones melt in your mouth, and there's no occasion to pick 'em; half a pound of seven and sixpenny green, so precious strong that if you mix it with biling water, it'll go nigh to blow the lid of the teapot off; a pound and a half of moist sugar that the niggers didn't work at all at, afore they got it up, to sitch a pitch of goodness, – oh no! . . .
>
> (39.259)

Charley Bates's irony comments both on the abolition of slavery in 1833, and on the further abolition of the apprenticeship of black labourers (which happened in 1838, the year of this comment: apprenticeship itself is a feature of the early parts of *Oliver Twist*). If Leeford's forced marriage takes him to an estate in the West Indies, he is followed by Edward Rochester in *Jane Eyre* whose autobiography is similar to the one Edward/Edwin Leeford might have given:

> When I left college, I was sent out to Jamaica, to espouse a bride already courted for me [by his father and Mr Mason, a West Indian planter and merchant] . . . I found her a fine woman, . . . tall, dark and majestic. Her family wished to secure me, because I was of a good race; and so did she. They showed her to me in parties splendidly dressed. I seldom saw her alone, and had very little private conversation with her. She flattered me, and lavishly displayed for my pleasure her charm and accomplishments. All

the men in her circle seemed to admire her and envy me. I was dazzled, stimulated: my senses were excited; and being ignorant, raw and inexperienced, I thought I loved her. There is no folly so besotted that the idiotic rivalries of society, the prurience, the rashness, the blindness of youth, will not hurry a man to its commission. Her relatives encouraged me: competitors piqued me: she allured me: a marriage was achieved almost before I knew where I was. Oh, I have no respect for myself when I think of that act! – an agony of inward contempt masters me.[7]

This now exists through the re-reading imposed on it by *Wide Sargasso Sea*, just as the creole implications of the subtext of *Jane Eyre* are brought out by *Absalom, Absalom*, another text which conditions reading of both Brontë and Dickens. Bertha Mason is creole as her mother was: I guess this is equally the case with Leeford's wife, however unstated, and that Brontë responds to this in her narrative. Monks's disorders, which seem to be epileptic (33.217, 38.251), seem strongly overdetermined. If inherited, they presumably come from the mother, and are similar to those of Bertha Mason's mother and younger brother, both crazy, and they suggest in their turn the possibility of miscegenation and Eurocentric fears of degeneration arising from that: hence Monks is described as 'dark' and Oliver thinks him mad. Perhaps that feature was what his father recognised once and for all in his twelve-year-old son: that the son was racially different.

But this dislike the father has is *also* overdetermined. Oliver seems to be twelve when the novel's main events take place,[8] and the age fits Dickens's autobiography: with the apparent abandonment by his family, and his being forced to work with (Bob) Fagin in the blacking factory. Monks is both the figure who, in a recall of the blacking factory episode, obliterates Oliver's identity and parentage in the ruined 'manufactory' overhanging the river, when he takes the gold locket off Mrs Bumble (Chapter 28), and, as a figure of rejection by the patriarch, he is what Dickens felt *he* might have become at the hands of his father, the Cain-like figure (see the 'broad red mark' on his throat (46.315)), who responds to Dickens's description of himself in his abandonment, 'small Cain that I was' (*Life*, 27). As the first of these two, he looks in through the window (as Dickens's father saw him at the window) at the sleeping Oliver (Chapter 34) in collusion with Fagin, himself, through his name, a recall of the blacking factory episode. Steven Marcus discusses the scene in 'Who is Fagin?' but there is a dimension there that his account misses: the character is overdetermined, being both the father and the dispossessed son who is pushed into colonial aggression. The purity of the Surrey home that Oliver finds himself in, the pleasantness of romantic reverie that holds the sleeping boy, these are maintained by the exclusion of the non-docile elements of that society, whose place is in the colonies. As the dispossessed son, Monks's epilepsy marks him off as frustrated by patriarchy. The text identifies consciously with Oliver but also, unconsciously, with Monks, and the epilepsy, which is a feature marking those so ambiguously constructed that I shall be discussing here, seems the outworking of absolute punishment by the power of patriarchy, just as in *The Idiot*, it seems to function as the marker of total loss and at the same time of unbearable insight.

Brownlow comments that the boy had been trained (by the mother) to hate the father: degenerate behaviour works through the mother to the son whereas Leeford had confidence in Agnes and believed 'that the child would share her gentle heart, and noble nature' (51.351). If Agnes were pure English, in terms of this colonial narrative, her effect would indeed be that. Mr Brownlow's references to vice and bad passions surely imply amongst anything else masturbation, that which threatens the codes of masculinity appropriate for empire which were being established in the period. In the context of a novel whose cast includes Master Bates this is not difficult to see: nor is it easy to imagine what else might be the substance of the charge. A commitment to passivity, which involves a fascination with its opposite state, runs through the text, and is found elsewhere in Dickens. Uriah Heep in *David Copperfield* seems to be another practiser of the solitary vice, and Dennis, the hangman in *Barnaby Rudge*, might be thought to allude to nothing else in his constant references to a man being 'worked off' when he is hanged. Ejaculation that follows hanging is the point here. If epilepsy in *The Idiot* suggests, along with much else in that text, the impossibility of the peaceful death that Sydney Carton is supposed to have on the scaffold, the impossibility of that wished-for passivity in termination, orgasm after death suggests too the impossibility of a going to death which is outside rebellious, even Oedipal assertion. (The comparable death of Billy Budd in Melville's text, hanged but with no 'muscular spasm' succeeding his execution – i.e. no ejaculation – implies the consummation that is so devoutly wished in this nineteenth-century ideology which negates the body.)[9] There is a withdrawal in Dickens from the body as likely to be stained and to lose its purity, but to this psychic desire for separation from the body's otherness, which is nonetheless recognised elsewhere in Dickens's texts, and contradicted, as in the instances of epilepsy which show the body not lying down, subject and passive, it is possible to add Foucault's argument. He discusses the 'strategy' set up in nineteenth-century power relations centring on sexuality. The second one of these strategies he calls 'the pedagogization of children's sex'. Here is:

> . . . a double assertion that practically all children indulge or are prone to indulge in sexual activity; and that, being unwarranted, at the same time 'natural' and 'contrary to nature,' this sexual activity posed physical and moral, individual and collective dangers; children were defined as 'preliminary' sexual beings, on this side of sex, yet within it, astride a dangerous dividing line. Parents, families, educators, doctors and eventually psychologists would have to take charge, in a continuous way, of this precious and perilous, dangerous and endangered sexual potential: this pedagogization was especially evident in the war against onanism, which in the West lasted nearly two centuries.[10]

The point is not just that children are defined as sexual beings, at least in potential, but that they *are defined*: demarcated in a moment when historically there were large numbers of people who could be classified into different subsections of 'children'. In the 1820s, a quarter of the population was between five and fourteen; in 1821, almost half the population were under twenty.[11] The strategy of power/knowledge Foucault discusses produces for the nineteenth century the category of the child – children such as Oliver Twist, Jane Eyre, David Copperfield. The investment made in Oliver is that he should be produced as a particular kind of child, fitting his class potential. The 'romantic' child (much use is made in this novel of Wordsworth's 'Intimations' Ode in relationship to Oliver) is constructed on a model that conceals its relationship to adult bourgeois values: Miss Wade deconstructs this ideology when she refers to the children around her in her childhood as 'little images of grown people' (*Little Dorrit*, 2.21.663). The middle-class child is a simulacrum: a copy of a copy (a copy of the adult who is supposed to be like the child in essential qualities, since, after all, 'the child is father to the man.') In contrast to Master Bates's working-class status which gives him a certain freedom, Oliver must be kept in a position of dependency, for:

> the onanistic child . . . was not the child of the people, the future worker who had to be taught the disciplines of the body, but rather the schoolboy, the child surrounded by domestic servants, tutors and governesses, who was in danger of compromising not so much his physical strength as his intellectual capacity, his moral fibre, and the obligation to preserve a healthy line of descent for his family and his social class.
>
> *(History of Sexuality*, p. 121)

This is what Oliver becomes: and to Foucault's class analysis which is also an analysis of state power might be added a colonial one: Edward Leeford must preserve a healthy line of descent in contrast to what he has produced in the West Indies.

The romantic child circulates through literary texts as a regulatory image: people of a certain age are to be produced as children in order to bring them under a surveillance which control their bodies. They are produced as 'others' who must become the 'same' through the operations of all around. Mr Leeford is determined, however unconsciously, that Oliver shall not become a masturbating child. If Oliver passes the test, it is only by sheer passivity on his part from the time he meets the Artful Dodger (but any action on Oliver's part would imply the movement of desire), but it is also by regulation: Mr Brownlow takes the credit that he has rescued Oliver 'from a life of vice and infamy' (49.335). Mr Brownlow has it both ways. The boy is pure, yet he is only pure because he is rescued. He both is and is not pure, therefore, or, as Foucault puts it, he is both 'on this side of sex, yet within it'. The pure child, Dick, who does not come under such beneficent surveillance, completes his cycle of passivity by dying. But Dick is not free from surveillance: he knows the doctor is right to tell the others he is dying, knows it because he dreams so much of Heaven and Angels and kind faces he never sees when he is awake (7.43) Charlotte Brontë's parody of this and attempt to break free from surveillance are apparent in Jane Eyre's reply to Mr Brocklehurst, much given to talking of angels and of dying children, and asking Jane how she can avoid hell, that 'I must keep in good health and not die' (*Jane Eyre*, 4.64). The gentleman in the white waistcoat and Mr Grimwig exemplify those responsible for actively creating the character of the child, both sustained by a paternalistic assumption that they know children. The novelist in the name of a romanticism which attacks weighing-and-measuring of human nature attacks their pretensions to knowledge, but it is certainly not in him to deny that the category of the child exists when it comes to Oliver and Dick, figures of bourgeois purity despite the workhouse, even though the concept of childhood receives contestation in the presentation of the non-genteel Artful Dodger and Charley Bates, and in what Nancy says – 'I thieved for you when I was a child not half as old as this' (16.104).

Oliver Twist and Dick are non-masturbating children, as David Copperfield and Mr Dick doubtless are also. These epitomise a pure Englishness, while Monks is the contrary: marked now by vices of all kinds. Hence the other causes of his 'disorder' which overdetermine it. His fits are also, perhaps, syphilitic, such is the drift of Brownlow's denunciation:

> 'You, who from your cradle were gall and bitterness to your own father's heart, and in whom all evil passions, vice and profligacy, festered, till they found a vent in a hideous disease which has made your face an index even to your mind.'
>
> (49:336)

Reading character(s), in Mr Brownlow's sense is a form of violence. Not surprisingly, the first time he is encountered in the text, he has, however unconsciously, purloined the book he reads. It is an image for what takes place in such confident reading of signs and construction of narrative. The acceptance of this narrative progression means that Monks has become what masturbation made him: the child is father of the man, or, in Foucault's terms:

> The child's 'vice' was not so much an enemy as a support; it may have been designated as the evil to be eliminated, but the extraordinary effort that went into the task that was bound to fail leads one to suspect that what was demanded of it was to persevere, to proliferate to the limits of the visible and the invisible, rather than to disappear for good.
>
> (*History of Sexuality*, p. 42)

The vice of masturbation licensed surveillance, both of the child and of the family, so in that sense it was a friend to doctors and teachers and to moral guardians. Foucault stresses that these guardians wished the vice to be seen in the life of the subject: it became a privileged way of reading the child's character, as also of creating it. The child's character would persist in later life: hence many adults in Dickens are – or call themselves – no more than children. Monks even has a boy with him, as if from 'an invincible repugnance to being left alone' (28.256). Perhaps this implies pederasty, but if so, it only repeats Fagin's set-up with the boys, and makes the temptations on Oliver as much sexual as concerned with infringements of bourgeois property. Monks is twenty-six and has a boy in attendance: so is Bradley Headstone who has Charley Hexam in attendance; so is John Jasper, whose nephew Edwin Drood is called 'the boy (for he is little more)' (*Edwin Drood*, 2.8). The Dickens text doubles its effects again and again through these figures of *ressentiment*, Monks, Headstone, Jasper, each deprived of status. The association of men with boys fits with what Sara Suleri calls the 'latent infantilism' at work in colonialism (especially expressed in the aspirations towards cross-cultural male friendship).[12] Each of these figures exist within the ideological framework necessary for the hegemonic stability of colonialism.

Monks rejects his mother whom he has robbed of jewels and money and hates his father who hates him. Mr Bumble is stuck for an image when he thinks of his putative love for Oliver: father–son relationships offer him no model:

> 'I always loved that boy as if he'd been my – my – my own grandfather,' said Mr Bumble, halting for an appropriate comparison.
> (51.353)

But Monks's grandfather, who insisted on his son's marriage for money, seems to be no one to set love upon either. The further back the narrative goes, in *Oliver Twist* and *Jane Eyre*, in the relating of offstage prior events, the more dangerous patriarchs become. But the text also rejects mothers. Agnes, the other mother who gives character to Oliver, despite the reference in the will to her noble nature and to her trust in Leeford – 'she had gone on, trusting patiently to him, until she trusted too far, and lost what none could ever give her back' (51.351) – is also called 'weak and erring' (the last line of the novel): a double ascription which accords with the double sense of the child projected in the text: as pure and not pure. In thus rejecting everything of the parental, the text repeats the motivations of Monks and is anti-bourgeois, since bourgeois order depends on the repression of the otherness that Monks implies. The bourgeois child, Oliver, becomes his father's child (gets the inheritance) by being his father's child (remaining pure).[13] But to that narrative, another decentred one is offered, the 'other' to Oliver's progress (birth in the workhouse for one; death in prison for the other) and an allegory of it. The economy of the colonies, miscegenation and racial hatred are what the novel's social critique of the Poor Law Amendment Act and of Benthamite philosophical radicalism do not recognise. The figure of Monks, obviously an impossible one from any critical reading which bases itself on realism, displaces several textual anxieties: fear of impurity besetting the bourgeois order; fear of the impact of the colonies which are nonetheless needed to sustain the myths of bourgeois existence, especially its commitment to purity; fear of the creation of a pariah class, through the division of society into those who use and those who are used by the colonies, a pariah grouping which has no investment in bourgeois stability. Above these, there is the overarching fear that bourgeois existence, because of its double standards and schizoid state which enables that, nonetheless produces a disaffected set of sons whose practices will destroy it at its ideological centre – the family.

II

These issues reappear in *Edwin Drood* but, before moving from *Oliver Twist* to that, I want to draw in another text for comparison. Wilkie Collins's *The Moonstone* (1868) links fear of the colonies with the necessity for the 'discovery of the truth' (the title of its second part). As Mr Brownlow had the confidence of the police in making discoveries and in reading the truth, so the Metropolitan Police Force, newly augmented in 1842 by the creation of a Detective Department, becomes an agency in detecting the foreigner (a foreigner is arrested for murder in *Bleak House*) and in perpetuating the British class system, as Inspector Bucket does. Against the fear of otherness which might provoke ideas of unintelligibility, everything becomes readable and significant. Sergeant Cuff in *The Moonstone* connects everything, even, in one investigation:

> a murder . . . and a spot of ink on a tablecloth that nobody could account for. In all my experience along the dirtiest ways of this dirty little world, I have never found such a thing as a trifle yet.[14]

Cuff is compared to an undertaker (First Period, p. 107) as if to suggest that the mind that finds every trifle significant invests in death. But Collins accepts the necessity of anatomising; as Dickens commented critically on his earlier novel *The Woman in White* (1859–60), 'the three people who write the narratives in these proofs have a DISSECTIVE property in common.'[15] Collins's novels work as fantasies of realism, believing in 'the discovery of the truth' (the title of the narrative's 'Second Period') , so that, as D.A. Miller argues, everyone in *The Moonstone* becomes the policeman, every one their own Gooseberry, and affected by detective fever.[16] But that in at least formal terms would have been true also of *The Mystery of Edwin Drood*: there seem to be no police in this novel; the normalising agents of society are its ordinary members, its establishment.

In *The Moonstone*, the excluded Monks-like figure is Ezra Jennings, who compels attention on many accounts: brought up 'in one of our colonies' he says that 'my father was an Englishman; but my mother –' leaving that narrative a blank. He is less than a younger brother: he is presumably illegitimate. He calls his weeping over Dr Candy's recovery from illness 'an hysterical relief', adding that 'Physiology says, and says truly, that some men are born with female constitutions – and I am one of them' which is the classic description of the homosexual in the nineteenth century: a female trapped in a male body (and the word 'homosexual', according to Foucault in *The History of Sexuality*, dates from 1869–70). Writing a book which nonetheless dies and is buried with him, so that it, like his mother (like 'Agnes') and his past, remains a blank, he also, importantly, blanks out at crucial moments and becomes 'other' – double:

> The grip of some terrible emotion seemed to have seized him and shaken him to the soul. His gipsy complexion had altered to a livid greyish paleness; his eyes had suddenly become wild and glittering; his voice had dropped to a tone – low, stern and reso-lute – which I now heard for the first time. The latent resources in the man, for good or for evil – it was hard, at that moment, to say which – leapt up in him and showed themselves to me, with the suddenness of a flash of light.
>
> (*The Moonstone*, 2.3.411, 414, 419)

The hero, Franklin Blake, has been about to tell him the truth about himself, to confess the accusation against him. The moment of 'em-barrassment' when Blake uses the word 'painful' and then the fit or shock quoted above, possibly epileptic, shows that Ezra Jennings sees himself as Blake's double, also accused, also in pain. Yet these two are not in fact doubles. Blake has stolen the diamond while unconscious, but though there may be a suggestion of the equation of the diamond with virginity, and entering Rachel's boudoir under shadow of night is of course suggestive, his instincts are patriarchal and bourgeois: he wants to protect property from the foreigners (the Indians); he does not think the property is safe with the woman, and he is not motivated by greed. There is, in short, little that is interesting to be discovered about his unconscious: detective awake, he is also a detective asleep. Jennings misreads if he connects Blake with himself. The text intimates, however, the question of desire: both Jennings's – and Dr Candy's (in his delirium he talks about Blake) – towards Franklin Blake. As Rachel says to Jennings, when she is caught kissing the sleeping Blake after the experiment: 'You would have done it in my place' (2.4.478). Hysteria and homosexual desire, in the very moment of the official encoding of that as a character-trait, are associated with Jennings's foreignness: the moment of crisis associates him with Monks and with Jasper, who, like Monks, has a weakness, which is either partly opium-induced (and Jennings also takes opium), or partly controlled by opium, which means that Jasper is in a state of dependency upon a drug, which leads him to moments of paratactic behaviour.

Dickens found *The Moonstone* 'wearisome beyond endurance', perhaps responding to the slow process by which everything in the text comes to a point of conclusion that could have been guessed from its origin, and there is no difference between the content of the conscious and unconscious mind. Thus *The Mystery of Edwin Drood* (1869–70) replaces the blameless bourgeois Franklin Blake with a sense of guilt and repressed violence in the bourgeois class, centred on Jasper's double consciousness. The colonial text of *Edwin Drood* accounts for the presence of the Lascar and the Chinese in the opium-den in the first chapter, Edwin Drood 'going to wake up Egypt a little' as an engineer, as his father was there before him; and the Landlesses. Neville and Helena are, as the name implies, the dispossessed produced in a colonial context, and neither colonised nor colonisers. They are from Ceylon, 'both very dark, and very rich in colour; she, of almost the gipsy type; something untamed about them both' (6.44). Neville Landless says they were brought up, after their mother died, by a stepfather in Ceylon, a miserly figure Neville would cheerfully have killed for his violence towards his sister.

Neville speaks of himself as brought up 'among abject and servile dependants, of an inferior race' which may have given him something 'tigerish' in his blood (7.49) and in argument with Edwin Drood, he says that his own 'ideas of civility were formed among Heathens' (8.56). This makes Drood say that Neville 'may know a black common fellow, or a black common boaster', adding that 'no doubt [he] has a large acquaintance that way' but that he is 'no judge of white men' (8.60). It does not need the narrator's comment on 'this insulting allusion to his dark skin' to make the point that Edwin has virtually said that Neville is black, which would make him and his sister products of miscegenation. But in addition to these people, who have no investment in bourgeois stability, there is Jasper, who seems respectable, but also has a dark skin (2.6), like Monks. He was brother-in-law to Mr Drood senior, who is buried in Cloisterham (his wife, Jasper's sister, is not). While the age difference between Jasper and Edwin Drood allows the assumption that the sister was considerably older than John Jasper, making Edwin and Jasper like brothers in terms of age, there is a missing narrative of the sister and of Drood's life in Egypt, which might mean that Jasper's birth itself is not European, and the missing dead wife not the sister, so that Jasper might be the racially different half-brother of Drood.[17]

The 1860s, the period of these novels, have been seen as the beginning of Britain's aggressive imperialism, as with Disraeli's Abyssianian campaign of 1867–68, and in this decade, empire was a matter of deep anxiety, as with the Governor Eyre controversy. This debate drew its vigour from the suppression of the Indian mutiny of 1857, which itself produced in Dickens highly authoritarian, racist and violent reactions, as in one letter:

And I wish I were commander in Chief in India. The first thing I would do to shake that Oriental race with amazement (not in the least regarding them as if they lived in the Strand, London, or at Camden Town), should be to proclaim to them in their language that I considered my holding that appointment by the leave of God to mean that I should do my utmost to exterminate the Race upon who the stain of the late cruelties rested and that I was there for that purpose and no other and was now proceeding with all convenient dispatch and merciful swiftness of execution to blot it out of mankind and raze it off the face of the earth.
(4 October 1857, to Angela Burdett-Coutts)

Dickens sounds like the later General Dyer at Amritsar in 1919 when 5,000 unarmed Indians were fired on, causing the deaths of nearly four hundred, with 1,200 wounded. And Dyer had the events of 1857 in mind. And so did Edward Eyre, Governor of Jamaica. He appealed to the excesses involved in quelling the Indian mutiny in justification for his own excesses in Jamaica in October 1865 when 439 people were shot without trial or hanged after court martial, 600 were flogged and 1,000 dwellings were burned – just as Rosa Dartle in a moment of true class hatred and sexual jealousy wanted Little Em'ly whipped, the house pulled down, and her to be branded on the face (*David Copperfield*, 31.533). An equivalent energy motivated Eyre, who removed one of the leaders of the blacks in Jamaica, George William Gordon, from an area where he had not proclaimed martial law to one where he had, and on this basis had him court martialled and executed. The news caused a scandal in Britain. John Bright – Mr Honeythunder in *Edwin Drood* – demanded that Eyre should stand trial for the death of Gordon, and between 1866 and 1868, public opinion was divided between the Jamaica Committee, which had Bright and Mill calling for Eyre's prosecution, and the Eyre Defence and Aid Fund. Carlyle, Dickens, Ruskin, Tennyson and Kingsley (who influences via his 'muscular Christianity' the portrait of Crisparkle) were pro-Eyre. Memory of this produces reference to Mr Honeythunder's radicalism: 'You were to abolish military force, but you were first to bring all commanding officers who had done their duty, to trial by court-martial for that offence, and shoot them' (6.45). There is also the satiric reference to 'a moral little Mill' in *Edwin Drood* (17.147). This is a reminder of Mill's hostility to Dickens over the portrait of Mrs Jellyby in *Bleak House*, where Dickens was faulted by Mill for anti-feminism and by others for attitudes that could be taken as anti-abolitionist.[18]

In Mill's anti-Eyre attitude, however, lies an ambiguity: readers of his *Autobiography* might hardly realise from his near silence about it that Mill was employed by the East India Company from 1823 till it was abolished in 1858, and that he approved of the governor-general Dalhousie's annexations, which were carried out between 1848 and 1856, including the taking of Oudh, which itself caused the unrest encouraging the mutiny of May 1857.[19] Mill's response to the abolition of the East India Company was to ask 'in what manner Great Britain can best provide for the government, not of three or four millions of English colonists, but of 150 millions of Asiatics, who cannot be trusted to govern themselves'.[20] In other words, he argued for more imperialism, not less.

John Stuart Mill had been taken into the East India Company through his father, James Mill, who, on the strength of his *History of British India* (1817), had already been taken into the company. Mill's history was written without the benefit of ever seeing India. This, 'the hegemonic textbook of Indian history' for the nineteenth century, [21] sets out the basis for governing India on Utilitarian lines, discarding the forms of Indian religion as merely the workings of the imagination. Mill's rejection of imagination is well known: it informs his *History* which is declared to be one based on facts (Majeed, p. 195). Leavis read *Hard Times* as a critique of Mill and Bentham's anti-imagination educational principles, but the analysis could go much further. Ronald Inden suggests the investment that was made by this Utilitarian in downplaying the imagination while constructing an India of imagination all compact:

> Implicit in this notion of Hinduism as exemplifying a mind that is imaginative and passionate rather than rational and wilful was, of course, the idea that the Indian mind requires an externally imported world-ordering rationality. This was important for the imperial project of the British as it appeared, piecemeal, in the course of the nineteenth-century. Why? Because the theist creeds and sects, activist and realist, were the world-ordering religions of precisely those in the Indian populace, among the Hindus, that the British themselves were in the process of displacing as the rulers of India. To provide India with a polarized religion, one that was, where rational thought was in evidence, cosmically idealist or parochially materialist, acted not simply to justify the presence of the conquering outsiders in some abstract way. Indology was as a discipline not merely reflective but agentive; it actually fashioned the ontological space that a British Indian empire occupied. Its leaders would, as had others before them beginning with the Aryans, inject the rational intellect and world-ordering will that the Indians themselves could not provide.
>
> (Inden, p. 128)

The construction of India in a process of Orientalism was designed, in Mill, to make India under instrumental Utilitarian rule 'a realization of the Panopticon' (Inden, p. 168). Unsurprisingly, the Landlesses' guardian (who knew Mr Honeythunder, a.k.a. John

Bright) is described as 'grinding' (7.47) which fits the *Hard Times* Mill-figure, Mr Gradgrind (and probably plays on his name). The 'mystery' of India (which had permitted, amongst other things, the practice of *sati*) was overridden by its compulsory Anglicisation (so *sati* was prohibited in 1829).

Mill's imperialism meant that he could not in consistency attack Eyre. To do so would be to will the deed – control – but not the violent means. Mill's position would be part of the schizoid state of public life that because of its own reliance upon colonialism cannot see its liberalism for what it is: a way of avoiding its dependence upon power relations. Hence the images of boxing associated with Mr Honeythunder fit not only a personal pugilism but also a systemic coerciveness in his approach to others. Dickens's position accepts a level of violence that actually recognises its necessity in imperial government. But there is an ambiguity about his own complicity with the idea of imperialism.

An India dominated by imagination, by the otherness this gives, in return haunts the imperialist mind as a fear – perhaps expressed in the discourse of Thuggee – that it will annihilate the imperialist's rational power, or that it will collapse difference altogether. As Miss Clack wonderfully and coyly puts it in *The Moonstone*, 'How soon may our own evil passions prove to be Oriental noblemen who pounce on us unawares!' (*The Moonstone*, 2.1.222). As opium and the diamond both come out of India to lay waste the English country house, and, in the case of the diamond, to feminise each person who steals it in turn, to make them unable to do anything, like everyone who thieves Poe's 'purloined letter', empowering and disempowering them at once, so also in *Edwin Drood*. There is the laying waste of Jasper, the most sensitive person in Cloisterham, through opium.

Opium, though it exists in literature as a bohemian and middle-class addiction (Colonel Herncastle, the younger son in *The Moonstone* (1.34) is rumoured to be smoking opium in his dissolute state), was sold in mass not only from India to the Chinese, but also to the British working class, especially the agricultural working class, and *Edwin Drood*, in making Jasper addicted, displaces attention from the working class to the disaffections of the middle class. The distribution of opium was limited to chemists in the Pharmacy Act of 1868, a year before *Edwin Drood* was started. But its use was widespread. The opium dens in the East End of London, where Jasper is found, were described as 'a merciful support in starvation and its consequent ills', which indicates their working-class status. The *Medical Times and Gazette* in 1873 described the opium-induced state as producing not violence, but a 'state in which people dream of virtue and goodness and piety and do nothing', but it seems clear it also induced feelings of melancholia and thoughts of suicide. Deep contradictions were at work in official perceptions of opium. It was less dangerous than alcohol; it was functional for the poor and the working classes; its effects could not be calculated, for there was no agreement whether it shortened life or lengthened it. At the same time it was dysfunctional in producing indolence; and the glamourisings of opium by the Romantics made it potentially subversive; and it was certainly addictive, as much as the mania for 'shares' in the 1860s was (and Dickens, in *Our Mutual Friend*, thinks of those buying shares being under the influence of opium).[22]

Edwin Drood opens with Jasper in an opium-stupor, visualising as in a return of the repressed, the English town called Cloisterham (Rochester). But this Rochester would repress even a Mr Rochester, as a dead city monumentalising a dead ideology, no more than a charnel house, returning as the uncanny, the *unheimlich*, to the man whose fantasies are elsewhere.

> An ancient English Cathedral Town? How can the ancient English Cathedral town be here! The well-known massive grey square tower of its old Cathedral? How can that be here? There is no spike of rusty iron in the air, between the eye and it, from the point of the real prospect. What IS the spike that intervenes, and who has set it up? Maybe, it is set up by the Sultan's orders for the impaling of a horde of Turkish robbers, one by one. It is so, for cymbals clash, and the Sultan goes by to his palace in long procession. Ten thousand scimitars flash in the sunlight, and thrice ten thousand dancing-girls strew flowers. Then, follow white elephants caparisoned in countless gorgeous colours, and infinite in number and attendants. Still, the Cathedral tower rises in the background, where it cannot be, and still no writhing figure is on the grim spike. Stay! Is the spike so low a thing as the rusty spike on the top of a post of an old bedstead that has tumbled all awry? Some vague period of drowsy laughter must be devoted to the consideration of this possibility.
>
> Shaking from head to foot, the man whose scattered consciousness has thus fantastically pieced itself together, at length rises, supports his trembling frame upon his arms, and looks around.

The narrative is of John Jasper struggling back into consciousness after taking opium in an East London opium den. In the opium-state, consciousness is pluralised; there is no repression of a schizoid state, and all speech becomes dialogic, just as the questions of the first paragraph also imply the presence of an other. Space is multiplied, as the visions are plural, for the cathedral town is no more visible than the fantastic Turkish palace, the 'here' of the second sentence. The setting is not India, but it nonetheless belongs to generalised Oriental fantasies, and to a dream of the scaffold, where the speaker has become an other, part of the Turkish harem.

The town gives way in the phantasmagoria to the tower, and then to the spike, whose existence is negated – 'there is no spike' before it is affirmed at all – 'What IS the spike . . .' The negation of the spike in fact is a repression, as the 'real prospect' – the one of the cathedral which is shown to visitors, displaying it as architecture – is also a repressed one (repressing the violence – the 'spike' – that underpins order and civilisation), just as architecture structures or reifies group relations and social existence (compare Edwin talking about Jasper's mobility: 'Your life is not laid down to scale and lined and dotted out for you like a surveyor's plan' (2.10)). In the dream, a fantasy succeeds of violence which is accepted – welcomed even – associated with the spike and of eroticism, but this cannot negate the other vision: 'Still, the Cathedral tower rises in the background, where it cannot be, and still – which may mean "as yet," as though it will happen – no writhing figure is on the grim spike.' 'Writhing' implies torment, perhaps caused by state violence, or erotic in character, or analogous to the failed play which is mentioned later, *The Thorn of Anxiety*. The phallic is a source of torment, which sets up a homosexual set of codings, or which relates to masturbation, or to fantasies of rape. The spike finally becomes part of the bed, which is an occasion for relief (something of the waking of Scrooge on Christmas Day has been carried into this). The 'shaking' then may also imply laughter, but it certainly continues the sense of being overpowered, and Miss Clack's remains the best commentary on it.

The second paragraph establishes a single consciousness which has been scattered: this consciousness is like Lacan's body in pieces, dismembered, which implies then that the composition of the self taking place in the second paragraph is no more than a rationalisation, its making itself one subject. Here the narrative becomes third person, omniscient and apparently offering 'the real prospect'. At the end of the first paragraph the speech begins to coincide with the point of view of the second paragraph: the text seems to have become centred.

The opening makes Cloisterham an 'other', where the known and familiar is the oriental world, which can be read and which turns out to be predictable – 'Maybe, it is set up . . . it is so'. In the first paragraph, the verb predominating is 'to be' and its cognates ('IS' is capitalised) and 'where it cannot be' is the attempted negation of being by another form of being where *both* forms of being are under erasure, because they belong to the opium dream. There is a movement to negate otherness, as when Jasper later in the chapter pronounces the word 'unintelligible' about the woman's mutterings and then those of the Chinese. If identity is plural, it also seeks in fantasy to repress signs of the other, a form of violence which would fit the imperialist's characteristic moves.

Jasper aims to cancel out otherness before entering into fantasy. As he says while under opium in the later sequence in the opium den:

> Yes! I always made the journey first, before the changes of colours and the great landscapes and glittering processions began. They couldn't begin till it was off my mind. I had no room then for anything else.
>
> (23.208)

The dream, which he has repeated 'over and over again' in his opium stupor, as if he is caught in a compulsion to repeat which suggests the organism readying itself for its own death, suggests De Quincey and Piranesi's imaginary prisons (Cloisterham's Gothic architecture takes on further *unheimlich* features), and Esther Summerson's dreams. 'When I could not bear my life, I came to get the relief, and I got it. It WAS one! It WAS one!' is how he describes his need for opium. Again, the capitalisation proclaims the fascination with a state of being. In contrast to the slow monotonous death of Cloisterham, he goes towards death in his own way, with a 'fellow-traveller' who never knew that this was his condition, and who never saw the road:

> It was a journey, a difficult and dangerous journey. That was the subject in my mind. A hazardous and perilous journey, over

abysses where a slip would be destruction. Look down, look down! You see what lies at the bottom there?

(23.207)

The impossible journey, as though on scaffolding with nothing below, suggests fascination with the idea of there being 'no thoroughfare'. The abyss, evocative perhaps of fear of the female, or fear of sexuality, suggestive of the state of *mise en abîme*, means that a perspective has been lost (there is no 'real prospect' – architecture, with its ability to stabilise spaces in relation to social identities, has gone). The direction 'look down' suggests the pointing of Allegory and those other figures pointing in Dickens, such as the Ghost of Christmas Future, all of whom direct the gaze to a dead body which both is and is not that of the self that looks. Similarly, the fellow-traveller is not definable as a single person: in De Quincey's version of Piranesi, it is always Piranesi, pluralised, seen at several moments of climbing. It is perhaps a desire for the other, like Esther's unknown friend to whom she writes, since for the other for whom the journey is nothing, it can be taken with ease.

The 'journey' permits the movement into the Orientalist fantasy which Cloisterham, as a 'return of the repressed' interrupts. The two stages of the dream – the crossing of the abyss and the Oriental fantasy – might stand comparison with the two paragraphs of the description of Staggs's Gardens being destroyed (*Dombey*, Chapter 6, quoted above, p. 73). No one can move where 'bridges . . . led nowhere', or where 'thoroughfares [were] wholly impassable'. The passage in *Dombey* suggests a dream landscape, with a dream's unintelligibility, and it is ready to become Esther's dream in her illness, Pip's delirious state and Jasper's recurrent opium-induced condition of risk, a risk which is as though gambled for in contrast to Cloisterham monotony. In *Dombey*, the confusion generates the railroad, which is envisaged as trailing smoothly away. The impossibility of the journey for Jasper makes the smoothness of the other vision with its 'glittering processions' the more wished-for, the more fantasised. Perhaps at the heart of the dream is the fear of arrest, of being unable to move, the fear of not being able to make narrative connections from one state to another.

Jasper uses opium to take him out of the existing order of things, the Lacanian symbolic order, hence his avoidance of the spike, which serves as the patriarchal phallic signifier, the privileged principle of difference which establishes meaning within the play of signifiers through its repression of difference. (Yet he is attracted to the spike, too, since it also is the marker of the scaffold, of punishment, of going to death.) His dream, an attempt to move into the Imaginary, is of participation in an Orientalist world, where *Robinson Crusoe*, the *Arabian Nights* and the *Tales of the Genii* have fed his imagination as they fed David Copperfield's (*David Copperfield* Chapter 5), and it is a colonialist's fancy and dream of escape from the ideology that is incarnated in an English cathedral town. His hatred of Cloisterham and the sound of the Cathedral service – which is self-hatred, since he epitomises it – makes him like a coloniser talking about 'heathen' practices:

> 'It often sounds to me quite *devilish*. I am so weary of it! The echoes of my own voice among the arches seem to mock me with my daily drudging sound. No wretched monk who droned his life away in that gloomy place, before me, can have been more tired of it than I am. He could take for relief (and did take) to carving *demons* out of the stalls and seats and desks. Must I take to carving them out of my heart?'
>
> (2.11, my emphasis)

The diabolical is the 'other' of the cathedral voice, and this other seems also to take over both Edwin Drood's life, and Neville Landless's, just as the woman in the opium den opium-smokes herself 'into a strange likeness of the Chinaman' (1.2). He says that his 'Diary is, in fact, a Diary of Ned's life too' (10.86). This resembles the changing of clothes in *Bleak House* or in *Our Mutual Friend*, or the changed clothes and changed destinies of *A Tale of Two Cities*; writing itself begins to shape itself into another identity. His desires are objectified onto Neville, the savage colonial subject – but Neville is also Edwin:

> The *demoniacal* passion of this Neville ['Edwin', MS] Landless, his strength in his fury, and his savage rage for the destruction of its object, appal me. So profound is the impression, that twice since have I gone into my dear boy's room, to assure myself of his sleeping safely, and not lying dead in his blood.
>
> (10.86, my emphasis)

Names interchange in the total reversibility of signs which I referred to in discussing *Little Dorrit*: the parapraxis is repeated in the next entry: '[Ned] laughed when I cautioned him and said he was as good a man as Neville ('Edwin', MS) Landless any day' (10.86). Yearning for and taking over the other takes place while the other is asleep, like Monks and Fagin with the half-sleeping Oliver Twist or David Copperfield with Uriah Heep or the sleeping Steerforth (6.140, 29.498). The superior knowing and desiring position could be colonising, where colonisation is the product of deep psychic desire to capture the desire of the other. Or it tests the reality – the otherness – of the people whose lives are so laid open.

The reversing of identities, the voices, and the impossible journey with an unknown fellow-traveller all suggest a schizophrenia at work in Jasper, and, I will suggest in the next section, in the text as well. Schizophrenia may be described in the language of Jameson, who, using Lacan, sees it as a condition of post-modernism (where signs do reverse), as a disease of language where:

> ... connections have broken down: continuity in speech, for Lacan, is a function of what he calls 'the slippage of signifieds' ... in other words, that relative semantic flux that allows us to disconnect a meaning from one word, or signifier, and attach it to its synonym. For Lacan ... the world of the schizophrenic is quite the opposite of meaningless: if anything, it is too meaningful; each instant, like each signifier, is a closed and full meaning in itself, from which it becomes increasingly difficult to lay a bridge to the next moment of time.[23]

Perhaps Piranesi's imaginary prisons, his dream scaffolds, portray a schizoid state, where the bridges are always down. The opium condition fits Jameson's reference to drugs which abolish 'the logic of time, which releases each instant, and the object in it, to glow and radiate a kind of undifferentiated and autonomous energy'. If Dickens's final investment is in the schizoid, it remains to be decided how far that is homologous with participation in 1860s society as schizoid.

III

As in some cases of drunkenness and in others of animal magnetism, there are two stages of consciousness which never clash, but each of which pursues its separate course as though it were continuous instead of broken (thus if I hide my watch when I am drunk, I must be drunk again before I can remember where), so Miss Twinkleton has two distinct and separate phases of being.

(*Edwin Drood*, 3.15)

In this quotation, Dickens plays with *The Moonstone*, using and assuming the reader's knowledge of that text, and Ezra Jennings's citations and quotations from Drs Carpenter and Elliotson (as though Collins had G.H. Lewes breathing over him) to substantiate the point that there can be a split-off consciousness (*The Moonstone*, 2.3.10, pp. 432-3), without which 'proof' Collins's narrative would be impossible. *Edwin Drood* has signs of being metafiction, not only with regard to Collins, but to earlier Dickens texts, as reference to 'the Circumlocutional Department' (11.93) recalls *Little Dorrit*. The love scenes in novels which Miss Twinkleton cuts and replaces by her own versions (22.201-2), where *both* forms of writing are fraudulent and parodied by Dickens, is another indicator, entailing the fictionality of narrative, the impossibility of a diegesis with any authority outside these relative and partial ones. Miss Twinkleton is not schizoid, since her duplicity throughout is deeply conscious, but the text signals, partly through its metafictionality, its awareness of schizoid states as well that it may also be complicit in.

Thus when Neville Landless is accused of Drood's murder, the narrative cites what people in Cloisterham say about him:

Before coming to England he had caused to be whipped to death sundry 'Natives' – nomadic persons, encamping now in Asia, now in Africa, now in the West Indies, and now at the North Pole – vaguely supposed in Cloisterham to be always black, always of great virtue, always undressed in coarse muslin, always calling themselves Me, and everybody else Massa or Missie (according to sex), and always reading tracts of the obscurest meaning, in broken English, but always accurately understanding them in the purest mother tongue ... He had been brought down to Cloisterham, from London, by an eminent Philanthropist, and why? Because that Philanthropist had expressly declared: 'I owe it to my fellow-creatures that he should be, in the words of BENTHAM, where he is the cause of the greatest danger to the smallest number.'

(16.143-4, MS reading)

Clearly these charges are no more than what the next paragraph calls 'the blunderbusses of blunderheadness'. But a satirical intention which this 'superior' diegesis points out does not exhaust the passage, which is rather demonstrative of the schizoid state of English ideology. Benthamism names that ideology, and the misquotation of Bentham by Cloisterham people who thereby turn themselves unconsciously into utter insignificance – into 'the smallest number' – continues the reversibility of signs commented on already. In fact, such reversibility is everywhere here. Neville is at least of mixed race, yet here appears to be analogous to a Southern slave-owner; states of dress are also states of undress; 'natives' call themselves Me which implies they recognise their subject-position to be that of the object; languages are interchangeable, as perhaps sexes are too. But that this text can speak every contradictory position also raises questions whether it can be differentiated from the superior diegesis I have referred to, or whether that too is to be read as schizoid; and it is not clear that the text does not replicate several contradictions elsewhere seen in the texts which make up 'Dickens' in terms of attitudes to foreigners and to colonialism, especially since this passage, quite clearly asking to be read against the grain, makes obvious its own contempt for the foreigners it thus objectifies. If natives can be thus undistinguished each from each (turned into a question of numbers, as in classical Benthamism), it is not clear that Dickens's romanticism which supports the individual does not, in fact, imply a Benthamism itself, in treating people as only of value as they are of use.[24]

In suggesting this, I see a schizoid tendency as basic to the text. Its incompleteness means that there is no closure placed on its plurality of possibilities which are implied in reading; but in any case it deals with opium which makes for a double-consciousness, and it has an overseas narrative of the East which necessitates a silence about otherness, as a necessary part of a virtually official state of secrecy involved in the doubleness of Britain's position as both a metropolitan and a colonial power, where speaking implies awareness of and complicity in state violence. Thirdly it thematises loss of identity or identity being shared, or moving over into another identity, or unacknowledged as a self-identity. (Durdles never says 'I' (4.29); in contrast, the native always has to say 'Me'.) Thus its central character, Jasper, shows the aporia involved in connecting together two halves of his dream: his whole dream is abyssal. And on Forster's evidence, it was to lead to confession.

In *The Moonstone*, Ezra Jennings's past is never given: it dies with him and his diary is buried with him; the secrets of this Wandering Jew figure (his 'glittering' eye quotes from 'The Ancient Mariner') remain what Mr Sapsea calls 'the secrets of the prison-house' (18.165, quoting *Hamlet*, 1.5.14). But the secrets of the prison-house are the secrets of the confessional. Jasper was to be made to speak, and confession implies the application of techniques to ensure the production of a single-subject. The originality 'was to consist in the review of the murderer's career by himself, when its temptations were to be dwelt upon as if not he the culprit, but some other man, were the tempted. The last chapters were to be written in the condemned cell, to which his wickedness, all elaborately elicited from him as if told of another, had brought him' (*Life*, p. 808).

If the confession was to be as Forster describes, it would present a schizoid mind. Murderous criminality and devotion to pursue the murderer (16.146), both of which subsist in Jasper, would have come apart completely. The existence of this schizoid state would allow for the discursive production of 'the criminal intellect' of which the text speaks as something which is different and exceptional: as that which:

> its own professed students perpetually misread, because they persist in trying to reconcile it with the average intellect of average men, instead of identifying it as a horrible wonder apart.
>
> (20.175)

The confession would have legitimated the idea of the 'criminal intellect'. It would have been complicit with official Victorian silencing of bourgeois guilt, and increased the novel's Panoptical tendencies, making the subject speak in the language assigned to him by the confessor. In the same way, Monks's discourse is swallowed up by Brownlow: where Monks is silent, Brownlow speaks fluently for him. In the project of Jasper's 'elaborately elicited' confession, Dickens practises the violence of the coloniser.

Yet what would this confession have meant? Ronald Thomas suggests that it would:

> ... disguise the self behind the mask of an alternative identity apparently unrecognisable to the 'confessing' agent. Beneath the confessional act of making the self intelligible ... is the deeper unintelligibility of a self censored from itself, speaking with a

voice not its own . . . this confession was to be an act of repression as well as revelation, a further sign of the opposing forces locked in contention within the 'criminal intellect' . . . a sign of the individual's inability to know and understand the operation of his or her own psychic agencies without the aid of the external agencies of detection.[25]

This would support the thesis of *The Novel and the Police* that the subject in nineteenth-century texts must be regulated, produced and constituted in conditions analogous to the carceral. Jasper's ignorance of his guilt would be a sign that he had 'repressed his own repression' (Thomas, p. 236). It would suggest that nineteenth-century bourgeois and imperialist society could not read its own ideological formation, its political unconscious, which would remain unintelligible, unless interpreted by the detective power of the realist text. Jasper's schizoid state parallels an evasiveness in the strategy by which official ideology sheds its responsibility (as the Indian sepoys, not the British, were made responsible for the Indian mutiny). In comparison, there is nothing of this in *The Moonstone* where each narrative belongs to a project interested in detection. The heroine, Rachel, who conceals her lover's 'crime' has therefore no narrative; nor does Godfrey Ablewhite, the bourgeois villain who has a double existence in the suburbs. Whatever the bohemianism of Collins, his pro-Indian writing and his awareness of female desire, his narrative offers little but comfort to the bourgeois reader.

But I would rather argue that *Edwin Drood*, beginning with the opium trance which sets up the plurality of the voice, conveys the *impossibility* of a confession where one speaker can be unconscious of the other speaking in his 'scattered consciousness'. Dickens's narratives are full of the confessions of those who have been hardened into a single-subject identity, in whom the mind-forged manacles operate as with Mrs Clennam saying that 'if the house was blazing from the roof to the ground, I would stay in it to justify myself against my righteous motives being classed with those of stabbers and thieves' (*Little Dorrit* 2.30.847–8). But it seems that something else is being offered here: that Jasper's confession would have a good faith behind it and yet be criminal. A schizoid tendency in Jasper would be inseparable from a narrational belief, in rendering the confession, in the power of repression to constitute a single subject. Yet, if Jasper can say 'I am self-repressed again' (19.173), that involves a textual commitment to the impossibility of repression. Repression cannot be that kind of conscious act: the self cannot repress its own repression.

In discussing *Dombey and Son* I asked whether the model of repression or monstration better fitted the text. Modernity – including in its practices the power of confession which produces the subject – brings everything to light, and repression only makes what by its mechanism therefore becomes unconscious the more evident, in pushing it into the parapraxes which make up the psychopathology of everyday life; in sending it into the various forms of displacement – metonymies and synecdoches of behaviour – that may themselves be read. Hence Lady Dedlock is not the 'inscrutable Being' she would like to think herself (*Bleak House* 2.59). Confession, as a monological project, aims at a single knowledge of the subject, but in turn it produces too much: it brings out the doubleness of the subject it would like to count and construct as single. If the Dickens text characteristically hovers between repression and monstration as two ways forward, it has to be emphasised that finally these are not two choices. To repress is also to show.

If the text had wanted to allow for a confession that would leave Jasper unconscious of his own criminality, it could only do so by asserting its own monologism, cutting out the dialogism of the speech that would speak its own otherness. The confessor-voice, demanding confession, and the colonising voice, are the same, and both are violent towards the other. Fagin applauds capital punishment for its silencing of voices: capital punishment makes an admirable repression, and Jasper, it seems, would have been hanged in this novel. There are ominous signs that there is a readiness for the text to become so repressive, as when Forster says that he thought Crisparkle was intended to marry Helena Landless and that Rosa would marry Tartar, the text thus endorsing 'the suburban establishment' (22.202) it parodies, and 'our glorious Constitution in Church and State' (Sapsea Fragment, 232). But the English ideology which supports colonialism creates Dickens as a double subject, and his half-awarenesses of that make for his identification with those figures of the colonies discussed in this chapter – Monks, Jasper – who have no shares in English public life.

The confession might have shown up the impossibility of the idea of confession save as a matter of state power in the condemned cell. If the confession had come voluntarily, it would have been part of Jasper's dream of the scaffold, part of his death-wish. But the desire for such a closure is also a desire for a repression, for a wish not to know, and the organism which desires its death is also trapped by the impossibility of such closure. The schizoid nature of British public life, despite its modernity, cannot see its own contradictoriness: this repeats Jasper's putative confession which does not know the other side of things: the violent side. The wish to confess is part of a too-easy desire to slough off the other side – to eliminate an otherness which cannot so easily be got rid of. It turns monstration – showing the character – into repression, by its staging of the self in the way it speaks of itself. Repression, however, turns just as quickly back into a full demonstration of a character that cannot be delimited. The confession in *Edwin Drood* would have shown by its very impossibility that only a bad faith constructs the discourse that would make it allowable, and that the public life, which is also a public lie, is sustained only by such procedures as work in those who try to produce confession – whether in the metropolitan centre, or in the colonies.

7

The Scum of Humanity:
Our Mutual Friend

A fascination with violence while having a violent reaction to its presence, hostility to surveillance and the carceral while perpetuating it, both a lackeying attitude with regard to the police and a sympathy with the criminal as Abel, a fascination with the transgressive woman while underwriting the doll in the doll's house, a hatred of middle-class attitudes doubled by a textual punishment of the non-bourgeois, a modernizing attitude that invests in nostalgia. In these contradictory moves in Dickens, presented in a writing marked by carnivalesque excess and proliferation but which also enforces restraint, there is a double attitude to the body which might be discussed by reference to Julia Kristeva on *abjection*, and which is activated by the drive towards modernity but also by a discursive *ressentiment*. In this last chapter I want to give space to this which, if named, would make Dickens's sympathies at some moments near to being proto-fascist.

In using that term, which I referred to before in discussing *A Tale of Two Cities* (3.2), I only partially imply a politics; more to the point is the affinity with the intellectual and above all the psychic roots of fascism. Kristeva offers an analysis of these in discussing abjection, but it is also important to draw on Bataille's essay 'The Psychological Structure of Fascism' (as Kristeva's work also uses Bataille).

For Bataille, a society which thinks in terms of the gift, of expenditure which is not calculable, has been replaced by bourgeois homogeneity, which resists waste, which hates everything non-productive and represses its existence. '*Heterogeneous* existence can be represented as something *other*, as *incommensurate*.'[1] The heterogeneous is nonetheless the object of attention of the homogeneous, which tries to get at it, to identify and classify it, while keeping its separation from it. The heterogeneous therefore is that which is outside representation, excluded from it, but which is to be represented on terms the homogeneous can use. For Bataille, in fascism the homogeneous aspects of society, those concerned with productive expenditure, with exchange and with conservation and recycling of energies so that nothing goes to waste, are directed by one aspect of the heterogeneous. The fascist leader, with his anarchism, subversion and pathologism, *is* heterogeneous but that takes the form of an oppression of the rest of the heterogeneous, the impoverished, the impure. The heterogeneity of fascism involves an attempt at purification of the state, by turning against other heterogeneous elements. The fascist revolts against his own heterogeneity: abjects it, tries to keep it out of representation. In doing so, he voices the attitudes of the homogeneous; nonetheless he is still other, still aware of being on excluded territory. To be bourgeois would mean being homogeneous; Dickens remains heterogeneous, both attracted to and repelled by elements of impurity, by that which is untouchable, by filth.

To trace this double movement, I want to look back at material and at novels referred to in earlier chapters and by giving two further examples of writing. I shall continue with the theme of the last chapter, with colonial material, for my first example is from a symptomatic text of 1858, 'The Perils of Certain English Prisoners'. The second is *Our Mutual Friend* (1864–65).

The first text was a response to the events of the Indian Mutiny.[2] The discussion of *Barnaby Rudge* and *A Tale of Two Cities* considered the violence of capital punishment in Britain and Dickens's increasing reaction away from abolition, and this can be linked to the general use of force and coercion which is involved in imperialism, which may be defined as 'the objectless disposition on the part of a state to unlimited forcible expansion'.[3] As an event within imperialism, the sepoy rebellion, as the Mutiny may be better called, began in Meerut, north India, in May 1857, and was repressed the following year. British Crown rule was proclaimed in eighteen languages on 1 November 1858 and read throughout district towns in India. De Schweinitz comments on the scope of the summary executions of that year carried out by the British, and quotes the army officer John Nicholson in the Punjab who suggested that a bill be proposed to allow the 'flaying alive, impalement or burning of the murderers of the women and children at Delhi. The idea of simply hanging the perpetrators of such atrocities is maddening' (de Schweinitz, p. 173). The sepoys had murdered Europeans in Delhi, but the massacre of hundreds of British at Cawnpore (17 July 1857) and the siege at Lucknow, which lasted from June to November 1857 caught the attention most of the British in Britain, and prompted Dickens's genocidal comments which I quoted when discussing *Edwin Drood*. It seems that British atrocities before Cawnpore, at Benares and Allahabad where thousands of Indians were executed after the bloody assizes of General Neill, acted to provoke revenge, and this was what Cawnpore represented.

There was no objection to the public execution of those Indians whose manner of death represented the way that British state power dealt with its imperial subjects, and in the chapter on *Edwin Drood* I argued that this was an element of an institutionalised schizoid attitude provoked through the presence of empire. Lord Canning, the Governor-General of India, wanted to regulate punishment after the rebellion so that there would be no needless bloodshed, a calming measure which further provoked Dickens's desire for revenge, believing that the army was being denied the chance for retribution, hence his letter to Angela Burdett-Coutts about exterminating the Indians. A further reaction was to write a Christmas number for *Household Words*, a story which he claimed would catch 'some of the best qualities of the English character that have been shown in India' (quoted, Oddie, p. 7). This piece, 'The Perils of Certain English Prisoners', which anticipates *A Tale of Two Cities*, was set in Central America. It involved a contribution from Wilkie Collins, but what follows is all Dickens.

The narrator, Gill Davis, a private in the Royal Marines, is involved in protecting an English mining colony against pirates. The pirates capture him and the rest of the English party; the party escapes down the river and all are rescued by the contingent sent in by Captain Carton, who shoots the central villain, Christian George King. He is introduced near the beginning, when the party arrive at the island, Silverstore:

> One of those Sambo fellows – they call these natives Sambos when they are half-negro and half-Indian – had come off outside the reef, to pilot us in and remained on board after we had let go our anchor. He was called Christian George King, and was fonder of all hands than anybody else was. Now, I confess, for myself, that on that first day, if I had been captain of the Christopher Columbus, instead of private in the Royal Marines, I should have kicked Christian George King – who was no more a Christian

than he was a King or a George – over the side, without exactly
knowing why, except that it was the right thing to do.

(*Christmas Stories*, p. 166)

Everything is here – the racism, the appeal to an adventurism
associated with Columbus, an appeal to an instinctualism that is
itself proto-fascist. But neither Oddie nor Brantlinger in discussing
this text (spliced in the middle by a less racist chapter by Collins,
describing life in captivity) bring out how the text is framed, the
way it constructs the narrator who becomes very similar to George
Silverman in the short story of 1868.[4]

It begins with the narrator declaring that he was a private off
the 'Mosquito shore' in 1744, but then breaks off in the second
paragraph:

> My Lady remarks to me, before I go any further that there is no
> such christian-name as Gill... she is certain to be right, but I
> never heard of it. I was a fondling child, picked up somewhere
> or another, and I always understood my christian name to be
> Gill. It is true that I was always called Gills when employed at
> Snorridge Bottom betwixt Chatham and Maidstone to frighten
> birds; but that had nothing to do with the baptism wherein I was
> made etc., and wherein a number of things were promised for me
> by somebody, who let me alone ever afterwards as to performing
> any of them, and who, I consider, must have been the Beadle.

(163)

Again, everything is here – echoes of *Oliver Twist*, of Dickens's autobiography in the reference to Chatham, anticipations of Magwitch,
the tone of Mr Bounderby. This is the voice of the heterogeneous,
who is called to defend the homogeneous aspects of society, and is
used by it for that. But what does not appear until the end is the
status of the 'lady'. She is not the genteel wife of Davis, the pleo-
nastically named Marion Maryon who is in danger throughout the
text, but Marion who has become the wife of Admiral Sir George
Carton, Baronet. The double hint of marriage in her name is disap-
pointed. Gill Davis himself is no Robin Hood to this Maid Marion:
class identities are fixed and annihilate adventurers:

> It was my Lady Carton who herself sought me out, over a great
> many miles of the wide world, and found me in Hospital

wounded, and brought me here. It is my Lady Carton who writes down these words. My Lady was Miss Maryon. And now, that I conclude what I had to tell, I see my Lady's honoured gray hair drop over her face, as she leans a little lower at her desk; and I fervently thank her for being so tender as I see she is towards the past pain and trouble of her poor, old, faithful, humble soldier.

(208)

This is a version of Lady Dedlock and Captain Hawdon: a relationship codified in respectable, domesticated class terms, repressed as to its sexuality where the underclass will not touch the woman and the woman will not stoop to conquer, despite her obvious feelings, and her awareness of sexuality. As though she has read the novels written subsequent to the Indian mutiny which featured the rape by Indians of English women, she asks Davis in the moment of crisis that if they are defeated and he is 'absolutely sure of [her] being taken' (185) he will kill her. The sexual must be refused, for the servant class cannot touch the woman when the discourse of imperialism depends to a great extent on the idea of the colonised threatening English women with rape.[5] A text so repressed ensures that the hero remains unpartnered, speaking a discourse of humility caricatured elsewhere in Dickens in Uriah Heep and repeated in Gabriel Betteredge in *The Moonstone*, whose terms of endearment about Lady Verinder are very similar, and who thus shows himself up to be Man Friday in the real-life of the British imperialist romance which he is so fond of reading. But however naive yet disingenuous the language of the text of 'The Perils of Certain English Prisoners', Dickens is not so naive as Collins with Betteredge, and the text's duplicity is apparent with this framing. The reader is intended to misread, to take the lady as Gill Davis's wife, so that Captain Carton is displaced – made as artifical and cardboard a character as the name suggests – and the hero enjoys a vicarious triumph, which is sexual and achieved through *ressentiment*, which *The Genealogy of Morals*, it will be remembered, associates with slave-revolt. The effect of the ending is to maximise the hero's sufferings by stressing his let-down: that he is not, after all, married, but is the injured soldier of one of Victoria's little wars.

The lower-class hero is encouraged in a permanent state of bitterness, and his first reactions to the people on Silverstore are not pleasant:

I had had a hard life, and the life of the English on the Island seemed too easy and too gay to please me. 'Here you are,' I thought to myself, 'good scholars and good livers; able to read what you like, able to write what you like, able to eat and drink what you like, and spend what you like; and much *you* care for a poor, ignorant Private in the Royal Marines! Yet it's hard, too, I think, that you should have all the halfpence, and I all the kicks; you all the smooth, and I all the rough; you all the oil, and I all the vinegar.' It was as envious a thing to think as might be, let alone its being nonsensical, but I thought it.

(167)

This heterogeneity is the language of Orlick to Pip, and it is recognised as being resentful, but disavowal cannot prevent the whingeing from being endorsed by the text. It institutionalises envy, makes it the character of the Anglo-Indians. That is ironic in so far as Dickens wished to describe that character and celebrate its heroism, but in the way the text works, it catches the unconscious of that dominant ideology of imperialism. The Anglo-Indian's attitudes to the English at home are caught in the *ressentiment* that supports the idea that their life is too easy.

In the suppressed anger that Davis has in fantasising other people's imagined privileges, he turns in a relay of oppression against Christian George King, another aspect of the heterogeneous, whose perfidy under a show of humility and zeal suggests both Uriah Heep and Mr Littimer in *David Copperfield*. But then much of Gill Davis (and not just by name) suggests some of the unconscious unpleasantness of David Copperfield in his own sense of *ressentiment* and belief in his class position. David, after all, has done a lot to come out of a tendential heterogeneity into homogeneity: he is at his lowest in travelling down from London to Dover. In this text, Christian George King, like Uriah Heep in relation to David Copperfield, is set up as a double of Davis:

If ever a man, Sambo or no Sambo, was trustful and trusted, to what may be called quite an infantine and sweetly beautiful extent, surely, I thought that morning when I did at last lie down to rest, it was that Sambo pilot, Christian George King.

This may account for my dreaming of him. He stuck in my sleep, cornerwise, and I couldn't get him out. He was always flitting about me, dancing round me, and peeping in over my hammock, though I woke and dozed off again fifty times.

(176)

Dancing around Davis is what Orlick does to Biddy. It is a gesture of excess – the very marker of heterogeneity – whose object is sexual. The obsession with the man in sleep reverses David Copperfield with Uriah Heep and Jasper with Edwin Drood, who both go to look at the man who possesses their thoughts while he sleeps (just as David Copperfield is also obsessed with the sleeping Steerforth), but it belongs to the same pattern. The explanation of why Davis dreams of the pilot is offered as a possibility only, but it is quite possible to argue in another way, such as that followed by Ashis Nandy referred to in discussing *Edwin Drood*. Nandy isolates the homoeroticism of the coloniser in relation to the colonised (Nandy, p. 10). If that is so, it is no wonder that, in conscious terms, Davis would like to kick him over the side of the ship.

King's fate is to be shot and left hanging in a tree (205), which makes him a figure of a man subject to capital punishment, but still, perhaps, a desired object. The sense that he doubles Davis in his lackeying and conscious/unconscious opposition to the class he serves is repressed: both figures of *ressentiment* have that quality characterised otherwise: King through a racist discourse which makes him both other and marginal and even on his own terms as colonised not racially pure, Davis through an ideology of self-sacrifice. The point, however, remains that an attempt to write affirmatively about the British in India does nothing more than try to sublimate feelings of envy, rancour and impotence, and is deliberately constructed as a self-justifying autobiography to maximise feelings of pity, even more significantly when these are articulated to emotions deemed fit for Christmas.

If the reader's identifications are to be with markers of repressed violence, it should be considered how this articulates with *A Tale of Two Cities*. The Carton of 'The Perils' speaks like Dickens discussing the Indians in the aftermath of the mutiny. Speaking about the pirates he says that:

'Believing that I hold my commission by the allowance of God, and not that I have received it direct from the Devil, I shall certainly use it, with all avoidance of unnecessary suffering and with all merciful swiftness of execution, to exterminate these people from the face of the earth.'

(179)

The other Carton, of course, allows himself to be killed. This Carton speaks as a cardboard cutout, or like a book, just as Antoinette in *Wide Sargasso Sea* feels that as she gets nearer to England and to the bookish world of English law, literature and patriarchal customs she is walking into a 'cardboard world'.[6] But however bookish, the tone still recalls the 'well directed gun' passage in *A Tale of Two Cities*. That desire for extermination gained its momentum from the perception of the revolutionaries as 'the wildest savages' whose barbarousness broke down all gender propriety. The passage curves back to the issues of 'The Perils of Certain English Prisoners', defining anew those perils as the sexual fear and desire of the man flitting dancing and peeping around the Englishman asleep, disturbing his unconscious, probing male English ideology at its most protected: its fears of homosexual rape. Yet those fears are nothing less than created by English ideology itself in its homogeneity. It is Davis, bought up by that ideology, who dreams, not Christian George King.

II

The wheels rolled on, and rolled down by the Monument and by the Tower, and by the Docks; down by Ratcliffe, and by Rotherhithe, down by where accumulated scum of humanity seemed to be washed from higher grounds, like so much moral sewage, and to be pausing until its own weight forced it over the bank and sunk it in the river.

(1.3.21)

'Scum of humanity' is strong language; so is 'moral sewage'. It comprises violent rejection of the other, different from the fascinated horror which Davis has in relation to Christian George King. As a rejection, as a gut-feeling about people, (if it is a gut-feeling, it becomes 'abjection') it has an archaelogy behind it of earlier utterances and metonymic connections in Dickens's writings which I will first try to unearth.

In *Oliver Twist*, Dickens describes the approaches to Jacob's

Island, 'near to that part of the Thames on which the church at Rotherhithe abuts'. The 'visitor' (the language parodies a guide-book, confident that no tourist will follow) makes his way, 'jostled', past 'unemployed labourers of the lowest class, ballast-heavers, coal-whippers, brazen women, ragged children and the very raff and refuse of the river' (50.338). The word 'raff' appears as the term of contempt used by the petit bourgeoisie in *Dombey and Son* (9.119) when Mrs MacStinger demands 'whether she was to be broke in upon by "raff"' with reference to Walter Gay, but in association with 'refuse' it is already virtually the language of *Our Mutual Friend*. In *Oliver Twist*, the 'refuse' came up from the river. In *Our Mutual Friend* it is about to go into it. The description of the approach to Jacob's Island 'beneath tottering housefronts projecting over the pavement, dismantled walls that seem to totter as [the visitor] passes, chimneys half crushed half hesitating to fall' evokes several other passages in Dickens: firstly the blacking factory, which Dickens described in his autobiographical fragment of 1847:

> The blacking warehouse was the last house on the left-hand side of the way, at old Hungerford-stairs. It was a crazy, tumble-down old house, abutting of course on the river and literally overrun with rats. Its wainscotted rooms and its rotten floors and stair-case, and the old grey rats swarming down in the cellars, and the sound of their squeaking and coming up the stairs at all times and the dirt and decay of the place, rise up visibly before me, as if I were there again. The counting-house was on the first floor, looking over the coal-barges and the river. There was a recess in it, where I was to sit and work.
>
> (*Life*, 1.2)

Significantly the other boys, including Bob Fagin, worked 'down-stairs'. The geography of space here suggests a protected bourgeois area for the young Dickens, while the cellarage might be seen in erotic terms: as the libidinal, always likely to invade, and that which must be kept down, as in Freud's 'Civilisation and its Discontents'. But the whole episode 'rising up' before Dickens in the 1840s sug-gests the return of repressed material (ghosts? making the gorge rise, in a comparison of the house to the body which is vomiting upwards? rising up like the rats coming up?), implying an erotic horror, the overdetermination of the sexual with issues of class (for a 'rising up' is also a revolution). Tom-all-Alone's in *Bleak House* is also anticipated: where, 'as on the ruined human wretch, vermin parasites appear, so these ruined shelters have bred a crowd of foul existence that crawls in and out of gaps in walls and boards; and coils itself to speak in maggot numbers' (*Bleak House* 16.272). The Clennam house in *Little Dorrit* also by the river is also suggested. Houses fall in Tom-all-Alone's, so does the Clennam house. Houses with vermin seem to be interchangeable with the human body and its vermin. The house in *Great Expectations* with its spiders and its spinster, Miss Havisham, continues the association.

In the Jacob's Island chapter of *Oliver Twist*, Bill Sikes and other convicts are cornered like rats: Sikes hopes to jump into the 'ditch' which is exposed as mud since the tide is out: the mud would, of course, be excrement, so there is a strong sense of an alignment of the criminal with the cloacal. The raff and scum begin in the chapter by being human; the scum at the end is the mud – the sewage – above which Bill Sikes swings, suspended. The word 'sewage', which appears in the passage from *Our Mutual Friend*, was first used in 1834 according to the OED, which gives 1868 as the date for its first use in a metaphorical sense, like Dickens's in the quotation above referring to 'newspaper sewage' in the *Saturday Review*. But then the 1860s were marked by several law-and-order scares, of which the Chatham riots, discussed in the first chapter, were an instance. A Garotters Act of 1863 restored corporal punishment for robbery with violence, after several celebrated 'garrotting' attacks, and a Penal Servitude Act followed in 1864, which made hard labour in prison routine, as imprisonment was now the routine punishment: a further Prison Act of 1865 specified details for hard labour. In such ways, the 'raff' of society was demarcated in an atmosphere of anxiety.

I am interested in the Dickens marked out by heterogeneity who nonetheless finds working-class humanity here to be 'scum' (as the Pirates in 'The Perils of Certain English Prisoners' are called 'scum of all nations' (p. 199)), thus aligning it with the rats overrunning Warren's blacking factory (where the name 'Warren' thus supports the idea of animal life taking over), and who further calls it 'moral sewage'. The history of Dickens's writing is coterminous with the history of the rise of a discourse of sewage and waste disposal and sanitation in Britain. Cholera made its initial appearance in Britain in 1831, with epidemics in 1846–49, 1853–54 and 1865–66, while influenza produced eight epidemics in sixteen years following 1833. Typhus fever came into prominence in the 1830s (compare the fever of Rose Maylie in *Oliver Twist*, Chapter 33: Mary Hogarth, on whom Rose Maylie seems to have been based, died, apparently, of heart disease). Smallpox epidemics appeared in 1837–40, and again in 1844–45 and 1848–52: Esther Summerson catches smallpox from Jo who seems to die of tuberculosis.

In 1839 the first Sanitary Commission, under the Benthamite Edwin Chadwick, reported, after a typhus epidemic of 1838, connecting the disease with sewage: a further epidemic occurred in 1848. Chadwick's Report on the Sanitary State of Large Towns appeared in 1842 and legislation continued throughout the 1840s, culminating in an act setting up a Board of Health (1848–58, re-established in 1865 during a cholera epidemic).[7] In 1847, legislation was passed to make sewage flow into public sewers which discharged themselves into the Thames, which is called a 'deadly sewer' in *Little Dorrit* (3.28), in a passage linked to the description of the Clennam house, making these two almost metonymies of each other. Drinking water was taken straight from the Thames. Dickens's brother-in-law, Henry Austin, secretary to the General Board of Health, began a scheme for sewage disposal in 1849 which Dickens promoted in *The Examiner* in 1849 and in *Household Words* in 1850 and through the 1850s.

A new medical discourse influenced by Benthamism names these diseases of the 1830s and 1840s and agitates and legislates to remove them in competition with another discourse that made illness a moral judgement upon the country. The names of Southwood Smith (1788–1861), who anatomised Bentham, Edwin Chadwick (1800–1890), Henry Austin (1812–1861), Lord Ashley, Earl of Shaftesbury (1801–1885) and the Earl of Carlisle (1802–1864) who introduced the Public Health Act of 1848 are prominent here. Dickens's writing of his autobiography belongs to the modernisation of the 1840s: the primal scene of the blacking factory is created within a discourse which is determined to speak about the rats (compare the rat that Jo sees in *Bleak House* (Chapter 16) near the grave of Nemo). The Dickens text *produces* the self as needing to keep the rats/scum/sewage at bay, not to let them rise up. Dickens, in the Preface to the 1850 Edition of *Oliver Twist*, discussing Jacob's Island, wrote that sanitary reform:

> ... must precede all other Social Reforms; that it must prepare the way for Education, even for Religion; and that without it, those classes of the people which increase the fastest, must

become so desperate and be made so miserable, as to bear within themselves the certain seeds of ruin to the whole community.[8]

A residual Malthusianism, if not fear of working-class fecundity, influences Dickens's own discourse, and the word 'desperate' indicates a class fear: fear of revolution brought about from the poorest classes who will ruin 'the whole community' – a ruin which seems to exclude themselves. This may be compared with the passage in *Dombey and Son* already quoted from:

> Those who study the physical sciences, and bring them to bear upon the health of Man, tell us that if the noxious particles that *rise* from vitiated air were palpable to the sight, we should see them lowering in a dense black cloud above such haunts and rolling slowly on to corrupt the better portions of a town. But if the moral pestilence that rises with them, and in the eternal laws of outraged Nature, is inseparable from them, could be made discernible too, how terrible the revelation! Then should we see depravity, impiety, drunkenness, theft, murder, and a long train of nameless sins against the natural affections and repulsions of mankind, overhanging the devoted spots, and creeping on, to blight the innocent and spread contagion among the pure.
>
> (*Dombey and Son*, 47.619–20, my emphasis)

The equations are apparent: the 'better parts of a town' are not so merely in economic terms, but in moral, and physical pestilence is inseparable from moral pestilence. There is no neutral illness. The innocent and the pure belong with the investment in Nature and natural affections: disease and morality are inseparable, as in the passage quoted above from *Our Mutual Friend*, where 'scum' – sewage – is washed down, as the poor are driven down from higher ground (ground that would not be quite so contaminated with sewage) to the bank and into the river, where so many drown in this text.

The discourse of sanitation was linked to surveillance and for social control of a still-feared poor: indeed it was attacked for its watchword of 'centralization', a word Mr Podsnap objects to (*Our Mutual Friend*, 11.140). But Mr Podsnap, with his belief in repression – 'there is in the Englishman a combination of qualities, a modesty, an independence, a responsibility, a repose, combined with an absence of everything calculated to call a blush to the cheek of a young person, which one would seek in vain among the Nations of the Earth' (11.133) – stands precisely for the elimination of such a discourse as Dickens's, which names sewage and scum, and names characters in relation to this – Murdstone, Turveydrop. Mr Podsnap's ancestor would be Sir Peter Laurie (1778–1861), the Alderman Cute of *The Chimes* who thought that Jacob's Island was fictitious.[9] A significant difference between Podsnap and Dickens is that Podsnap names the bourgeois who ignores and represses sexuality, the excremental and the body itself, while Dickens stands for the fascinated spirit of excess that writes about – and hence produces – and rejects these things at once.

Rotten houses, rats, vermin and scum – moral sewage – all these figure people in the Dickens's texts.[10] *Bleak House* connects the partly euphemistic 'mud' in the streets with a 'general *infection* of ill-temper' that plays through that novel, just as *Little Dorrit*, which starts with people in a quarantined port just arrived from Asia and generally from outside Europe, has a chapter-title called 'The Progress of an Epidemic' that evokes the fever to invest in *Merdle* enterprises, so linking infection, money-making/trade and faeces together. 'Mr Merdle was never the gentleman' the Chief Butler says, making clearer the novel's own reading of Merdle in death (the moment of truth) as 'a heavily-made man, with an obtuse head, and coarse, mean, common features' (2.25.705). Mr Merdle turns out to be no more than a piece of shit in his death. He does not properly belong to the 'better parts of the town'.

In discussing *Little Dorrit* I suggested that the Marshalsea prison had features of the mother for Amy: the prison suggests the mother's body. But that fits with other images. Like Tom-all-Alone's, Jacob's Island's collapse is overdetermined: 'thirty or forty years ago, before losses and chancery suits came upon it, it was a thriving place, but now it is a desolate island indeed' (*Oliver Twist*, 50.339). Chancery, and parental neglect which puts the father in jail and the child to work, seem to come together. Chancery itself, as the relic of equity law, might be represented in feminine terms as I think it is in *Bleak House* – it has wards in court; it has the mad Miss Flite associated with it; it is associated with the hysterical warning of 'Suffer any wrong that can be done you, rather than come here!' (1.51); it even seems to fit Mr Gridley's combativeness, as Skimpole points out (15.269); its Lord Chancellor is in manner 'courtly and kind' (3.78) and above all it has a capacious holding quality about it. It is that hysterical, female body, I believe, that is spontaneously combusted, that leaves behind it 'a thick yellow liquor . . . offensive to the touch and sight and more offensive to the smell. A stagnant, sickening oil, with some natural repulsion in it . . .' (32.509). In contrast, common law, which would involve Mr Bucket and the underhand secrecy he practises, is representable in masculine terms.[11] The fate of Jacob's Island and of Tom-all-Alone's, then, might be connected with that which is imaged as the mother, just as in *Our Mutual Friend*, Gaffer Hexam declares the river the source of fire and warmth and protection to Lizzie (1.3). But this is the river that is filthy and fills Lizzie with a feeling of revulsion, and it is inseparable from the other element of detritus and filth that the text makes so much of: the dust mounds.

The association of the mother with filth and refuse, with that which must be repudiated, corresponds in Julia Kristeva's *Powers of Horror* to abjection, which is the violent state of denial of the mother, a rejection of her body being essential for the establishment of borders, for the creation of the narcissistically complete ego (which, in Bataille's terms, would belong to the homogeneous). Kristeva places such a denial of the mother outside the Oedipal struggle with the father: however, this abjection of the mother, where she is seen as split, divided rather than as whole, produces the melancholy subject that is 'abject' as well, not certain of its boundaries, neither constituted singly as a subject, nor part of the object, the mother. To speak about an abjection of the mother in Dickens's case is not necessarily to psychologise that particular mother–son relationship as Edmund Wilson's approach would do, in spite of Dickens's indignation that his mother was warm for his being sent back to the blacking factory after he had perforce left it because of a quarrel with the owners. In the same way, the disavowal of resentment ('I do not write resentfully or angrily') does not comment on any personal *ressentiment* in the novelist (*Life*, 35). Rather, the rejection of the mother is systemic, though the contradictions it produces in Dickens show up on every page in the violence of the writings. In Kristeva, excrement, blood and body fluids and dead bodies are instances of the abject. Separations from these elements of 'filth' are enforced by the mother in early training procedures, and in turn the subject internalises that demarcation from filth by an identification of the mother with these things.

In *Bleak House* and *Little Dorrit*, the narrative reduces things to Baudelaire-like allegory, destroys their coherence and, in the world of reified objects, demystifies their status as commodities by a process of destruction. The fragment is all that there is. In *Our Mutual Friend*, there seems no need of the allegorist: London in its melancholy modernity seems post-industrial, unable to cope with waste:

> Between Battle Bridge and that part of the Holloway district in which [Mr Wilfer] dwelt, was a tract of suburban Sahara, where tiles and bricks were burnt, bones were boiled, carpets were beat, rubbish was shot, dogs were fought, and dust was heaped by contractors.
>
> (1.4.33)

The random nature of everything, as in the account of the Deptford area, south of the Thames, suggests the detritus of a culture, as though T.S. Eliot took everything from this novel, down to the inspiration for the title for *The Waste Land*:

> [The schools] were in a neighbourhood which looked like a toy neighbourhood taken in blocks out of a box by a child of particularly incoherent mind, and set up anyhow, here, one side of a new street; there, a large solitary public-house facing nowhere; here, another unfinished street already in ruins; there, a church; here, an immense new warehouse; there, a dilapidated old country villa; then, a medley of black ditch, sparkling cucumber-frame, rank field, richly cultivated kitchen-garden, brick viaduct, arch-spanned canal, and disorder of frowsiness and fog. As if the child had given the table a kick and gone to sleep.
>
> (2.1.218)

The desire for order is an authoritarian wish to homogenise the heterotopic, at a time when all of England (in 1862) had just been brought under the power of the Ordnance Survey[12] (another form of defence, this time on a national scale). The anxiety that there can be no comprehensive modernisation structures a retentive attitude to waste. In *Our Mutual Friend* the fragment is part of an industrial recycling. Jenny Wren makes 'pincushions and penwipers to use up my waste' (2.1.223), and this is waste of waste, since her primary material for the dolls is also waste – the waste products of Pubsey and Co. (2.5.280). Mr Venus's shop is another indication that entropy can always be reclaimed: nothing is ever lost. The dust mounds are all to be cleared: everything is recycled. In the text there are the deaths which turn back into lives: Catherine Gallagher argues that in this there is a pattern where 'suspending the body's animation allows the liberation of value'.[13] This suspension of process and the image it generates would be like Benjamin's 'dialectics at a standstill',[14] a suspension analogous to the photograph where something dialectical, because something of tension remains in the frozen image. In the reduction of things to waste, to the abject, 'more dead than alive' (to quote from the title to one illustration in the text), some form of cognition may be released. Yet while the process of reduction suggests the possibility of recycling rather than the hoarding that is associated with Chancery and Krook in *Bleak House*, the process also continues much further in *Our Mutual Friend* for not only is there the continued power of reification (as with the Veneerings) but there is an identification of the fragment with filth and with the abject and a fear that it cannot be put back into circulation:

> My lords and gentlemen and honourable boards, when you in the course of your dust-shovelling and cinder-raking have piled up a mountain of pretentious failure, you must off with your honourable coats for the removal of it, and fall to the work with the power of all the queen's horses and all the queen's men, or it will come rushing down and bury us alive.
>
> (3.8.503)

The satire is against Parliamentarians, but the anxiety goes back to the reference to 'accumulated scum' and the word 'us' may be exclusionary: keeping out the waste that cannot be recycled.

The text does not hide that abject, however, any more than Dickens's own tendency made him avoid dead bodies. Here it may be necessary to think of abjection alongside *ressentiment*. 'All truly noble morality grows out of triumphant self-affirmation. Slave ethics, on the other hand, begins by saying *no* to an outside, an "other," a nonself, and that *no* is its creative act. This reversal of direction of the evaluating look, this invariable looking outward instead of inward, is a fundamental feature of rancor. Slave ethics requires for its inception a sphere different from and hostile to its own. Physiologically speaking, it requires an outside stimulus in order to act at all; all its action is reaction.'[15] The Kristevan argument by itself may seem essentialist, producing the abject at all times and in all places. But the Nietzschean argument might help situate it in nineteenth-century class terms. The inequality the slave suffers from produces a violent repudiation of the outside: all that is other is likely to be registered as filth, and rejected. The violence stems from a fear of having been identified already with the disgusting and with the outside. Putting abjection into these terms suggests that the requirement for a narcissistic ego-establishment is the repudiation of the other as 'scum', as 'sewage'. The repudiation that Nietzsche identifies is perhaps patriarchal in character, in that it has to do with the state and state power, but in Kristeva, it is of the mother; thus one of its productions is a masculinity that is defined by its hatred of everything that would upset its insecurely held borders. This leads Kristeva to read Céline's fascism and anti-semitic writings as produced from a writer who is on the inside of abjection – both fascinated and horrified by the idea of something 'defiling' his borders. He is fascinated in that this other outside speaks of the mother. Céline's excess in signification, to say nothing of his taking his mother's family name in his writing, and his thesis on Semmelweiss, the Hungarian doctor who demonstrated the horror of puerperal disease which killed off so many mothers in childbirth, attended by people like Mrs Gamp just come tainted from laying-out bodies, shows his identification with the mother. At the same time he is appalled by this otherness and from the standpoint of his adherence to the symbolic order and therefore to patriarchy, he denounces it in virtually fascist terms.

III

The figure of *ressentiment* in *Our Mutual Friend*, but also the abject figure, whose behaviour (certainly proto-fascist in its violence) is soon revealed to be absolutely heterogeneous, is Bradley Headstone. As the producer of a calculated discourse about him, the heterogeneous novelist who writes for and with the homogeneous, shows his violence. The text creates him as a 'criminal', with this generalisation:

> If great criminals told the truth – which being great criminals they do not – they would very rarely tell of their struggles against the crime. Their struggles are towards it. They buffet with opposing waves to gain the opposing shore, not to recede from it. This man perfectly comprehended that he hated his rival with his strongest and worst forces ...
>
> (3.11.546)

In contrast to this sense of the criminal as Macbeth, the nineteenth-century creation of the criminal (together with techniques of confession to make him 'tell the truth') was aimed at dividing the working class, isolating a delinquent class within it, containing the potential outbreaks of the 'perishing class' – the sector of the working class most likely to break out. In 1865, 35 per cent of male prisoners could neither read nor write.[16] Bradley Headstone is thus pure fiction as a 'criminal' but he is not therefore to be dismissed, for the fascination he has as a 'great criminal' towards a crime mirrors a Dickensian fascination which is horrified and abject, and derived from *ressentiment*. Dickens and Bradley Headstone have much in common. The pauper figure (like Uriah Heep), who might have made a good seaman and has the energy for it but has become a Schoolmaster, is taunted by the aristocratic Eugene Wrayburn for being that petit-bourgeois thing (2.6), so that his every emotion is forced into reaction. He tries to buy into 'decency', which would make him fit for the Podsnap world and separate him from the abject:

> Bradley Headstone, with his decent black coat and waistcoat, and decent white shirt, and decent formal black tie and decent pantaloons of pepper and salt, with his decent silver watch in his pocket and its decent hair-guard round his neck, looked a thoroughly decent young man of six-and-twenty.
>
> (2.1.217)

'Decent', which according to the *OED* does not take on the meaning of 'pleasant' till the twentieth century, takes on new class tones in the nineteenth century: the *OED* refers to *Crotchet Castle* (1831) for an example of its then new implications: 'Respectable means rich and decent means poor. I should die if I heard my family called decent.' In this presentation of the self, the head is drawn attention to, appropriately for Bradley Headstone's surname, and the description implies the importance of retention, of nothing being lost, of there being no waste:

> From his early childhood up, his mind had been a place of mechanical stowage. The arrangement of his wholesale warehouse, so that it might be always ready to meet the demands of retail dealers ... – this care had imparted to his countenance a look of care; while the habit of questioning and being questioned had

given him a suspicious manner, or a manner which would be better described as one of lying in wait. There was a kind of settled trouble in the face. It was the face belonging to a naturally slow or inattentive intellect that had toiled hard to get what it had won, and that had to hold it now that it was gotten. He always seemed to be uneasy lest anything should be missing from his mental warehouse, and taking stock to reassure himself.

(2.1.217)

The repetitions and balances in this passage: care/care; manner/ manner, questioning/being questioned; settled trouble; face/face; warehouse/warehouse, belongs to the desire for retention that tries hard to be complete (like the complete narrative of a headstone). He circulates entirely amongst males (Hexam, Wrayburn, Riderhood) as if this male economy were a way of protecting himself against the waste of spirit associated with the feminine. Marriage to Lizzie Hexam would be part of a relationship with Charley Hexam which would mean that there would be no entropy in that relationship or loss of investment in Hexam, or a leaking out of the pauper origins of them both.

Headstone as the slave figure of *ressentiment* tries to capture the desire of the master, Eugene, and he constructs himself as the abject, while desiring to colonise the unconscious of Eugene, to be in his thoughts:

'You think me of no more value than the dirt under your feet,' said Bradley to Eugene, speaking in a carefully weighed and measured tone, or he could not have spoken at all.

'I assure you, Schoolmaster,' replied Eugene, 'I don't think about you.'

'That's not true,' said the other, 'you know better.'

(2.6.291)

Masochistically, he *wants* to be thought of as 'dirt', and must construct himself as someone who is in Wrayburn's thoughts as a despised object – he cannot bear the other possibility that he is not thought of at all, which would make him a neutral, not abject figure. The abjection appears in his self-division, in the double use of the word 'man' alongside 'himself' and 'I', when he admits that he is not content being a schoolmaster. 'Do you suppose that a man, in forming himself for the duties I discharge, and in watching and repressing himself daily to discharge them well, dismisses a man's nature?' 'Discharge' speaks the language of waste; what is wasted, however, is the passion he negates in his effort to establish the 'decent' ego.

Yet the discourse which marginalises him as the failure is also subject to something else which produces something much less delimitable, and this brings about a return of power, indeed. I am referring to the way the text articulates him as a masochist, just as Miss Wade in *Little Dorrit*, a figure with whom he has some affinities, is called a 'self-tormentor'. I will move to this masochism by discussing the name and its different valencies. Bradley Headstone's name was once in Dickens's planning Amos Deadstone – which unpacks Old Testament Puritanism and Nonconformity caught in a first name that has a privative quality in it in the prefix A-. That last point is still imaged in the way he rubs out his name (4.15.795), in the same scene when Riderhood points out the finally chosen name's analogy with death – 'Headstone! Why, that's in a churchyard' (4.15.793). In the same chapter Headstone puns on his name in a reference to his class and poverty: 'you can't get blood out of a stone' (4.15.798). Bradley seems not to have been a first name in the nineteenth century, which hints that the character is to be assumed to have adopted it from a surname, so that the name suggests his utter deracination, as in 'I am a man who has lived a retired life. I have no resources beyond myself. I have absolutely no friends' (4.15.799).[17] His own name may not be his.

Being nameless institutes marginalisation, just as Miss Wade, that comparable figure with no recorded first name, says about herself and Tattycoram as two marginalised figures: 'She has no name. I have no name' (*Little Dorrit*, 1.27.330). No name means illegitimacy, in which Miss Wade shadows Arthur Clennam's status, and it accuses patriarchy, which is what he refuses to do, but is what her 'history of a self-tormentor' (2.21) – an attempt to legitimate herself – does. And namelessness also names the sexual deviance through the 'perverted delight' Mr Meagles refers to (1.27.330), which the text produces and maps onto masochism.

Headstone, as opposed to deadstone, comes more into focus with the imagery of the head, which images the ego. When talking to Lizzie Hexam in the churchyard:

The working of his face as she shrank from it, glancing round for her brother, and uncertain what to do, might have extorted a cry

from her in another instant; but all at once he sternly stopped it
and fixed it, as if Death itself had done so.

(2.15. 398)

Recalling both the name and the reference to the Medusa given
in the description of Mrs Lammle's aunt, 'a widowed female of a
Medusa sort, in a stony cap, glaring petrifaction' (1.10.120 – this
recalls Mrs Clennam), this figure becomes both castrated and cas-
trating, a death's head, like someone decapitated, guillotined, so
that when he is in rivalry with Wrayburn, he is described as a head
only:

> Looking like the hunted, and not the hunter, baffled, worn, with
> the exhaustion of deferred hope and consuming hate and anger
> in his face, white-lipped, wild-eyed, draggle-haired, seamed with
> jealousy and anger, and torturing himself with the conviction
> that he showed it all and they exulted in it, he went by them in
> the dark, like a haggard head suspended in the air; so completely
> did the force of his expression cancel his figure.

(3.10.544)

One 'source' for this last image may be the armed head that appears in *Macbeth* – Macbeth's or Macduff's, or the past Thane of
Cawdor's, but which suggests a helpless attempt at self-defence:
the thoughts armoured, the man told to 'beware' any threat to the
thoroughly masculinised self. The dissociation of body and head
leads to the next chapter, 'the state of the man was murderous, and
he knew it' which reifies him as the great criminal, the transgressive force who in his transgression is strongly parallel to the character of modernity, and to the artist of modernity.

> This man perfectly comprehended that he hated his rival with his
> strongest and worst forces, and that if he tracked him to Lizzie
> Hexam, his so doing would never serve himself with her, or serve
> her. All his pains were taken, to the end that he might incense
> himself with the sight of the detested figure in her company and
> favour, in her place of concealment. And he knew as well what
> act of his would follow if he did, as he knew that his mother had
> borne him. Granted, that he may not have held it necessary to
> make express mention to himself of the one familiar truth any
> more than of the other.

(3.11.546)

In this chapter, the conceit of the disappearance of the body has become basic to the text: 'the haggard head floated up the dark staircase' (3.11.547) and so on, when the 'head' is listening at the keyhole for signs of Lizzie Hexam. Bradley Headstone's rivalry with Eugene Wrayburn replays the Carton/Darnay rivalry in *A Tale of Two Cities* and, as it were, comically mocks the endstopping of that rivalry in Carton's death: the head goes on, a mobile part, a mobile passion, a rolling stone.

This freezing of a mobile self, getting and spending, into nothing more than a head, like the death masks in Mr Jaggers's office in *Great Expectations*, all that is left of the person after he has been turned off, and like photographic representations of the person which reduce the subject to a portrait of the head only, all this suggests that Bradley Headstone is an image for the text: repressed, resentful, castrated, abject in the loss of the body: all that the mad Mr Dick in *David Copperfield* fears when he is haunted by King Charles's head. But being reduced to his head implies a doubleness. He is not just a head, he is also headless. In the earlier quotation from 3.10, there is a marked ambiguity of 'expression' and 'figure' where these both further suggest the tropological power of language, its ability to give a face and to efface, to name the body in the production of discourse, and to repress it. Head and body – either can both be crossed out. In surrealist thought, recalling Bataille's society of the 1930s known as Acéphale (Headless), 'headlessness' may be defined as 'the condition of being, like Sade, a "conscience without a head," as Klossowski called it '.... an overwhelming desire to be guilty ... a glorious, ecstatic self-loss' characteristic of Bataille.[18] Walking around the streets all night looking for your enemy is suggestive of excess (Dickens also walked round streets all night); it is a labyrinthine activity, where the labyrinth has also the character of excess. Denis Hollier, discussing Bataille, says that 'labyrinthine structure is acephalous: antihierarchical (anarchic)',[19] but also a figure of masochism which feminises the self, a headlessness.

Masochism, which I discussed earlier in reference to *Great Expectations*, works differently in Miss Wade and Headstone. In the woman, as the 'passive' partner in heterosexual relations, masochism has been argued to be a way of negotiating an earlier trauma to do with the father, a way of regaining a certain control through suffering. 'The individual tries to achieve freedom through slavery, release through submission to control. Once we understand

submission to be the *desire* of the dominated, as well as their helpless fate, we may hope to answer the central question, How is
domination anchored in the hearts of those who submit to it?'[20]
Reading back to Miss Wade in the light of that, the angry woman,
deprived of parents and so of status, repeats and translates other
motifs in the text associated with women.[21] She reads the (unconscious) ideology of middle-class patronage she suffers from as its
power, and thus she puts herself into a position of masochism in
order to deal with it, to give herself a certain control. The power she
sees to be at work shows itself, for instance, in the ambiguity of
the word 'unhappy' as it is repeatedly used about her, which slides
from meaning 'not content' to 'non-quiescent' and thus changes in
the user from implying a sympathy into an attitude of surveillance
and control and a reminder that an 'unhappy temper' is the marker
of a revolutionary spirit.[22]

Her behaviour, after seduction by Gowan, involves a self-
assertive *ressentiment* which directs itself towards Pet Meagles
whom she seeks out, as Bradley Headstone seeks out Wrayburn,
but it is also masochism in assuming a marginalised position as
a lesbian, and it seems to have some relation to her response to
Gowan. Whatever the status of her relationship with Tattycoram
(it changes between the two encounters Clennam has with them –
culminating in 'Clennam felt how each of the two natures must be
constantly tearing the other to pieces' (2.20.661)), there is certainly
a masochism there, as it is masochism, too, in the demand to be
loved.

Male masochism in comparison, as in Pip, is a surrender of
masculinity, a desire for self-loss, constitutive of sexuality and a
revaluation of powerlessness.[23] In Headstone, there are strong
signs of masochism, however strongly protected by the ego. When
he woos Lizzie Hexam, he is obsessed with the prior place that
Wrayburn has with her; he speaks to her, proposing marriage, while
pulling at the stones of the wall of the burial ground in a way
which seems to affirm his desire to be taken out of the symbolic
order itself, and when Lizzie refuses to marry him:

'Then,' said he, suddenly changing his tone and turning to her,
and bringing his clenched hand down upon the stone with a
force that laid the knuckes raw and bleeding; 'then I hope that I
may never kill him!'

(2.15.398)

The split, seen on his body, is evident. His words are marked by 'hatred and revenge' – *ressentiment* – but the body speaks otherwise, in a drive towards masochism.

Headstone's criminality ends with his death in the mud (not drowned at sea like a sailor but drowned in excremental sludge – 'the ooze and scum behind one of the rotting gates' (4.15.802)), locked in an embrace with Riderhood, like a homosexual rape, as Eve Kosofsky Sedgwick argues in *Between Men*. As he has tried to displace Wrayburn, so he has also dressed up as Riderhood, in an unconscious throwing away of his own ego-identity: a headlessness indeed. The masochistic wish to have torture lengthened out shows itself not only in the last instance where he actually fails to kill Wrayburn in his murderous attack, but earlier, in following him about as if wishing to provoke him to a reponse, like the Underground Man with the army officer in *Notes from Underground*. Wrayburn goads Headstone to madness by playing a game with him; the effectiveness of this is seen in the repetition both men go in for: this pursuit happens every night. Wrayburn describes it to Lightwood:

> I study and get up abstruse No Thoroughfares in the course of the day. With Venetian mystery I seek those No Thoroughfares at night, glide into them by means of dark courts, tempt the schoolmaster to follow, turn suddenly, and catch him before he can retreat. Then we face one another, and I pass him as unaware of his existence, and he undergoes grinding torments . . . Thus I enjoy the pleasures of the chase, and derive great benefit from the healthful exercise.
>
> (3.10.542–3)

Wrayburn's lightness and talk of healthful exercise, which belongs to the discourse of the healthy body (referred to in relation to *Edwin Drood*) and which represents one way in which society reacts to scum and filth, is compromised by his profession that he studies how to do this through the day. What he does is not spontaneous: unconsciously he has been taken over by Headstone. Master and slave are in a contest with each other, as in Hegel, and it is by no means clear who is hunter and who hunted. This is akin to the no less Venetian mystery of Aschenbach's masochistic pursuit of Tadzio in *Death in Venice*, and in both cases the question is whether the unconscious of the other can be seduced. Both men are dependent on each other in a way which suggests that Bradley Headstone cannot, as the name of an abject other, be shaken off. *Ressentiment* has become something else, a masochism which undercuts hard-held identities: so that in the triangulation of Wrayburn–Headstone–Riderhood, first Headstone follows Wrayburn about, but at the last, Riderhood follows Headstone, proposing to be parasitic on him, undercutting separate identities.

Such masochism is deeply threatening to Dickens, as another marker of the heterogeneous. Dickens wrote about Miss Wade's intercalated narrative that he had the idea of 'making the introduced story so fit into surroundings impossible of separation from the main story as to make the blood of the book circulate through both' (*Life*, p. 626). Miss Wade's text is discussed by Dickens as though it were a Fielding-like story placed in the midst of another narrative, but the failure of marginal and main narrative to come together is suggestive. Her deviance must still be placed on the margin, made the *parergon*, and named 'The History of a Self-Tormentor', the chapter title being the voice of the dominant discourse, of the homogeneous, which would see such energy as she has as simply wasteful. In *Our Mutual Friend*, Bradley Headstone cannot belong to the *parergon*, and being a male, his heterogeneousness is more threatening to the text, less marginal. His progress describes an arc through the text, from the scum to scum – from pauperism to the literal mud – but at all times he belongs to that which must be abjected, but which cannot be. It follows the respectable about, undermining personality itself.

After he has tried to kill Wrayburn, who is restored to health like Rochester by Jane Eyre, the chapter title 'Better to be Abel than Cain' (4.7) appears. Dickens calls himself Cain; Monks is a Cain, so too Blandois (*Little Dorrit*, 1.11.124). Magwitch was Abel, and in *Edwin Drood*, Mr Honeythunder thinks of Edwin Drood as Abel, and Neville Landless (the foreigner, marked for death) as Cain – 'Bloodshed! Abel! Cain! I hold no terms with Cain' (*Edwin Drood*, 17.149). Deleuze, discussing masochism, disagrees that it is better to be Abel, just as Dickens's chapter title may be putting the case – that it is better to be Abel – for possible disagreement. For Deleuze, Cain is the figure loved by Eve, the mother (the mother punishes, in masochism). His words to God after he has killed his brother who is aligned with patriarchy, 'My punishment is more than I can bear' make him the masochist. So better to be Cain? Masochism is an impossible solution, but belongs to a transgression which is also essential.[24]

IV

The opening lines of *Our Mutual Friend* are:

In these times of ours, though concerning the exact year there is
no need to be precise, a boat of dirty and disreputable appearance
... floated on the Thames, between Southwark Bridge, which is
of iron, and London Bridge, which is of stone ...

Southwark Bridge opened in 1819 and this particular London Bridge
in 1831. 'These times' looks back for a reference point to the title
Hard Times: For These Times – Dickens's text dealing with machinery
in all its forms. There is a sense of regression in the opening sentence of the novel, as though time were going backwards, from the
Iron Age to the Stone Age, despite the 'iron ring' in which Bradley
Headstone holds Riderhood as they die together. Perhaps life, with
its cannibalism which is implicit in the first chapter of the novel, is
regressing to the stone age: the term the 'Stone Age' as an archaeo-
logical term is first recorded, according to the OED, in 1863.

Nonetheless, the keyword of the second chapter is 'new', and
'these times' are modern. The text encourages some regressive
moments, as in 'come up and be dead' (2.5.282), and as in the kitsch
elements of the description of the country around Plashwater Weir,
and in the narrative of the Boffins and Bella and John Harmon
which has so strong an investment in bourgeois stability. And its
whole drive is different from *Bleak House, Little Dorrit* and *Great
Expectations* in that it does not situate the text's events as having
happened in the past, its characters caught by the past, with its
tradition, its violence and Oedipal struggle. There is a drive to
disconnect the text from 'these times', as though trying to invest
only lightly in them, giving the characters more wished-for autonomy. That seems another element of its kitsch (some critics have
described it in terms of a tendential Christianity). If it is kitsch, it is
part of the effort to disengage from the 'scum' which is seen, in the
descriptions of urban squalor, to be inseparable from modernity.

In 1863, Charing Cross railway station opened in London, so
adding to the railway world that runs through Deptford in *Our
Mutual Friend*. On Friday, 9 June 1865, six years to the day before
Dickens collapsed and died, in one of the coincidences he was
so eager to draw attention to, he was involved in a railway crash.
This was when his train leapt over a forty-two-foot bridge in

the Staplehurst accident, when he was travelling from Folkestone to Charing Cross with Ellen Ternan and her mother, and with the manuscript of no. 16 of *Our Mutual Friend* in the carriage.[25] The ill-effects of this are drawn out by Forster, as in a letter from Dickens of 1866: 'I am not quite right within, but believe it to be an effect of the railway shaking. There is no doubt of the fact that, after the Staplehurst experience, it tells more and more (railway shaking that is), instead of, as one might have expected, less and less' (*Life*, p. 705). There is the sense of being a convalescent, and an inability to take speed (*Life*, p. 743).

Shock, for Benjamin, defines modernity, and convalescence is the condition in which the modern such as Baudelaire exists.[26] A sense of death in Dickens was seized on by Carlyle, in his comments on what of Dickens's personality could be found in Forster's *Life*: '. . . deeper than all, if one had the eye to see deep enough, dark, fateful silent elements, tragical to look upon, and hiding amid dazzling radiances as of the sun, the elements of death itself'.[27] Perhaps Pip's death-wish in his delirium in *Great Expectations* (reminiscent of Esther's state in her illness) is strongly anticipative not only of Dickens's death, but of this accident which took place four years later than the novel:

> I was a brick in the house-wall [anticipating Bradley Headstone in name and gesture with the churchyard stones] and yet entreating to be released from the giddy place where the builders had set me [if the building is moving, this recalls again the dizziness of Piranesi's *Carceri*]; that I was a steel beam of a vast engine, clashing and whirling over a gulf, and . . . I implored in my own person to have the engine stopped, and my part in it hammered off . . .
>
> (*Great Expectations*, 57.458)

These are dreams of scaffolds indeed. The description of Mr Carker's death, going back further to 1848, again in retrospect seems a moment of preparation for an accident from whose trauma Dickens never fully recovered. The grindstone and the guillotine of *A Tale of Two Cities* seem two more elements of that machinery and scaffolding which has such pulverising effects, causing a dispersal of the body, but doing so horrifically.

This is to read Dickens in the light of *Beyond the Pleasure Principle*, where Freud describes 'traumatic neurosis' as a 'a condition . . .

which occurs after severe mechanical concussions, railway disasters and other accidents involving a risk to life' and the compulsion to repeat the trauma involved in such shock-experiences leads him to refer to 'the mysterious masochistic trends of the ego' – trends whose functions are, by repetition, to weaken the ego's sense of being able to defend itself.[28] The tendency of the death-drive to undermine everything of deep subjectivity and rationality I have already referred to in relation to *Great Expectations*. Perhaps the paradox of modernity is a dual tendency to push things into the open and to fuller self-expression, and also to weaken their being. Certainly Dickens linked the ending of the text with his own death, as he put it in the Postscript to *Our Mutual Friend*: 'I remember with devout thankfulness that I can never be much nearer parting company with my readers for ever than I was then [at the accident] until there shall be written against my life, the two words with which I have this day closed this book – THE END.' Writing *Our Mutual Friend* for serial publication seems to take on the character of a series of staged movements towards death. Yet such autonomy of repetition was also denied to the author. It may be that the railway disaster acted for Dickens as a metaphor for the machinery of modernity which caught up with him himself – producing the incessant momentum of the public readings, which virtually killed him by making it impossible to stop. That machinery his own art did so much to encourage by its praise of modernity. If the art had a masochistic drive, as Freud implies, perhaps there is an identification with the energy of Bradley Headstone, as in the following passage. It was written after the railway accident, and, like that, involves a fall into the abyss, like the one John Jasper feared. The language of 'come down' means there is no transcendental coming up to be dead. Having commented on this passage before, I now want to quote it in full to notice its obsessiveness, its masochism which is sadism, the attempt to turn suicide into mastery, the informing of its language by machinery, modernity, and sense of the interchange of identities, as well as the vertiginousness whereby there can be any holding back from the abject and from filth:

> Bradley had caught him round the body. He seemed to be girdled with an iron ring. They were on the brink of the Lock, about midway between the two sets of gates.
> 'Let go!' said Riderhood, 'or I'll get my knife out and slash you wherever I can cut you. Let go!'

Bradley was drawing to the Lock-edge. Riderhood was drawing away from it. It was a strong grapple, and a fierce struggle,
arm and leg. Bradley got him round, with his back to the Lock,
and still worked him backward.

'Let go!' said Riderhood. 'Stop! What are you trying at? You
can't drown me. Ain't I told you that the man as has come through
drowning can never be drowned? I can't be drowned.'

'I can be!' returned Bradley in a desperate, clenched voice. 'I
am resolved to be. I'll hold you living and I'll hold you dead.
Come down!'

Riderhood went over the smooth pit backward, and Bradley
Headstone upon him. When the two were found, lying under the
ooze and scum behind one of the rotting gates, Riderhood's hold
had relaxed, and his eyes were staring upward. But he was girdled
still with Bradley's iron ring, and the rivets of the iron ring held
tight.

(4.15.801–2)

'I'll hold you living.' We may ask who holds who? It is as though
scaffolding which supports turns out to be the scaffolding that hangs.
Dickens is held and as if destroyed by the modernity he articulates.

But I want to finish not there but with a reference to his power
to unveil that bourgeois ideology that never quite accepted him
and which has done so much to evade his challenge by its smooth-
ing out of his work into harmless caricature. This is Headstone's
pupil, Charley Hexam, *ressentiment* and abjection combined, in his
last encounter with Headstone with whom relations have had a
quasi-homoerotic tendency, now trying to become respectable at
the price of not recognising that violent murder (as he thinks) has
been done, but, unlike Headstone, not giving way to masochism
but allowing the sexual utter repression:

I hope, before many years are out, to succeed the master in my
present school, and the mistress being a single woman, though
some years older than I am, I might even marry her. If it is some
comfort to you to know what plans I may work out by keeping
myself strictly respectable in the scale of society, these are the
plans at present occurring to me.

(4.7.713)

If we assume that Hexam marries as he says, and perhaps his wife
has children, we may date their birth at somewhere around the

1870s. Their children would be born before the First World War, their children around the time of the Second.

I have not approached Dickens with any sense of him in terms of mimetic realism. Yet here I would like to stop with that, in order to think how fully he has understood the soil and roots of present-day English bourgeois and petit-bourgeois ideology, particularly the ideology of such Home Counties areas of Britain as Surrey or Kent, formed by descendants of Charley Hexam who have got away from London as the place belonging to 'the scum of humanity'. Charley Hexam's great expectations in their combination of repression and calculation are an appalling genealogy of the unconscious of present-day respectable society.

Notes

INTRODUCTION: DICKENS AND DREAMS OF THE SCAFFOLD

1. John Carey, *The Violent Effigy: A Study of Dickens's Imagination* (London: Faber, 1973), pp. 91–93 cites the various references to wooden legs in Dickens. This book, which is informative and useful, also seems to me dismissive in reducing Dickens to comedy and the grotesque.
2. Jacques Lacan, *Ecrits: A Selection*, trans. Alan Sheridan (London: Tavistock, 1977), p. 4.
3. See on this Alexander Welsh, *George Eliot and Blackmail* (Cambridge, Mass.: Harvard University Press, 1985).
4. *The Theory of Moral Sentiments*, 1759, quoted in David Garland, *Punishment and Modern Society* (Oxford: Clarendon Press, 1990), p. 62.
5. Edmund Wilson, 'Dickens: The Two Scrooges', *The Wound and the Bow* (Oxford: Oxford University Press, 1941); Steven Marcus, *Dickens From Pickwick to Dombey* (London: Chatto, 1965). Both these Freudian readings try, however, to affirm a single identity for Dickens. I am more interested in the split subject, who is constituted by difference.
6. The *Letters*, which along with Forster's *Life* make up the best biography of Dickens; the Clarendon edition of the works (both of these still in progress); the scholarship starting with Humphry House, *The Dickens World* (Oxford: Oxford University Press, 1951) and Kathleen Tillotson, *Novels of the Eighteen-Forties* (Oxford: Oxford University Press 1954), and John Butt and Kathleen Tillotson, *Dickens at Work* (Oxford: Oxford University Press, 1958).
7. Lionel Trilling's essay is reprinted in the Oxford Dickens edition of *Little Dorrit* (1953). J. Hillis Miller, *Charles Dickens: The World of His Novels* (Cambridge, Mass.: Harvard University Press, 1958); Lawrence Frank, *Dickens and the Romantic Self* (Lincoln: University of Nebraska Press 1984); D.A. Miller, *The Novel and the Police* (Cambridge, Mass.: Harvard University Press, 1988).
8. F.R. and Q.D. Leavis, *Dickens the Novelist* (London: Chatto, 1970).
9. 'Prison-bound: Dickens and Foucault', *Essays in Criticism*, Vol. 36 (1986), pp. 11–31; see also my *Confession: Sexuality, Sin, the Subject* (Manchester, Manchester University Press 1990) for discussion of *David Copperfield* and 'George Silverman's Explanation'. A first draft of my *Dombey* chapter appeared as 'Death and modernity in *Dombey and Son*', *Essays in Criticism*, Vol. 43 (1993), pp. 308–329. I say little about *David Copperfield* here, but see my forthcoming edition of the text for Penguin (1995).
10. On this subject see Ned Lukacher, *Primal Scenes: Literature, Philosophy, Psychoanalysis* (New York: Cornell University Press, 1986) for some very suggestive pages on Dickens.

CHAPTER 1 PRISON-BOUND: DICKENS, FOUCAULT AND *GREAT EXPECTATIONS*

1. F.R. and Q.D. Leavis, *Dickens the Novelist* (London: Chatto & Windus, 1970), p. 331.
2. Barry Smart, *Foucault, Marxism and Critique* (1983), p. 90.
3. Michel Foucault, *Discipline and Punish*, trans. Alan Sheridan (Harmondsworth: Penguin, 1979). All textual references are to this edition.
4. Foucault, p. 207, quoting from the Preface to Bentham's *Panopticon, or, The Inspection-House: Containing the idea of a new principle of construction applicable to any sort of establishment, in which persons of any description are to be kept under inspection and in particular to Penitentiary-Houses, Prisons, Poor-Houses, Lazarettos, Houses of Industry, Manufactories, Hospitals, Work-Houses, Mad-Houses and Schools: With a Plan of Management attached to the principle: in a series of Letters, written in the year 1787, from Crecheff in White Russia to a Friend in England.*
5. Robin Evans, *The Fabrication of Virtue: English Prison Architecture 1750–1840* (Cambridge: Cambridge University Press, 1982), pp. 43–45, cp. p. 409.
6. Quoted, Denis Hollier, *Against Architecture: The Writings of Georges Bataille*, trans. Betsy Wing (Cambridge, Mass.: MIT Press, 1989), pp. 46–47.
7. Quotations from *Great Expectations* are from the Oxford edition, ed. Margaret Cardwell, 1993, and page references are to this, but chapter references in parentheses are to more standard editions of the novel, which do not break at the end of each stage of Pip's expectations: thus the text may be followed in, for example, the useful Penguin edition of Angus Calder (1965). Here, Chapter 27, p. 222.
8. A recent study of the Panopticon, Janet Semple, *Bentham's Prison: A Study of the Panopticon Penitentiary* (Oxford: Clarendon Press, 1993), defends Bentham against all-comers, especially Foucault, for whom, she says, 'the panopticon is a cruel and ingenious mechanism of the new physics of power designed to subjugate the individual' (p. 316). But the Panopticon is for Foucault the production of the individual.

   David Garland, in *Punishment and Welfare* (Aldershot: Gower, 1985), p. 46, sees prison architecture of the nineteenth century enforcing the freedom of the subject to choose: making it 'a market option, chosen by free individuals'. Solitary cells repeat the lessons of individual responsibility: architecture embodies the logic of *laissez-faire*. The subject that is constituted is Utilitarianism's 'economic man'.
9. The theme is dealt with in Michael Ignatieff, *A Just Measure of Pain: the Penitentiary in the Industrial Revolution, 1750–1850* (London: Macmillan, 1978). Ignatieff points out that the suspension of transportation in 1853 meant that prison sentences became longer. 'Until the late 1840s, the longest sentences in English prisons were three years. Lord John Russell was only repeating a commonplace when

he said in 1837 that a ten-year imprisonment would be a punishment worse than death. By the mid-1850s, sentences of such a length had become common . . .' (p. 201).

10. Jeremy Bentham, quoted in *Dickens and Crime* (London: Macmillan, 1962), p. 18.

11. See the *Letters of Charles Dickens*, Vol. 3, 1842–43, eds Madeline House and Graham Storey (Oxford: Clarendon Press, 1974), pp. 50 (Boston), 69 (Hartford), 104–105 (Auburn system), 110 (Philadelphia), 181 (Pittsburgh), 436 (Gloucester) for details on these prisons. See also *Michel Foucault* by Mark Cousins and Athar Hussain (1984), pp. 183, 192, for further details.

12. George Eliot, *Letters*, ed. Gordon Haight, Vol. 5 (New Haven: Yale University Press, 1955), p. 226.

13. *Martin Chuzzlewit*, ed. Margaret Cardwell (Oxford: Clarendon Press, 1982), Chapter 9, p. 129.

14. Dickens's comments on Washington as a planned city (*American Notes*, Chapter 8) are interesting in this context. Jonathan Arac, *Commissioned Spirits: The Shaping of Social Motion in Dickens, Carlyle, Melville and Hawthorne* (New Brunswick: Rutgers University Press, 1979), pp. 58–93, writes on *Martin Chuzzlewit*, focusing on 'the view from Todgers's' (the title of Dorothy van Ghent's famous essay, of course), and on the relationship between Dickens's realism, and determination to see the city whole. My own comments on *Martin Chuzzlewit* and America are in debt to Steven Marcus, though I feel he idealises the view from Todgers's.

15. Marx, *Capital*, Vol. 1, trans. Ernest Mandel (Harmondsworth: Penguin, 1976), p. 759. As a characterisation of Bentham, I also like Wilberforce, in a letter to Bentham, 1810, 'I am delighted by seeing with my mind's Eye your Honour like a great Spider seated in the Centre of your Panopticon' (quoted, Semple, op. cit., p. 264).

16. Collins, op. cit., pp. 20–21. Cp. Ignatieff, op. cit.: 'In 1861, when the prison directors ordered a major reduction in diet as part of an attempt to tighten up deterrence in the convict system, prisoners at Portland and Chatham staged a two-day riot that caused substantial damage. The prisoners doused the principal warder with gruel from their soup tins, overpowered the guards, unlocked the cells, and took over complete control of Chatham for several hours, until a contingent of armed Royal Marines succeeded in retaking the institution (p. 203).

The words 'at that time' raise the question of the book's date: Amy Sadrin (see note 23) answers this in her Chapter 4, dating Pip as about ten years older than Dickens, and seeing the action as Regency. This distancing might have something to do with the book's implicit backing of violence: violence is taken out of the context of mid-Victorian Britain.

17. Freud, 'Fragment of an Analysis of a Case of Hysteria', *Penguin Freud*, Vol. 8 (Harmondsworth: Penguin, 1977), pp. 66–67.

18. Lionel Trilling, *Sincerity and Authenticity* (Oxford: Oxford University Press, 1972), p. 24.

19. Michel Foucault, *The History of Sexuality*, Vol. 1 (Harmondsworth, Penguin, 1981), p. 60.
20. F.R. and Q.D. Leavis, *op. cit.*, p. 288. Apart from this account of the novel, I am in debt to Julian Moynahan, 'The Hero's Guilt: the Case of *Great Expectations*', *Essays in Criticism*, Vol. 10 (1960), pp. 60–79, and A.L. French, 'Beating and Cringing: *Great Expectations*', *Essays in Criticism*, Vol. 24 (1974), pp. 147–168.
21. *Ressentiment* is translated as 'rancour' and discussed in detail in the first essay of Nietzsche's *The Genealogy of Morals*, trans. Francis Golffing (New York, Doubleday, 1956); see especially p. 170.
22. This, which I will develop in Chapter 3 on *Bleak House*, derives from Paul de Man's discussion of Wordsworth's 'Essay on Epitaphs', where the traveller is silenced by the voice from the tomb: see de Man's 'Autobiography as De-facement', *The Rhetoric of Romanticism* (New York: Columbia University Press, 1984).
23. I owe this point to Amy Sadrin, *Great Expectations* (London: Unwin Hyman, 1988), p. 231. On some of the motifs here, see James E. Marlow, 'English Cannibalism: Dickens After 1859', *Studies in English Literature*, Vol. 23 (1983), pp. 647–666.
24. Forster, *Life of Dickens*, ed. J.W.T. Ley (1928), Vol. I, Chapter 2, p. 34. On the incident, see Steven Marcus, 'Who is Fagin?', in *Dickens from Pickwick to Dombey* (London: Chatto, 1965).
25. Robert Newsom, 'The Hero's Shame', *Dickens Studies Annual*, Vol. 11 (1983), pp. 1–24.
26. Freud, 'Civilization and its Discontents', *Penguin Freud*, Vol. 12 (Harmondsworth: Penguin, 1985), pp. 327, 328.
27. Freud, 'The Economic Problem of Masochism', *Penguin Freud*, Vol. 11 (Harmondsworth: Penguin, 1984), pp. 413–426. This essay depends on 'Beyond the Pleasure Principle' for its identification of masochism with the death-drive (p. 419): in reference to this, Laplanche refers to Freud's own 'compulsion to demolish life' (Jean Laplanche, *Life and Death is Psychoanalysis* (Baltimore: Johns Hopkins University Press, 1976), p. 123.
28. Gilles Deleuze, *Masochism: An Interpretation of Coldness and Cruelty* (New York: George Braziller, 1971). This also reprints Leopold von Sacher-Masoch's *Venus in Furs*. For an application of Deleuze, see Gaylyn Studlar, *In the Realm of Pleasure: Von Sternberg, Dietrich, the Masochistic Aesthetic* (Chicago: University of Chicago Press, 1988).
29. Amy Sadrin (note 23, p. 57) reads Miss Havisham as having become a double of Compeyson, to be fought with like Magwitch with Compeyson.
30. Cp. Foucault on the cases of Buffet and Bontemps (referred to in *Discipline and Punish*, p. 15), guillotined in November 1972 for crimes committed in prison. 'Foucault argued that the guillotine was merely the visible symbol of a system governed by death. The possibility of death, especially by suicide, was inherent in any prison sentence. Life sentences and the death sentence meant the same thing. 'When you are certain of never getting out, what is there left to do? Except risk death in order to save your life, risk your life even though you

may die. That is what Buffet and Bontemps did.' Foucault ended up by accusing the prison system of murder' – David Macey, *The Lives of Michel Foucault* (London: Hutchinson, 1993), p. 287.

CHAPTER 2 'AN IMPERSONATION OF THE WINTRY EIGHTEEN-HUNDRED AND FORTY-SIX': *DOMBEY AND SON*

1. Quoted, Philip Collins (ed.), *Dickens: the Critical Heritage* (London: Routledge & Kegan Paul, 1971), p. 443.
2. F.R. and Q.D. Leavis, *Dickens the Novelist* (London: Chatto & Windus, 1970), p. 11.The Asa Briggs I refer to is *The Age of Improvement* (London: Longman, 1959).
3. Steven Marcus, *Dickens From Pickwick to Dombey* (London: Chatto & Windus, 1965), pp. 306, 311.
4. 'Riddling the Family Firm: the Sexual Economy in *Dombey and Son*', *English Literary History*, Vol. 51 (1984), pp. 69–84 at p. 79.
5. Nina Auerbach, 'Dickens and Dombey: A Daughter After All', in Alan Shelston (ed.) *Charles Dickens: Dombey and Son and Little Dorrit* (London: Macmillan, 1985), p. 105. On feminist issues in the text see Louise Yelin, 'Strategies for Survival: Florence and Edith in *Dombey and Son*', *Victorian Studies*, Vol. 22 (1979), pp. 297–319, and Lynda Zwinger, 'The Fear of the Father: Dombey and Daughter', *Nineteenth-century Fiction* Vol. 39 (1985), pp. 420–440.
6. Marx, *The Revolutions of 1848*, ed. David Fernbach (Harmondsworth: Penguin, 1973), p. 70.
7. Quoted, Bernard Semmel, *The Rise of Free Trade Imperialism* (Cambridge: Cambridge University Press, 1970), p. 153.
8. Suvendrini Perera, 'Wholesale, Retail and For Exportation: Empire and the Family Business in *Dombey and Son*', *Victorian Studies*, Vol. 33 (1990), 603–620 at p. 608. On the details about South American trade, see R.A. Humphreys, *Tradition and Revolt in Latin America* (London: Weidenfeld & Nicolson), Chapter 7, and for the Caribbean, Eric Williams, *From Columbus to Castro: The History of the Caribbean 1492–1969* (London: André Deutsch, 1970). For Dickens's radicalism as a Free Trader, see Michael Shelden, 'Dickens, 'The Chimes,' and the Anti-Corn Law League', *Victorian Studies*, Vol. 25 (1982), pp. 329–353. On the crisis of 1825, see Norman Russell, *The Novelist and Mammon* (Oxford: Clarendon Press, 1986), Chapter 2.
9. The suggestion, implicit in Marcus, is made by Lawrence Frank, *Charles Dickens and the Romantic Self* (Lincoln: University of Nebraska Press, 1984), pp. 39–59, who gives a suggestive reading of Carker as would-be son.
10. See Paul Virilio, *Speed and Politics* (New York: Semiotexte, 1986) for a discussion of the interrelationship between speed and modern warfare.
11. On the issues of time in the novel, see N.N. Feltes, 'To Saunter, to Hurry: Dickens, Time and Industrial Capitalism', *Victorian Studies*, (1977), pp. 245–267; Murray Baumgarten, 'Railway/Reading/Time:

Dombey and Son and the Industrial World', *Dickens Studies Annual*, Vol. 19 (1990), pp. 65–89. For Heidegger, see Martin Heidegger, *The Question Concerning Technology and Other Essays*, translated by William Lovitt, (New York: Harper Torchbooks, 1977).

12. *Wordsworth's Poetical Works*, ed. Thomas Hutchinson (Oxford: Oxford University Press, 1969), p. 224. Wordsworth's footnote to the first sentence of the poem runs: 'The degree and kind of attachment which many of the yeomanry feel to their small inheritances can scarcely be overrated. Near the house of one of them stands a magnificent tree, which a neighbour of the owner advised him to sell for profit's sake. 'Fell it!' exclaimed the yeoman, 'I had rather fall on my knees and worship it.' It happens, I believe, that the intended railway would pass through this little property, and I hope that an apology for the answer will not be thought necessary by one who enters into the strength of the feeling.' See Wordsworth's letters on the railway and discussion thereon in *The Prose Works of William Wordsworth*, ed. W.J.B. Owen and Jane Worthington Smyser, Vol. 3 (Oxford: Clarendon Press, 1974), pp. 322–366, and on the general context, Stephen Gill, *William Wordsworth: A Life* (Oxford: Oxford University Press, 1990), pp. 413–414. Presumably Dickens quoted from memory, hence 'rood' for 'nook' (a more Wordsworthian word). Behind Wordsworth is Cowper's *Task* 2, line 207, and perhaps behind Dickens's 'rood' Goldsmith's *Deserted Village* line 58, 'a time there was . . . when every rood of ground maintained its man.'

13. See Norman Russell (note 8) on the 'stag' in relation to the stock market, 'a man who applied for a new issue of shares in the hope of making a quick profit when dealings began' – hence the 'deceased capitalist'. Russell connects this phenomenon of the 1840s with railway mania (pp. 31–33).

14. For Dickens's interest in corpses, see John Carey, *The Violent Effigy: A Study of Dickens's Imagination* (London: Faber, 1973), pp. 80–84. According to the *Letters*, 4.677, unidentified bodies were exposed at the Morgue for three days for public inspection; about 300 were exposed annually. For Dickens and the morgue, see *Letters*, 4.677, 5.3, 6.120. For *The Birth of the Clinic* see my '*Middlemarch*, Realism and *The Birth of the Clinic*', *English Literary History*, 57 (1990), pp. 939–960. See also Albert D.Hutter, 'The Novelist as Resurrectionist: Dickens and the Dilemma of Death', *Dickens Studies Annual*, Vol. 12 (1983), pp. 1–39.

15. Quoted, David Trotter, *Circulation: Defoe, Dickens and the Economics of the Novel* (London: Macmillan, 1988), p. 114.

16. John Butt and Kathleen Tillotson, *Dickens at Work* (London: Methuen, 1968), p. 106.

CHAPTER 3   'A PARALYSED DUMB WITNESS': ALLEGORY IN *BLEAK HOUSE*

1. Baudelaire, 'Le Cygne', *Les Fleurs du Mal* (London: Picador, 1987), p. 269, my translation. For Dickens in Benjamin, see Walter Benjamin,

Charles Baudelaire: A Lyric Poet in the Era of High Capitalism (London: Verso, 1983), pp. 49–50, 69–70. This book is part of the uncompleted *Passagenarbeit*. The earlier text is translated by John Osborne as *The Origin of German Tragic Drama* (London: Verso, 1977). References to both appear in the text. Comparison of Dickens and Benjamin is made by Ned Lukacher, *Primal Scenes: Literature, Philosophy, Psychoanalysis* (New York: Cornell University Press, 1986), Chapter 8.

2.   Quoted, J. Hillis Miller, *Charles Dickens: The World of his Novels* (1958: Bloomington: Indiana University Press, 1969), p. 293.

3.   On the phantasmagoria and the quotation from *Capital*, see Gillian Rose, *The Melancholy Science: An Introduction to the Thought of Theodor W. Adorno* (London: Macmillan, 1978), p. 31.

4.   Walter Benjamin, 'Central Park', trans. Lloyd Spencer, *New German Critique*, Vol. 34 (1985), p. 34.

5.   'Theses on the Philosophy of History', *Illuminations* (London: Jonathan Cape, 1970), p. 259.

6.   Paul de Man, 'Autobiography as De-Facement', *The Rhetoric of Romanticism* (New York: Columbia University Press, 1984), p. 78, first emphasis mine. Further citation given in the text.

7.   Paul de Man, *Allegories of Reading* (New Haven, Conn.: Yale University Press, 1979), p. 205.

8.   *Othello*, IV. i. 54–55. Susan Shatto, who notes several references to *Othello* in the text (but not this one), derives Allegory from Pope's 'Epistle to Burlington', lines 145–8: Susan Shatto, *The Companion to Bleak House* (London: Unwin Hyman, 1988), p. 102. See also on *Bleak House*, for deconstruction, apart from Hillis Miller, especially Michael Ragussis, 'The Ghostly Signs of *Bleak House*', *Nineteenth-Century Fiction*, Vol. 34 (1979), pp. 253–280. For pointing, see Nancy Aycock Metz, 'Narrative Gesturing in *Bleak House*', *Dickensian*, Vol. 77 (1981), pp. 13–22.

9.   Michel Foucault, *The Birth of the Clinic*, trans. A.M. Sheridan (London: Tavistock Publications, 1973), p. 166. I have discussed this theme in '*Middlemarch*, Realism and The Birth of the Clinic', *English Literary History*, Vol. 57 (1990), pp. 939–960.

10.   Quoted, Rosemary Ashton, *G.H. Lewes: A Life* (Oxford: Clarendon Press, 1991), p. 144. Dickens's sources for spontaneous combustion – Bianchini, (1704–1764), Le Cat (1700–1768) – belong to a different medical episteme from that of Bichat who leads toward Positivist science, an episteme followed by Foderé and Marc (called Mere by Dickens), both writing in 1813. On Dickens and spontaneous combustion, see E. Gaskell, 'More About Spontaneous Combustion', *Dickensian*, 69 (1973), pp. 25–35, and Peter Denman, 'Krook's Death and Dickens's Authorities', *Dickensian*, 82 (1986), pp. 131–141. For Dickens and Lewes, see Gordon S. Haight, *George Eliot's Originals and Contemporaries* (London: Macmillan, 1992), Chapters 8 and 9. For Lewes on art, see his 'Realism in Art: Recent German Fiction', *Westminster Review*, October 1858, p. 493 – 'Art is a Representation of Reality – a Representation which, inasmuch as it is not the thing

itself, but only represents it, must necessarily be limited by the nature of its medium . . . but while thus limited, while thus regulated by the necessities imposed on it by each medium of expression, Art always aims at the representation of Reality, i.e. of Truth; and no departure from truth is permissible, except such as inevitably lies in the nature of the medium itself. Realism is thus the basis of all Art, and its antithesis is not Idealism but Falsism.' Here is Lewes's commitment to George Eliot's work – which could only be a contrast to Dickens's.

11. This connects Dickens to the Gothic, to Hawthorne's 'romances' and to such a text as *Wuthering Heights*. See Allan Pritchard, 'The Urban Gothic of *Bleak House*', *Nineteenth-Century Literature*, Vol. 45 (1990–91), pp. 432–452.

12. Review of Robert William Mackay, *The Progress of the Intellect*, in *Westminster Review*, Vol. 54 (1851), 'Three Novels', *Westminster Review*, 66 (1856), both reprinted in *The Essays of George Eliot* (London: Routledge & Kegan Paul, 1968), pp. 27–45, 325–334.

13. Quoted, *Dickens: The Critical Heritage*, ed. Philip Collins (London: Routledge & Kegan Paul, 1971), pp. 281, 283. Further references to Collins in the text.

14. Jonathan Arac in *Commissioned Spirits: The Shaping of Social Motion in Dickens, Carlyle, Melville and Hawthorne* (New Brunswick: Rutgers University Press, 1979), Chapter 5, draws attention to Carlyle's use of imagery of spontaneous combustion to characterise the *ancien régime* before the revolution.

15. Marx, *The Revolutions of 1848*, ed. David Fernbach (Penguin: Harmondsworth, 1973), pp. 70–71, my emphases.

16. Walter Benjamin, *One Way Street And Other Writings*, trans. Edmund Jephcott and Kingsley Shorter (London: Verso, 1979), p. 65.

17. See George H. Ford and Lauriat Lane Jr, *The Dickens Critics* (Ithaca, NY: Cornell University Press, 1961), p. 69. Further references in the text.

18. Gordon S. Haight (ed.), *The George Eliot Letters* (New Haven, Conn.: Yale University Press, 1954), Vol. II, p. 309 (letter of 14 March 1857).

19. Wordsworth, *The Prelude* (1805), 6.525–530.

20. On Piranesi, see Jennifer Bloomer, *Architecture and the Text: The (S)crypts of Joyce and Piranesi* (New Haven, Conn.: Yale University Press, 1993) pp. 117–122. See also Arden Reed, 'Abysmal Influence: Baudelaire, Coleridge, De Quincey, Piranesi, Wordsworth', *Glyph*, Vol. 4 (1978), pp. 189–206.

21. See Sergei Eisenstein, 'Dickens, Griffith and the Film Today', *Film Form*, ed. Jay Leydu (New York: Meridian, 1957). For Eisenstein on Piranesi, see Manfredo Tafuri, *The Sphere and the Labyrinth: Avant-Gardes and Architecture from, Piranesi to the 1970s*, trans. Pelligrino d'Acierno and Robert Connolly (Cambridge, Mass.: MIT Press, 1990), Chapters 1 and 2.

22. Paul de Man discusses fragments that do not add up to a whole in his 'Task of the Translator', *The Resistance to Theory* (Minneapolis: University of Minnesota Press, 1986), pp. 90–91. On discontinuities

between the narratives, see Diane Sadoff, *Monsters of Affection: Dickens, Eliot and Brontë on Fatherhood* (Baltimore, Md.: Johns Hopkins University Press, 1982), pp. 16–17.

23. See Bruce Robbins, *The Servant's Hand* (New York: Columbia University Press, 1986), pp. 1541–55.

24. George Eliot, *Middlemarch* (1871–72), ed. W.J. Harvey (Harmondsworth: Penguin, 1965), pp. 224, 225, 226.

CHAPTER 4   FINDING THE PASSWORD: *LITTLE DORRIT*

1. For photographs of the Crimea, see those by Roger Fenton, who, under the patronage of Victoria, was charged to record evidence to refute newspaper accounts of hardship as reported by William Russell, in Frances Fralin, *The Indelible Image: Photographs of War, 1846 to the Present* (New York: Harry N. Abrams, 1986), pp. 26–29. See also Matthew Lalumia, 'Realism and Anti-Aristocratic Sentiment in Victorian Depictions of the Crimean War', *Victorian Studies*, Vol. 27 (1983), pp. 25–51. For photography and early surveillance, see John Tagg, *The Burden of Representation* (London: Macmillan, 1984), p. 74.

2. Natalie McKnight, *Idiots, Madmen and Other Prisoners in Dickens* (New York: St Martin's Press, 1993), Chapter 8.

3. Armand Audiganne, quoted, William H. Sewell, Jr, *Structure and Mobility: The Men and Women of Marseille, 1820–1870* (Cambridge: Cambridge University Press, 1985), p. 101.

4. Christian Metz, 'Photography and Fetish', in Carol Squiers (ed.), *The Critical Image: Essays on Contemporary Photography* (London: Lawrence and Wishart, 1990), p. 161. *Camera Lucida* is quoted from Richard Howard's translation (New York: Hill and Wang, 1981), see pp. 4, 76, 92, for the citations given.

5. Colin MacCabe, *James Joyce and the Revolution of the Word* (London: Macmillan, 1979), 35.

6. Nietzsche: *Beyond Good and Evil*, trans. R.J. Hollingdale (Harmondsworth: Penguin, 1973), p. 15.

7. Nancy Aycock Metz, '*Little Dorrit*'s London: Babylon Revisited', *Victorian Studies*, Vol. 34 (1990), pp. 465–486 at p. 467.

8. *Speech and Language in Psychoanalysis*, translated by Anthony Wilden as *The Language of the Self* (Baltimore, Md.: Johns Hopkins University Press, 1968), p. 57. Freud refers to Champollion when discussing Leonardo: see *The Penguin Freud*, Vol. 14 (Harmondsworth: Penguin, 1985), p. 178.

9. *Genealogy of Morals*, trans. Francis Golffing (New York: Doubleday Anchor, 1956), pp. 253–254.

10. 'The Fetishism of the Commodity and its Secret', *Capital* (Harmondsworth: Penguin, 1976), 1.1.4, pp. 163–164.

11. *One Way Street and Other Writings*, trans. Edmund Jephcott (London: Verso, 1979), pp. 158–159.

12. Abjection recalls Julia Kristeva, *Powers of Horror* (New York: Columbia University Press, 1981); for discussion of the 'vacancy' (the

vide) see Neil Hertz, 'Afterword: The End of the Line', in *The End of the Line* (New York: Columbia University Press, 1985), especially pp. 231–232.

13. The passages were first put together by Q.D. Leavis, 'Dickens, George Eliot, Henry James', *Hudson Review* 7 (1955), pp. 423–428. The passage from *Middlemarch* is discussed by Hertz (pp. 88–92); see also Jim Reilly, *Shadowtime: History and Representation in Hardy, Conrad and George Eliot* (London: Routledge, 1993), pp. 45–51.

14. On this, see Alexander Welsh, *The City of Dickens* (Oxford: Clarendon Press, 1971), pp. 134–135. For other critiques of the novel to which I am indebted, see Sarah Winter, 'Domestic Fictions: Feminine Deference and Maternal Shadow Labour in Dickens's *Little Dorrit*', *Dickens Studies Annual*, Vol. 18 (1989), pp. 243–254. On the protection of patriarchy, see Diane Sadoff, 'Storytelling, and the Figure of the Father in *Little Dorrit*', *PMLA*, Vol. 95 (1980), pp. 234–245. See also Elaine Showalter, 'Guilt, Authority and the Shadows of *Little Dorrit*', *Nineteenth-Century Fiction*, Vol. 34 (1979), pp. 20–41.

15. 'Encrypting' comes from Nicolas Abraham and Maria Torok, *The Wolf Man's Magic Word: A Cryptonomy*, translated by Nicholas Rand (Minneapolis: University of Minnesota Press, 1986). See Esther Rashkin, 'Tools for a New Psychoanalytic Literary Criticism: The Work of Abraham and Torok', *Diacritics*, Winter (1988), pp. 31–52. In encrypting, the subject incorporates into itself material which it thus represses and which is therefore not acknowledged: the repression of knowledge is carried over from the previous generation, and Abraham illustrates it with his reading of *Hamlet* where the ghost is guilty (of having killed old Fortinbras with a poisoned sword in a duel under the instruction of Polonius) hence Laertes follows his father using the encrypted material about poisoning within him. See the same issue of *Diacritics*, pp. 2–30.

16. Quoted, Peter Ward Fay, *The Opium War 1840–42* (Chapel Hill: University of North Carolina Press, 1975), pp. 332–333.

17. Quoted, Jack Beeching, *The Chinese Opium Wars* (London: Hutchison, 1975), p. 111.

18. Compare Marx on the 'illegal opium trade which yearly feeds the British treasury at the expense of human life and morality' (journalism of 22/3/57, *Collected Works of Marx and Engels* (London: Lawrence & Wishart), Vol. 15 (1986), p. 234).

It is worth considering one figure in the China wars who exemplifies the dualism that a dominant ideology imposes upon him. Sir John Bowring (1792–1872), Governor of Hong Kong (1854–59) did more than anyone else to provoke war with China, launching an offensive against Canton in 1856, the aim being to make the opium trade fully legal, and calling on the help of the 'mother-country' which sent five thousand men to China under Lord Elgin (the son of the man who took the marbles from Greece). The contradictions constructing Bowring run deep. The man who forced a war in 1816 had been President of the Peace society, which aimed to promote conciliation to settle international pursuits: as a Utilitarian, he was first editor of the radical and rationalist *Westminister Review* (1824), and editor of Bentham's works. As secretary for the Greek Society, he had corresponded with Byron for his expedition to Greece, and had arranged for his body to be returned. Intermittently, he was an MP from 1833–49, standing for radicalism, free trade (hence the desire to open up China and Siam (which he visited in a spirit of coercion in 1855)) and pacific politics. He stood for Deontology (the science of duty), but added to this a Christianity which made him write Evangelical hymns, and a literary sense which made him a minor poet and translator and writer for *All the Year Round* in 1865. He defended his position with regard to China – 'The powers of reason fail when coming in contact with the unreasoning and the unconvincable. No man was ever a more ardent lover of peace than I . . . but with barbarians, ay, and sometimes with civilized nations the words of peace are uttered in vain – as with children too often the word of reproof' (quoted, *Autobiographical Recollections of Sir John Bowring*, London, 1877, p. 217.) Yet that incomprehension which makes him finally an imperialist and party to violence, runs through Victorian ideology.

19. Abigail Solomon-Godeau, *Photography at the Dock* (Minneapolis: University of Minnesota Press, 1991), p. 172. The book contains several reproductions of nineteenth-century photographs of the Sphinx.

20. Cigarettes were popularised during the Crimean War. Dickens's first reference to them is in 1854: see *Letters*, Vol. 7, p. 418n.

21. Norman Russell, *The Novelist and Mammon* (Oxford: Clarendon Press, 1986), p. 1. See also his discussion of Merdle, Chapter 6.

22. *Charles Baudelaire: A Lyric Poet in the Era of High Capitalism* (London: Verso, 1973), p. 176.

23. Another example is Harold Skimpole talking to Sir Leicester: 'The owners of such places as Chesney Wold . . . are public benefactors. They are good enough to maintain a number of delightful objects for the admiration and pleasure of us poor men; and not to reap all the admiration and pleasure that they yield, is to be ungrateful to our benefactors' – *Bleak House*, 43.659.

24. See Barbara Weiss, *The Hell of the English: Bankruptcy and the Victorian Novel* (Lewisburg, W. Va.: Associated Universities Press 1986), and N.N. Feltes, 'Community and the Limits of Liability in Two Mid-Victorian Novels', *Victorian Studies*, Vol. 17 (1973–4), pp. 355–369.

25. Walter Benjamin, *Illuminations* (London: Cape, 1970), p. 77.

26. Lacan discusses the power of the symbol in his 'Rome discourse' of 1953: 'The function and field of speech and language in psychoanalysis'. He argues that psychoanalysis can work with nothing else than the patient's speech (p. 40). The text distinguishes between 'empty' and 'full' speech and says that analysis has for its goal 'the advent of a true speech' (p. 88).

27. See Geoffrey Hartman, *Saving the Text: Literature, Derrida, Philosophy* (Baltimore, Md.: Johns Hopkins University Press, 1981), p. 134. The password enables an arrival at the destination: it opens up the unconscious.

28. On these points in Lacan, see Wilden pp. 43, 101, 51, 109.
29. Jean Baudrillard, *Selected Writings* (Oxford: Polity Press, 1988), p. 175.

CHAPTER 5 DICKENS AND DOSTOEVSKY: CAPITAL PUNISHMENT IN *BARNABY RUDGE, A TALE OF TWO CITIES* AND *THE IDIOT*

1. David D. Cooper, *The Lesson of the Scaffold: The Public Execution Controversy in Victorian England* (Athens, Ohio: Ohio University Press, 1974), p. 85.
2. Martin J. Wiener, *Reconstructing the Criminal: Culture, Law and Policy in England, 1830–1914* (Cambridge: Cambridge University Press, 1990), p. 61.
3. N.M. Lary, *Dostoevsky and Dickens: A Study of Literary Influence* (London: Routledge, 1973) discusses *The Idiot* in relation to *Dombey and Son* and *Little Dorrit* and *The Possessed* in relation to *Barnaby Rudge*.
4. See Joseph Frank, *Dostoevsky: The Years of Ordeal, 1850–1859*, (Princeton, NJ: Princeton University Press, 1983), Chapter 5.
5. Fyodor Dostoevsky, *The Idiot*, 1.5, trans. David Magarshack (Harmondsworth: Penguin, 1955), pp. 86–88.
6. Peter Linebaugh, *The London Hanged: Crime and Civil Society in the Eighteenth Century* (Cambridge: Cambridge University Press, 1992), Chapter 10.
7. J.M. Rignall, 'Dickens and the Catastrophic Continuum of History in *A Tale of Two Cities*', *English Literary History*, Vol. 51 (1984), p. 577.
8. Carlyle, *The French Revolution*, eds K.J. Fielding and D. Sorensen (Oxford: Oxford University Press, 1989), 6.1.222. Further references in the text.
9. See Lee Sterrenburg, 'Psychoanalysis and the Iconography of Revolution', *Victorian Studies*, Vol. 19 (1975), pp. 241–264, and Carl Schorske, 'Politics and Patricide in Freud's *Interpretation of Dreams*', *American Historical Review*, Vol. 78 (1973), pp. 328–347.
10. *Interpretation of Dreams* (Harmondsworth: Penguin, 1976), p. 769.
11. 'The Work of Art in the Age of Mechanical Reproduction', *Illuminations*, trans. Harry Zohn (London: Jonathan Cape, 1970), p. 224.
12. Elizabeth Dalton, *Unconscious Structure in The Idiot: A Study in Literature and Psychoanalysis* (Princeton, NJ: Princeton University Press, 1979); see especially pp. 123–144 (p. 137). The dead Christ would then be an image of castration. See also Julia Kristeva, *Black Sun: Depression and Melancholia* (New York: Columbia University Press, 1989), Chapters 5 and 7. Kristeva discusses Holbein's 'Dead Christ', following Dostoevsky. Myshkin says of it that 'some people may lose their faith by looking at that picture.' Ippolit discusses it in his 'Explanation', thinking of the disciples looking at the body which in life had said '*Talitha cumi* and the damsel arose, who cried *Lazarus come forth* and the dead man came forth.' The body now gives the impression of being entirely subject to the laws of nature, where nature is

'some enormous, implacable, and dumb beast, or, to put it more correctly . . . as some huge engine of the latest design, which has senselessly seized, cut to pieces, and swallowed up – impassively and unfeelingly – a great and priceless Being.' It causes Ippolit to attempt to evoke 'in a vivid image' that which 'has no image' as a 'dark, deaf-and-dumb creature' (*The Idiot*, trans. David Magarshack (Harmondsworth: Penguin, 1955), pp. 90, 250–51, 446–8). The body torn to pieces and swallowed by this monster is a reference to cannibalism, discussed by Lebedev as a widespread practice in medieval Europe. Lebedev says that at least people felt guilty about it then, the implication being that with the approach of the Apocalypse, that is not permitted now. (See the discussion of cannibalism in *Great Expectations*.)

13. The aristocrat's fear of the guillotine contrasts interestingly with Freud's sense of the aristocrat as the libidinal force put down by the crowd as superego, when he writes, with reference to dreams of being guillotined, 'Who . . . could fail to be gripped by narratives of the Reign of Terror, when the men and women of the aristocracy, the flower of the nation, showed that they could die with a cheerful mind and could retain the liveliness of their wit and elegance of their manners till the very moment of the fatal summons?' *The Interpretation of Dreams*, p. 638.

14. Victor Brombert, *Victor Hugo and the Visionary Novel* (Cambridge, Mass.: Harvard University Press, 1989), p. 33. For the likelihood of the influence of Hugo (first translated in 1840) on Dickens, see Duane De Vries, *Dickens's Apprentice Years: The Making of a Novelist* (Brighton: Harvester, 1976), p. 115ff.

15. Nietzsche, *The Gay Science*, trans. Walter Kaufmann (New York: Vintage, 1974), p. 269.

16. *Twilight of the Idols*, trans. R.J. Hollingdale (Harmondsworth: Penguin, 1968), pp. 30, 45.

17. John Kucich, *Excess and Restraint in the Novels of Charles Dickens* (Athens: University of Georgia Press, 1981). See pp. 118–120 for discussion of Carton and Darnay. Relevant essays of Bataille are 'The Notion of Expenditure', and 'The Psychological Basis of Fascism', *Visions of Excess: Selected Writings 1927–1939*, Georges Bataille, edited Allan Stoekl (Minneapolis: University of Minnesota Press, 1985).

CHAPTER 6   FROM *JANE EYRE* TO GOVERNOR EYRE, OR *OLIVER TWIST* TO *EDWIN DROOD*

1. Edward Said, *Culture and Imperialism* (London: Chatto & Windus, 1992), p. 61.

2. On imperialism in *Jane Eyre*, see Susan L. Meyer, 'Colonialism and the Figurative Strategy of *Jane Eyre*', *Victorian Studies*, Vol. 33 (1990), pp. 247–268; Gayatri Chakravorty Spivak, 'Three Women's Texts and a Critique of Imperialism', *Critical Inquiry*, Vol. 12 (1985), pp. 243–261;

John Barrell, *The Infection of Thomas De Quincey: The Psychopathology of Imperialism* (New Haven, Conn.: Yale University Press, 1991) makes links between De Quincey's terror of the Orient and psychosexual fears which may be linked to his opium state. See the discussion of *Edwin Drood* by Eve Kosofsky Sedgwick, *Between Men: English Literature and Male Homosocial Desire*, (New York: Columbia University Press, 1985). She relates the text to 'the homophobia of empire'. The same book contains an analysis of *Our Mutual Friend* in relation to Bradley Headstone's desire for Eugene Wrayburn.

3.   Suvendrini Perera, *Reaches of Empire* (New York: Cornell University Press, 1991), p. 110.

4.   For Dickens's sources for opium, see Cardwell, Introduction to *Edwin Drood*, xvi–xviii, including a letter to Sir John Bowring, 'the authority whom he consulted on the effects of opium-smoking in the east'. Howard Duffield, 'John Jasper – Strangler', *American Bookman*, Vol. 70 (1930), pp. 526–537 makes Jasper a Thuggee: he is followed by Edmund Wilson. See, for a negative view, Wendy S. Jacobson, 'John Jasper and Thuggee', *MLR* 72 (1977), pp. 526–537.

5.   For an application of Nandy's work, see Rustom Bharucha, 'Forster's Friends' in *E.M.Forster: New Casebooks*, ed. Jeremy Tambling (London: Macmillan, 1995).

6.   Ashis Nandy, *The Intimate Enemy: Loss and Recovery of Self Under Colonialism* (Oxford: Oxford University Press, 1983), pp. 32–35.

7.   Charlotte Brontë, *Jane Eyre*, ed. Q.D. Leavis (Harmondsworth: Penguin, 1966), pp. 332–333.

8.   The point, as part of a general revising upwards of Oliver's age, is brought out by David Paroissen in his *Companion to* Oliver Twist (Edinburgh: Edinburgh University Press, 1992).

9.   'Billy Budd' in *The Portable Melville*, ed. Jay Leyda (New York: Viking, 1952), p. 730. William A Cohen, 'Manual Conduct in *Great Expectations*', *English Literary History*, Vol. 60 (1993), pp. 217–259 finds masturbation to be the 'master-trope' in *Great Expectations* (p. 224), though he does not make it cohere through the text, and for me forces readings where it is not necessary to go further than to assert a powerful and non-specific sense of guilt which belongs to all males constructed to assert their masculinity in that and other Dickens's texts.

10. Michel Foucault, *The History of Sexuality* (Harmondsworth: Penguin, 1981), p. 104.

11. Martin J. Wiener, *Reconstructing the Criminal: Culture, Law and Policy in England, 1830–1914* (Cambridge: Cambridge University Press 1990), p. 17.

12. Sara Suleri (Goodyear), 'Forster's Imperial Erotic', reprinted in *E.M. Forster: New Casebooks*, ed. Jeremy Tambling (London: Macmillan, 1995), p. 151.

13. The point is made by Cynthia Chase, 'The De-composition of the Elephants: Double-Reading *Daniel Deronda*', *PMLA*, Vol. 93 (1978), p. 222.

14. *The Moonstone*, ed. Anthea Trodd (Oxford: Oxford University Press, 1982), First Period, Chapter 12, p. 110.

15. Quoted, Norman Page, *Wilkie Collins: The Critical Heritage* (London: Routledge, 1974), p. 80.

16. 'The monologism of the narration is exactly analogous to the work of detection in the representation. Just as a common detection transcends the single efforts of various detective figures, a common narration subsumes the individual reports of various narrators. The world resolves its difficulties, and language finds its truth, according to the same principle of quasi-automatic self-regulation.' D.A. Miller, *The Novel and the Police* (Berkeley: University of California Press, 1988), p. 156. On Miller's case against Collins, with implications for the realist text generally, see Lilian Nayder, 'Robinson Crusoe and Friday in Victorian Britain: 'Discipline', 'Dialogue' and Collins's Critique of Empire in *The Moonstone*', *Dickens Studies Annual*, Vol. 21 (1992), pp. 213–231; and her 'Agents of Empire in *The Woman in White*', *Victorian Newsletter*, (1993), pp. 1–7. For Collins as pro-Indian, see John R. Reed, 'English Imperialism and the Unacknowledged Crime of *The Moonstone*', *Clio*, Vol. 2 (1973), pp. 281–290. For Collins's scientific realism, see Ira Bruce Nadel, 'Science and *The Moonstone*', *Dickens Studies Annual*, Vol. 11 (1983), pp. 239–260. On Dickens and Collins, see Jerome Meckier, *Hidden Rivalries in Victorian Fiction* (Lexington: University Press of Kentucky, 1987), Chapter 6.

17. Richard M. Baker, *The Drood Murder Case* (Berkeley: University of California Press, 1951), argues that Jasper is the younger brother of Drood's (Egyptian) mother.

18. See Brahma Chaudhuri, 'Dickens and the Question of Slavery', *Dickens Quarterly*, Vol. 6 (1989), pp. 3–10. On the Eyre controversy, see Gillian Workman, 'Thomas Carlyle and the Governor Eyre Controversy: An Account with Some New Material', *Victorian Studies*, Vol. 18 (1974), pp. 77–102.

19. See Lynn Zastoupil, 'J.S. Mill and India', *Victorian Studies*, Vol. 32 (1988), pp. 31–54; Trevor Lloyd, 'Mill and the East India Company', in *A Cultivated Mind: Essays Presented to John M Robson*, ed. Michael Laine (Toronto: University of Toronto Press, 1991).

20. Quoted, Javed Majeed, *Ungoverned Imaginings: James Mill's The History of British India and Orientalism* (Oxford: Clarendon Press, 1992), p. 125.

21. Ronald Inden, *Imagining India* (Oxford: Blackwell, 1990), p. 45.

22. Virginia Berridge's work on 'Fenland opium eating in the nineteenth century', *British Journal of Addiction*, Vol. 72 (1977), pp. 275–284 establishes how Norfolk and Lincolnshire consumed half the opium import (on 1859 figures, 30,000 lb) so that the agricultural worker in an area of rheumatism, ague and neuralgia survived with 'Godfrey's Cordial,' with thirty grains a pennyworth a day. It was cheaper than alcohol; sold quite openly in pills, and even regularly added to beer. The drainage of the Fens entailed the use in the mid-nineteenth century of itinerant 'public gangs' comprising women and children and led by a 'gang master' who ranged over wide areas. While the mothers were away from home, their children were kept quiet with opium. The mortality rate in Wisbech in the Fens was 206 to a thousand,

which put it higher than Sheffield. Opium was used universally: as cattle medicine and to kill unwanted babies (twins and the illegitimate); and public opinion was not above seeing its use in the Fens as a general cure-all and cheaper than either doctors or drink as a justification for its growth in India. Opium was a working-class addiction, and specifically a woman's – certainly no luxury. *The Lancet* in 1879 described opium-eaters as not public-house goers, but 'the careworn and miserable, who prefer to take their solace alone'. On the subject generally, see Virginia Berridge, *Opium and the People: Opiate Use in the Nineteenth-century* (New Haven, Conn.: Yale University Press, 1987).

    Michael Cotsell, 'The Book of Insolvent Fates: Financial Speculation in *Our Mutual Friend*', *Dickens Studies Annual*, Vol. 14 (1984), pp. 125–142, argues that Veneering's money is from drugs.

23. Fredric Jameson, *The Ideologies of Theory*, Vol. 1 (Minneapolis: University of Minnesota Press, 1988), p. 70. See also Jameson's *Postmodernism, or The Cultural Logic of Late Capitalism* (Durham, NC: Duke University Press, 1991), pp. 25–31.

24. Note the reference to surveillance in one of the cancelled MS passages here: 'and always posing overseer with'.

25. Ronald R. Thomas, *Dreams of Authority: Freud and the Fictions of the Unconscious* (Ithaca, NY: Cornell University Press, 1990), p. 222.

CHAPTER 7   THE SCUM OF HUMANITY: *OUR MUTUAL FRIEND*

1. *Visions of Excess: Selected Writings of Georges Bataille*, ed. Allan Stoekl (Manchester: Manchester University Press, 1985), p. 143.

2. See William Oddie, 'Dickens and the Indian Mutiny', *Dickensian*, Vol. 8 (1972), pp. 3–15. See also Patrick Brantlinger, *Rule of Darkness: British Literature and Imperialism, 1830–1914* (Ithaca, NY: Cornell University Press, 1988), Chapter 7, and Lilian Nayder, 'Class Consciousness and the Indian Mutiny in Dickens's "The Perils of Certain English Prisoners"', *Studies in English Literature*, Vol. 32 (1992), pp. 689–705.

3. Joseph Schumpeter, quoted in Karl de Schweinitz, Jr, *The Rise and Fall of British India: Imperialism as Inequality* (London: Methuen, 1983), p. 26.

4. I discussed this text in my *Confession: Sexuality, Sin, the Subject* (Manchester: Manchester University Press, 1990), pp. 151–154.

5. See Nancy L. Paxton, 'Mobilizing Chivalry: Rape in British Novels About the Indian Uprising of 1857', *Victorian Studies*, Vol. 35 (1992), pp. 5–30.

6. Jean Rhys, *Wide Sargasso Sea* (Harmondsworth: Penguin, 1968), p. 148.

7. See Susan Shatto, *The Companion to Bleak House*, (London: Unwin Hyman 1988), pp. 251–252. See Chapter 46 of *Bleak House*. See also A. Susan Williams, *The Rich Man and the Diseased Poor in Early Victorian*

Literature (London: Macmillan, 1987), and Bruce Haley, *The Healthy Body and Victorian Culture* (Cambridge, Mass.: Harvard University Press, 1978).

8. *Oliver Twist*, p. 382. On the drive within Dickens's Prefaces to *Oliver Twist*, see Paul Foss, 'The Lottery of Life' in Meaghan Morris and Paul Patton, *Michel Foucault: Power, Truth, Strategy* (Sydney: Feral Publications, 1979).

9. Laurie is 'put down' by Dickens in the 1850 Preface to *Oliver Twist*, as he was also put down in Dickens's speeches to the Metropolitan Sanitary Association. See *Speeches of Charles Dickens*, ed. K.J. Fielding (Oxford: Clarendon Press, 1960), pp. 104–113, 127–132. See also pp. 42–43. See p. 130 for Dickens's satire against the enemies of 'Centralization'. On Podsnap, see Ruth Bernard Yeazell, 'Podsnappery, Sexuality and the English Novel', *Critical Inquiry*, Vol. 9 (1982), pp. 339–357.

10. See Michael Steig, 'Dickens's Excremental Vision', *Victorian Studies*, Vol. 13 (1970), pp. 339–354. For an application to *Our Mutual Friend* see Nancy Aycock Metz, 'The Artistic Reclamation of Waste in *Our Mutual Friend*', *Nineteenth-Century Fiction*, Vol. 34 (1979), pp. 59–72.

11. I owe this point to a paper of a colleague in jurisprudence, William P. Macneil, 'Law/History – Living On: Borderlines', to be published in *Law and Social Problems*, eds Tom Campbell and Phil Thomas (1995), which uses the legal historian F.W. Maitland to argue that this kind of gender identification is instinct in legal history writing.

12. See Jonathan Arac, *Commissioned Spirits* (New Brunswick, NJ: Rutgers University Press, 1979), p. 182.

13. Catherine Gallagher, 'The Bio-Economics of *Our Mutual Friend*', *Fragments for a History of the Body*, (New York: Zone, 1990 p. 361. See also for reclamation of waste, Michael Peled Ginsburg, 'The Case Against Plot in *Bleak House* and *Our Mutual Friend*', *English Literary History*, Vol. 59 (1992), pp. 175–195.

14. *One Way Street and other Writings*, trans. Edmund Jephcott (London: Verso, 1979), p. 65.

15. *The Genealogy of Morals*, 1.10, trans. Francis Golffing (New York: Doubleday Anchor, 1956), pp. 170–171.

16. David Garland, *Punishment and Welfare* (Aldershot: Gower, 1985), p. 67; compare pp. 38–39, 67.

17. Pam Morris, *Dickens's Class Consciousness* (London: Macmillan, 1991), p. 131ff draws out well the implications of this endstopped language of Headstone's. On Headstone, see also Eve Kosofsky Sedgwick (see chapter 6, note 2).

18. See Carolyn J. Dean, *The Self and Its Pleasures: Bataille, Lacan and the History of the Decentred Subject* (Ithaca, NY: Cornell University Press, 1992), p. 203.

19. Denis Hollier, *Against Architecture: The Writings of Georges Bataille* (Cambridge, Mass.: MIT Press, 1989), p. 64.

20. Jessica Benjamin, *The Bonds of Love* (New York: Pantheon Books, 1988), p. 52, quoted in Michelle A. Massé, *In the Name of Love: Women,*

Masochism and the Gothic (Ithaca, NY: Cornell University Press, 1992), p. 45.

21. She is not a fool, she says, (2.21.663), recalling Mr F's Aunt's 'I hate a fool' (1.13.159). Henry Gowan tells her after their relationship that there is no such thing as romance, just as Mr Finching tells Flora that he wants a sexless marriage ('romance was fled' – her words to him – his reply: 'he was perfectly aware of it and even preferred that state of things' – 1.24.283). She pursues Pet Meagles in the same way that Mrs Clennam goes after Arthur's mother and her anger at Gowan replicates Mrs Clennam's anger at her husband. Her stress on 'hate' repeats Mrs Clennam's prayers for divine judgement. But she also translates motifs in Clennam. Her 'grandmother' and Mrs Clennam parallel each other; so do their childhoods.

22. I discussed Miss Wade in my *Confession*, pp. 144–148, as in a continuum with Charlotte Brontë's heroines. The death of Charlotte Brontë on 31 March 1855, and Dickens's letter about her and refusal to carry a story about her life in *Household Words* (*Letters*, 7.610), are interesting in this context. Miss Wade's first friend is called Charlotte. See also for source material for Miss Wade the references in the *Letters* to Emily Jolly's 'A Wife's Story' in *Household Words*, September 1855, where the wife reveals knowledge of 'one dark phase of human nature' (*Letters*, p. 674, 676–7), and Eliza Lynn's 'Sentiment and Action', *Household Words*, November 1855 (*Letters*, p. 681), for the woman discontented with what her husband offers in marriage.

23. See, for example, Leo Bersani, *The Freudian Body: Psychoanalysis and Art* (New York: Columbia University Press, 1986), pp. 38–39.

24. Gilles Deleuze, *Masochism: An Interpretation of Coldness and Cruelty* (New York: George Braziller, 1971), p. 83. Ian Duncan, *Modern Romance and Transformations of the Novel* (Cambridge: Cambridge University Press, 1992), p. 215 says, with reference to Cain and Abel, that in Dickens 'the original sin – the creation of death – is … a civilizing and *family-splitting* violence of social competition' (my emphasis). On the feminising of Bradley Headstone, see Mary Saunders,'Lady Dedlock Prostrate: Drama, Melodrama and Expressionism in Dickens's Floor Scenes' in Carol Hanbery MacKay (ed.), *Dramatic Dickens* (London: Macmillan, 1990).

25. See Claire Tomalin, *The Invisible Woman: The Story of Nelly Ternan and Charles Dickens* (Harmondsworth: Penguin, 1990), pp. 145ff; Fred Kaplan, *Dickens: A Biography* (New York: William Morrow, 1988), pp. 458–461.

26. Barbara Spackman, *Decadent Genealogies: The Rhetoric of Sickness from Baudelaire to D'Annunzio* (New York: Cornell University Press, 1989).

27. Quoted, Philip Collins, *Dickens: Interviews and Recollections*, Vol. 1 (London: Macmillan, 1981), p. 63.

28. Freud, 'Beyond the Pleasure Principle', *The Penguin Freud*, Vol. 11 (Harmondsworth: Penguin, 1977), pp. 281–283.

Index